The Other Half of Me

Annabel Lovick

An inspirational story of one woman's journey through heartbreak.

Copyright © 2022 Annabel Lovick
All rights reserved.

No part of this publication may be reproduced or transmitted in any form or by any means, electronic or mechanical, including photography, recording, or any information storage and retrieval system without the prior written consent from the publisher and author, except in the instance of quotes for reviews. No part of this book may be uploaded without the permission of the publisher and author, nor be otherwise circulated in any form of binding or cover other than that in which it is originally published.

This is a work of fiction and any resemblance to persons, living or dead, or places, actual events or locales is purely coincidental. The characters and names are products of the authors imagination and used fictitiously.

The publisher and author acknowledge the trademark status and trademark ownership of all trademarks, service marks and word marks mentioned in this book.

Dedicated to Mum and Dad
To credit you with creating me, just the way I am.
I am enough.
Thank you
X

Acknowledgements

Someone once told me that the most therapeutic and successful way to make it through heartbreak was to write it down. All the emotions, the ever-changing feelings and every little one of my rational or irrational thoughts and behaviours. I took that advice and wrote for years, believing I was writing for me alone.

No one else would ever read my words.

It became a deeply cathartic process that I truly believed saved me. It enabled me to evolve into a better person, a more present mother, a more resilient human being and most certainly, a better divorcee.

Several years later, after hundreds of rewrites, I can proudly put my name to over ninety-seven thousand words of fiction. I wish I could remember that person. If it's you, thank you!

However, that process alone didn't make me a good writer, nor result in a good book. So, I want to thank my editor, Jessica Ryn, for all her advice, honesty, and words of encouragement throughout the many edits and changes that were essential to transforming my emotional ramblings into a fictional story for others to read.

Lastly, I want to thank my parents for giving me the most balanced childhood ever, my friends for never rolling their eyes when they were constantly being told, 'It's nearly finished', and most importantly, my boys.

Thank you, boys, for your adjustment to a situation unwantedly forced upon you, and your unquestioning adaptability to it. I love you for the new relationship we now have. We are closer, we understand each other better, and I now believe you will have a greater chance of becoming the sort of man your *mother* would want you to be.

We all learnt some life lessons. It affected a lot of people. So once again, thank you all.

'Forever? A person might not last forever, but what they teach us … that lasts a lifetime. That's their legacy.'

Unknown

Prologue

Tuesday, 30th August 2011

Today should not have been memorable. It started as just another pleasant day in Sophie's uncomplicated life. She had two young children, a cottage in the country, a loving husband, and two little dogs.

She was perfectly content, but her nature had always been to strive for more. A bigger house, more children and someday, a stable in the back garden for horses. Since early childhood, she could remember the power behind her parents' words. *Never give up, Sophie. You'll always get what you always want if you work hard enough.* So she had. She'd worked hard and achieved a good education, a successful career, and when she happily married her soulmate and created a future together, her parents couldn't have been prouder.

Today, Sophie's life was exactly where she planned it to be, moving in precisely the direction she felt she deserved. She would never tire of working hard to keep it that way.

The sun was shining and the smell of freshly cut grass

sweetened the air. Sophie had taken William and Michael and the two Jack Russells for a picnic in the fields behind the cottage when she heard the familiar buzz of her mobile, throwing its tinkling tune throughout the peaceful, Northalton countryside. Lunch outside was a regular occurrence, breaking up the long summer days of entertaining young children whilst simultaneously walking energetic dogs.

There was no caller ID on the screen. Just an unrecognised female voice.

'You don't know me. I work with your husband. He's playing away from home. I thought you deserved to know.'

The line went dead.

Sophie laughed awkwardly, looking around the field, nonchalantly glancing across to the far trees, trying to spot the caller. Surely, someone was about to jump out and shout, 'Only joking!'

No one did.

She frowned, returning her gaze to the silent phone. Someone must be mucking about. Maybe someone at work didn't like Toby. Maybe someone didn't like her? It didn't cross her mind for one moment that what the caller said was true.

Sophie shook her head and put her phone in her back pocket, then returned her focus to the half-eaten picnic. One of the dogs had disappeared, taking advantage of her lapse in attention, and Michael, her youngest at five years old, had helped himself to a carton of juice, squirting the orange, sticky liquid all over himself in the process. By the time the mess was cleared up and the dog was retrieved from a rabbit hole, she had pushed the unwelcome message to the back of her mind.

She mentioned the call to Toby later that night. After ten years of being happily married, she expected him to quickly laugh it off, maybe explain it as a friendly prank or a colleague with a grudge. After months of looking for a new, more challenging role, he had recently secured a high-level position in Drema Ltd. His first task had been to issue redundancies, so Sophie guessed a disgruntled employee could be out for revenge.

'What *exactly* did she say?' Toby said, reaching across the kitchen table for her phone.

'I can't remember. Something about how you were playing away from home.' Sophie laughed. 'It's funny because I thought they might have been talking about your golf match this weekend.'

Toby didn't return the laugh. He started pressing buttons on her phone, checking her call log, verifying her story. 'Yes, but what did she sound like? Did she have an accent?'

Sophie related what she could, but really, there hadn't been much to remember. The caller was female. She sounded posh. She was quite pleasant as she delivered her brief message.

Toby seemed to know who it could have been. He mentioned an expense department and his itemised phone bills. He muttered that *she* must have deciphered Sophie's number from the one most regularly rung.

'Right. I'm not having that. We'll have to change your number.' His voice was harsh, and he was already trying to prise out the sim card.

'Why? I really don't care if she rings again. I've had that number for years, there's no way I want it changed.' Sophie thrust out her hand, trying to reclaim her identity, her voice raised, angry at his insistence. She wasn't troubled by the call; she hadn't believed a word. She felt as secure in her marriage and Toby's fidelity as she had since the day they met.

But perhaps Toby didn't. Perhaps he couldn't trust this person not to divulge more unfounded truths.

As if to confirm, the phone beeped twice before Toby secured its demise, but not before Sophie caught a glimpse of the simple message.

Unknown:
He's lying to you.

1

Thursday, 3rd May 2012

Sophie approached her destination, listening carefully to the directions from the posh American lady on the satellite navigation system. Normally, she would have silenced it, but she was in an unfamiliar area and was already late for her appointment.

She chastised herself for not planning the day's appointments more carefully. Being late made her stressed. She was usually more diligent and organised, but this search for their dream home was becoming a desperate rush. Toby's appointment to Drema Ltd last year had meant agreeing to relocate, leaving rural Northalton behind. Motivated by the significant increase in budget this new job would allow, Sophie had willingly agreed to sacrifice their charming, thatched cottage.

It had sold the day it was put on the market, and they'd moved out quickly into a nearby rental property. Their dream home continued to elude them, so now at the end of their tenancy, the day's viewings held even more significance.

Sophie's long, dark hair hung loosely around her shoulders. She'd selected dangly earrings and a matching necklace to complement her smart jeans and shirt, keen to make a good impression on the estate agent. Toby had helped get the boys off to school, surprisingly starting work late so that she could make this appointment on time.

Eight-year-old William would have frowned at the change of routine. His worrying nature was likely to make relocating schools hard. Michael, who was six going on sixteen, wouldn't have a problem. His carefree demeanour was likely to carry him through most of life's obstacles.

Sophie's destination was loudly announced by the pompous American, and she spotted the big, red brick property she had come to see. She'd already made her mind up about this house. Despite the pull of its rustic five-bar gate, gravel drive, and charming wooden nameplate, she would not be buying Nettlefield House. She'd only kept the appointment to demonstrate how serious they were as buyers, ensuring they would be the agent's first call when their perfect home eventually did come onto the market.

It wasn't that the house and grounds were wrong; it was simply the location. It sat on a main road a few metres behind an ancient yew hedge, just a stone's throw from a major service station. Comparing this position to the charming, old, thatched cottage sitting quietly alongside a bridleway, with just a stony track for access, was ridiculous. Sophie could never be happy in such a congested environment. It reminded her of her chaotic roots in

London, where heavy traffic was always just a few feet away.

She drove onto the side driveway of the house and stepped onto the deep gravel, enjoying the sound it made as she walked towards the house. After deliberating which door to knock on; front or side, she chose the latter. She shouldn't have.

'You're s'posed to come in the front.' The ginger-haired lady stepped to the side, huffing loudly as she waved Sophie through. 'T'is ain't the best way in. And you're late. But now you're here, I s'pose you'd better come in. You must be Sophie Cooper. Call me Roxy.'

Feeling suitably chastised, but politely smiling, Sophie shook the offered hand and stepped across the threshold to view this house she wasn't going to buy.

The small side lobby she now stood in had its original black and white, geometric floor tiles. It opened onto a charming, rustic kitchen, with cabinets painted an unexpected shade of blue. It was not a colour Sophie would have chosen, but alongside the rough floorboards and wooden farmhouse table, it blended in perfectly. There was even a subtle aroma of fresh coffee.

'Is the agent here yet?' Sophie enquired, somewhat doubtfully and with an air of retaliatory hostility. *I don't want your stupid house anyway, so stop being so stroppy.* Hopefully, she'd soon be saved from this unwelcoming owner by a more amenable estate agent.

'They're not coming. Can't bear it when they drag every Tom, Dick, 'n' Arry off the streets. Most of 'em can't afford it anyway. Just nosy parkers from the village. I'm showing you round. Agents are bloody useless anyway.' She strode through the kitchen door, beckoning Sophie to follow like a troublesome child.

They walked into the main hallway and Sophie gasped. 'Oh wow,' she said, captivated by the large, glass chandelier hanging from the floor above, passing down through the stairwell. Its reflection in the floor to ceiling mirror magnified its dramatic effect.

'Impressive, isn't it? *That's* why you should've come in the front.'

Sophie ignored the rebuke. 'Bet it's a nightmare to clean though?'

'Well … yes t'is but leave that to the cleaner. I'll give you her number.' Roxy smiled for the first time.

The Victorian house continued to impress as they progressed from one large, well-furnished room to another, but Sophie's original thought was foremost in her mind.

She would not be buying this house.

'Right. Outside now,' Roxy announced. She pulled on some wellies and walked out the boot room door.

Sophie loved the idea of a boot room, and this one was massive. Plenty of room for saddles, she found herself thinking.

'Yes, please. The sales particulars didn't show the stables. D'you use them?'

'Only for storage. Oh, the kids did one of 'em up into a glorified party room. Bit of paint, lights across … you know the sort of thing. Used to 'ave some damn good parties over the summer. Hardly come up here now,' Roxy admitted, striding across the freshly mown lawn.

Sophie was captivated as they walked through the large,

mature orchard full of apple trees; their fragrant blossom showing such promise for bountiful times ahead. The horses would love it, Sophie thought as she spotted the stables, mentally moving them in.

Snowy had been bought for William last year. A common white Welsh pony, a classic schoolmistress who knew her job well. Then Juno, Sophie's own prized horse, was bought earlier this year in her defiance of being forced to run faster and for longer as William dictated, leading him from the ground. Being able to control him and Snowy, led from the back of her own stead meant they could roam the countryside together, and Sophie loved it.

She imagined the run-down stables spruced up with a good wash, a bit of paint, and some new fences. She'd dreamt of this for as long as she could remember. As soon as Sophie could talk, she had desperately wanted to own a dog. When she'd turned sixteen and finally accepted there was never going to be a cardboard box with holes and a red bow waiting under the Christmas tree, she changed her ambitions to a horse. Surprisingly, due to her father's allergies, this had been easier to achieve than the elusive dog, and the dream rapidly expanded into fields and stables in the back garden.

Perhaps a back garden like this? Nope. Not an option. She quickly corrected herself.

I am not buying this house. Not so close to the main road. Sophie turned her back on the stables and concluded the tour with her smile contained and her mind made up.

*

Later that night, as the boys slept in their tiny, shared bedroom, Sophie updated Toby on the day's viewings.

'Don't get me wrong, it was lovely. Too lovely really. The house is bigger than we need, but the stables and grounds were great. Such a shame about that road.'

'Well, what about the others? This is getting silly. How is it possible to have over half a million pounds and a search area across three counties, yet still not be able to find anything?' Toby leant over her shoulder, looking at the various house details strewn across the kitchen table. 'Are you sure you're not being too fussy?'

'They were no good, I'm telling you.' Sophie pulled out one of the morning's brochures to illustrate her case. 'Look, that one's got pylons! Great ugly pylons in the garden. Can you imagine? You've seen all the details; we've just got to be patient. It's got to be right.'

'Yeah, but patience is not going to put a roof over our heads, and I refuse to keep wasting money on rent.' Toby dragged his hand through his receding hairline. The signs of stress with the new job, the desperately long commute, and the inability to find a house were showing in the lines around his eyes.

Sophie wondered if she *should* be more compromising, but her dream was for all of them, and she knew the wait would be worth it in the end.

'Well, we can't live on a main road. I won't. For goodness' sake, it's a few hundred yards from the motorway services. That's not the country house we dreamt of.' Sophie gathered up the brochures, tossing them into the recycling bin to make her point, and left the kitchen.

Invariably, it was always Sophie who concluded the conversations. Toby seemed to be getting more and more passive. Sometimes she wished he would argue back, just a bit. He'd always say, 'You only need one decision-maker in a relationship. Otherwise, it creates arguments. I'll trust your decision.'

Sometimes it might be nice to have a proper argument, the way most couples do.

2

Monday, 10th September 2012

Today should have been like any other Monday. A pleasantly short commute into work, then straight into the morning sales meeting. Toby would discuss with his colleagues business updates from the week before, the sales trend for the week ahead, and the team's excesses from the weekend. He never had much to say about the latter. He was approaching forty-two, and not for the first time, had the feeling life was passing him by.

He loved his wife and kids. He loved his new life in Nettlefield House. Did it matter that everyone else in the office seemed to have had a more fulfilling weekend?

Toby thought back to the night he insisted Sophie compromise on the big, red brick house near the motorway services. He knew she hated the location, but for once, he'd stood up to her decision and changed her mind. He'd retrieved the details for Nettlefield House from the bin, won over by the image of a large old barn. It sounded like the perfect man cave, so he'd insisted they all attend a second viewing.

Sophie had agreed, and whilst she continued to complain about the location, she couldn't disagree with him that it was otherwise perfect. Toby knew the way to Sophie's heart so had spoken quietly to her in the stables, successfully bribing her with the promise of an all-weather arena and thus the deal was done. He remembered back to the day just a few weeks before, when bursting with excitement she had moved the horses into their newly painted stables.

Finally, she had her dream and she'd been overjoyed. Even her own muck heap was considered an achievement. The boys had been in their element too, running free-range through the orchard, climbing trees, and freely kicking a football without it disappearing into a neighbour's garden.

It had felt like the start of the next twenty years of happy family life, so why now was he feeling so disheartened?

Toby studied his reflection in the office toilets, conceding defeat to the increasingly bald, shiny head accentuated by the unforgiving fluorescent lights. He had never minded wrinkles, he successfully convinced himself they added character, but perhaps he *should* invest in a moisturiser.

Was forty-two too young to start worrying about growing old?

He didn't feel young. He didn't exactly feel old, but he did feel like he'd stopped living. Maybe he would join a gym, get fit, and ask Sophie to buy him some special wrinkle cream. With those decisive thoughts to his vanity, he left the washroom.

*

His self-deprecating mood didn't subside, so Toby decided to leave work early to clear his muddled mind.

Striding purposefully, he let himself in through the side door of Nettlefield House, keen to surprise Sophie. The boys would soon be home from school, excited to find him already there, and he was hopeful for an evening of family time to compensate for the melancholy he'd felt during the day. Sadly, he'd forgotten Monday was the boys' Study Class night.

'Gosh, what are you doing back already?' Sophie said, picking up her car keys. 'You should've phoned. I'm just off to collect the boys from school. We won't be back till six.'

'Damn. Of course. Well shall *I* take them to Study Class?' Toby wished his wife had been more pleased to see him. 'You stay here. I'll collect them.'

Sophie put down her keys. The brightness in her eyes gave away her joy at being released from the task. 'But you've never taken them. You don't know where to go.'

Toby opened his mouth to interject.

'But okay then.' Sophie carried on. 'I haven't walked the dogs yet, and the horses still need doing. See if you can encourage William to try harder. Last week, he really struggled with the work.'

Sophie continued with a bombardment of instructions which made Toby want to rebel, disappear with the boys to McDonald's, and boycott Study Class altogether. They would love it, and he could really do with a Big Mac and apple pie.

He wouldn't though. He knew it would be wrong. It was

easier to just do as Sophie said, even if her long list of instructions had seemed excessive.

'Right. Right, yes, I've got it.' Although, he wasn't sure he had.

Toby made himself a quick tea in his travel flask, grabbed an apple to substitute for the apple pie, and jumped back into his car to go about his duties as instructed.

*

The venue for Study Class hadn't needed the extensive directions. He found it easily. The parents waited in a small, windowless lobby whilst the children proceeded into the large hall with their week's worksheets and the required positive attitude.

Only two other parents were waiting, and the silence in such a small room was nearly tangible. The chairs were too close for any privacy, so Toby positioned himself between a radiator and an exhausted-looking young mother, then took out his phone to check emails. Ten or so minutes went by without any change. The only movement came from a toddler, who was opening and closing the main door with much squeaking, sudden gusts of air, and parental warnings of, 'Watch for fingers.'

He had barely noticed the other lady in the room. She was quietly sitting with her head in a book, the sign of a mother who had sat there many times before. A boy exited the study hall, and the weary young mother stood up to claim him, then gathered up her annoying toddler and swiftly departed the dingy room.

Toby turned in his chair and looked up from his phone. He felt obliged to break the awkward silence now there were only two of them in the room. 'I suppose you can be in here for quite a while?'

She lifted her head out from the book. 'Oh, yes, it can take forever. I've been coming for years. Can't imagine the hours I've wasted sitting here, playing on my phone, or trying to read.'

'First time I've been. My wife, Sophie, usually comes. You've probably met her?' He noticed her bright, sparkly blue eyes light up as she recognised the name.

'Oh, Sophie, yes. We have a good gossip every week, makes the time go faster. You must be William and Michael's dad. Pleased to meet you. My name's Abigail.' She stretched out her hand, moving to a closer chair.

Toby could smell her. An unfamiliar, sweet scent that travelled up his nostrils and settled in his mouth. He could almost taste her, and he wondered why Sophie never wore perfume. He found himself drawn into an easy, informal conversation about children, schools, and the benefit of Study Class.

'I feel so silly, sitting here in this outfit. Normally, I'd have changed, but today's been one of those days, you know, when things just work against you?' Abigail was dressed in a flight attendant's uniform, so obviously felt compelled to explain her livelihood.

'That's a great look though. I love red on women. Such a bold colour and so smart and sassy.' Toby smirked. 'You look just like the women on those adverts. Virgin, isn't it?'

Toby hoped he wasn't being too familiar, but Abigail seemed not to mind and replied with equal openness.

'I'd rather strip this off right now and put my running gear on to go round the park for a bit, blow away the cobwebs. Planes are so claustrophobic; don't know how I still do it at my age.'

Toby smiled. 'I haven't run for years. Golf's my game. Still good for those cobwebs though.' He found himself describing his hobby, his work and the unusual day that had led him to this slightly less dingy little room.

Now that the toddler had stopped playing with the door, the room seemed to have warmed up. Toby stood and walked across the small space to glance through the narrow window into the hall, both to dispel the heat from his body and to gauge how long the boys might be.

He couldn't see them. He turned and instantly locked eyes with Abigail, drawn back by an invisible winch. He allowed the winch to pull him forwards and he sat to the side of her, away from the radiator he attributed to his heated body.

Abigail started talking again. Toby listened to her soft, well-spoken voice with an unexpected awareness of her attractiveness. She had the sort of face that if each individual feature was studied separately, she would be quite unattractive, but somehow, putting them all together with her long, wavy blonde hair, she became rather beautiful.

It was her mention of the Triathlon Club that prompted Toby to re-enter the conversation. Up until then, he had nodded and answered but now realised how little he'd heard and how much he'd enjoyed just looking at her animated face as she spoke.

'The club's a good starting point. I've been a member for years, and they're a great bunch of people. We meet up socially quite a bit, and there's enough of us that you're never short of an invitation for a run, swim, or bike ride.'

Toby was surprised at how exciting she made the exertion of running, swimming, and cycling all in one day sound. He'd always thought running would be good for his fitness and he knew he could ride a bike, but he had never enjoyed swimming in open water. As a child, his family had capsized in a raft on a white-water course in California. The memory of his younger sister being sucked under by the currents and of his own legs entangled in river weeds terrified him. However, many years later, sitting in this dingy room with this sparkly woman, he felt capable of tackling anything. For the first time that day, that week, or even that year, he didn't feel old. He felt like he might have found his 'gym', the thing that may help him to start feeling alive again.

'Sounds great. Might be just what I need.'

'How'd it go, sweethearts?' Abigail spoke lovingly to her children as they exited the hall. 'You've been in there ages. Hope you finished it all this week?'

Toby noticed the way she spoke. So tender and fragile. They locked eyes again with a new, more acquainted bond as she stood, gathering up her things and making to leave.

'Why don't you come along to the club one night? I can introduce you to everyone. There's a run next Sunday.' She spoke whilst simultaneously checking under seats and passing coats to her kids. 'A few of us are going. It might be a good starting point.'

Toby had a flashback to his displeasure with his increasing baldness. 'Let me get the door for you. Looks like you've got your hands full.' He stood quickly, thankful for his height of six-foot-two and held open the door.

'Thanks. Anyway, nice to have met you. I'll get your number from Sophie and message you. Hopefully see you Sunday.' She touched his arm as she left and held eye contact just a fraction longer as she walked through the door, away from the little, now desolate room.

Toby was left with a heated body, a confused look on his face, and a surprising change in his mood. He felt ten years younger, capable, and optimistic about life, and he revelled in the unfamiliar feelings.

Physically shaking his thoughts away from the woman who could light up this room, he watched as his much-loved boys came out from the hall, animating the space with a different, more powerful light.

*

Toby and the boys returned home to find Sophie out, no doubt walking the dogs across the fields behind the house. He switched on the kettle and began making tea whilst the boys disappeared to play.

His phone vibrated, and he began reading the emails that continually fed into his inbox, expecting a reply. Drema Ltd was a 24/7 operation, which meant he felt obliged to provide a 24/7 response, and he knew it drove Sophie mad.

Sophie could never understand why he couldn't leave things till the morning. She had been well trained in the art of time management throughout her successful career as a senior buyer in a large retailer and knew how and when to say no. She had been a corporate highflyer when they met, but at heart, she was a wife and mother, needing little to make her happy. Society's pressure and her parents' expectations drove her forward, but in the end, it was simply love that had halted her in her tracks.

They were both Capricorns, born just eight days apart, and in their first week of meeting, spiritual words appeared in the horoscope section of the free London newspaper.

Times are changing fast and for the better. Your cloud has burst, there is a silver lining, and yes ... you can be this lucky in love.

They both believed it had been a sign and had talked of magical bursting clouds with silver linings ever since. Within the year they were married, and they felt like two halves that had become whole. Soul mates.

As Toby reminisced on the memories of that period in his life, he became weighed down once again by feelings of life passing him by. He drank his tea, immersed in thought, until his subconscious mind and the contraction in his stomach alerted him to either something great or something bad about to happen. His heart pumped faster in response as the thought manifested in his mind.

Has she asked Sophie for his number yet? Has she already messaged him?

Toby recalled the look she gave as she left the room. Goosebumps raced up his arm from the place she had touched, and he opened his phone, checking for a message. No new message had appeared, and the goosebumps deflated as his subdued, conscious mind took over, reminding him of his earlier self-deprecating mood and disappointment in life. He couldn't even remember her name.

He slumped further down in his chair, returning to the security of emails, waiting for his wife's return.

3

Monday, September 10th 2012

'Sorry I've been so long. How was Study Class?' Sophie bustled into the kitchen with the two hungry dogs following. 'It's a lovely evening. It's so nice now the rapeseed's been cut. I could see the dogs and where they were hunting. Poor bunnies had nowhere to hide.'

She had wasted many hours over the years, sitting at the edge of a field of tall bright yellow, calling for the Jack Russells to reappear. They returned only when *they* decided the time was right. When they did, they would be exhausted from chasing bunnies, their eyes rubbed raw from pushing through the hard stems of rapeseed plants.

'Where are the boys? Boys!' Sophie shouted, not waiting for Toby to answer. 'Boys,' she repeated, cupping her mouth with her hands. Her voice echoed across the empty rooms. She knew her shout may not have been heard, and even if it had, it was unlikely the boys would have reacted, knowing it was time for bed.

She turned back to Toby, immersed in his phone at the table. 'Where are they?' She suspected he'd have been unaware if the boys were outside, riding their bikes around the service station.

'They were here just now. Not sure where they've gone,' he finally replied, but Sophie was already walking out, searching for the bleeps and pops from the Wii.

'Pop me. Pop me! You have to pop me,' said Michael as the miniature Mario figure floated by in its bubble of doom, waiting for a remaining player to pop him back to life.

'No, I can't. I've got to finish this world. You're too slow.' William entered the next level of the game, seemingly unaware of his mother's entry, her hands firmly on her hips.

'Who said it was time to go on the Wii?' Sophie asked the intensely focused gamers. She knew from experience they wouldn't move, even if an ice cream van pulling a pic 'n' mix counter drove in front of the television. 'Come on. It's seven o'clock. It's bedtime.' Sophie moved in front of the screen, obscuring their view to elicit a response.

Michael spoke first. 'Daddy said we could. He promised us. Didn't he, William?' He looked to his older brother for backup.

'Well, yes ... yes. He said we could. Earlier.' William lied. He was far less convincing than his brother.

Sophie knew all too well the promises Toby made, without thought to the consequences. 'Children don't forget a promise'. She remembered that from reading parenting books. 'Never promise anything you can't deliver, and never use a punishment you can't or won't enforce'.

Sophie loved reading self-help books and learning from others' experiences. Unfortunately, the only things Toby read were Twitter and the sporting news. He certainly hadn't read any parenting books.

Asserting her authority, she said, 'Right, turn it off. It's bath time.'

'I'm still hungry,' William said. It was a phrase he used regularly when trying to delay bedtime. 'Have we even had tea yet?' he continued, looking up from the screen, furrowing his brow.

'You can't be hungry. Did you not finish your fish and chips?'

'No, we didn't get any. Daddy went a different way. We didn't pass the chip van.'

Sophie's realisation that the boys had not been fed redirected her annoyance onto her husband. With her temper rising she found him where she'd left him, sitting at the kitchen table, consumed by Drema.

'Toby! The boys are starving. Why didn't you stop at the van?' She spoke whilst filling the microwave with beans and the toaster with bread, glaring as she moved around the kitchen.

'What?' Toby looked up from his phone, visibly shaking Drema from his mind.

'I told you to stop at the van. I know I did. God, Toby, I couldn't have been clearer in my instructions. Were you even listening to me earlier?

'Well, yes. But I didn't go through the village, it slipped my mind. They shouldn't eat that rubbish anyway,' he offered as an excuse.

'So why didn't you make them something when you got in then?' Sophie noisily pulled out some plates from the clean dishwasher. 'They're in there playing games, and you're in here, oblivious to anything other than Drema.' She threw her arms up. 'What *was* the point in coming home early?'

'Okay. I'm sorry.' He stood and slipped his phone into his back pocket. 'Look, I'll feed the dogs for you.'

Sophie ignored his waving white flag. She had thoroughly enjoyed sorting out the horses without the boys in tow and had spent longer than usual grooming Juno, brushing away the dust from his coat, returning the black, dense hair to an ebony shine. She would never have done that if she had known the boys had not yet had dinner.

What would have happened if she'd stayed out even longer? No one would have realised until their tummies started rumbling louder than the Wii. Feeling like a mother of three, she dolloped piles of beans onto toast and yelled for William and Michael to go wash their hands.

*

Reassured that Sophie had taken control of the evening meal and with the dogs happily fed, Toby took his phone into the lounge, quietly closing the door behind him.

The Wii was still playing, and the background noise and movement was surprisingly calming, so he left it on. His phone had vibrated as he fed the dogs, and his anticipation had been building.

Childishly counting to three, he opened his phone to be rewarded with a message.

Unknown:
Hope you weren't there too long?
Anyway, if you're interested, the next
club run is Sunday at Bottomley Lakes.
Meeting in car park at 9. About 8 miles.
Happy to introduce you to everyone!
Should be fun! Oh, it's Abigail!

It was a simple, informative text. Nothing more than an innocent arrangement between two parents, recently acquainted at their children's tutoring session. Yet his breathing had quickened as he re-read the message, searching for any double meanings to her words. Finding none, he responded with a simple, friendly message, but he couldn't stop a rising surge of anticipation spread through his body. He reassured himself this was due to the prospect of the run, not to the company, yet he couldn't help but recall her bright, sparkly eyes as he hit send.

Toby:
Wasn't too much longer. Goodness
knows what they do in there! Sunday
shouldn't be a problem. Not sure about
the 8 miles though. Might need some
help there!

Toby continued to watch the little Mario figure travel across the screen on his solo journey and waited in anticipation for Abigail's reply. He added her details to his contacts list then silenced his phone, relying on its vibration to alert him, but frequently checked the screen regardless. No response came.

He couldn't help but feel a decline in his expectations. Perhaps he had misread the situation, or maybe she was just busy, feeding her own family.

He walked back to the kitchen to offer his help with dinner and watched Sophie.

She was filling up the empty dishwasher with dirty plates. Her long, dark hair was tucked behind her ears, and she was encouraging the boys to hurry up and finish their dinners. He knew she craved the few hours that would be left of the evening. Time to relax with a glass of wine and sit together on the sofa, in front of the television. Quality time he had unintentionally reduced.

Watching her now, he could see she had probably accepted the loss of those hours. He felt he should sidle up next to her, hug her close, kiss her gently on the cheek, and apologise for his earlier lapse. He knew it would feel nice and that it would make him feel better when she responded with a gentle hug and loving words.

But he didn't.

Instead, he poured himself a glass of wine. He felt a bit hungry too but wasn't brave enough to ask what was for *his* dinner. Sophie seemed to have forgotten about his oversight and was having a lively discussion with William.

'He needs a new pony.' She brought Toby into the discussion. 'If he's to start Tetrathlons this year, he'll need something bigger.'

'What's wrong with Snowy?'

'She's seventeen! You can't expect her to carry an eight-year-old over a sixty-centimetre cross country course. Don't be daft. Snowy can be Michael's pony now.'

Toby wasn't sure why she thought he had an opinion. When it came to the horses, Sophie made all the decisions, and that suited him fine. He hadn't even considered that ponies could be hand-me-downs too, like a pair of trousers or shoes.

'How much would a new pony cost?' Toby asked.

'Well, five hundred pounds at least. Probably more for a good one, but I think we should be giving Michael the opportunities William had. It'd be great if they could both do pony club camp next summer on their own ponies.'

Toby looked across at his wife and admired her for her dedication to the children's activities. She put them first all the time and he didn't know how she managed it. He loved watching the boys in their competitions and events, but the day-to-day care of the horses bored him.

'What about Juno? He's bigger and younger, isn't he?'

'Are you crazy? William can't manage Juno. He'd fall off before he got on!' Sophie looked across at William's equally shocked face, and they both laughed at the obvious absurdity of Toby's suggestion.

'Well, I don't know, do I? Ponies are your department.' He went to the freezer to see what he could find to microwave for his dinner.

*

It had been an unseasonably warm September and it was a muggy night. As Toby climbed into bed, he noticed that Sophie hadn't pulled on her usual pyjamas, socks, and anything else to keep out the cold. She was possibly naked; he couldn't be sure.

As he turned off the light and snuggled down close, he wasn't thinking of new little ponies, but of more primal, selfish pleasures.

Toby was naked as always. He loved the feel of the cold sheets on his body. He couldn't understand how Sophie could bear the heat from her side of the electric blanket. As he settled into his spoon shape behind her, he allowed his lean, muscular body to press up close. He may have been going bald, but he still had a decent physique, and the touch of his skin on her unexpectedly naked body caused a welcome, rousing sensation.

He allowed the cool and throbbing pressure to the back of her thigh to continue asking for permission, with a subtlety he found hard to control. It had been a long time since Toby had any luck with this approach, and it didn't look like tonight was going to be any different. He was sure Sophie couldn't be asleep, but she wasn't picking up on his obvious need, and his efforts began to wane.

He hadn't felt up to it anyway. He was tired from his emotionally draining day and the full bottle of wine he knew he shouldn't have finished. Not on a Monday.

He rolled over, accepting defeat, and began imagining a pair of sparkly blue eyes watching him run effortlessly around the edge of a beautiful lake, before quickly falling into a deep, dreamless sleep.

*

Sophie remained motionless, ensuring the moment had passed. She knew his intentions yet couldn't bring herself to partake.

She would have loved to have enjoyed the intimacy they used to share, but somehow, after this evening's disjointed dinner and his distractions with Drema, she felt a chill in her heart she couldn't warm up. Wishing she had worn her pyjamas to cushion the void between them, she gently moved away and slept fitfully, dreaming about new ponies.

4

Sunday, 14th October 2012

It took just two weeks to find the new member of the Cooper family. Chicco was a sour-looking pony, but his willingness to jump and his calm disposition compensated for his lack of charm.

Since his arrival, William had bonded well, and today was their first test as a combination, competing for a place on the Pony Club Tetrathlon Team.

It was 6:30 a.m., and Sophie woke to find Toby on the iPad. In the old days, they would have woken slowly, drank tea, chatted, and occasionally made love. Now she barely got a hug, and she missed it. She had always tried to avoid having a television in the bedroom for this exact reason, and she was now trying—unsuccessfully—to get the iPhones and iPads banned from the bedroom too.

She rolled over and put her arm around Toby, pulling herself in close, savouring the last few minutes before starting her day, but her movement seemed to be the signal it was time to get up.

He rolled away from her, put down his iPad, and jumped out of bed, heading towards the shower.

Feeling discarded, Sophie climbed out her side, cursing the coldness in the room. She pulled back the curtains to confirm, as she did every morning, that the ponies were happily grazing, irrespective of today's heavy mist, then went downstairs to organise an early breakfast for them all.

Sophie was disappointed that William's selection day clashed with Toby's first attempt at a half marathon. She couldn't think of a worse activity than running for thirteen miles round the streets of Desborough, but Toby was relishing the occasion. She had been surprised at his enthusiasm for his new sport over the last month. He had joined a triathlon club, bought some padded Lycra (which she couldn't help but laugh at when he first put it on), and surprisingly was even swimming in open water. His golf clubs had been relegated to the back of the barn, and in their place stood his new road bike that cost the same as a small pony.

Sophie hadn't minded the change of sport, but she found his intense addiction to it, and the hours spent training, out of character.

By eight a.m., Toby had left without the family breakfast and without the words of encouragement for William, Sophie would have expected. She had a busy day ahead with the boys, the dogs, and the ponies, yet she felt abandoned and neglected on behalf of them all by Toby's devotion to his new hobby. Even worse was that he was missing, even forgetting, a significant day for William.

But there was no time for melancholy. There was plenty to do, and whilst Sophie was an expert at getting boys and ponies ready for such events, she would have welcomed some help from the rider.

'William, get those jodhpurs on *now!* We're going to be late.'

'Okay. When Liverpool have beaten Man U.' He remained transfixed to the screen.

'It's a recording. The result won't change, you can watch it later. Now turn it off.' Sophie silently cursed Toby for reminding William that the recording was waiting to be watched.

William didn't move.

'Chicco's waiting in the trailer going crazy. Now come on.' Sophie was disappointed by William's reluctance to go to his pony, all clean and ready, through no effort of his own. He would probably have been happier sitting in front of the football for the next two hours, rather than cantering through the countryside, leaping over fences, ditches, and banks.

Sophie reached across to power it off.

'Wait!' William thrust out his hand, covering the button. 'I need to ring Daddy. Liverpool just scored a goal. Gerrard flipped it in from outside the box. It was amazing. Where is Daddy?'

'You can't speak to him. He's running round Desborough. You can watch it with him later, he'll be home before us.' Sophie had an edge to her voice she realised was annoyance. Whilst Toby was out enjoying himself, she was struggling on her own with the boys.

'But Daddy won't mind. It was a really good goal.'

Sophie pressed down hard on the button, hearing the electricity flick off as the screen turned black. 'Look, he won't have his phone on him. He's running. He doesn't have any pockets, does he? You can message him when we get in the car, and he'll pick it up when he finishes. Now please, can we get on the road before your pony climbs out of the trailer?'

'Okay, okay. Liverpool's gonna win anyway. They're two goals ahead already. I'll message Daddy in the car.' He slowly stood and noticed the cream jodhpurs and stripey tie next to him.

Tilting his head, he looked up and asked, 'Where are we going again?'

*

As it was, William and Chicco did a great job. There were no rosettes to be won, but they had navigated the course of ditches, water jumps, and log piles, interspersed with long gallops up and down hills, and secured a place on the team. A big achievement for an eight-year-old. Sophie was annoyed she didn't have a camera to capture the action. She may even have put the photos on Facebook. She rarely updated her profile and she only ever looked at her newsfeed to be nosy.

Toby frequently frustrated her with the amount of time he devoted to social media. They joked that he probably knew more about his celebrity friends from Twitter than he knew about his own family from real life, and today was no exception.

It was one p.m. when Sophie received a message. She'd

been waiting for the end of Toby's run so she could share William's success.

Toby:
Phew ... finished. 2hr 5mins. Not the best time but really enjoyed it! Bit of a crap route round streets. Just stopping for a bacon sandwich, then back to car and home. Hope you're having a nice day even though the weather's rubbish. What you all up to? X

Well, at least he made it round in one piece.

Sophie was in much better spirits now William's event was over, and she could see how thrilled he was with his achievement. He hadn't stopped patting Chicco on the neck and kissing his muzzle, thanking him for jumping so well and was now rapidly feeding him a lifetime of polo mints.

She loved seeing the boys enjoy their ponies, making all her efforts worthwhile, yet it pained her that Toby had not asked after William. He was usually so keen on being an integral part of their sporting activities, encouraging them to try their hardest and to always be great sportsmen. But today, he appeared to have forgotten his eldest son was achieving something special too.

She sent a quick congratulatory message in reply, then began the chaotic task of getting everyone back home.

*

Once Chicco was back in his field, the trailer unhitched and cleaned, the car unloaded, and the boys sat in front of the television, Sophie made a much-needed cup of tea. It was three p.m., and she had expected Toby to be home by now.

She hoped for a cosy family afternoon. Maybe they could watch a film, put some logs on the fire, and toast some marshmallows. She longed for this quality time, but she suspected she was the only one who did. The boys were back playing on the Wii, and she sat alone in the silent kitchen with her second cup of tea, feeling abandoned, unwanted.

She spotted the pile of sketches on the side and began to look through the rough pencil drawings of their new conservatory. It was the one downfall of Nettlefield House that the best view of the garden was from the downstairs toilet. Building the new structure would bring the garden into the heart of the house and have a captivating space to watch the seasons go by and the sunsets go down.

They had still not decided on the final design and the mass of sketches proved their indecision. Sophie didn't think they were too far away now and hoped that by Christmas they would be eating dinner inside the special space.

As another rough sketch began to take shape on paper, Sophie's phone rang.

'Hiya, it's me. I was just thinking of you all and how William got on at his event today?'

Rani was Sophie's best friend, conveniently married to Toby's best friend Ant. They had known each other since their first babies were born within days of each other and had lived around the corner in Northalton. They'd spent many enjoyable weekends together at Nettlefield House and were as relaxed in each other's company as if they were family.

Sophie and Rani could tell each other everything, and over a bottle of wine, they regularly did.

'He did great, Chicco was a star. They got a place on the team.'

'Cool, bet Toby loved that, another place on another team. Your boys are *so* sporty!' Rani often shared her friendly envy at how competitive the boys were in contrast to her two girls.

Sophie found herself doodling a collection of stars above the roof of her new sketch. 'Toby wasn't there. He had his half marathon today; he didn't even remember it was on. Didn't ask after William once.' Sophie went on to explain how even now she was still waiting for him to come home to spend some time together as a family.

Rani and Ant did everything together and seemed to have the perfect marriage. 'Bet Ant wouldn't leave you and the girls as much as Toby does? I felt really lonely before you rang.'

'Yeah, but think of how fit and athletic he's gonna get with all that training,' Rani laughed. 'He's going to have a six-pack and pecs; Ant's barely got a one-pack and wouldn't know what a pec was if it pecked him!'

Rani always had the capacity to make Sophie laugh and visualising Toby now, Sophie realised he *had* got fitter and toned. She made a mental note to check him out later, fully.

'True. But that doesn't help with the loneliness if he's never here. Plus, that makes me look even worse, I still can't shift this last half stone, and if I don't do it before Christmas, I'm going to be enormous by January!' Sophie rolled her eyes as she realised the newly recognised importance of losing her last half stone.

'Talking of Christmas, are we still coming to you?' Rani changed the subject. 'I've got the wine sorted, Tesco had a special on and Ant nearly bought the whole shelf. Some nice stuff too. He found that red wine Toby loves so much.'

Sophie remembered back to Christmas Day 2000, the day they discovered their favourite wine and the magical day Toby had proposed. Her father had been ecstatic that at last, one of his four daughters was getting married, so he offered his best wine in celebration. They had drunk it over many occasions since, happily reliving the memories of the day they first realised they were going to be together, forever. The wine had since become harder and harder to find and more and more expensive.

'Can't believe you found it! Toby will be well chuffed.' Sophie brushed her loneliness and worries aside. 'So yes, definitely still on for Christmas in that case. I'm hoping the conservatory will be built by then.' She drew a childish, triangular Christmas tree inside her sketch, then added an oversized bottle of wine to complement it and smiled. Christmas this year was going to be great.

Plus, that design, with its stars and Christmas wine, looked perfect now. That was definitely the one.

*

Toby didn't get home till four p.m. and required a long, hot bath and an equally long glass of wine to get over his ordeal. Sophie had no sympathy.

If you're gonna run thirteen miles, you're going to have to suffer the consequences.

Whilst Toby relaxed and chatted to William about his earlier achievements, Sophie sorted out the mundane Sunday night chores of finishing homework, ironing, cleaning football boots, and sorting dinner.

She finished the horses, walked the dogs, fed the family, bathed the boys, and put them to bed. She finally allowed herself a glass of pinot grigio and went through to the lounge to join Toby who had been sitting on the sofa since his bath, allowing his muscles to regain their strength.

She sank alongside him, smiling, deliberately pushing her previous annoyance aside. 'What are you watching?'

'Oh, it's just the darts. Taylor's on in a minute. I can go in the other room if you want to watch something.'

He was already standing, picking up his wine to leave.

'Don't you want to watch that drama on the BBC everyone's talking about?'

Sophie used to enjoy sitting together before the week ahead, relaxing and watching Sunday night dramas. There would be one dog on the side of the sofa, nestled between herself and the armrest, then the other sprawled across Toby's lap.

But Toby had already left the room, and the dogs reassumed their positions, unconcerned at the missing piece of the puzzle. Sophie, however, was concerned. She missed that piece and cursed the darts for removing it from her Sunday night jigsaw.

She only watched the first part of the drama anyway before she lost interest, settling instead for an early night. She left the lounge, leaving the dogs in ecstasy at being able to stretch out into her warm patch, and went to find Toby.

He was standing in front of the television in the family room, watching the darts, playing darts, and holding his phone open on Twitter. He had recently hung a dartboard on the wall beside the television, and the boys had loved it. The newly decorated walls, floorboards and small dogs walking beneath had not.

'I'm going to bed. I'm knackered and it's flipping cold in there. Shall I put your side of the blanket on?' Sophie said.

'No, don't worry. I won't be up for a bit. Taylor's only just coming on.'

Toby placed his phone in his pocket and sipped his wine. More darts flew at the wall. One, Sophie noticed, fell from the board, embedding itself into the Victorian skirting below.

She flinched and turned away, too tired to argue about the suitability of playing darts in the house.

'Well, don't be long.'

Why he wasn't tired, she couldn't understand. If she had just run thirteen miles, she would certainly be in bed by now, asking for an all-over body massage accompanied with love and sympathy. But then *she* would never have considered running thirteen miles, and if Toby thought a massage would be on offer, he should have put down the darts and asked for it.

Feeling no guilt at not offering yet annoyed she couldn't now check out his newly toned physique, she continued up to bed.

*

The darts are such good entertainment, Toby thought as Sophie left the room. He turned the volume up, knowing she wouldn't hear it in their bedroom. He wished he could be there live, absorbing the adrenaline-fuelled atmosphere, the hyped-up entry songs, and the theatrical players with their scantily clad, walk-on girls.

He remembered the days when he would sit on the sofa with Sophie, watching the Sunday night drama with a dog on his lap, and it seemed so dull in comparison. Excitement, adrenaline, and feeling alive was what he craved. Not for the first time, he considered he was staring a mid-life crisis in the face.

It must be all that adrenaline from earlier. Those endorphins from his run were making him feel alive again.

As if on cue, he felt his silent phone vibrate. His adrenaline line was refuelled as he read the text.

Abigail:
Hope you're still feeling high. Told you it
feels good! Glad we caught up at the
end. It's nice to see a friendly face
after 13 miles. Maybe next time you'll
manage to beat me? Thanks for lunch.
Sorry I kept you for so long. LOL

Toby smiled as he read and re-read the message. Taylor had walked on, and he'd barely noticed. He smirked at Abigail's comment about managing to beat her, promising himself that he would achieve that gauntlet very soon. His time today was the slowest of all the club members, but he hadn't minded.

This was just the start. He would quickly get faster. Roused by the adrenaline, with a buzz from the wine and a roar from the crowds, he wrote his reply.

> Toby:
> Definitely still high and not just from the run! Really enjoyed chatting. Could talk to you all day long! But watch out. Next run I'm coming to get you!

5

Sunday, 28th October 2012

Toby's phone vibrated on the bedside table. He rapidly reached across, deadening the vibration a second after it began, but it didn't go unnoticed by the lightly sleeping Sophie.

'Who's that? It's only seven a.m.'

Toby glanced at the message as he quickly climbed out of bed, entangling himself in the sheets in his eagerness to get out. 'Um … oh, it's Ant. He's messaging about the football.'

Ant was another dedicated Liverpool fan, so Toby knew this answer would satisfy Sophie.

She turned over with a groan, grabbing the duvet, obviously trying to hang onto sleep as long as possible.

Abigail:
Hope you're ready for today's big run.
My start time's way before you, so I'll
wait at the finish. Hope you haven't

> forgotten our bet on who gets the
> winning time? Bring your wallet, it won't
> be you! xxx

Tugging free from the sheets, his heart rate pounding, he re-read what Abigail had written, aware he had just lied to his wife.

He had his second half marathon in two hours and had simply received a friendly message regarding a bet he was determined to win.

So why had he felt the need to lie?

He and Abigail had met several times over the last few weeks, at swimming practice, organised runs, and the occasional bike ride. It was always as part of the club and always innocent. So, why hadn't he told Sophie? He reasoned he would never find *her* waiting at the finishing line and as Abigail seemed certain she would be there before him, there was no reason to involve Sophie. Was there?

With the self-reassurance he had done no wrong, he made his way to the boys' shower room instead of his own en suite. It had underfloor heating, was more like a wet room, and was a quieter option for his sleeping wife.

It also had a lockable door.

> Toby:
> I've been training hard you know. I'm
> going to be faster than ever today, so
> the drinks will definitely be on you! X

As the message left his phone, Toby wondered where the kisses at the end had come from. He scrolled through his recent history. He and Abigail had exchanged just a few messages every couple of days, all about the club, start times, and runs. He noted the first kiss had come from him a few days ago, after Abigail had been upset at swim practice. A few members had huddled round, offering sympathy, but Toby hadn't known what was wrong so didn't like to intrude. He had sent a polite, 'Hope all is okay?' message later that night, and his reply to her answer had delivered the first kiss.

Abigail:
I'm fine. I was just a bit of a mess earlier. Bad argument with Matthew. Everyone knows things have been rough and it's just getting worse. Thanks for asking though!

Toby:
I didn't want to intrude. Glad you're OK, but happy to listen if you want to offload anytime. See you soon. X

Brushing aside his growing guilt, Toby accessed the contacts list on his phone and searched for Abigail's name. He replaced it with 'James B.'

James was, in fact, a real person from the club, so it didn't feel too deceitful.

He was not exactly a friend but someone Toby might talk to about bets and runs. He made a conscious note to be careful with the kisses and delete the text history. There was a brief moment when the voices inside his head questioned his actions and where this deceit was going, but he brushed them aside, feeling relaxed about the concealment. He was startled into reality by a new text.

It simply read, 'Tea!'

This one-word demand made him smile, quickly dispelling his worries about the lie he was cultivating. It was a long-standing joke between him and Sophie. Whoever woke first at the weekend would make the morning tea and bring it up to bed. When it fell to Toby, he would invariably get caught up reading the news, watching sporting re-runs, or just playing with the boys, so Sophie would eventually send the one-word quip to prompt him.

'Coming!' was his simple reply. He left the shower room and went downstairs to complete his task.

*

'Are you not having yours here?' Sophie asked, as Toby put down the single cup.

She was sitting up, writing her diary.

She had written daily for over twenty years and had every diary sitting on the bookcase. She said she wanted to capture her memories and have something meaningful to read when she became old, deaf, and immobile.

Toby had loved that sentiment, imagining them together as an old decrepit couple, bringing their memories back to life, but now her words worried him. For the first time, he pondered what she might be writing, speculating it might not all be good.

'Mine's downstairs. I've got to be off in a bit. Registration's at nine. I'm just jumping in the shower first.' He spoke quickly, trying to hide his building excitement.

He had done plenty of training for this run and was convinced he could achieve a personal best. He was desperate to beat Abigail and impress her. Last year she had completed the London Marathon in under four hours and Toby admired her dedication and success. She was lean and strong, and he couldn't help but compare her to his wife.

Sophie was strong in many ways: certainly mentally and when dealing with half-tonne animals, but she had lost her strength in her identity and physical appearance. She held no passion or interest in anything other than the dogs and the horses, and typically, that was all on behalf of the boys. He could never imagine sharing his new interest with her, not like he was doing with Abigail. Running made him feel alive, and he wouldn't allow himself to feel bad about that.

Sophie was probably happily planning another day with the boys and their ponies, requiring and expecting little input from him anyway.

He searched his mind for anything of importance for the boys (he had felt bad about forgetting William's tetrathlon event,) but he couldn't find anything.

Sophie was absorbed with filling in her diary and drinking tea, offering no last-minute instructions or reminders, so he felt free to go.

He gave her a quick kiss on the side of her face and left the bedroom, fully focused on his game plan for beating Abigail.

*

Several hours later, covered in mud and dried sweat, Toby pulled onto the driveway of Nettlefield House, waiting for normality to sink in.

He didn't want to be here.

He'd had an amazing run and a thoroughly fulfilling day, which he had prolonged ending for as long as he thought acceptable. The buzz from achieving his personal best was overwhelming in a different way than from winning a round of golf and he loved it.

Yet now, at home, his endorphins were running away, replaced with an oppressive cloud.

He thought back to the hour or two after the race when he'd sat with Abigail in a rather scruffy café, both oblivious to the state they were in. He smiled as he remembered how relaxed he had felt in her company.

They'd had an emotional conversation. Abigail's marriage of fourteen years was disintegrating, and she felt powerless to stop it. The cracks had become craters, and they were making each other miserable.

Toby worried these signs were evident in his marriage too, and he'd been surprised at the extent of his empathy. He found himself discussing his own examples, some slightly fabricated, to demonstrate he knew how she felt.

Being back home now made him feel like a hypocrite.

'I'm home.' Toby walked through the kitchen, listening for a response. Silence. Not even the dogs came to greet him.

He knew he was back later than expected, so he assumed everyone was outside, tending to the animals. The boot room door, locked from the outside, confirmed this.

As he made a cup of tea, alone with his thoughts, he reran the marathon in his mind, enticing back the endorphins.

But he couldn't separate the feelings for the run from his feelings for Abigail. She released a different side to him; a more masculine, yet more sensitive, protective side. He laughed and felt exhilarated in her presence. She could ignite his whole body.

For a moment, he began to question his intentions and morals, but not liking his answers, he quickly crushed the seed of guilt.

They were just friends who enjoyed each other's company and shared a mutual interest, nothing more.

I can have close female friends, can't I?

Without answering himself, Toby decided it was time to stop confusing his endorphins and go find his family.

*

Sophie returned from putting the animals to bed with two reluctant children in tow. The encroaching darkness was getting faster each night and the expanding mud brought a challenge of its own.

She walked through the boot room door just as Toby was pulling on his wellies. 'Oh, finally. You're back.' She scowled. 'How was your race?'

'Great. Really good. I did a personal best: two hours five.'

Sophie was bent over, trying to pull off Michael's muddy boots. 'For goodness sake, stop fidgeting, you're flicking mud everywhere!'

Successfully de-booting both boys, she stood up, looking into Toby's face, frowning. 'Two hours five? You must have finished ages ago then? I've had to drag the boys out to do the horses and they were a real pain. They just won't stand on the concrete and stay out the way. Twice Chicco nearly knocked Michael over at the gateway.' She paused, tilting her head. 'Why are you so late then?'

'I'm not that late.' He ran his hand through his decreasing hair, then looked at his watch for confirmation. 'I couldn't just leave. We had to wait for everyone in the club to finish. Then there was the usual few drinks and food afterwards. I was knackered, so I had to eat something before I drove home.' He was looking at her now, a massive smile across his face. 'Two hours five I did it in. That's flipping brilliant you know!'

'Okay. Well ... well done you. Dinner's nearly ready, and I promised the boys a film night. You need to join in too. They've barely seen you all weekend. They must've asked a hundred times when you'd be back. It would've been good if you'd let me know. They've been desperate to play football, and I'm just no good ... supposedly!'

Toby didn't answer. 'Right, boys, I'll be back in a bit. We can watch the recording of the Grand Prix. Apparently, it was an exciting race. Just got to have a shower first.' He screwed up his face for effect.

'Yeah, you smell Daddy. You've got really muddy legs.' Michael said. 'Think you splashed it all over Mummy's white walls.' And he pointed at the sploshes of mud he himself had left, relinquishing all blame.

Sophie watched as the boys rushed after their dad, exclaiming at the gold medal with its bright silver writing, hanging off an elaborate red ribbon. She felt tired and bored after her day of chores and childcare, and Toby's late arrival home had done nothing to lift her mood.

Ridiculously, she was even looking forward to Monday morning, when the new week could begin, and everything would go back to normality. Then she could forget about weekend disappointments and the loneliness of being by herself, at least for five more days.

*

After a dinner of homemade lasagne and ice cream, they all sat in the lounge watching *Harry Potter*.

Sophie sat on the sofa with Michael and the two dogs. Toby lay on the floor with William across his back. The iPad was next to them, with the Grand Prix playing silently. It didn't help Sophie's mood. They couldn't even watch a film as a family without the iPad joining in. It felt like there were five in this family.

They had been watching for less than thirty minutes when Sophie noticed Michael was fast asleep. Not enjoying the film and feeling tired herself, she called an end to film night and carried Michael upstairs, dragging a reluctant William behind. As she left the room with a chorus of good nights, she heard the Grand Prix volume increase.

*

Toby relocated to the sofa, pushing a dog from its spot and contently caressing his glass of red wine.

The text from 'James B' appeared the instant Sophie left the room. The phone had been lying on the floor, face-up, and Toby thanked the timeliness of its arrival.

James B:
Finally got some time to myself.
Matthew's like a bear with a sore head.
I can't bear his company. Would much
rather be with you! I'm sitting in a hot
bath, really starting to ache. You
should be here massaging my muscles.
It's your fault I had to run so fast! Hope
you're suffering too! LOL xxx

Toby smiled broadly as he typed his reply.

Toby:
Can't believe you still beat me. Again! I
was trying really hard too! Still, I didn't
mind buying lunch. Just means you
now owe me dinner! X

Her reply was instant.

James B:

Well, how about tomorrow night? After swimming practise? I'll buy you a drink!

xxx

Toby's heart rate quickened, both from Abigail's suggestion and because he could hear Sophie coming down the stairs.

He quickly replied with a thumbs-up emoji, then deleted her messages.

*

Sophie entered the room and saw the familiar rapid movement of Toby's phone. A movement she was beginning to distrust.

'Toby, it's nine o'clock. You're not writing emails, are you?'

'Oh, it's just to get a head start on tomorrow.' He picked up his phone, then quickly put it down again. 'Just clearing out some emails. Don't want to start the week with a full inbox.'

'Please put it away. And why not turn off the iPad too? Shall we watch the next episode of *24*? It's been ages since we've sat down together.' Sophie found the DVD and placed it in the machine.

They adopted their familiar positions on the sofa, complete with two dogs.

Twenty minutes later, Toby was asleep. His head was tilted back, and his mouth was open just enough to let the flies in. His chest was deeply rising and falling.

He had an almost narcoleptic ability to sleep in a blink

of an eye. How he managed it, watching such an adrenaline-packed program, Sophie didn't understand.

She pressed pause and nudged him awake. 'There's not much point in me watching it if you keep falling asleep. D'you even know what's going on now?'

Toby pulled himself into an upright position. 'I just nodded off quickly. I know what's happened. It's all the same as the last series anyway. Press play again. I'm awake now.'

Five minutes later, he was snoring. 'For goodness' sake, we might as well go to bed.' Sophie shook him awake. 'Let's get an early night and I'll give you a massage, eh? We've got that edible massage oil upstairs. It's barely been used!' She stood and dropped a kiss on his forehead, smiling as she flirtatiously flicked back her hair as it fell forward.

Toby wiped a wet dribble from the corner of his mouth. 'Oh. Yeah. Maybe. Might be nice. I'll be up in a sec. Just need to catch up on the last few laps of the Grand Prix. Think I must have slept through that too.' His smirk indicated that he found it amusing.

Sophie didn't.

'Well, don't be long. You're tired, I'm tired, let's just snuggle in bed.' She let the dogs out for their last run, locked up the house, turned off all the other lights, and went upstairs.

She burrowed under the artificially heated covers and waited for Toby, eager to check out his aching pecs and re-boost his adrenaline with her new, matching, lacy underwear.

Twenty minutes later, she felt him climb into bed,

allowing a gust of cold air to follow. She waited for the warmth of his naked skin to touch hers and his increasing caresses as he realised she was virtually naked, but he seemed not to notice and was in no hurry to claim the promised massage.

She willed him to turn off the light and snuggle down into their familiar spoon shape, anticipating that moment where they were as close as they physically could be, united, side by side.

But a few minutes later, feeling no movement, she turned over to find him sitting upright, still on his phone.

Not more emails?

'Toby,' she chastised. 'For goodness sake, surely you're tired? Put down your phone, let's snuggle up.'

'Yeah, yeah. In a minute.'

She lifted her head and shoulders off the pillow and looked closely at his screen. 'What *are* you doing? You're flipping Twittering.' She answered her own question. 'You've spent all evening falling asleep, and now we're finally in bed, you're reading tweets from people you don't even know. Plus, you've made me cold now.'

She dashed across the room to get her pyjamas, quickly pulling them over her new red lace underwear, then with more movement than necessary, feeling totally unwanted, she climbed back into bed, bashed her head into the pillow, and sighed her disapproval.

Bloody phones in bed.

*

Sophie's annoyance hadn't gone unnoticed. Toby knew how much she hated him 'wasting time,' as she put it, on social media.

He may have felt sleepy earlier, but when he finally got into bed, he felt wide awake. Normally, it would be work issues keeping sleep at bay, but tonight it was a different emotion.

He glanced across at Sophie's back and glimpsed the pink collar of her pyjamas, knowing that underneath was some bright red underwear. He had spotted it from the corner of his eye as she'd jumped out of bed but he'd rapidly looked away, not wanting to see, not wanting to acknowledge the bottle of edible oil on the side.

She now had her ear plugs in, so he assumed she had given up on the promised massage.

He knew she would simply want his arm around her as they fell asleep, side by side, but tonight he couldn't provide that. Even Twitter wasn't calming his mind.

Ignoring the faint, guilty feeling and embracing the anticipation, he typed his last response to the message frenzy that had occurred over the last twenty minutes.

> Toby;
>
> Can't sleep. Still buzzing from earlier. Still replaying that mental image of your Lyrca clad backside running in front of me! Looking forward to that drink. Night night. X

With all his willpower, he powered off his phone, placed it face-down, and turned off the light.

Even as he did so, he knew he would be checking for a reply before he could let sleep finally claim him.

6

Tuesday, 1ˢᵗ January 2013

By six p.m. on the 1ˢᵗ of January, Sophie had had enough of 2013. She fled to her room as she felt the tears welling and threw her head onto the pillow to muffle her sobs. Why they had come on so suddenly, she didn't know, but she did nothing to resist them and would have screamed out loud if the boys hadn't been within earshot.

Toby would have seen the tears forming in her eyes as she'd fled from the kitchen. He would have felt the sadness emanating from her as she'd hurried out the door and surely he would have heard her quickened footsteps as she raced up the stairs.

She expected he would follow. Would help her understand these emotions seeping into her pillow. He would tell her she was being silly, would reassure her that this was going to be a great year. But he didn't seem to be coming.

As the sobs reduced in their intensity, Sophie sat up and

dried her eyes with her sleeve. She gazed out the window at the fairy lights, twinkling in the new conservatory below, reflected a thousand times in the angular glass of the ceiling. The final design had been perfect, and it had effortlessly hosted several fun and intoxicating evenings with Rani and Ant over Christmas.

Sophie pulled out her diary and re-read what she had written at the end of those magical, messy evenings. She laughed at how bad her handwriting was after several glasses too many.

Gosh, they'd been drunk. Rani was such a bad influence! But Sophie knew they were equally to blame, and she wouldn't have it any other way.

But Christmas hadn't been all good. Sophie read over her entry for Christmas day, reliving the moment when the boys opened their stockings, still innocently believing in Father Christmas.

Her smile vanished as she remembered the moment she exchanged presents with Toby. He'd always said he'd like to learn how to ride a horse, so Sophie had bought him a day's polo lesson with an overnight stay at the local prestigious polo grounds and country house hotel.

Sophie thought it would be a unique way to spend some quality time together, so she had booked herself in too, hoping they could find a slot in his schedule of runs and training sessions which had become ever more frequent over the last few months.

Sophie's present in return had been less thoughtful and, in Sophie's mind, odd. Normally, Toby was overly generous and spot-on with his choice of gifts. There was the waxed Barbour jacket one year, the Le Chameau wellies the next, and the expensive Timberland watch another.

This year's gift had shown promise, gift-wrapped in white branded paper from John Lewis. She'd opened it with expectation but was baffled as to what was inside, even after reading the details and seeing the picture on the box. Toby had explained to her bemused face that it was the latest in wireless, surround sound speakers.

'Imagine. All our music transmitted by our phones, anywhere in the house and with no wires. Clever, isn't it?'

'Crikey, Toby. It says here it was three hundred and fifty pounds?' Unimpressed at such an unnecessary gadget for someone with zero songs on her iPhone, she hadn't hidden her disappointment. 'I hope you've kept the receipt?'

'I kind of did wonder if you'd know what it was.' Toby gave a sheepish smile and reached across to take it from her. 'Don't worry. I think it's terrific. It's powerful enough to sound great in the garden. You don't even need to dock your phone.'

Sophie pushed his hand away and carefully returned the gadget to its box. 'I think we should exchange it, it's too much.' She made a mental note to find the receipt.

The day had continued quite adequately with the arrival of their best friends, without any surround sound.

*

Toby *had* noticed Sophie's emotions as she'd suddenly departed the kitchen. He had only just returned from cleaning his bike after his New Year's Day ride and was excitedly chatting to the boys about the darts match later that night.

'Phil Taylor's bound to win, it's the World Championships you know.'

'Can we watch it too, Daddy? William had asked.

Sophie had stepped in before he'd been able to respond. 'No, boys. It's on far too late, you'll be in bed.' She'd finished putting the cheese on top of the lasagne and put it in the oven. 'Anyway, I thought we were having a family night tonight? There's bound to be a suitable film on. It is New Year's Day after all.'

'Sorry, no chance Sophie. This'll be his sixteenth win. Man's a legend. Not gonna miss that.' He'd turned to William, 'Might be a bit late but ignore Mummy. We can watch it whilst playing darts and see if we can score as well as him. You're really good now. Reckon you could beat him?' He'd laughed, tickling William under the arms, then he'd poured himself a wine.

He really couldn't work out why Sophie had suddenly left the room, so had finished planning the evening with William, then put down his glass and went to find out. He knocked gently and entered the bedroom.

She put down her diary and turned away from him as he tentatively sat on the bed, placing his hand across her back. She didn't recoil, or push him away, so he felt safe to vocalize his concern.

'Darling, what's wrong? Why are you crying? What's happened? Have *I* done something?'

'I ... I'm just fed up with it all.' She wiped away the tears as they slid down her cheeks. 'I'm dreading another new year; it feels like it's going to be really shit.'

There was silence for a moment as she seemed to absorb her realisation. The tears began to slide down her cheeks again. She roughly swept her wet hair out of her eyes as she turned to look at him.

Toby remained silent and removed his hand from her back, awkwardly laying it in his lap.

'You. The boys,' she continued. 'You all take me for granted. The sodding animals too. I look after everyone. Who the hell looks after me? No one, that's who.'

She seemed to find certainty in her emotions, raising her voice higher with each word. Her contorted red face was now directly in front of Toby's confused one.

'No one gives a shit about me. No one cares what I'm doing or what I want. You've been out all day, *again*, with your bike and I've been stuck in with the boys, *again*. Where has the *us* gone? We don't do anything together anymore; I don't even think you liked the polo idea. A night away just you and me, you didn't even ask where or when it was.' She turned away and took a few deep sobs.

Before he had a chance to respond she continued. 'Oh and let's all watch the damn darts. On New Year's Day!' She turned her back on Toby as the tears came back in force. 'I'm just so tired and fed up with it all.' She buried her head into the wet pillow.

Realising these emotions were down to him, he replaced his hand on her back and moved in closer. 'I'm sorry, darling. I'm sorry if you think we take you for granted. We don't. We all love you. We know it's you who holds us together. Please don't cry.' He turned her shoulder, leant in close, and dropped a kiss into her hair, hoping to quell the tears.

Perhaps she was right. Perhaps he did take her for granted. It wasn't something he'd ever thought about. Perhaps that was half the problem. He hated seeing her so upset.

'Sophie, you're so good at hiding your emotions, and it takes a lot for you to get to this stage. I've not noticed. I'm sorry. I promise I'll consider you more.' He felt ashamed as his mind recalled his earlier conversation, excitedly talking about the darts. Of course she would have hated that, on New Year's Day, especially as he had left her for most of it to go on his bike ride. 'Look, it's been such a busy time, we've forgotten to check in with each other. I think the polo thing is a great idea. I'm really looking forward to it. Can't wait to learn how to fall off a horse properly.' He laughed, attempting to lighten the situation. 'We don't have to watch the darts. What d'you want to watch? We'll have a film night. I'll light the fire.'

He thought of all the Christmas entertaining and organisation over the last few days. The new conservatory had looked so festive, with its twinkling lights and beautifully laid table. He remembered feeling full of pride as they entertained Ant and his family, and it was Sophie who'd managed it all. Apart from the simple online purchase from John Lewis, he hadn't purchased a single present, sent a single card, nor made a single mince pie. His only contribution had been to light a fire each night.

'You did such a fantastic job with Christmas, and I haven't even thanked you. I'm sorry. I do appreciate everything you do. I promise to show it more.' And at that moment, he really meant it.

*

Toby's reassuring words were comforting. Sophie rolled over to face him and looked him in the eyes, noticing they were wet too. He was right. It took a lot for her to break down, and she knew these feelings had been establishing themselves over a long time. Maybe this was the release she needed, and she felt better for it.

'I just want things to be like they used to be. When it was just you and me and we spent all our time together. I want the other half of me back, not out on some never-ending marathon or bike ride.' She smiled, returning his humour, showing that she was okay.

Toby flattened out the duvet, standing and awkwardly smiling. He was unaccustomed to her showing vulnerability.

'I know. So do I. Remember how we used to finish each other's sentences? Bet I know what you're about to say.' He smiled. 'Something abooouuut … a gin and tonic?'

'Ha ha. Well now you mention it, yes please, oh and could you also check on the lasagne? It should be nearly ready.' She watched him turn and leave, noticing him wipe his hand across his eyes. She let out a deep shuddering breath and felt her shoulders relax. Maybe everything *was* going to be okay.

Sophie leant back against the pillows. Back in control of her emotions and reached for her diary to write her new year's resolutions.

Every year, they would start with 'must lose weight', then she would continue with many other declarations that would never make it past January. But this year, there was an unexpected entry:

'Focus on the stuff that makes me happy. Do less of the stuff that doesn't. Must understand the difference!'

She had barely finished writing when the boys crept into the room and clumsily climbed onto her bed.

'I love you, Mummy,' they chorused. It was a sweet gesture, most likely orchestrated by Toby.

'What's wrong, Mummy? Why are you crying?' William had a hitch in his voice as he spoke. He was always the one that worried the most. 'Are you sad?'

'I know why she's crying,' Michael offered, with far more certainty. 'Mummy's sad cause Daddy went on that bike ride.'

Sophie thought back to earlier that morning and realised how much her children subconsciously picked up. She *had* been cross with Toby. It was New Year's Day, and his first thought had been a damn bike ride on his precious bike.

She may well have sworn her disapproval when Toby left for his ride, so Michael had allotted it as the reason for tonight's tears. In Michael's mind, two plus two equalled four and if it didn't, he would happily keep changing it till it did.

William was less convinced. Sophie could see the concern

building across his tight frown, trying to understand a situation he had no solution for.

Reassuring them both, she said, 'Mummy's being silly. I'm okay. Just a bit sad because Christmas is all over, and we have to go back to school next week. Don't worry. It's nothing to do with Daddy and his bike ride.'

Sophie hugged them as close as they would allow, kissing them both. Michael instantly brushed the kiss away with the back of his hand, taking it as the sign they were free to go. William followed, but not before glancing over his shoulder with a small, but loving smile.

Instructing the boys to go wash their hands for dinner, Toby returned and placed the medicinal drink on Sophie's bedside table, accompanied by a left-over Christmas cracker. 'The lasagne's nearly ready, let's pull the cracker?'

Sophie took hold and pulled, rolling her eyes as it gave a feeble snap, leaving the winning end in Toby's hand. 'Great. Can't even win a cracker. Sums up 2013 really!'

'Don't be silly, we'll share it. You put on the hat, I'll read out the joke.'

Sophie put the creased red tissue over her head, trying to stop it falling across her eyes as she watched Toby unravel the small piece of paper.

'Oh, it's not a joke. It's a saying … It's quite relevant, really.' He stood back and read. 'It's not what we *give*, but how much *love* we put into the giving.'

Sophie laughed, 'Very relevant. Not sure how much love was in that Wi-Fi music thingy! So who said those wise words?'

'Mother Theresa, apparently.'

'Yup, that's about right. Can't get more loving than her.' Sophie concurred.

'I promise to put more love into you, Sophie Cooper. Come down when you've finished your drink and we can have a nice evening. All together.'

It wasn't quite the intimate, loving kiss and making-up hug Sophie was hoping for but as she watched him leave, she took a massive gulp of gin, relishing the strong, astringent liquid as it revived her throat.

Good old Mother Theresa. Much easier to be a saint without a marriage or kids.

*

Toby had a reason for holding back physical affection tonight. New Year's Day had been upsetting for him too, but he couldn't share these emotions with his wife.

Abigail had had a terrible Christmas. Matthew had shown his true colours by being forced to admit he'd been having an affair and Toby had been the person Abigail turned to.

James B:
I don't know what to do. I'm so shocked. I caught him on the phone talking to another woman, saying he loved her. He admitted it when I confronted him. I'm so sad. I can't believe it. 14yrs of marriage. Oh God,

what am I going to do? I know it's a
difficult time to get away, but I wish I
could see you. xxx

Bloody Bastard, Toby had thought.

Each time they had managed to speak, he felt his heart tighten. She was a good, close friend, but something had changed. The intimacy they now shared at such an emotional time had given a whole new vocabulary to their dialogue.

Toby felt an overwhelming sense of importance, knowing he was the first person she shared her sadness with. He was her support system, her rock. It crossed his mind he'd never been Sophie's rock. She had never needed him to be.

Being someone's rock felt good.

This morning's bike ride was the first time they'd met since the discovery of the affair. They'd cycled to Bottomley Lake from their respective homes but had spent little time cycling once there. The lake was surrounded by families enjoying their new start to the year, blowing away the cobwebs from the night before.

The surface of the lake was unusually tranquil, offering no waves to lap at the sandy shore, enabling the noise from the visitors to hang around eerily in the still air.

Toby and Abigail had sat on the grass near the edge of the lake, a hundred yards from the coffee shop. It wasn't cold, but they sat close, legs touching, holding their coffees, joking that their padded Lycra pants were keeping the damp at bay.

It was the first time they had deliberately touched. Still innocently. Still just as friends.

They'd remained in close conversation for over an hour. Abigail told Toby everything about her marriage and why she felt it had failed. Toby tried to comfort her with situations from his own eleven-year marriage, exaggerating some of its failings to console her.

At one point, Toby hugged Abigail close, and he couldn't deny the feelings it gave him. He tried to mentally subdue it, but the tingling sensation as he felt her chest compress against his, made his lungs jump. He couldn't recoil from her like he knew he should, nor did she.

For the first time since they'd met, he knew for certain that this was not just a close, platonic friendship. Perhaps on some level, he'd always known. He sensed Abigail felt the same but didn't dare ask in case her answer made it real.

'I'm so sorry to burden you with all this.' Abigail had said as they moved apart, ready for the cycle home. 'It's going to be okay. I know it is. I just feel so guilty for the kids.'

'They've got you as a mum, they'll be fine.' Toby had tried to placate her. 'They're old enough to comprehend a divorce a bit better now. You'll help them to understand, I know you will.'

'It's not me I'm worried about. Matthew will make things hard; I know he will. He was a shit dad before the marriage started to go wrong, can't imagine he's going to step up now. He's going to make it all my fault.'

Toby had imagined for a moment how a divorce might look for him. Sophie would never forgive him if he had an affair, and she would certainly turn the boys against him. He would fight that with every bone in his body. Matthew wouldn't; he wouldn't give a second thought to the welfare of the mother of his children. He'd felt a surge of protectiveness and held onto her arm to ensure she looked into his eyes. He wanted her to see it. He couldn't remember the last time he'd felt such a fierce, possessive emotion for someone, and he revelled in it. If he ever met Matthew, he wouldn't want to be held accountable for his actions.

'Don't you dare feel guilty. This is all his fault. I can't believe he's been having this affair for so long, and you didn't realise.'

'He was clever, he made sure he'd deleted everything on his phone. He'd never let that phone out of his sight. I wish I'd been more questioning. I knew something was going on with him.'

'Hey, don't beat yourself up about it, modern technology makes it all so easy. He couldn't have hidden it without text messages and delete buttons. You weren't to know.'

Toby felt a chill as he recognised the relevance of what he'd just said and how it mimicked his own behaviour. He ignored it. 'Come on, we should go.'

They'd picked up their bikes and threw their empty coffee cups into the bin. Toby moved alongside Abigail as they walked to the exit.

'You'll be fine. He doesn't deserve you anyway,' he'd said, awkwardly using his right hand to brush her cheek where the earlier tears had fallen. 'I hate to rush away. I could sit with you all day, but Sophie wants us all to go on a dog walk or a flipping pony ride or something. Be strong, Abigail. Things *will* be okay.'

'Oh, sweetheart, I know you're right. I'm so lucky to have you. You're such a good friend.'

Toby beamed, holding his head high. 'We'll keep talking. You mustn't bottle anything up or feel bad about any of it. We'll catch up soon. It'll be a happy New Year, I promise.'

He'd looked into her eyes and saw the light that first entranced him a few months ago, sparkling bright. He knew he'd crossed an emotional line there was no coming back from.

Both had left the lake knowing this was not going to be a normal or simple year.

7

Monday, 28th January 2013

The anti-climax of the festive period lingered, prolonged by the equally depressing, inevitable diet. Sophie's birthday, falling at the end of the longest month ever did little to uplift her mood. There were still twenty-eight days of February's torture to get through before March brought the optimism of the clocks moving forward and the new grass creeping in as the mud retreated.

The sun had not yet risen, and Toby had left for work, offering no surprise treats or suggestions of a night out. At only seven a.m., this birthday already felt more of a non-event than usual, and Sophie shoved a pillow over her head and sighed.

Minutes later the boys rushed in, carrying their homemade card. 'Wake up Mummy. Wake up!' Michael shouted, jumping on the bed. 'It's your birthday. Can we have pancakes for breakfast?'

'We've made you a card, I did all the writing. Can we

have cake for breakfast too?' William asked.

Sophie forced herself from under the covers and took the offered card, opening it with a smile across her face. 'It's lovely, boys. Your writing's really good, William, and that picture of me is so lifelike, I look so fat!'

'Here's your present. It's from Daddy and us.' William handed her a small box.

'Oooo, thanks. I wonder what it is?'

'Don't know. Don't know!' Michael shrieked, bouncing up and down, 'Open it, Mummy. Quickly. Let me help.'

Sophie knew what was inside. It had been delivered last week and the delivery note stated, 'The Watch Shop'. The small, hard box wrapped with a red ribbon now confirmed it. She'd smiled when she signed for it, fondly remembering the Timberland watch he'd bought her many birthdays ago, which had only recently perished. Toby believed in a good quality watch. A 'proper' watch, like the Tag Heuer his parents bought him for his eighteenth birthday, which he still wore today.

The boys were tucked under the covers, watching in anticipation as she unwrapped the package, helping where they could. She needed a new watch and would appreciate a decent quality one. She'd been struggling with her cheap one for a few months, using a paper clip to hold the strap in place whilst the pins rattled in their worn holes.

She carefully pushed the red ribbon off, not wanting to ruin the elaborate bow, and pulled out the container, revealing her new timepiece.

Instantly, her anticipation at such a thoughtful present

turned to worry and annoyance. The shop had made a huge mistake. This was obviously not *her* watch. This one was far too ostentatious. Toby would never have bought her this.

First, it was white. A quality leather, but white. White was not a colour suited to Sophie's lifestyle, and Toby would have known it. Second, it was huge. The strap was at least an inch wide, and the silver face was the size of a small saucer. It was totally inappropriate for someone whose engagement ring had been chosen based on how prone the small protruding diamond would be to catching on haynets and reins.

'I can't have a white watch. It's ridiculous. It'll be black by next week.' Sophie was speaking to herself more than to the boys, who had turned their attention to the box of Christmas decorations that had still not made it into the loft.

She carefully placed the watch back in its box before any mucky fingers marked the leather, then phoned Toby. He answered immediately.

'Happy birthday, darling. Did you like my present?'

'The watch. Yes, thanks it's a great gift. But I think there's been a mix-up. They've sent the wrong one. It's white.'

There was a moment's pause.

'Yes. I know it's white. Don't you like it? I thought you could do with a change from your normal brown ones.'

'Well, it's huge as well. It's far too big,' Sophie said, hurt that Toby was trying to change her rustic tastes.

'Is it? Oh. It didn't look big on the screen. I didn't measure it. Sorry, I've got to go. I've a conference call from China in a sec. I'll be home early tonight, and you can show me then. See you later.'

Then he was gone.

Sophie laid her head back on the pillows and stared blankly at the ceiling, a frown across her face, feeling dismissed. China was waiting and Toby had gone. How the tables had turned. She remembered back to her first birthday as a wife, when it was *her* dealing with the pressures of a high-level job and Toby was unemployed, struggling to find work. She had managed to leave the office early and Toby had surprised her by collecting her from the train station. He'd had a self-satisfied glint in his eye and a dusting of something white across his face.

Sophie had walked into their house and was hit with a heavy, sweet smell she could almost taste of home baking. The cake had still been warm, and she had teased him at how she would never have believed he had made it if it hadn't been for the covering of flour and drips of mixture all over the kitchen. He had known her so well, put so much thought behind her birthday and it had tasted amazing.

Why now had he got it so wrong? What with the wireless music thing at Christmas and now this, she wondered if he knew her at all anymore.

She thought back to their emotional conversation at the beginning of the year. Had that not meant anything to him? Had anything changed since then? She had still spent the weekends doing homework, cooking, cleaning, and looking after everyone else's needs.

Toby had still spent every waking moment with Drema, running, or tweeting.

So much for finishing each other's sentences; we don't

even speak the same language anymore.

'Damn this new year. Bloody 2013. I hate odd numbers. Come on, boys. Time to get ready for school. Let's go and eat pancakes and cake.' Sophie flung the covers forcibly off the bed and began another day of her next year of life.

*

Toby's proposed early arrival home was 6:30 p.m. 'Sorry, darling. Traffic was a nightmare. I left the office at five, then had to stop for petrol.' He brushed her cheek with an untouching kiss. 'Happy birthday.'

Sophie's eyes narrowed. 'It's always bad traffic, Toby. You've been commuting for three years, and you still don't seem to register it's always bad.' She turned away. 'Dinner's ready. I've assumed you're not taking me out?'

'Oh gosh, sorry no. Monday's a terrible day for a birthday, isn't it. Maybe we could book somewhere for next weekend?'

'Or what about a whole day out for all of us? Even if it's just bowling or something simple. Boys would like that.' Sophie offered. 'Could you take a day off work in half-term?'

'Well, yes, probably. Depends on this China deal, things are really busy.'

Sophie delivered his dinner, landing the plate roughly on the table, nearly slopping it onto his lap. 'Yup, let's make sure China's happy first.' She muttered.

Toby hadn't heard. He was hungrily tucking into his spaghetti and meatballs and sipping a freshly poured glass of wine, having made no attempt to pour one for Sophie. By the time he was halfway through eating, Sophie surmised he had totally forgotten about his wife's birthday and the unsuitable gift.

She was sitting opposite him with her small portion already finished and wondered for the hundredth time why the iPad had to share the table with them. Tonight, it was a 'cars for sale' website. Toby had been addicted to it since his New Year resolution to buy a new car. No longer did the BMW estate satisfy him. On the screen now was a convertible, two-door Audi sports car. It didn't even have full-size seats in the back, and Sophie couldn't believe he was considering it.

'You can't buy that,' she said as she leaned over the table, angling the screen towards her. 'The seats in the back are tiny. They can't be safe, can they?'

In disbelief, she listened to his argument that the few times he needed four seats, he would take her car. He drove a lot during his working week, so he wanted to enjoy it in style, with more speed.

'I deserve a nice car. The boys will love it. Look, it's convertible too.'

Sophie could already hear the arguments over who was going to sit in the front.

'Anyway, I'm seeing it first thing tomorrow,' he continued. 'I'm taking cash as it won't stay around for long.'

Sophie didn't understand her husband and this new, irrational mindset. He was only focused on himself, and she couldn't remember when she last felt in tune with him. In the early stages of their relationship, when they would finish each other's sentences and answer a question unasked, they would laugh and say, 'We're the same.'

What happened to that sameness? How does it just not exist anymore?

'You're crazy, Toby. You have two young children, and you think you can get a silly sports car? It's just so impractical.' She knew her words were falling on deaf ears. His mind had been made up, and he probably wasn't even listening anymore. She just couldn't accept this was the new normal.

Where did her old Toby go?

She may have joked with Rani recently about their ageing husbands going through a mid-life crisis, but now Sophie no longer found it funny. Toby was removed and self-absorbed, and this new car proved it.

Sophie gathered up the empty plates. 'D'you want any pudding?' She began filling the dishwasher, waiting for his answer. There was a half-eaten birthday cake on the side, candles extinguished earlier with help from the boys. Even though she had eaten several pieces, she wanted an excuse to take yet another slice. The best thing about her birthday was the total abandonment of her diet so baking a cake had never been in question.

Toby didn't answer. He just began pressing buttons, invariably composing an email to some other work crazed Drema employee still working at eight p.m. Sophie roughly closed the door of the dishwasher, purposefully causing the crockery to clash against itself.

She was striving for a reaction, waiting for an

acknowledgement, but she received nothing. Glancing angrily at the square white box on the table, in full view yet unnoticed by Toby, she left the room to get the boys ready for bed.

At least she'd get a birthday kiss from them. What a shit birthday. She hated January.

*

Once Sophie had left the room, Toby took a slice of the cake she had put in front of him. He didn't have a sweet tooth, he would have preferred cheese and biscuits, but he knew Sophie could eat vast quantities of cake if she let herself.

He glanced at the remaining portions and concluded that she had, most likely already succumbed to her weakness. He frowned as he realised she would have totally abandoned her diet today and would likely never shift that weight he knew was creeping around her middle.

Thank goodness his running was keeping him trim. He took a large bite of the cake.

As he let the sweet chocolate coat his teeth and cover his fingers, he noticed the little square box. He stopped himself from touching it just in time, preventing his brown, sticky fingers from ruining the pristine white case.

Abigail had helped him choose the watch. They'd been sitting close in a bar after swimming practice last week. He had no idea what to get Sophie for her birthday, so he thought a clever solution was to consult another female around the same age.

He had been grateful for her help and took her suggestion

of the white leather watch without hesitation. Now he was kicking himself for not first checking its dimensions. He knew Sophie hated pretentious things and would never have wanted anything too large. He consulted his personal shopper.

> Toby:
> Sophie hated the watch! Think you got that one a bit wrong. Last time I ask you for advice. X

He pressed send, took another bite of the cake, then panicked that the message may come across too abrupt, rude even. He *had* been grateful for her help; it wasn't *her* fault Sophie didn't like it. He wiped his hands on his trousers and added:

> Toby:
> Sorry, didn't mean to sound rude. You can have the watch if you want it. Probably suits you better anyway. At least you liked my choice of new car. Sophie hated that too. I'm going to buy it though. I'll swing by and take you for a blast with the roof down. Might be a bit cold, but I can warm you up afterwards! X

Not waiting for a reply, he put his phone in his pocket, poured another wine, and went to say goodnight to the boys.

8

Monday, 18th February 2013

Three weeks after Sophie's birthday, they were finally having the family day out she craved. It was the start of the boys' half term holiday and Toby was able to take a day off, having now completed the China deal.

The weather forecast was rubbish, so Sophie had planned a day inside with some bowling, cinema, and plenty of high calorie, inappropriate food and treats.

She glanced across at the bedside clock. It was 7:04. She rarely had the chance to sleep in, so she leisurely stretched out, relaxed and smiled, turning to put her arm around Toby to snuggle in for a few more minutes of slumber. He wasn't there. Sitting up to check, she noticed his phone and iPad were gone too. He obviously wasn't coming back.

If he was in the office working, she was going to be annoyed. And anyway, if he was, where was her tea?

Receiving no response to her familiar request via text, she went downstairs to make the tea herself but first walked into the office. As expected, Toby was sitting in his dressing-gown on the swivel chair, concentrating on a spreadsheet. There was an empty cup of tea to his side.

'Hiya.' He turned in his chair. 'I'm just finishing off this spreadsheet. Needs to be done today, and there's a formula wrong somewhere. Nigel's such a tosser. He didn't check it, so now I've got to put it right.'

Sophie could tell he was annoyed and trying to appease her, but not for the first time, she recognised that as a team player and a manager, Toby was quick to rescue his colleagues. No doubt Nigel was still in bed, aware that his boss would sort out any inaccuracies.

Biting her tongue, she said, 'Well shall I make a tea, and we can go back upstairs for a bit?' She picked up his empty cup. 'The boys are still asleep; I could bring up those biscuits you like?'

'No, you go. I've got to get this done.' He turned back to his screen. Sophie felt dismissed, rejected. 'I'll have another tea though,' he shouted to her back as she walked out the room. 'And that biscuit, if you're offering!'

The chickens hadn't been let out, and the dogs were still shut in the boot room. The bins were not out on the roadside, and Sophie was sure she could hear the lorries coming. But all of Drema's demands, wants and needs had been dealt with the moment Toby woke.

'Lucky bitch, Drema,' Sophie said out loud. Her annoyance would have been clear to anyone who may have seen her dragging the bins out into the street, wearing nothing but her pyjamas, uncaring of who saw her on this busy main road.

After flicking the switch on the kettle, she released the dogs, let out the chickens, and checked on the horses, still only in her pyjamas but this time with her wellies and coat on top.

After filling Toby's mug, she took her own and went back to bed. Sophie cherished her early mornings snuggled under the duvet, drinking tea, watching the horses graze in the field beyond the garden. This morning she had just the dogs to snuggle with, even the boys had gone straight down to play on the Wii the moment they woke.

She was in no rush to get dressed. No one else in the house seemed bothered to start their family day out. No one had even questioned where they were going. Perhaps they hadn't even remembered?

Sophie finished her tea and logged onto Google to check the timings for the day's activities, suddenly realising if they wanted to fit it all in, they would have to leave within the hour.

'Right dogs, action stations. Time to get up.'

Both dogs lifted a head, and one tail gave a gentle wag, but neither moved. Sophie ignored their lack of response and went downstairs to chivvy everyone along.

'Come on boys. Time to get dressed. We're leaving in an hour, so chop-chop. Turn off the Wii, please.' She was met with no response, not even a metaphorical wag of a tail.

She continued down the hallway into the office and received a glance and a smile from Toby, still engrossed in the spreadsheet.

'How's it going? You done yet?'

'Oh, it's a nightmare. Think I've finished it though. Just got a few phone calls to make.'

'Really? Come on, you're supposed to be off today. If we want to do the bowling, we need to leave within the hour.' Sophie couldn't help but feel she was the only one interested in going out for the day.

She walked back into the hallway, shouting as she went. 'Come on boys. Hurry up and get dressed. What d'you want for breakfast?' She busied herself in the kitchen getting bowls and cereal out.

Eventually, the boys and Sophie were dressed and sitting down eating breakfast, talking about who was going to win the bowling.

William believed it would be him, and he was probably right. She could still hear Toby in the office on the phone, talking about purchase order numbers and lost deliveries. He was still in his dressing-gown, not showered, and was showing no sign of moving.

Considerately, Sophie waited till his phone call had finished before entering the office. This proved to be far longer than necessary; the last five minutes were seemingly just general chit-chat. It would appear he was in no hurry.

'Come on, Toby,' she implored. 'We're all ready to go. You're not supposed to be working.'

'Okay, *okay!*' he replied, emphasizing his words with an accompanying deep sigh. 'I just need five minutes more.'

'Oh, come on. Why can't this wait? It's never five minutes. Bowling starts soon, and you're not even dressed. This is supposed to be a family day out. Just leave it, can't you?'

'All right, all right. I'll leave it now then.' He slammed his laptop shut and shoved back the chair like an angry child. 'Stop hassling me, will you?'

'I'm not hassling,' Sophie protested, standing away from the door as he stormed past. 'I'm just trying to get this family out for the day.' She followed his raging path as he walked into the hallway. With a sarcastic tone, she called out, 'Gosh, anyone would think you'd rather be at work.'

'Yeah, maybe I would,' he said. Then more quietly, 'Didn't exactly have a choice.'

It wasn't quiet enough.

Sophie's face fell, and the hurt momentarily drained her of energy. A day out with his family, even if it was only bowling and the cinema, was obviously second place to a day with Drema.

If she hadn't made the effort—and she wished she hadn't—this day would not be happening. For the sake of the boys, now excited by the fun ahead, she would be damned if she was going to let Toby spoil it.

Far too late, they got into the new little sports car. Toby's mood, now he'd left Drema at home, seemed to improve. He was mucking about with the boys over who was going to sit in the front.

Sophie was surprised it wasn't automatically assumed it would be her sitting beside him. Instead, she had to fold herself like a leaf into the cramped space in the back, which didn't amuse her. Even Toby's golf clubs got more space in this car, as they had to travel with the passenger seat forward. Her head was just a few inches from the soft fabric roof and even less from the chair in front.

She felt unsafe and claustrophobic as she picked a long, wavy blonde hair from the headrest of the passenger's seat.

Great, they didn't even clean it properly. She discarded it out the window, not wanting to create an atmosphere in the tiny space.

They only just made the start of the bowling session, and within ten minutes, Sophie was being thrashed by a six and eight-year-old.

'Stupid game. I need the sides up,' she complained as another ball snaked into the gutter. The boys loved it, probably loving their mother's humiliation more.

Toby was his usual competitive, successful self. The only reason he wasn't winning, was due to his secret rigging of the game to ensure one of the boys won.

'I'll go and get some coffees, see if that helps you,' he joked, nudging Sophie in the side with an affectionate but slightly patronizing look. 'Boys, what d'you want to drink? The hot chocolates look great.'

'Yes please. Can I have mine with a flake and marshmallows too?' William pleaded unnecessarily. Toby was in a carefree mood and would happily give the boys whatever they wanted.

'Well, in that case, I'll have a bottle of beer.' It was nearly lunchtime, and if they were all having whipped cream and marshmallows, Sophie reasoned she could have a beer.

'Right. Three full works of hot chocolates and a beer it is.' He walked off towards the bar, pulling his phone out of his back pocket as he went.

Sophie turned her attention to the silly balls with holes.

She selected her lucky orange one. At least this one had hit the pins last time, even if it was only the outer two. She needn't have bothered; it made no difference. Her thumb managed to get stuck inside the hole just long enough after the other fingers had let go to swerve the ball off to one side. It too rolled into the gutter.

'Mummy you're rubbish!' William laughed, theatrically clutching his sides.

'That's it. I can't do it. You boys can have my go, I'll just watch.'

'No, Mummy, you can't give up. It'll ruin the scores. You have to keep playing.' William was taking the game seriously.

'Well, put the sides up then. I'm never going to hit anything otherwise.'

Giving in to his mother's weakness, William agreed. He took his turn, adding another cricket score to his leading position on the electronic scorecard.

Glancing across at Toby, Sophie could see he was still at the bar. She could see him typing into his phone. Another email, no doubt. She thought they had left Drema at home, allowing them all to enjoy the refreshing change to his mood. If she had hackles she would have felt them rising.

He returned a few minutes later, just in time for his turn, with a tray laden with calories. He had added two bags of nuts and two bags of crisps to the order. As much as Sophie salivated, she was cross he had put more temptation in her way. She still hadn't managed to shift the excesses from Christmas and hated being on the wrong side of sixty kilos. She gave up the fight before it started and opened the nuts.

William took the winning position as expected. Michael didn't seem to mind defeat. Coming ahead of his mother was success enough for him. On the way to the kiosk to change out of the ugly bowling shoes, the boys hung back at the bank of pool tables.

'Can we have a go? Can I play you, Daddy?' William said.

'Play Mummy. I'll go and change the shoes.' Toby put a pound in the slot, releasing the balls.

'Mummy's rubbish. She can't play. I want to play with you.' William crossed his arms, pouting.

Toby didn't disagree with his statement. 'Okay, well play with Michael first then. Give me your shoes and I'll be back in a bit.'

Neither noticed Sophie's face drop. She turned away from the tables, hugging her coat around her.

She dragged over a barstool to watch the boys play, avoiding having to stand in her socks on the sticky floor. The game was progressing well and was evenly matched until William was caught cheating. Michael was convinced he had fouled, but William didn't see it that way, and Sophie hadn't been looking.

She'd been watching Toby at the desk, engrossed in his phone, with their returned shoes neatly in front of him.

She shifted her stool, concealed behind a pillar. He couldn't see her, but she could lean out and peer around the side to watch him. Having resolved the boys' argument, she continued watching Toby, getting increasingly more annoyed.

While the boys were walking about on the disgusting, cold floor in their socks, he was standing there with their shoes, unable to put Drema back in his pocket.

William's scream as the white cue ball hit him in the chest brought Sophie back into the game. She was sure it had been overdramatized, meant for effect, but she had to get off her stool, braving the stickiness through her socks, to begin the referee, inquisition, and punishment routine she had lots of practice in. Even after getting the boys back on speaking terms to finish their game, Toby still hadn't returned.

Sophie took her phone out of her bag and rang Toby. She watched his head jolt as he was electronically reminded of his family just a few metres away. Sophie raised her arms out to the side, now in full view and gave him a wide-eyed glare.

Immediately, he put his phone back in his pocket, gathered up the shoes, and made his way back.

'Blimey, Toby, you've been ages. What were you doing?'

'They took forever to find the shoes,' he replied without hesitation. 'William's, I think. Someone must have mixed up the slots. I was waiting forever.'

Either well-rehearsed or the absolute truth, Sophie couldn't tell. His precise answer had flummoxed her. She knew he was on his phone for over ten minutes. She had watched him and timed it. She also knew the shoes were in front of him throughout.

But how many? Three pairs or four? She couldn't be sure; she hadn't thought to check. She just wanted to get out of this oppressive dark environment and go for lunch.

She gave the boys their shoes, and with her own back on her feet, she brightly said,

'Come on. Let's go. Lunch time, who wants pizza!?'

'One more game. Please? Daddy, can I play with you now?' William asked.

'No. Come on. Aren't you hungry? I am, let's go.' Sophie picked up her bag and began walking away from the tables.

'One more game won't hurt,' Toby interjected. 'I haven't played yet. Come on William, I'll give you fifty pence if you can beat me.'

William was quick to take the offered bet, and the balls were in play.

'Oh, for goodness' sake. We've been here for ages. They've already kicked off half a dozen times. Can't we just get out of here?'

But her protesting fell on deaf ears, and she knew it was pointless. Michael didn't seem to mind he had been excluded from a game with Daddy. He had found a group of children playing with the fruit machines and was just as happy watching them waste a few months' pocket money.

Another game turned into three, and not once did anyone ask her if she wanted to play. She wasn't rubbish as William thought, she was a damn site better at pool than bowling. She consoled herself by indulging in one of her favourite lonely pastimes: people watching.

Everyone looked so happy. Families enjoying a day out in half-term, laughing and joking, drinking beer and hot chocolate in their little bubbles of fun.

What do we look like? Do we look happy?

She wasn't sure they did.

9

Monday, 18th February 2013

Lunch had been a rushed affair. Sophie was relieved when they finally made it to their cinema seats; clutching popcorn, sweets, and large fizzy drinks no one really needed. The film was the latest Disney release, with a loud soundtrack, impressive graphics, and a bright colour palette from every arc of the rainbow.

Sophie and the boys were fully captivated for the whole ninety minutes. Toby was not. He didn't allow himself to be. Although on silent, Sophie had seen his dimmed phone screen light up on at least three occasions. He was being discreet, hiding it behind the massive carton of popcorn, but Sophie's eye was as keen as an eagle's when it came to that phone.

Before the film was halfway through, he was asleep, sitting bolt upright with his mouth open, enticing her to throw a piece of popcorn into it. She smiled, remembering doing exactly that several years ago. Toby had been asleep on the sofa during a family film night, and William had casually thrown a single piece of popcorn into his open mouth. Everyone laughed hysterically as the corn hit the spot with perfect accuracy. Toby had jolted awake, looking shocked, before grinning and munching away. He then prolonged the fun by pretending to fall back to sleep so the boys could continue throwing popcorn into his mouth. Sophie had joined in, and they had all bent over laughing as Toby, mouth full, showered them with the slightly soggy popcorn. She couldn't play that game now, but if she had been closer, not separated by the boys, she would have nudged him awake before allowing herself to be fully caught up in the Disney magic.

It was only four o'clock when they shuffled out into the startling daylight. Sophie thought they might go into town for an early meal or a drink to finish off their day, but before she had a chance to suggest it, Toby was making a beeline for the car.

Having not particularly enjoyed her family's company today, she held her tongue and followed silently. Besides, it would be good to get home early to walk the dogs and finish the horses with the small amount of daylight that was left.

*

As dusk fell to darkness, Sophie returned from sorting out the animals to find Toby back in the office.

'What d'you fancy for dinner?' She held back her annoyance as she spotted a spreadsheet on the screen. 'Shall we get a takeaway?'

He didn't look up. 'I've got to go out. I told you earlier, didn't I? I got a message from Tom. You remember him?' He rubbed the prominent vein on his neck and turned in his chair to face her.

Sophie didn't remember and said as much.

'It's only to the pub in the next village. He wants to come back to Drema and hopes I can get his foot in the door, or at least give him an insight into what's going on with the new structure. I won't be late.'

'Really? Would you rather not stay at home? We could put the boys to bed early, then sit in the conservatory with a curry. We've still got our favourite wine that Rani and Ant gave us for Christmas. Let's open it.'

'I'm not hungry. I won't be long.' Toby shut the lid of his laptop and gathered up his papers.

'How long?' Sophie said, but he had already walked away.

Sophie had hoped that today could be a turning point in their relationship, a chance to bring them closer. Quality time, sitting in the conservatory with the memorable wine and a takeaway, the fairy lights still up from Christmas. It would have been a perfect end to the day. But she seemed to have failed in her plan.

She turned her back on Toby's rejection as he shut the door behind him and focused on what easy meal she could feed the boys. They were probably not even hungry after such a carb-rich lunch, followed by all those unnecessary sweets and popcorn. Why worry about healthy eating now?

Sod it. She'd do them beans on toast.

She pulled out the special red wine from the top of the

rack, and in defiance to Toby's indifference, poured herself a large glass, trying to understand how someone called Tom now had a status above hers in Toby's hierarchical list. As she took her first sip, anticipating the warm feelings of hope and love from their earlier years to cascade over her, she realised how she now cared less for red wine, she would have preferred a white, a pinot grigio. She drank it regardless, in several large gulps, savouring nothing.

*

Once the boys were in bed, Sophie felt the painful feelings from New Year's Day resurface.

As she poured her second glass of wine, she rang Rani. She needed to offload about the day's events, and Rani was the best person to listen without judging.

'Hiya. Everything okay?'

'No, not really. Toby's pissed me off. I've had a few glasses of that special wine you gave us, so I'm being silly. I'm just *so* fed up with it all.'

'Still? Why what's happened? Wasn't it today you all went out?

Sophie proceeded to tell her friend how Drema accompanied them for the day and how her husband was, even now, still talking, to *her*. When exactly Drema Ltd first took on a feminine status, Sophie wasn't sure, but it felt appropriate.

'Oh, Sophie, I'm sorry. I know he was texting Ant recently about how much work he had on with the China thing. I guess he just finds it hard to switch off?'

Sophie walked into the hallway to check the boys were still upstairs asleep, out of earshot. She climbed back onto her soapbox in the kitchen. 'Yeah, but that China thing is finished. He should have loads more time now. He should want to spend it with us.'

She thought again to that night on New Year's Day, when he had promised her everything was going to be all right. He said he was going to think of her needs and not take her for granted. Love her more. But he hadn't. He hadn't thought of her needs more, nor took her for granted any less. Drema was emotionally bleeding him dry, and there was nothing left over for her.

'I don't think it could be worse if he were having an affair.' Sophie hadn't vocalised this before, but after two glasses of wine, it suddenly seemed to be her answer.

'Don't be silly. Of course he won't be. He's not that type,' Rani reassured.

'D'you know, I almost wish he were. At least then I could go and punch the stupid bitch in the face and get rid of her without damaging his pay packet.' Sophie laughed at the sheer ridiculousness of the conversation. 'How could he have an affair with an actual woman? She'd have to get past *Demanding Diva Drema* first.'

'Stop thinking like that. Can you imagine the implications if he were? He would never do that to the boys … to you. He loves you all too much.'

'Oh, I know. He certainly wouldn't do anything to hurt the boys. They idolise him and he knows it. He would never let them down. He's their flipping hero. I'm just the hired help!'

They both laughed. 'It would just be nice to have something tangible to explain his behaviour. It'll all blow over. We'll be okay.' Two large glasses of wine or not, Sophie was certain their marriage was solid, and she would stop at nothing to keep it that way. 'Anyway, how's you and Ant? When's your romantic getaway?'

The change of conversation led to a discussion on Rani's early birthday present from Ant: a weekend away in a Spa hotel. Sophie couldn't stop the twinge of jealousy as she thought back to her recent present of the large, white watch and for the first time, wondered what had happened to it and why it hadn't yet been replaced with something more suitable.

*

Nerves flooded through Toby as he left Nettlefield House. He had felt terrible at leaving Sophie so suddenly, but he couldn't have eaten a thing. He had been debating his options all day and knew he had been subdued and withdrawn as a result.

When Sophie had challenged him about the wait for the shoes, he was convinced she knew what he had been doing. She could have guessed it all, there and then, and when he imagined the faces of the boys as she told them of his deceit, his constricted heart gave him the push he needed.

As he drove to a pub several miles away, he gave himself a massive pat on the back for not yet succumbing to his primal desires for Abigail, regardless of how much he had wanted to. He knew he had been weak and had made some doubtful choices, but this important fact meant it had never been a proper affair, so today's realisations and tonight's decision were just in time.

Abigail looked amazing as she walked into the pub in a tight pair of jeans and ankle boots. A simple white blouse floated around her shoulders, only just obscuring her underwear beneath. She smelt of sweetness and warmth, and Toby could feel his whole torso heat as she reached in for a kiss.

'I'm so glad you called. You sounded really stressed. I hope you had a nice day out?' She sat next to him. 'Did the boys enjoy it?'

'Listen, Abigail.' Toby pushed a glass of pinot grigio towards her and took a sip of his beer. 'I can't do this anymore; we have to stop. I'm not risking the boys.'

Abigail glanced over her shoulder, then moved in closer, thigh pressed into thigh. 'I won't let you, Toby. We need to see where this goes. It's too good not to, surely you agree?'

Toby prayed she wouldn't cry. She seemed close to tears. He was desperate to comfort her, but he moved away, sensing the sudden coldness of the gap between them and repeated his decision to end things.

There were no explosive outbursts, no emotional tears, just one drink and several long moments of silence as they mutually allowed time for Toby's choices to sink in.

Abigail left the pub first. She was visibly holding back tears, leaving Toby to sit alone, tearing a beer mat into tiny pieces. It should never have gone as far as it had, and this had been the only way to stop it.

Toby could now look ahead to life without the lies and

deceit, without the massive burden he'd been carrying, preventing him from being present in his marriage and his family.

He was empowered by his decision and the strength of his conviction. He was climbing off his slippery slope, and it felt good. He would miss the running and the club, but he knew he had to break all ties for this to work. Maybe he could get his golf clubs out again. Heck, he could even burn that damn Lyrca. That would please Sophie, he would let her light the match!

And he smiled a guilt-free smile for the first time that year.

10

Saturday, 23rd February 2013

Toby had been surprisingly good company the last few days. It was as if he had a new lease of life, finally free of the demands of China, or Drema in general. He simply seemed happy.

'I've made you a tea,' he announced as he placed the mug on Sophie's bedside table. 'I've let the dogs out and checked the horses. Oh, and I've filled up the chickens' water too, it was really low.' He beamed at his successful morning's chores.

'Really, that's great, thanks, I didn't realise you knew chickens drank water.' Sophie chuckled at her joke, pleased to see Toby's beam grow bigger.

She noticed the accompaniment to her tea. In a little china vase, was a delicate posy of wildflowers. Sophie couldn't believe there were flowers so beautiful in her garden at this time of year. She recognised bright yellow celandine from the orchard, fragrant winter jasmine from around the back door, some snowdrops, crocuses, and a single yellow daffodil.

'Blimey. That's so sweet, they're lovely. Have you broken something?' She raised her eyebrows with a nudge of a smile.

'Nope. Just thinking of you and feel like I've got some making up to do. I know I don't show it, but I do love you, Sophie Cooper.'

Sophie quickly flicked a black bug from the arrangement, watching it land feet first and scuttle away. She looked across at Toby, sitting beside her, drinking his tea and her heart melted.

If only they weren't on a tight timescale this morning, they could prolong such an unexpected, intimate moment. It had been a lifetime since she'd felt this warmth from him, felt like she mattered.

They lay side by side, legs touching, toes entwined, drinking their tea. The intimacy was still there. The love, the affection, the togetherness. There were no electronic devices between them. Sophie couldn't even see the hated iPad.

They just talked. Finished each other's sentences, answered questions unasked. Back together as one. Their devotion didn't need validating by sex. The posy of flowers, delivered with a bug and a smile and their intertwining of toes, was worth so much more to Sophie.

She knew relationships were complicated. They just needed to work a bit harder on theirs, and this was feeling like a good start. They had their issues, but Sophie was convinced they were purely a result of a brilliant relationship stuck in a rut caused by just living.

Oh, and Drema.

They finished their tea and took a few moments more to

discuss the plans for the weekend.

Today the boys were taking part in their first official Pony Club tetrathlon event. It was too early in the year and too wet and muddy for the full, two-day tetrathlon. This weekend would be the winter version, starting with the triathlon (a one-kilometre run, a two-minute swim, and a two-handed pistol shoot), followed by the show jumping event in an all-weather arena tomorrow.

Until now, Toby hadn't known what the boys would be doing. He was intrigued to find out that Michael was also competing as an unofficial team member, so he was becoming more and more enthralled about the day ahead.

'Seriously, Michael's got to run one kilometre? D'you think he'll make it? He can barely run to the toilet.'

'Well, he said he wanted to. I think he felt left out. He can't do the shooting though. He's too young, it's like a biathlon for him.'

Sophie went on to explain that until children are eight, they can't legally shoot in competitions. This was a shame, as Michael had been surprisingly good at this phase in training.

'It's his swim I'm more worried about,' Sophie continued. 'Two minutes swimming, and I'm not sure he will make half a length. I just hope he doesn't get upset when everyone else overtakes him.'

'Blimey, my Mum and Dad will be having kittens. Michael swims like he's about to drown. They'll be covering their eyes.'

Dot and Frank had travelled up from Kent the night before,

eager to watch their only grandchildren in a competitive, sporting event.

They were only a few years older than Sophie's parents, but to her, they were a generation apart. She had offered them the ensuite double bedroom when they'd arrived, but they'd insisted on the room across the hallway with the two single beds. The double had recently been decorated and was a far superior room, already laid with fresh flowers and a tea tray. Sophie tried to insist they take it, but they'd declined, not wanting to impose; they didn't want to mess up the smart room. Sophie bit her tongue and moved the flowers and tray into the chosen room, struggling to turn up the thermostat on the radiator.

'Don't worry, we don't need it on,' Frank had said.

'Don't be daft, it's freezing in here,' Sophie had replied abruptly. 'I'll get Toby to sort it out, but for now, leave your bags and come downstairs. I'll make you a tea; you must be gasping after your journey?'

'Well yes, okay. That would be nice,' Dot had said. 'So long as it's not too much trouble?'

'OMG it's a cup of tea, not a three-course meal!' Sophie had muttered under her breath before she'd gone briskly downstairs to get a head start on her in-laws and the troublesome chore of turning on the kettle.

Now, Sophie could hear Dot and Frank going downstairs, most likely fully dressed, ahead of schedule, desperate to be helpful with the boys and animals. Sophie had made the most of their visit and scheduled their babysitting service for later that night, whilst she and Toby went on a rare night out with friends.

Following the recent weeks of Toby's inattentive company, Sophie had wanted to cancel, but after the last few days and with their toes now entwined, she was beginning to look forward to their evening out.

*

Once everyone was ready, Sophie left with all the equipment, refreshments, and Dot. Toby followed with his dad and the two boys, squashed in the silly sports car.

The shooting phase came first and was not a spectator event. No one was allowed into the hall, apart from Sophie, who was officiating as William's loader, responsible for reloading the gun and releasing the safety catch before handing it to him to fire.

Sophie was surprised at how nervous she felt in her official role. Somehow, loading a real metal gun was terrifying, especially as she handed it to her eight-year-old.

William didn't seem to notice his mother's shaking hands. He began his round by hitting the target with a score of two out of a possible ten. Not great. Following a rather smooth reload, he then managed to shoot a four, and Sophie began to relax.

His third bullet had a mind of its own and missed the target altogether. He blushed fiercely as the boy next to him yelled out his ten and high fived his father, which Sophie wasn't sure was shooting etiquette. She was mortified for William but knew talking was not permitted, so she threw him a loving look of confidence as she shakily reloaded.

William's hands remained steady, and his fourth bullet responded by hitting the bullseye.

Sophie saw him glance across at her, a controlled upturn to his mouth. She responded with a big smile and leant in close to secretly whisper her praise. By the end of the phase, William had scored 540 out of a possible 1000, placing him well down in the rankings.

Sophie led him out of the hall giving him a huge pat on the back for remaining calm and doing so well, then stood back to watch as he proudly recounted the event, shot by shot, to his captivated family audience.

*

After both boys had finished their run and swim events; William's at record speed and Michael's miraculously completed without falling over or drowning, they all sat in the February sun to eat. Sophie had organized a large picnic, which was devoured quickly, then subsequently added to, courtesy of the burger van.

Toby was being particularly attentive towards her, showing his appreciation of her efforts. Sophie knew how much he enjoyed watching the boys compete and she was relieved it had all gone so well. She felt proud of their little family and had no doubts that today, they did look happy.

'It's lovely here, isn't it?' Toby said, as they sat on a large grassy space between elegant stone buildings of the prestigious private school where the event was being held. 'We should come again. I saw some interesting shops on the high street as we drove in. Bet there's some lovely walks around here too.' Toby took a bite of his burger. 'I wonder how much it costs to send your kids to school here?'

'Masses, I should think. I'd have to start working for Drema too. Plus, I think the children have to be super clever as well.'

'It would be nice though, wouldn't it?' Toby put his hand on Sophie's leg, gently massaging her thigh. He was likely caught up in a different world, where money was no object, the boys had the best of everything, and he was lord of his manor.

Sophie couldn't disagree, but she knew no matter how much money they had, they would never fit in with the tweedy, Land Rover brigade. They hadn't introduced the pony part to these events yet, so it had the potential to become even more tweedy as immaculate ponies and posh horse boxes came onto the scene.

'It might be nice, Toby, but it's not really us, is it? I would still look for bargains at boot sales, and you'd soon get fed up with all the drinking port and smoking cigars.'

They both laughed. Toby vehemently disagreed and playfully pushed Sophie away by the shoulder.

Enjoying the teasing, Sophie continued. 'Besides, you'd have to wear corduroy trousers and start hunting and shooting. You'd have to get rid of your Lycra and stop running marathons.' Sophie smirked at her vision and nudged him affectionately in the side. 'Although, I could quite fancy you in tweed, riding a big black horse. Far more attractive than that effeminate, padded Lycra on that skinny bike. When is your next marathon?'

'I've no idea.' The words rushed out of his mouth as he shrugged dismissively.

'Really? Surely at this time of year, marathons are everywhere. It won't be long till the London one, will it?'

'I'm not sure I'm running them anymore.' Toby looked down at the ground, crossing his long legs.

Sophie brushed the crumbs from her lap. 'Don't be silly, why would you give it up? You've worked so hard, and you're really fit now.' She squeezed his bicep and poked his six-pack. 'I'm only joking about the big black horse thing; I think it's great you've committed so much to the triathlon club. Makes me feel I should try and get fit too.'

'Oh, I don't know, it's just not the same anymore.' Toby said.

'Same as what? What's changed?' Sophie raised an eyebrow. 'You haven't lost the padding in your Lyrca pants have you, or got sores where you shouldn't,' and she winked across at Dot, who was stifling a laugh.

Toby's jaw twitched but it wasn't due to a smile. 'No, it's nothing like that.' And with no further explanation why, he turned to speak to his dad about the upcoming match for Liverpool.

*

Toby couldn't fault Sophie's organisational skills on this busy day. She may not have run one kilometre, nor swam several lengths, but she had timed everything to perfection for warm-ups, course walking, and heats for both children. Plus, she had ensured three adults and herself were in the right place for the action and were suitably refreshed throughout.

He had always loved her ability to organise and plan for any occasion. Even their wedding had been solely orchestrated by her and had run fluidly and effortlessly. She had been so intent on proving to her parents they were meant to be together after less than a year, that she had organised and paid for the whole thing herself.

Today, she had seemed in her element, busily moving them from event to event, totally in control and always smiling. Up until now, he had been able to ignore the insistent messages from Abigail, but Sophie had kept on going on about marathons. Insisting he should keep training. Unknowingly pushing him back towards her. He knew he should have blocked her number as soon as she'd left the pub last week, but he had genuinely hoped they would remain friends, eventually both being part of the club without the attraction.

Now he wasn't sure what his conflicted mind was thinking. He needed time to think. An opportunity to remind Abigail to leave him alone, before he would finally block her number. So with the help of a little white lie about staying behind to help clear up, he watched Sophie bundle everyone into her car and drive off, before sitting on the wall and pulling out his phone.

> Toby:
> Please stop messaging me. You're making this too hard. Even Sophie has tried to push me back into the club and into running. I need to forget it all.

>At least for a while. I'm hoping we can
>still be friends.

James B:
You're kidding yourself if you think you
can stop this. You'll realise soon
enough. I'm going to wait for you.
Besides, you haven't beaten me yet at
a half marathon. You still need to win
that bet! xxx

>Toby:
>I love Sophie, I really do. We've got
>things to work on I know, but I can't risk
>it all. I won't risk the boys' happiness. I
>will beat you though one day. I feel it's
>my duty ... but it might not be just yet.

James B:
Listen, why don't we meet up and chat
some more. I don't mind sharing you
for a bit. I'm still so wrecked by my own
divorce. I don't want anything serious.
Can't we just have fun? Don't be a fun
sponge! LOL. Who will it hurt? You want
to keep running and be part of the
club, don't you? Why let me stop you?
I can do it if you can? No strings? No
commitment? Why not? xxx

> Toby:
> I don't know how that would work. Look, I'll call you in a minute, just leaving this pony club thing. No strings or commitment? What does that even look like?
> p.s. What on earth is a fun sponge!? LOL.

He had an alarming bolt of adrenaline to his heart as he sent the last message, then powered off his phone. He felt like a teenager again, ridiculously excited by a message from a girl that sent him giddy with lust.

He didn't want to read her reply. He didn't like the way her messages were making him feel, but he couldn't, just yet block her number.

Maybe a no strings, no commitment thing could work? It wouldn't mean anything then, would it?

Toby went to offer his help. He rolled up a hundred-metre rope barrier, pulled up twenty-course flags and loaded them onto a trailer. He then climbed into his little sports car and began the journey home.

He pulled out of the car park, automatically plugging his phone into Bluetooth, and made the call he thought he'd be strong enough to resist. He drove home the long way, and didn't finish his conversation till he pulled onto the driveway of Nettlefield House, by which point, Abigail had convinced him, not to be a fun sponge.

He unplugged his phone, deleted the evidence, and entered his home.

'Sorry it took so long. There was so much to tidy up, and I had to stop for petrol. I only need two minutes, and I'll be ready.' He knew he was later than expected by Sophie's stiff stance and tightly pursed lips, not saying a thing. True to his word, he returned to the kitchen two minutes later.

'Are you wearing that? They're not even clean. Did you get them out of the wash basket?' Sophie said.

'Well, I haven't got any other jeans. These are my only ones without a rip,' Toby threw back, taking no notice of her heels and dress.

'Oh, I give up. Let's just go. We're late.'

She walked out the kitchen door, yelling goodbye to her in-laws and the boys. Toby closed the door behind them, yearning for the sofa and the re-run of the Liverpool game.

*

The well-fed group left the restaurant at eleven and were welcomed into their neighbour's home for a nightcap just a few doors down from Nettlefield House.

Toby had not made much effort to enjoy himself. He was usually more animated and chattier. Normally, he would talk to anyone about anything, and Sophie loved him for it. But tonight, it was as if he didn't want to be there.

Cliff and Heather were a hospitable couple and generously offered around the port and wine. Sophie, once comfy on the sofa, craved a peppermint tea and her bed, but she was enjoying the conversation, so she accepted a small glass of wine and sank deeper into the comfy chair.

The living room contained far too many sofas for its size

and its walls were painted deep red, so they looked as if they were closing in on them. The darkness of the carpet added to the slightly seedy atmosphere as everyone found their position on comfy but mismatched upholstery, barely visible in the dimmed lights.

As quick as Sophie began to feel sleepy, Toby came alive. He was being surprisingly vocal. The conversation had moved on to Formula One, and he was unaware he was in the minority in his opinion of what makes the sport so great.

'At the end of the day, the best car will always go to the best driver. That's just life,' he slurred, holding his large glass of port.

'Yes, but it shouldn't. There shouldn't be a best car,' Cliff responded. He continued discussing how other sports would never allow such massive disadvantages due to differing equipment or budgets.

Toby seemed to lose interest in his argument, and as the topic moved on to the speed limits in the village, he pulled his phone out of his pocket.

Sophie began to feel weary, both from her energetic day and the subsequent conversation about speed patrols, which she found even duller than the Grand Prix debate.

It was more exciting watching Toby on his phone. He could only have been surfing the web, but his facial expressions and his rhythm of typing implied something else. It was as if he were writing an email, then he'd pause, take a sip of port, perhaps add to the conversation in the room, then write some more.

Sophie watched him intently without leaving the

conversation, frustrated she couldn't see his screen. If he was surfing the net, then that was rude. If he was sending emails, then that was just silly. It was past midnight, and he had far too much to drink to represent Drema appropriately.

If he was texting, then who? Why? And what on earth about at this time of night?

'So, what d'you think the new head is going to do first?' Cliff's question jolted Sophie back into the conversation. All eyes turned to her, eager to hear the answer.

Her appointment to Parent Governor of the village school last year meant she did have an opinion, so she offered what she could. Then, as quickly as was polite, she passed the conversation on and returned to spying on her husband.

He was fast asleep. His head was angled back in the chair, and his mouth was open, catching flies. He was possibly dribbling, it was too dark to see, but his phone was back in his pocket, and his glass was empty.

Sophie knew from experience that this was the end of the night for Toby, so she made their excuses, apologized for her husband's embarrassing behaviour, and shoved him awake and out into the night.

They walked apart, silently, the few doors to Nettlefield House and to bed, where the small, floral posy was drooping sadly. Underneath, surrounded by fallen petals, the little black bug lay motionless, legs in the air.

11

Sunday, 24th February 2013

Sophie woke, planning to ignore last night's disappointment, hoping to replicate the intimacy from the morning before. But Toby was out of bed before she had even turned over.

She reached across to the bedside cabinet for his phone, grabbing the opportunity to find out what he had been doing last night, but it wasn't there. She foolishly realised it must have accompanied him into the shower. She could hear the water pumping.

It was flipping 6:30 on a Sunday. Why on earth did he need his phone in the shower?

She could feel the significant distance between them growing once again as she listened to the pulsating water, straining to hear what else might be happening in the shower. It was no longer just her jealousy of Drema bothering her.

There was something else, something harder to explain. She thought back to yesterday's restorative moments of intimacy and tried to understand what had changed. Why had Toby morphed from the kind, loving, other half of her, back to this phone-obsessed, sullen new man?

Today, she was going to 'borrow' his phone and carry out some detective work to understand what was capturing his attention so fully. If that failed, she would just have it out with him later. She couldn't continue with this uncertainty anymore.

Charged with a plan of action and focused on getting everyone ready for the show jumping event, she got out of bed, threw the little posy of dead flowers in the bin, and went downstairs to make a tea, just for herself.

*

The boys' ponies lived out in the fields most of the year. They found great enjoyment rolling in the mud, engraining it into every strand of their long, white, Welsh pony hair.

Sophie had left them overnight, wearing rugs from ears to tails, which kept them mostly clean. So, apart from eight mucky brown legs and two mud-clumped tails, her work this morning was minimized.

Even so, she would have welcomed some help from the riders to load the saddles and other paraphernalia, or some manly muscle to hitch up the trailer. But the three generations of men in her life were all watching the re-run of the Liverpool match.

The event was held at a local equestrian centre with ample parking and two all-weather arenas. The first class had been delayed due to a loose pony and the burger van still hadn't arrived, so Sophie had to work hard to keep everyone happy.

Nana and Grandad, who understood less about ponies than Toby, had retreated into their car to escape the bitterly cold wind sweeping across the showground and Toby, missing the expected bacon rolls, kept asking how much longer she thought it would be.

Eventually, it was time for Michael's class, and it was the first time he was jumping a proper course of over one foot. Although still being led by Sophie, he was showing great confidence and an ability to hang on and steer in the right direction. Sophie would retain control of Snowy's forward speed, shouting instructions to match the course of jumps, but in Michael's opinion, he would be controlling it all.

Sadly, at the first jump, the little mare rattled the pole with her back legs, probably in protest to the jab in the mouth she received whilst in the air.

'Mummy, you knocked it down,' Michael said through clenched teeth.

Sophie accepted the blame. There was no time to protest her innocence before the second jump appeared. 'Let's just concentrate on the next one. It's bigger, so get ready ... and ... jump!' She lifted her legs a bit higher to absolutely make sure it wasn't going to be her to blame if another pole fell.

Michael sat deep to several large jumps and although he might have looked as near to falling off as he had done to drowning the day before, the rest of his round was clear. As they exited the ring and the announcer declared the four faults, Michael once again made it clear in a loud voice, it was mummy's fault, not his, that the pole had fallen.

It meant he progressed no further, the next class was too high, so in his mind, his job was done. Mummy had messed it up and he wanted to play on daddy's phone, sitting in the warm car.

Sophie was embarrassed by her spoilt and rude child, discarding his pony aimlessly and running off with the electronic gadget Toby willingly handed over.

William's class came next, and this would be hands-off for Sophie. She was no longer permitted by her eight-year-old to touch the pony's reins, nor offer instruction. New pony or not, William was in charge in the warm-up ring.

If Sophie said, 'Canter,' William would trot; if Sophie shouted, 'Shorten your reins,' William would lengthen them.

Unfortunately, he hadn't yet mastered this new pony in this environment, and he really did need to listen to his mother's instructions. Chicco had quickly learnt that his new rider didn't have the length of leg or power to push him into a canter, so he remained trotting. The more Sophie tried to help; the worse William's mood became. The warm-up ring became a battleground, and Sophie came close to giving up and going home.

Why had she bothered? She might as well have left them all in front of the television and brought Juno to jump the classes herself.

'God, he's a brat,' she said to Toby, standing at the rails of the warm-up ring. 'He won't listen, and now he's in a foul mood. Let him trot around and see how many faults he gets. I don't care anymore.'

'D'you want me to have a word?' Toby offered.

Sophie knew Toby hadn't yet worked out how ponies operated, but he did know that William's attitude was wrong and would know what to do about that.

'Yes, go on then. Quickly. It's nearly his turn. Tell him to put his gloves back on too. It's freezing.'

Sophie watched as Toby awkwardly climbed through the railings, dodging a few carefree kids on unruly ponies, before flagging down William. She couldn't hear what was being said, but William's stony face broke into a smile, and he seemed to willingly put on his gloves.

'Last to go, we have number 257, William Cooper, riding Chicco,' announced the commentator.

Sophie went to yell across to William to hurry up and come through to the ring, but he was already on his way, high-fiving Toby as he went. His face was intensely set in concentration, eyes staring forward, mouth tightly closed and cheeks taut. He looked every inch a committed and confident horseman, most likely a direct response to the conversation with Toby.

'I'm not going to canter. Chicco doesn't want to,' he announced as he trotted past Sophie, not making eye contact, focusing on the jumps ahead. Sophie wanted to tell him to shorten his reins, but she knew better than to offer advice at this stage.

'Okay darling. Good luck.' She joined Toby and his parents, pulled out from the warmth of their car, at the side of the ring to watch.

'Where's Michael?' she asked, suddenly aware that a loose

six-year-old wandering around thirty half-ton horses was not safe.

'He's still in the car, on my phone. He didn't want to come and watch.'

Typical, Sophie thought. That's where Michael is happiest, on an electronic gadget.

Reassured he could come to no harm, she concentrated on her older son.

William did indeed just trot around the course. The pony made a genuine effort, leaping over the two-foot fences with limited impulsion and forward momentum. William didn't seem to mind the slow and ungraceful movement as he trotted into a fence, virtually stopped, then successfully leapt over with the skill of a pony that knew his job better than the rider.

Miraculously, he went clear and received a big round of applause for a job well done. William rode out of the ring beaming. He had remembered the course, been kind to the pony, and above all, stayed on board over some uncomfortable looking jumps.

'Well done, William,' Toby and his parents chorused.

'That was brilliant, William. It would have felt better at a canter, but you did great. The poles all stayed up. Well done.' Sophie took the reins and patted the pony. 'Don't get off,' she exclaimed as William went to dismount. 'You've got to learn the jump-off course now.'

They moved over to see the numbers on the board, indicating the new order of the jumps. This course would be shorter in length, but the poles would be set a few inches higher.

The winning tactic was not only to go clear but to go fast. William would need a grenade up his backside to stand a chance of winning a prize now.

'Just focus on going clear, William. You're up against a lot of older people on bigger ponies, so give Chicco a good line in, and don't worry about cutting the corners. Though, you might need to liven him up a bit. Look, they're putting them up quite a bit higher. Number five's a whopper. You're gonna have to kick hard over that one.'

William seemed to listen, absorbing the advice. His mood had significantly changed from the stroppy, spoilt child from earlier to a committed sportsman who did not want to disappoint.

In the end, William came fourth. There were ten in the jump-off, and he was one of only four who went clear. He was well behind the pace of the third-placed rider, but due to the steady and genuine nature of an old pony that knew his job, he had succeeded where faster, riskier riders had failed.

He was immensely pleased with himself and beamed from ear to ear. Winning did matter, but to come fourth was a good result for an eight-year-old who started the day in a real sulk.

'That deserves a hot chocolate, don't you think?' Toby said as William dismounted and dismissively handed his pony to his groom.

Sophie didn't mind. 'I'll get Chicco back to the trailer and get ready for loading. Why don't you get him one with a flake and marshmallows?'

She quickly led the pony to the trailer, hoping for a few

minutes' head start on her husband. Sophie had a growing feeling of mischievousness at what she was about to do, but with enough silliness to wash it away.

For goodness' sake. What was she expecting to find? Nothing, she was sure. But a quick look wouldn't hurt. As soon as Sophie got back to the trailer, she quickly tied Chicco up, threw a rug over his back, and opened the car door, startling her son inside.

'Hiya. We're all done now. Pass me Daddy's phone. I need to do something.'

Michael's eyes didn't move from the screen. 'No, I'm in the middle of a game.'

'Quickly. I only need a second. You can have it straight back.'

Michael still didn't comply.

'Michael. Now.' She thrust out her open hand.

Accepting he was not going to win this situation, he defiantly switched it off, then smacked it into her palm. 'There you are. Have it.'

'Thank you,' she retorted sarcastically. She had virtually no time to lose, so ignoring her insolent son, she switched Toby's phone back on and typed in his password.

INCORRECT PASSWORD, it flashed.

She was confused. She was sure she'd put it in correctly. She keyed it in again, more slowly, but she got the same message.

'What's the password, Michael? Has Daddy changed it?'

'Don't know.' He brushed past her to go and stroke his tethered pony, calmly eating hay.

Sophie tried the code again. Her pulse quickened. Toby had used the same password on his phone for as long as she could remember. It further fuelled her sense of foreboding and increased her determination to access his phone. She tried one last time in a panic as she saw Toby and his parents walking back across the field.

'Damn it.' She tried again, with a slight variation in the code. 'Oh, bugger.'

A new message appeared: IPHONE BLOCKED FOR 1 MIN.

'Shit. Oh, flipping shit.' Toby was closer now, so she shoved the phone under the driver's seat and began to get the ponies ready for loading.

'Where's my phone, Michael?' she heard Toby ask.

Nana and Granddad had gone back to their car to escape the wind, sipping tea out of polystyrene cups. William paraded his extravagant hot drink in front of Michael, along with his green rosette. Surprisingly, Michael didn't rise to it. He climbed into his grandparents' car instead and began to raid the travel sweet tin in the glove box.

'Well, where is it?' Toby ineffectively yelled after him. He turned to Sophie. 'Mummy, where's my phone?'

Judging that one minute had passed, Sophie gave away its position. 'Come on, William. Let's get these saddles off.' She turned her attention back to the ponies.

Sophie carried the saddles from the ponies' backs to the tack container at the front of the trailer. Standing inside, she looked through the little window to the car hitched in front. She saw Toby standing by the driver's door, phone in hand, no indication he had noticed anything wrong. She was deflated that her plan to inspect his phone had failed, but she now felt more justified. It really did need to be investigated.

Why had he changed his password?

She busied herself getting the ponies ready to load, admonishing William for the hundredth time to not leave his pony untied. Allowing the mare to graze with her reins hanging under her feet, the quickest way to snap the leather.

Each time Sophie had to carry items into the trailer, she watched her husband through the little window, unobserved. She was fascinated by how he could have anything to do on that damn phone, in a field, on a cold Sunday. He was obviously not going to offer any help to get the ponies loaded; he just kept tapping away on his mobile friend with an animated but unreadable facial expression.

Sophie took her phone out of her pocket to see what sort of signal was present in this field, in the middle of nowhere. As she expected, she had a phone signal but no 3G. Clicking onto her most frequently used internet page, she waited for the BBC weather to load. It didn't. If it were going to, the weather would have already happened.

So, he couldn't be surfing, she concluded. Or sending emails. So what was he doing on that damn phone?

Detective work done, evidence (or the lack of it) collected, she returned to the task of getting everyone home.

*

The moment to interrogate her husband came later. Toby's parents had gone home. The boys were in bed, and the kitchen had been cleared away. The animals were all done, and it should have been time for a couple of hours before bed, snuggled on the sofa, to start the new week refreshed.

Toby seemed reluctant to leave the kitchen table, satisfied from dinner and unaware that, all around him, the chores had been completed.

Sophie peered around the side of the fridge, and under the pretext of sorting out Monday's packed lunches, watched him. She could see his changing expressions and his satisfied grin as he typed away on his phone. He suddenly stood up.

'Right. I've just got to pop out. Tom wants to chat again. He's got an interview next week and is keen to get some tips. I won't be long.'

Toby's smile as he put his phone back in his pocket convinced her that her instincts were right. Tonight, she had been watching him closer than he knew, and it wasn't someone called Tom that was igniting his mind. She came out from the cool of the fridge and stood directly in front of him, feeling strong and empowered, yet a little bit silly and scared. Before she could reconsider her approach, she had spoken a strong and direct four words that would change her life forever.

'Show me your phone.'

12

Sunday, 24th February 2013

Sophie's words hung in the air as Toby froze. Her voice sounded alien. The anticipation at finally uncovering the truth felt like excitement riddled with dread, but there was guilt too. Guilt at how awful she must be making Toby feel.

He pushed his chair away from the table, sitting with his back to the wall, unable to make eye contact. She stood rock solid and still, towering over him, holding out her hand, showing no hint of a shake. She repeated her words, empowered by her strength and her heightened position.

His silence lasted an eternity, and it allowed her to imagine how things would play out. He would hand over his phone without delay, showing her everything her suspicious mind had imagined. They would share a joke at the ludicrousness of it all, then finally go and snuggle up on the sofa.

Sophie waited for him to concede, to conform to her imaginary scenario, but she noticed an ominous change in his face. His soft features were hardening and becoming rigid. His blue eyes darkened, and his pupils became lost. He grew taller as his shoulders stiffened, yet he remained seated and just stared.

With her outstretched hand moving closer to his face but a little less steady, Sophie repeated, 'Toby. Please. Show me your phone.'

'No.' He lifted his stare to challenge hers. 'What's wrong with you?' His tone was icy, and each word drove a single stab of steel into Sophie's stomach. He spoke and looked like a stranger. She had never seen him so spikey, so mean.

'There's nothing wrong with me. I simply want to see your phone.'

'Why? What for? Well, you're not getting it.' Toby stood abruptly, scraping his chair across the floor. 'Get lost. Just leave me alone.'

The harshness of his words simultaneously drove the cold steel upwards, towards Sophie's head, and trickled its coldness through her legs, making her whole body shiver. She'd started something now so she had to finish it.

'Look, okay, so maybe I am being silly. I just want to see what you're doing on the phone all the time.' Sophie was trying a softer approach, hoping to take the tension out of the room. 'Show me if it's nothing. Show me what you were smiling at just now. Please?'

'I'm doing emails and stuff. You know me. I can't help it.' His tone began to match hers.

'But it's Sunday night. You've been on it loads today; I can't believe you're simply emailing.'

Toby did a complete three-sixty. He slumped, pulled his

chair back under the table, and rested his head on his hands. 'Well, okay, I might've been surfing the net a bit too. You know me. I can't help myself, can I?' He gave a nervous laugh and stood to leave the room. 'Come on. Let's go and watch that programme. I'll tell Tom I'll meet him another night.'

But Sophie wasn't giving in. 'Then show me. Show me your phone. If that's all it is, then just let me see.'

She held out her hand once again, but this time it felt like the upper hand. He had admitted surfing, so if he were telling the truth, why was he now trying to run away and change the subject? She knew there was something to see on that phone. His actions had proved it, and as he continued to flee from the kitchen, she decisively managed to pluck the phone from his back pocket.

But as easily as the pocket gave it up, Toby snatched it back. The coldness returned, accompanied by his pulsating neck vein. He moved quickly, half-running up the hallway and into the lounge, slamming the door behind him. Sophie followed in this mad pursuit and entered the room to see him retreating backwards, frantically pressing buttons on his phone.

'Toby, stop it. Are you deleting stuff?' Her voice became louder, not quite shouting but with enough underlying anger to frighten the sleeping dog off the sofa. 'Bloody hell, Toby, stop deleting things!'

She grabbed his arm to see what his fingers were doing but he held the phone high, out of her reach, and spun round so that his back was to the wall. He had over a foot height advantage, and with his arms in the air, Sophie stood no chance of seeing the screen. She could feel her whole body pulsing with adrenaline.

They had never had such an unusual and tense altercation, and it scared her. She sensed his physical strength, so much greater than hers, but she had no choice but to face the fight if she wanted to uncover his secrets.

'Jesus, Toby, what's happening to you? You've turned crazy. I only asked to see your phone. How bad can it be?' Sophie backed away, realizing she could never win this physical fight so tried a more level-headed approach. 'You have to tell me, Toby. There's no choice now. Your actions have proved there is something you are trying to hide. You need to tell me. Now.'

She felt superior again. She could sense he felt beaten, as his arm began to lower. How could he possibly deny it now, whatever *it* was? She gave him some space, moving to sit on the far sofa, waiting for his next move.

*

Toby saw the determination in Sophie's eyes. He sat on the opposite sofa, defeated and mortified. He did have to tell her, or at least he had to tell her something. His heart was beating so fast, panicking on the inside.

What could he say? He'd done the right thing. He'd already ended it. It had been Abigail pushing him into the no-strings thing, pressurising him to meet up to discuss it tonight. No strings wouldn't have meant anything, would it?

He looked at Sophie as she waited for his answer, but all he could see was the boys' destroyed faces and the love he would have risked if the truth came out. She would have every right to kick him out once he told her, and the thought of leaving tore him in two.

Instead, he would force himself to erase his unwanted emotions from the last few months for good. Stop thinking of no strings. Stop believing that no commitment was a good thing. Charged with the depth of his love for the boys, he would protect and repair his family unit and he thanked God that he hadn't left to meet up with Abigail. He hadn't done what she so obviously wanted him to do, and which would have so brutally damaged his marriage.

He keyed in his password, metaphorically crossed his fingers, and held out his phone to do the talking for him.

'Thank you,' Sophie said and began scanning through the phone, obviously unsure what she was looking for. Toby could see her reading his emails, checking text messages, waiting for something to jump out, but nothing did.

She handed it back. 'I don't even know what I'm looking for. You've probably deleted it all anyway. What was it, Toby? What did you delete?'

Toby struggled to find his answer. 'It's … it's just … silly stuff. Photos. Games, you know.' He looked down at the phone in his hand, uncertain he was convincing in his cover-up.

Sophie's tilted head and narrowing eyes confirmed it. 'Games? Photos? I don't understand.'

'You don't need to worry. I'm embarrassed, that's all. I'm not doing it anymore.'

He wasn't telling her what *it* was, but he knew in his heart he wouldn't go back to it. The last few minutes had made him feel like a deceitful, lying creep, and he hated it. He couldn't go through that again. He couldn't bear the fear on Sophie's face and her desperation as she searched for the incriminating evidence.

He was embarrassed at how he had behaved and surprised by his commitment and speed to eradicate the evidence. It *had* just been some photos and texts, and he did play Candy Crush sometimes. Yes, he was certain. He was not going to go there again and this time it would be for good.

But Sophie was not letting this drop. 'So, what were you doing, hiding behind the trailer at the show? I could see you. You looked like you were texting, smiling at something?'

Toby needed something more believable, something unexpected to put her off the scent.

The bombshell he promptly found was perfect. 'It's porn. It's just porn.'

Sophie appeared momentarily stunned. 'Porn? You're joking, right?' She smiled broadly as if she were about to laugh, but it didn't travel across the vast space between them. 'On your phone? In a field? At a horse show? What are you? Eighteen?'

'I know. It's embarrassing.' Toby felt more comfortable than he thought he would by his lie.

'But your screen's so small.' Sophie's brow was so creased, she could have been sucking lemons. 'Michael was on your phone this morning, for goodness' sake. He could have seen it.'

Sensing he wasn't quite convincing her, Toby continued.

'Ant was the one who told me about this site, we joke about it all the time. Men like porn. People save photos of things they like. Look, I'll show you.' He typed into Google and waited for the site he hadn't used for years to load.

*

Sophie stood, awkwardly looking over Toby's shoulder, beginning to blush. She was surprised that Toby was interested in porn. She found it so alien, so unlikely.

But why would he lie? It would certainly explain his unusual behaviour, his lightning-fast reactions to hide his phone whenever she walked into a room, like a child stealing biscuits.

She felt somehow to blame. Did men seek out porn because their partners were sexually disinterested or unexciting? Toby used to joke about how unattractive she was in bed with her warm and comfy pyjamas, bed socks, eye mask, and earplugs.

Could it be enough to send him to porn sites? She *had* bought some new underwear recently, and tried to wear less in bed some nights, but he had never noticed. He'd been too occupied with his phone—could that have been porn?

She looked at the screen Toby was showing her. The full-scale sex scene was taking place in front of her eyes on a screen no bigger than a credit card. She felt naïve. Surely, you had to subscribe to these sites. Toby's salary would easily cover it, but she was meticulous in checking their joint bank statements. She would have spotted it, even if it was under a pseudo name.

Toby continued to explain his use of the site in knowledgeable detail until Sophie interrupted him.

'But the photos. You said you were deleting photos. What of?'

'Of women. Off the sites. Here, look.' He smiled and showed her the simple act of saving a screenshot of a film in progress, quite obviously enjoying his unexpected browsing session.

'Okay, stop. Look, I don't get why you didn't tell me. Why keep it a secret? I could have helped … it might have been fun. We could have watched it together.'

His eyes widened. 'Really? You'd have done that?'

'Well, yes, I suppose. Lots of couples do, don't they? Although, I can't believe Rani and Ant watch it. I'll have to ring her and find out.' She turned away from the screen with an awkward giggle.

'No don't. Don't tell Rani I've told you, eh? You'll get me in trouble with Ant if he finds out. Promise me?'

Sophie did, but she knew she wouldn't be able to keep it.

*

As Toby listened to Sophie's enthusiasm for watching porn together, he wasn't sure if his feelings were of guilt or pleasure. Would she really do that? Maybe she was calling his bluff. Either way, he was terrified she might put on an X-rated channel and get naked right here, right now. He would have felt terrible, knowing she was doing it for him, because of him and his lies.

Oh, blimey, please don't.

Fortunately, her clothes stayed on, and she continued with her questioning.

'I still can't see why there's been so much secrecy. So many times, your phone comes first. Are you sure there's nothing else you need to tell me?'

'No, of course not. I'm going to stop now. I promise. No more secret porn.' Toby was trying to convince himself as much as Sophie. His obsession over work, over Abigail, over his lies; it was all going to stop. 'I'm sorry, Sophie. I'm so embarrassed.'

He looked directly into her face, hopeful his eyes appeared soft, drooping at the edges like a puppy's, begging through their gaze to be loved, to be cherished and forgiven.

Sophie held out her hand, a metaphorical olive branch. 'Come on, let's go to bed. Don't do this again. It was like I didn't know you. It's only porn. It should never have gotten like this. Come on. Maybe you should leave that page loaded and bring your phone to bed? I've got some new red underwear I think you'll like.' She smiled, and for a moment, Toby thought she winked.

'I'm sorry. I won't do it again, I promise.' He quickly deleted the page.

Several minutes later, as he heard Sophie close the bathroom door, Toby sent the essential text that would indeed end it. It wasn't just a repeat of the messages before. This one felt different. This time he genuinely meant it.

> Toby:
> Sophie's been watching me. We were messaging far too much today, and she nearly found out. I managed to lie

> my way out of it, and I'm mortified at what I've become. This is now my chance to put things right. I know I've said this before, but today frightened me. I cannot risk her finding out. I know I said we could try the no commitment thing, but I can't. I'm truly sorry for all the hurt I'm causing. I must put things right. I have to man up and do what I should have done a long time ago. I'm sorry, Abigail. It's over. It has to be.

He deliberately left off any kisses and powered off his phone, praying Sophie wouldn't ask him to turn it back on to refresh the previous internet page.

It was going to take a lot longer for him to restore *that* part of his marriage.

13

Monday, 25th February 2013

Before leaving for work, Toby had delivered tea to the side of Sophie's bed. He had put it in a flask to keep it warm. Propped up beside it, in full view, was a handwritten note.

> My Darling Sophie,
>
> I'm so sorry for yesterday and the way I've been. I'm embarrassed, guilty, and distraught that I've hurt you and lost your trust. I can promise you, my darling, that I will get off my phone, leave it where it belongs, and start to focus on what matters: you, me, and the boys. I found this fascinating world and was drawn in. Combined with work, I've become selfish, uncaring, and lost in my own little world. Well, it's time for that to change. I love you, sweetheart, and I love our life. I'm so sorry.
>
> Toby x

The more Sophie read, the more the knot in her stomach untied. She could feel through his words that her old Toby would be back. She desperately wanted to forget the drama of the night before and this note would permit it. Her shoulders began to relax as the warmth of optimism replaced the dread and fear.

Today, she had even more reason to be in a good mood. She was planning for the annual Drema Ball, being held in a few weeks at a prestigious London hotel. She was immensely looking forward to this opportunity for her and Toby to spend some quality time together.

She was going to blow his socks off with a seductive new dress and some sexy, inviting lingerie. It couldn't have come at a better time.

Rani had generously offered Sophie a recce of her numerous extravagant dresses that had barely been worn, so she wouldn't have to resort to the high street. Tonight, they had organised a fun, dressing up evening, which combined with a bottle or two and with Rani as judge, would be a great start to the week.

Sophie finished her tea, tucked the loving note in her diary, then climbed out of bed with a lightness to her body she hadn't felt in a long time.

*

'It's just not right. It's lovely. Don't get me wrong. It's just … not enough?' Sophie removed the tight material from her body.

'Enough? It's barely there. You couldn't wear less and still call it a dress.' Rani replied.

'I know. It's just a bit … cheap.' Sophie paused, seeing the insult hit Rani's face. 'Oh, I didn't mean the dress was cheap. I know it's a Karen Millen, I bet it looks amazing on you, but it makes me look like a slapper.'

'Thought that's what you wanted?' Rani mumbled, taking the discarded dress and putting it back on its hanger. 'How about this one?'

She handed Sophie a greater mass of tightly ruched and tucked turquoise satin. Sophie intuitively knew it was not her colour and sank onto the bed shaking her head. She had now tried on six dresses and wouldn't have worn one.

'Last one, then,' Rani said, taking an elegant but simple black dress out of the wardrobe. 'I think it's going to be too long for you, though. It's long on me, and I've got a couple of inches on you,' she joked.

'I like it. Looks very classy.' Sophie pulled it over her head, letting the silky material cascade down her body. It did indeed hang with a few inches gathered on the floor.

'High heels, that's what you need.' Rani scuttled back into the wardrobe and retrieved a pair of black stilettos at least four inches high. They were a size too small for Sophie, but once on, they transformed the dress into a perfect fit with an extremely sexy look.

The neckline plunged to her waist, revealing a sharp, deep triangle of flesh. Her cleavage was encouraged by the boned sides and the material clung to her curves, elongating her body. The full-length split to the side cut the dress nearly in two.

Sophie loved it. She could barely walk in the shoes, but

all girls suffered the pain of racy heels with a fixed smile on their faces, and Sophie would be no different. The perfect dress for a perfect night.

She couldn't wait to see Toby's face as she stood in front of him dressed like this. She wouldn't even need any underwear. The thought scared her with the excitement this might bring.

'This will knock the socks off him,' she said. 'See if he needs to watch porn with me wearing this.'

'Yeah, you look great, better than I ever did. Toby's gonna love it. Now let's open that wine.'

*

Sophie watched as Rani went into the kitchen and returned with the expected bottle of Prosecco. She looked uneasy, fussing unnecessarily about the choice of glasses.

'So, what's the latest? Have you and Ant got a favourite porn channel I should know about?' Sophie perched on the arm of the sofa, enjoying the first few sips of the sparkling, ice-cold wine as it slipped down her throat, loosening her vocal cords.

'Blimey.' Rani spluttered on her drink, covering her mouth with her hand as the bubbles escaped down her chin. 'Just come right out with it, won't you?'

'I'm intrigued. That's all. Don't say if you'd rather not.' Sophie knew her friend wouldn't be able to resist such a conversation, particularly over a glass of wine.

'Well, no, we haven't.' Rani hung her head a little lower, taking another gulp. 'How about you?'

'Nope. It's not that I wasn't up for it, but to tell you the truth, I'm not sure Toby was even that keen.'

'Really?' Rani leant back in her chair, watching a half-dead fly repeatedly fall into the corner of the window.

'It's as if I've put him off. You know, like the idea is suddenly a turn-off if it's me he's watching it with.' Sophie said this as a joke but felt the truth behind it.

Rani continued just staring at the window.

Sophie poured some more wine. 'Earth to Rani? Some advice would be good here, please. How d'you approach it with Ant? I know I've put on a bit of weight but d'you think Toby's stopped fancying me?'

Rani had trouble maintaining eye contact as she spoke. 'Are you sure there couldn't be another reason?'

'What d'you mean?' Rani's odd behaviour began to unnerve Sophie.

Rani continued, 'I'm sorry. The whole situation is just odd. So unlikely.'

'I know. I agree. But why would he admit to it if it were untrue?'

Rani took a big swig of the happy, sparkly stuff. 'To cover up something else?'

'Cover-up what?' Sophie's volume began to increase. 'What else can it be? It's driving me mad.'

'Look … I don't mean to be cruel, but d'you think he could be having an affair?'

'For goodness' sake, Rani, this is Toby we're talking about. We've already had this conversation. He hasn't got it in him. He's in bed with Drema. He's always with her.

Anyway, we agreed, Toby's just not that type. He couldn't cope with anything more in his life, could he?'

Rani was staring at her now, saying nothing.

Sophie felt compelled to continue her defence of her husband. 'Besides, he'd never risk losing the boys.' She was convinced of this. 'I'd flipping kick him out of the house for a start!'

'Okay, I agree he's the last person you'd expect it from. It's just—' Rani paused to drain the last of her glass. She quickly refilled before speaking. 'I spoke to Ant about it all. I hope you don't mind, but I wanted to see how much time he devoted to that website you told me they were on.' More wine slid down her throat in a large, uncomfortable-looking gulp.

'Well of course I don't mind. It was your bloody husband that got Toby into it.'

'Yes, but that's just it.' Rani took more gulps of wine. 'Ant didn't know anything about it. He said he's never been on that site and has never even spoken to Toby about porn. Ever.'

'Oh come on. He probably just doesn't want to admit it, that's all.' Sophie reasoned, but something inside her doubted Ant would be lying. Her breathing quickened. Could Ant be telling the truth? Was it Toby who was lying?

'I know you don't want to believe it, Sophie, but Ant is never on his phone. Most of the time he doesn't even know where it is, and I have to retrieve it from under the sofa or somewhere. He doesn't even have an iPad and the computer is in the kids' room, so I know he's not going to be on that!'

Sophie knew this was the truth. She had often heard Rani chastising Ant about misplacing his phone. She'd never known such a close couple or as solid a marriage as theirs. This wouldn't be something Ant would lie about.

'Ha. One good thing, then.' She took a big swig of wine to loosen the lump in her throat. 'At least now I know it wasn't my suggestion of watching it with *me* that frightened him off. He was probably scared to death, if he never watched it anyway. Even more reason to seduce his socks off at the ball.'

'Well, that dress is certainly gonna do that! Cheers,' and Rani raised her glass.

'Cheers.' Sophie replied with a false optimism to her voice. She pushed back her shoulders, raised her glass, then took a large swig and coughed a little to brush away the tear that was threatening to slide down her face.

What has he been deleting? If it's not porn, then what is it and why is he lying? As Rani poured another glass, Sophie gave up all worries to the second bottle of Prosecco and the person she now trusted most in the world.

14

Saturday, 16th March 2013

The few weeks since Porngate hadn't been perfect; Sophie accepted that much. But that night had not been mentioned again. Whatever had been going on, Sophie felt it had stopped, and Toby's behaviour towards her had improved. She simply wanted to put it all behind them.

He *had* spent less time on his phone, and most evenings, it had remained on the side in the kitchen. Even Drema was taking up less of his time and Sophie made sure to show him how much she appreciated that.

Sometimes, she saw the old Toby, the other half of her, and she knew she was winning. Moments such as when they were all trying to catch the chicken that had escaped into the neighbour's vegetable patch. Sophie and the boys were rolling around in laughter as Toby pretended he was the world's best chicken whisperer, acting and 'talking' like a chicken. More amusing than that was that the chicken was entranced by him, following him back to her run, gazing up like a dog, not leaving his side.

But there were other times, when she felt like Toby's counsellor, trying to interpret the mid-life crisis he was going through, and she'd have to keep reminding herself of her Father's words. 'Never give up Sophie. You'll always get what you always want if you work hard enough.'

She knew Toby had believed her father's words too. A large part of the Father of the Bride speech had been directed to the groom and Sophie remembered it well.

Her father had said to their wedding guests, 'When Toby came to me and asked for Sophie's hand, I told him straight. I've three other daughters, are you sure you're choosing the best one? Won't be able to change your mind you know.' He had then paused, looking around the surprised faces, before squaring up to Toby and with a piercing stare continued, 'Marriage takes hard work and sacrifice to last forever, are you fully prepared for this?' Then he had stood still, silent, for an eternity. The guests went quiet; you could have heard a pin drop. Toby looked worried, uncertain as to what was expected of him.

'I'll take that silence as confirmation then, shall I?' Sophie's dad had continued. 'You're happy with the daughter you've chosen … yes?' And he had burst into a broad smile, full of pride and pleasure, raising a toast of longevity to the well-matched couple. Toby had visibly released a lung full of air, and he and Sophie had gazed at each other with the shared, unquestionable belief that nothing between them could ever be hard.

She knew she would keep working, keep being strong, to

save this marriage, but would Toby?

Ultimately, Sophie was waiting for the Drema Annual Ball, nervously pinning all her hopes on this extravagant weekend to bring them fully together again. Toby seemed to share her enthusiasm, dry-cleaning his suit, polishing his shoes, and fully briefing Sophie's parents (who had travelled up from their home in Sussex), on the logistics of the boys' football matches. All so they could leave early to make the most of the weekend.

But as Sophie looked across at Toby now, she could sense a change in his enthusiasm. He was just sitting on the bed with his phone in his hand and his head bowed low. He had quickly thrown his things into his overnight bag, not caring about the creases, and looked as disinterested about the weekend ahead as she now knew he was about porn.

'You wait till you see me in this.' She teased, trying to get a reaction. 'Gonna see a *lot* of my flesh tonight, you lucky man!' And she carefully placed the folded black dress into her case as Toby continued staring at his phone.

*

Toby's hands had shaken as he'd caught sight of the text. He nervously glanced across at Sophie as she delicately placed a folded, silky black fabric into her case, praying she hadn't spotted his emotional reaction, not hearing what she had just said.

It had been twenty days. For twenty days, he had maintained his resolve and had ignored the messages of, 'no strings', 'just for fun', from Abigail and in the last ten days, even those had dried up. There had been moments where he had been tempted to respond, but like an addict, he knew the only way through was to suffer his abstinence, and this knowledge had given him the strength to keep his demons at bay.

Now, here was temptation, held in his hand. It was a message he mustn't read, a test he must pass. But before his mind acknowledged this, Toby knew he had weakened. This text had a different tone from the rest. It meant a lot more. He knew he would reply. He just didn't have the strength not to.

James B:
Please call me. I have to see you.
Today. It's really important. Things are
so bad. It's been 20 days without you.
I'm so sorry, but I can't stay away, not
now. I need you more than ever.
Please. I just need to talk. xxx

As he looked across at his wife, Toby shamefully accepted that he would see Abigail today, and it would have to be before they left for London. She was in trouble and crying for help, and he felt compelled to respond. At this moment, he saw Sophie as a strong and challenging obstacle that would break his heart as he moved it away. He couldn't look her in the eye as he explained the fabricated reason for needing to take William to his football game.

'I'm sorry, sweetheart. It's a league match, and they beat

us last time. They've messaged me to help.'

'Seriously. Now? Is there no one else who can wave a flipping flag? We're supposed to be leaving.'

'I know, its crap timing, but the boys have only just learnt the offside rule, so they need someone who knows what they're doing.'

It was only a 'friendly' match, not part of the league, so any of the other dads could have run the line, but Sophie wouldn't know. He couldn't look her in the eye as her face fell in disappointment.

'I'll go and tell Grandpa he doesn't have to take William now.' He left the room before his obstacle of a wife saw through his lies. 'I've got time to give the dogs a quick blast for you before I go.' He shouted over his shoulder. He knew Sophie would appreciate the offer, and it helped him feel better about his deceit.

He began to relax as he walked across the garden and through the orchard. The two dogs raced off toward their secret gaps in the fencing, escaping into the hundred acres beyond and the more exciting prey. Their disappearance went unnoticed as Toby read the reply to his arranged meeting time and place.

James B:
Thanks for not ignoring me. This morning, when my decree nisi came through, I just needed you so much. I couldn't stop it. I had to reach out. I haven't got anyone else to talk to. I

know I said no strings, and that's okay,
but you know I want more. See you in a
bit. Can't wait. xxx

*

'He couldn't even bloody walk the dogs without losing them,' Sophie cursed as the two white blobs in the distance reappeared.

Toby had sent a message, letting her know they hadn't returned before he'd had to leave for the game. She had traipsed across the fields, yelling for them to return to her loving, open arms. Her fake smile secretly concealing her anger towards Toby for allowing them to disappear. They were filthy from digging, and one had rolled in something disgusting.

'Great. Now I've got to scrub shit off you!' she declared to the countryside. 'That's me! I'm just the shit shoveler of Nettlefield House. I spend my life clearing up shit. Dog shit, horse shit, chicken shit, all the kids' shit, and even trying to sort out my husband's shit. Who deals with my shit? Oh, yes. *Me.*'

Sophie thought back to that night on New Year's Day, when Toby had said, 'Things will be different now, I promise. We're going to have a great year.' They weren't different enough, not in a good way, and it still didn't feel like a good year. Her optimism for the weekend ahead faded and she returned to the house to hose off the dogs.

*

Toby hadn't seen much of the football. He certainly hadn't called any offsides or even got close to a flag. He had spent a large part of its duration sitting in Abigail's car, comforting her, assuring her everything would get better.

The official process to end her marriage seemed to be her signal she could now claim another partner. Toby was overcome with jealousy it might not be him. They had talked it through, and Abigail was right. They could do the 'no strings thing', at least to get it out of their system, then see what happens.

He couldn't stop this. He couldn't risk losing her. She needed him and he wanted her. He had so many questions in his head as he drove home from the match that he could only nod, emitting monosyllabic answers to William's questions about the amazing goals and some blatant fouls.

Did he love her? Did he love Sophie? Could he love two people at the same time? He couldn't stop the feelings, could he? Should he?

Toby had all these questions and no one to answer them. When did life get so complicated? He now had to spend the night with his wife but with Abigail dominating his thoughts. How was he going to do that?

He arrived home to find out.

15

Saturday, 16th March 2013

As they drove through central London, Sophie attempted to leave her annoyance behind. Toby was subdued, and she didn't want to spoil the mood further by complaining about their late start and his lack of enthusiasm.

She reclined her seat and pulled down the visor against the vibrant sun, relaxing in the leather upholstery of the little sports car. The verges were alive with random bursts of yellow from daffodils at their peak, in vibrant contrast against the fresh green shoots of spring.

They may have been arriving late but the sights and sounds of London in Spring boosted Sophie's mood. She glanced across at Toby, his sunglasses obscuring his eyes, longing to see the same effect on his face.

Their hotel room had incredible views over Hyde Park, a massive bed with crisp, white cotton sheets, and a lavish bathroom with an impressive shower for two. There was even a welcome gift from Toby's director: a Jo Malone room diffuser and a large black box of premium chocolates, elaborately tied up with a gold bow.

It was only three p.m., but Sophie collapsed on the bed, turned on the TV, and opened the all-expenses minibar. It irritated her that Toby's mood hadn't lightened. He didn't relax and join her on the bed, choosing instead to sit on the chair by the desk, looking around awkwardly, as if afraid to touch anything.

'D'you want a drink?' Sophie broke the silence. 'It's not too early for a gin and tonic, is it? D'you think there's ice anywhere?'

'Probably. Somewhere.' He put his hands in his pockets and gazed out of the panoramic window. 'I might just go for a walk. Selfridges is up the road.'

'Really? You want to go shopping? We hate shopping. Why don't we stay here and have a drink and a snooze?' She didn't wink, but she hoped her eyes gave a similar invitation as she patted the bed. 'Shall we open those chocolates and just devour them all? They look amazing.'

To Sophie, it felt like conditions were perfect for a couple struggling with their marriage. A cheeky afternoon gin and tonic, an indulgent box of chocolates, and over four hours till they had to be anywhere. She could even envision them intimately sharing the walk-in shower, something she wasn't sure they had ever done before.

But Toby didn't seem to share the same fantasy. 'You stay here if you'd rather. I fancy a walk,' and without waiting for an answer, he made his way to the door.

Sophie abandoned her half-made gin with an exasperated sigh. 'I'm coming, I'm coming. I don't want to stay here on my own do I?' She slipped back into her shoes to accompany him on this absurd shopping excursion, quickly catching up as he strode down the corridor.

Selfridges was, as she thought, packed with tourists and overpriced clothes. It was the complete antithesis of where she would want to be.

Toby browsed the men's sections as if he did it every week, whereas, in reality, he did it once a decade. Sophie just watched, longing to return to her drink and the chocolates. Toby bought nothing and tried on nothing. He even said nothing on the walk back.

Sophie wasn't surprised the weekend was panning out like this. She was disappointed and annoyed but not surprised, and she was adamant he was not going to spoil the night ahead. She began to plan like a predator, sizing up her prey, then fine-tuning her tactics to achieve her aim.

Tonight's target was Toby, and with a few drinks and *that* dress, he would succumb to her as any warm-blooded male should.

*

An hour after they returned to the hotel, Sophie walked out of the bathroom surprisingly steady, given the shoes and the two gins she had gulped down. Even with her nerves, she knew she looked ravishing. She was reminded of the night of their honeymoon when she'd spent ages squeezing into a skinny red dress, revealing her slender, pre-childbirth figure, in the best possible way. She'd felt so confident, stepping out of the bathroom that night, ready to embrace their first evening together as a married couple. She had watched Toby's face as he absorbed her, sucking her in. She smiled now, thinking of how easily that dress had come off, in comparison to how hard it had been to put on.

She willed herself to feel that confidence now and she couldn't wait to see Toby double-take as he saw his wife looking better than the day they got married. Even her weight seemed to have taken a back seat in her troubles over the last few weeks.

Toby looked up from the television, his half-drunk gin warm in his hands, 'You look nice,' he said.

Nice? *Nice!* Sophie screamed internally. *He said nice.* Rani would have a fit. The dress looked incredible, alluring, hot, seductive, provocative. Not bloody NICE.

'Nice' was a word she was banned from using in English lessons as a child. She could hear her teacher's admonishment now: 'It's wishy-washy, lacking precision and intensity. It's meaningless.'

She knew he wasn't going to elaborate. He wasn't going to mention the plunging neckline, the cleavage, the shoes. He certainly wasn't going to try and undress her, if only with his eyes. She bit her tongue, not wanting to create a scene just as they were about to leave.

'Thanks. You look nice too.'

With that simple exchange of compliments, they left the room. The space between them growing to the size of a football pitch.

*

Toby could see Sophie was enjoying herself. She didn't know anyone in the room, but she had always been good in a crowd and found conversation easy, particularly after a few drinks. Her years spent working for a large corporation meant she could hold her own in the business chat that dominated these events.

Sometimes, he even felt beneath her in her knowledge, her strong self-belief, and in the confident way she held a conversation. He used to massively admire that, but somehow, tonight, he found it belittling and unattractive.

Abigail was humbler. She was still eloquent, just quieter with it. Abigail would voice her opinion but never if it meant stepping on someone else's. She was too docile for that. Toby recognised how much he enjoyed the contrasting characters of his two women.

Sophie returned from the ladies, just as a slow dance came over the speakers. Toby saw the suggestive smile on her face and noticed her flick her hair and lick her lips. Before he had the chance to escape, she coerced him onto the dance floor. He tried to resist, but she was a lot less drunk than him and was clearly not going to let him go.

He held her clumsily as they swayed to the music. He could feel her hands delicately massaging the back of his neck and willed himself to enjoy it. He gently caressed her back, noticing it was completely devoid of material or underwear.

'I'm not a car, you know.' Sophie peered into his eyes, with a teasing smile. 'I don't need a polish.'

'Sorry. Is this better?' He slowed his caresses till his hands lay still on her hips.

'This feels good, doesn't it?' Sophie offered.

'Yes, it's ... lovely,' Toby responded, not believing either statement.

They had been so close, their faces nearly touching, and he could no longer endure the expectation in her eyes. As the music came to an end, he took the opportunity to abruptly escape to the gents.

*

Sophie decided it was time for bed. Toby was so drunk, he couldn't even dance properly, and her feet were killing her from the heels. Toby seemed happy to call it a night and eagerly said goodbye to his colleagues, before leading the way upstairs, oblivious to the impediment of her shoes.

Less than ten minutes later, Toby was asleep, seemingly overcome with alcohol. The large room was cold; they should have adjusted the air conditioning earlier. The cool air lingered in the large expanse between them in the super king bed.

Sophie had no choice but to snuggle up close for body warmth, regretting the absence of her pyjamas, yet their closeness felt a million miles away.

*

Sophie slept terribly and woke early, made worse by the fact that Toby appeared to have slept so well. Even the earplugs and face mask hadn't helped, and they were usually a godsend at shutting off the outside world. But last night, it had been her inside world keeping her awake.

She opened the curtains and gazed out across Hyde Park. Joggers, dog walkers, lovers, and all-nighters, all enjoying the luxury of a large piece of countryside in the capital.

She longed to open the window and smell the sweet freshness of the greenery outside, but there was no catch. It might not have been the real countryside, but if she squinted, she could piece together the components enough to bolster her mood. She was looking forward to exploring the park after an extravagant, leisurely breakfast.

Sophie heard the bathroom door close and turned around, observing the empty bed. She wondered how Toby had missed her, stood as she was, naked and silhouetted against the morning sun. She climbed back into bed and found the warm spot he had vacated, pulling up the covers to keep in the heat.

'You hungry?' Toby asked as he came out of the bathroom. He grabbed his boxers and jeans off the chair and started to get dressed. 'I'm starving.'

'Seriously? It's only seven a.m. We don't need to rush do we?' Sophie sat up, purposefully not pulling the duvet with her, displaying more than enough flesh to help her cause. 'Come back to bed, and I'll make us a cup of tea.' She flicked across the alluring eyes that had failed to work last night.

'Well ... Okay then. I'll fill the kettle.' And he retreated into the bathroom.

Satisfied she had persuaded him, Sophie set a plan in her head for the ultimate seduction. This, she had decided, was going to be a test. An irresistible, perfectly executed test of their marriage.

She was going to seduce her husband like never before and her nerves and excitement began to build.

Toby climbed back into bed, having flicked the switch on the kettle, and reached for his phone.

'Please put that down,' Sophie asked in a low, soft voice.

She leant across him, took the phone from his hand, and placed it on the side table. She felt her heart race as she purposely allowed her naked body to slide across his chest. She lifted her eyes level to his, then planted a full kiss on his lips, tasting the wine from the night before.

It wasn't altogether a nice taste. There wasn't yet enough passion in the room to counteract morning breath, but now she had started, she was going to finish. The challenge had become such a task in her mind that she didn't think she would enjoy it, but she was going to make sure Toby did.

She couldn't yet tell how she was doing. His hands were behind her back, holding her close, but they weren't exploring. They weren't even polishing. Sophie willed him with her tongue to relax and enjoy the nakedness of their bodies, which was such a rarity these days.

She wasn't quite getting the response she expected. There was no excitement pressing from beneath. She soldiered on determinedly, desperate to get things moving.

It had never been her favourite sex act, but it was always the most successful. She took him by surprise, sliding under the covers and arranging herself between his thighs. She was beginning to enjoy herself more than she thought she would. The primal, controlling, predatory nature of holding a man's most precious asset between her lips was creating a lust of its own.

She adjusted her position to gain increased penetration and used her hands to cup and caress his delicate parts, increasing her movements.

Usually, by this point, she would have bet money on any man being rock-hard and fully engrossed by the activities, but not Toby. Not now. It all seemed like a bit of a non-event. As soon as the realisation dawned on her that the plan was failing, the momentum and her confidence was shattered.

'I'm sorry.' Toby said as Sophie reappeared from under the covers, slightly red, with hair askew from her endeavours. 'It was lovely. I'm sorry. I think I drank too much wine last night.'

Never used to affect you, Sophie thought. *I didn't enjoy it either,* she lied to herself. *No, don't worry about me. I'm okay. Don't need anything, thanks.*

She continued with the sarcastic voices in her head, wondering why and how she could have failed. Her embarrassment would have been obvious in her face if Toby had paused long enough to look, he was already reaching for his phone.

'Guess I'll make that tea, then.' She climbed out of bed and pulled on the hotel robe to cover her nakedness, preserving what dignity she had left.

'Let's not bother with the tea. We can have one downstairs. I'm starving. Breakfast is meant to be brilliant. Besides, I think we should get going quite soon.' Toby lightly sprung out of bed, obviously relieved it was over and he was free to go.

'Really? I thought we were staying all day. We could hire

out a boat on the Serpentine. It'll be fun.' Although, her fake smile said differently.

'No, the parking ticket will be up. We should get back.'

He had made up his mind. Toby was not interested in spending any more time with her than necessary. His stomach was calling, and she knew how loudly it called when it wanted something. There was no point in arguing, this wasn't the time or the place.

Sod it. I give up.

Sophie went into the bathroom to get ready for a breakfast she didn't want with a man who quite obviously didn't want her, in a place that wasn't right for either of them.

At that moment, she wanted nothing more than to be back home with her boys, drinking tea with her parents, before taking the dogs for a walk across the fields in the spring sunshine.

Without Toby.

16

Monday, 18th March 2013

Sophie did well to act normal on this typical Monday morning. She had seen to the horses, the dogs had been walked, the boys were happily ensconced at school, and the kitchen was tidy after the breakfast chaos. It was 10:30 a.m., and the whole day loomed ahead. The whole week.

The whole month.

She sat at the kitchen table, a coffee in front of her and reached for the elaborate black box, discarding the gold bow. Unashamedly, she began to devour the one good thing that had come out of the weekend away. She consumed the intricate mouthfuls piece by piece without any thought to the excessive calories.

Sophie had placed so much expectation on the weekend that now it was over, she was scared by the magnitude of the anti-climax. It hadn't just failed to resolve things; she now had an even greater certainty something was wrong. She was defeated. Every part of her conscious mind had questioned the last few months yet could find no answers.

She rubbed away the newly formed tears, a reaction to this unaccustomed experience of failure and for the first time, wondered if she could win this battle. Her marriage was collapsing, and she was doubting her ability to rescue it.

She needed to capture these unwanted feelings. To bring them to life in words, to face up to them, then eliminate them in a burning, fiery blaze. She was not equipped to deal with this greyness, she needed to see these emotions in black and white, ink on paper, even if she didn't yet have the answers to change them.

Inspired by her images of flames, Sophie reached for her notebook and another luxury chocolate, and continued her fight on paper.

The words flew in front of her eyes. Her hand couldn't keep up with the thoughts as they tumbled out, jostling to be first. Motivated by the songs on the radio, she wondered when words and lyrics began to mean so much. She paused for a moment, listening, stealing the words from the latest song by *PINK*, Just give me a reason. Gaining reassurance that these feelings were not isolated to her alone.

I need a reason too. Why are we not fixing this marriage, this love? Surely, we can? Can't we?

Six pages later, she stopped. The tear-stained papers full of urgent scrawling simply ended with:

What did you delete?

Sophie didn't read the pages through. She downloaded the song from where she had stolen so many lines, and sang out loud, following the lyrics on her phone. Three times she ran through the verses, hoarse with the unaccustomed use of her voice. She felt cleansed. Better.

She no longer felt the need to burn the words, they were too precious, meant too much. Instead, she ran upstairs and placed them in her diary. Now they were captured, she could discard them from her mind and make better use of this clear Monday, this empty week, this full month ahead.

Reverting to type, she collected her fork and wheelbarrow and went into the fields. Whilst her world might be falling apart, the rest of civilisation went on regardless, including the production of vast quantities of horse poo.

*

The field kept Sophie busy for hours, providing plenty of time to align her thoughts. By the time she ran up the slope, tipping her second full wheelbarrow onto the muck heap, she was speaking her thoughts out loud. 'Right life, you big pile of shit.' She laughed at her play on words. 'I am NOT going to let this marriage defeat me.'

By the third wheelbarrow her convictions were growing, and she told the muck heap so. 'You can shit on me all you want, I'm *never* gonna stop trying to mend this.' And as she exerted herself with the fourth wheelbarrow, she felt lighter and empowered, not noticing the heaviness of the wet muck as she effortlessly tipped it over the heap.

'I can't control what you do Toby, but I *can* control how I'm gonna react to it and that's with positivity and conviction and I'm starting tonight!'

She would plan a special 'adult-only night'. She would get an expensive ready meal out of the freezer, and the microwave could do the cooking, allowing more time for conversation. The boys, encouraged by sweets, popcorn, and freedom on the iPad, would be restricted to their bedroom. The conservatory would provide a romantic backdrop, with its twinkling lights and the promise of a fading sunset.

Sophie smiled as she sent Toby a text to invite him.

His mid-life crisis won't stand a chance.

*

Things hadn't gone to plan. Toby had been late home; the sunset had faded into a dull grey and the expensive ready meal had not been the finest as the label suggested.

'Toby, just look at your body language. It looks like you're not bothered we're falling apart.' Sophie leant across the table, hands outstretched, indicating his posture.

He didn't seem to hear. He remained casually reclined, legs resting on the adjacent chair, gazing out of the long pane of glass to the darkness beyond.

'Can't you sit up and actually look at me? Are you even listening?'

'I am listening. I am. I'm just relaxed … that's all.' But Toby didn't change the direction of his gaze.

'Relaxed? How can you be relaxed? We are in crisis here and you're relaxed?' Sophie stood quickly, smacking her chair, on the wall behind. 'What the hell is happening to you? I can't mend this on my own, Toby.'

*

Toby finally brought his mind in from the darkness and looked at his wife, who was virtually climbing across the table in her efforts to get through to him. He could see her anxiety seeping through every pore.

He could almost feel her trembling heartbeat and hear the catches in her voice as she tried to control her emotions. But all he could offer in return was weakness, deceit, and his crumbling strength as he faced this force in front of him, and he hated himself for it.

But *his* emotions were important too. His happiness had to be his priority. He couldn't keep feeding this internal conflict, and this weekend had been evidence of that. Her efforts at trying to resolve this thing she couldn't see had been painful to endure.

Why did she have to try so hard? And why couldn't he love her more for it?

He felt a monumental pressure to come clean, to admit his feelings. Feelings for both women. He knew Abigail was waiting for him, so if he told Sophie, *she* could decide what happened next, take the decision away from him. He wouldn't allow himself to think of the boys' happiness, which would place confusion and turmoil in his mind. He would put them in a box and worry about them when things were clearer.

Yes, I'm gonna tell her. One more glass of wine.

He opened the second bottle of red, ignoring Sophie's sideways glance. He knew she didn't agree with how much he was drinking, but she had no idea of the demons in his head and the stress he was currently under.

Sophie picked up her empty glass as he put the bottle down. 'No thanks. No more for me.' She had an edge to her voice he realised was annoyance as she poured her own glass. 'I think you should stop drinking so much. It's clouding your judgment. You're turning into someone else.'

Sophie then punched him square in the stomach with her next words. Words that could finish it all and give him the coward's way out he craved.

'Are you having an affair?'

He lifted his glass to deflect the shockwave, but his hand was shaking. He put it down without taking a sip. 'Oh, Sophie. I … I'm so sorry.'

His brain was speaking to him in two parts. The demon on his shoulder exclaimed its sudden relief: *At last, it can all come out. Sophie's asked for it.* But then a louder voice, from deep within, screamed at him not to do it. *Deny, deny, deny. You can work it out afterwards. You still love her.*

The louder voice won. He took a sip of wine, his heartbeat racing. 'Of course I'm not. I've just been in my own little bubble. I've got to find a way out.' He couldn't hide his tears as the massive impact of what he had nearly said hit him. 'I love you, Sophie.'

And at that moment, he meant it. His heart burst open in his relief and awareness of this fact, and he looked up into Sophie's eyes with conviction.

'Really?' Sophie enquired with a touch of sarcasm. 'You're not seeing anyone? Not even someone as a friend? Maybe someone you just get on well with?'

The demon on his shoulder spoke. *Jeez, she's so flipping*

persistent. Just tell her if that's what she wants.

Toby didn't listen. 'No, don't be silly. There's no one.' And he nearly believed it himself.

'Then what's happening here, Toby? What are we doing? Look at us both crying over something we don't understand. It just doesn't make sense. I need to make sense of this.' Sophie continued to plead as her tears matched his for pace.

Toby reverted his gaze to the darkness beyond and wished it could suck him into its nothingness.

In his silence, Sophie got up and left the room. 'Wait there. I'm going to get something. Something you need to see.'

Uncertain where his wife had gone, Toby took the opportunity to dry his eyes and check his silent phone. He thought he felt it vibrate earlier, but there was no way he could have checked. The phone showed no notifications. He was disappointed. He was confused.

Just a few moments ago, he'd had the conviction to tell Sophie everything, relieved he could finally admit the truth. Then, instantly, his overpowering relief was because he hadn't told her. He had maintained the lie, even though the question had been asked directly.

Now here he was, checking his phone for an imagined message and feeling no satisfaction it wasn't there. He was mortified by his weakness. He felt the emotional swell of tears return as his conflicted mind continued to direct the somersaults in his heart.

Sophie reappeared with some paper in her hand and pushed it across the table. She looked angelic as the lights flickered across her teary face. Her long hair, dishevelled from the countless times her hand had dragged through it, hung down, shaping her oval face like a cameo in a brooch.

At that moment, he knew he loved her, but he acknowledged he wasn't *in* love with her, and that realisation shattered his heart. He picked up the six sheets of paper and began to read.

Sophie sat silently throughout. She didn't hurry him, just sat and watched.

He consciously displayed his emotions. He wiped his eyes and snuffled a sob, but he knew the truth about everything she had written. He knew what devastation he was bringing to her world, and he felt as lowly and cowardly as anyone could.

The note ended with a simple question he couldn't truthfully answer.

What did you delete?

He could offer nothing other than, 'Sorry.'

*

Sophie took the note from him as he finished reading, anticipating an emotional response. But her eyes widened under arched eyebrows as he simply turned and stared out into the night.

He didn't look across at her, nor offer any words of love or support. The fairies dancing across the lit wires were providing her with more affection than her husband.

She had played the only card she had, and it had achieved nothing. Her much-loved conservatory had become her Room of Pain, and she was furious; not just because Toby was still sitting in it, indifferent, tainting its very existence, but with herself for thinking she could resolve this.

How could she think that some silly words on a piece of paper could have triggered him into becoming the man he used to be? She had allowed him to read her innermost thoughts. She had shown him the open scars on her heart that only he could mend and he had acted like he couldn't care less.

The lyrics of the song came back to her, and for the first time, she wondered if this marriage was indeed broken, not simply bent as PINK had sung. Toby was breaking them and he wasn't going to stop.

Sophie could stand the insolence of the man no longer and violently thumped her hands on the table, alarming Toby, who jolted in his chair. This anger was consuming her, creating an energy that wasn't healthy, especially in the presence of this weak man. Her blood was pumping forcefully, racing in combat with the alcohol in her system and she effortlessly flipped over the table.

Glasses smashed on the solid floor, sending minute daggers in every direction. Toby didn't move, just grabbed the falling wine bottle, relief across his face as he saved it, then casually brushed a fallen fork off his lap.

Sophie marched from the conservatory and out the boot room door. The grass was crunchy beneath her feet, but she couldn't feel the cold stinging her face. It was a black night; stars appeared as her eyes adjusted, but there was no moon. She could barely see her hand in front of her face.

She scrambled through the electric fencing; a movement

so familiar she didn't need the light to see. She wouldn't have felt the electric pulse even if she had connected.

Sophie could just about make out the outline of the brightly coloured show jumps, set up in the middle of the field. She made her way to them, sat down on a plastic drum, then angled her head to the sky and screamed, not caring who might hear.

The tears had come now, and she felt their warmth dissipate as they slid down her cheeks. As the adrenaline began to fade, she felt the cold encroach.

She heard them coming from across the field before she saw them. Could feel their speed through the trembling ground as their hooves struck the hardness and their dark shapes made a hole in the starry night.

Juno slid to a halt in front of her, and he lowered his head to hers, gently whickering as she stroked his nose. With a sudden leap to the side and a backward kick into the dark, he threatened the others to stay away. It was an impressive display of power, dominance, and protection.

Why couldn't a man treat her this way, be like her horse?

She remained seated, unthreatened by her vulnerability, trusting her connection and bond with Juno. He pushed his nose against her body, nuzzling gently. His breath was warm, and she could feel it blowing through her light clothing. She ran her hands up his face and over his ears.

Ordinarily, he hated his ears being touched and would hold his head out of reach, but tonight he allowed her to caress him, and he nuzzled more intently. If he pushed any harder, she would fall to the ground, and he may trample her.

That would make Toby sorry. That would teach him.

'What's happening, Juno? How have things gotten so bad? Oh, when does this end?'

Sophie stroked his neck, enjoying gaining emotional support from her vulnerable proximity to a half-tonne horse.

She wondered if Toby would come to find her, try to heal her pain. If he did, she would position herself behind Juno and coax the horse into a display of unconditional, animalistic love.

Juno would lower his head, ears flat against his neck and snort like a dragon, staring Toby in the eye. He would then stamp his front hoof before threateningly striding forwards. Toby would sense the horse's sinister intention and retreat behind the gate, acknowledging the power of the bond and loyalty he himself had lost.

This isn't a film, you silly woman, Juno is not Black Beauty, and Toby is too emotionally detached to recognise a horse is showing more feeling towards you than he is.

Whether Juno sensed it or not, he had helped Sophie's mood. Her tears had declined and enough time had passed to know that Toby was not coming to find her.

As Juno walked off to continue eating the cold grass, Sophie slowly made her way back to the house, stepping carefully through the electric fence. She noticed how bright the conservatory with its twinkling lights looked against the darkness of the house. Instinctively, she paused, motionless, watching Toby through the glass as he drank his wine and spoke on his phone.

He was talking quietly; she couldn't hear what was being said and with his back to her she couldn't even attempt to lip read.

But she *could* see his body language and he had his head leaning on one hand, elbow on the table and was slumped right over, he might even have been crying from the way his body was moving, she couldn't be sure.

The phone call ended, and he began typing. It could have been emails, but after all that wine, it was doubtful. It was too long to be a text message. Finally, he put the phone down and his head fell into his hands again.

Sophie was desperate to know what was in his thoughts and having shared her own deepest emotions she felt she now had the right to ask. She slowly crept back into the house, praying the dogs didn't give away her approach.

'Jeez.' Toby visibly jumped in the chair as she suddenly appeared. 'You frightened me.' He clasped his hands to his chest, involuntarily dropping the phone on the table with a clatter.

Sophie ignored his theatrics and placed her hands on her hips. 'What were you doing just now on your phone?' She watched the panic rise through the blush on his face.

He confirmed his guilt by pushing the phone away and flipping it face-down. 'Nothing,' he predictably replied, like a child caught with their fingers in the biscuit tin.

Sophie remained calm on the outside, but inside, she was awash with dread and trepidation. Using as much strength as she could muster from her panicked body, she spoke the four simple words she had used before, but this time, she wasn't accepting porn as the answer.

'Show me your phone.' She didn't say please, but her tone was softer and gentler than the last time. She wanted to avoid a repeat of the previous irrational, frightening scene. She just needed to know what was happening to her husband. 'Just let me see it?' She held out her hand.

'God, not again, Sophie. What's wrong with you? There's nothing to see.' Toby pushed back his chair and abruptly went to stand up. 'Don't start this again. I'm doing emails. It's work.'

'No, you're not. I've been watching you through the glass.' She pointed out to the darkness. 'I've been in the field; I could see everything you were doing. Who were you on the phone to? You were crying.'

'Shit, Sophie, you're turning into a nutcase. Stop hassling me. I'm scheduling meetings, writing notes, filling in my online diary. I wasn't crying, it's work, for goodness' sake.' His voice rose and his face reddened. He slammed his hand on the table and pushed back his chair.

'Please don't do this again,' Sophie pleaded, shocked at his tone. Feeling once again as if she were in battle with her husband. The man she had been trying to help for the last four months.

Her eyes spotted the abandoned evidence and she lunged at the table, making a successful, unexpected grab at his phone. Clutching it against her chest, she ran out through the kitchen and into the enclosed courtyard, but there was nowhere left to run.

Toby rushed through the doorway in pursuit, a total stranger, his eyes wide, like a rabbit caught in the headlights. A contrast to his clenched fists and angry tight lips drawn across his teeth.

'Give. Me. Back. My. Phone.'

'No way. What's on it? I'm going to look.' Sophie held the phone behind her back, her heart racing as his tone confirmed there was indeed evidence to be found.

She wanted to run back into the field and jump onto Juno. She'd gallop off into the dark to explore the phone in isolation. However, the padlocked courtyard gates held her in.

She could smell the neighbour's dinner, surprised at something so familiar amongst the alien scene in front of her and it gave her increased confidence to fight.

Toby grabbed the tops of her arms. He was hurting her now as his hands clenched and tightened their grip. She was scared, but her defiance grew stronger than the fear.

'You're hurting me. Let me go, or I'll scream.' Her adrenaline had taken over, and combined with the cold air, made her tremble. 'I'll scream. Let. GO!' She raised her voice such that the neighbours eating their dinner a few metres away would hear.

*

Toby lessened his grip just a fraction. He didn't doubt for a second that she would scream, and it would be heard all the way to the service station. When Sophie needed to chastise a half tonne horse or call for a hunting Jack Russell, she had plenty of decibels in reserve.

He looked into her scared but challenging eyes and felt defeated. Not by the strength of his wife but by his own weakness. His adrenaline seemed to have involuntarily transplanted into Sophie and he no longer recognised himself, who he had become. A lying, deceitful man chasing his wife outside and now aggressively clutching her arms, hurting her.

He stood back releasing his grasp, and awash with shame, he watched as Sophie ran past him, back into the house through to the boot room, locking herself in the toilet. He followed her path slowly and considered kicking in the door. He pushed hard against it, more for effect than anything but Sophie's words stopped him.

'I'm ringing Cliff. He'll be up here in seconds. I mean it, Toby. Leave me alone, or I'll ring him. I will.'

Sophie's threat forced Toby to retreat. 'Okay, okay. Look at the phone then. It's just my thoughts. It's nothing.' And he slumped to the floor with his back to the door, clutching his knees.

He could hear his sad, pathetic voice, and he almost didn't care anymore. He deserved everything he got. He was giving up. This was killing him.

Yet what Sophie would find now would kill her just a little bit more. It wasn't even the messages she would be reading; he had become competent at their timely deletion.

What she was going to uncover now, he could never take back.

17

Monday, 18th March 2013

Sophie relaxed as her adrenaline declined. She put down the lid and sat on the toilet experiencing déjà vu as she held the enemy's phone, searching for an unknown truth.

After extracting the password through the door from her defeated husband, the phone gave up its secrets. On the screen were Toby's words, his true feelings in black and white which he had been too cowardly to say to her face. Even after everything she had tried to help him with, it came down to this note, written to himself.

```
Notes:
I don't feel loved.
I don't think S feels loved.
I only love her as the boys' mother. I'm
not in love with her.
I've changed. I want something different.
I don't enjoy her company. No spark.
```

No affection. No laughing.

No shared interests.

Feel like I'm getting old before my time.

Would we get together if we met now?

Probably not.

Would we be together now if it weren't for the boys? Doubt it.

Is it right to stay together for the sake of the boys? No.

So, what shall I do?

Option 1. Stay, carry on, work at it. Is the relationship recoverable? Don't know. Doesn't feel like it.

Option 2. S leaves me. She takes the boys.

Option 3. I leave S. I rent a small flat.

Could I cope with 2 or 3?

- I'd only see boys every other wknd.
- We would have to sell the house and ponies.
- The boys and S would have less money.
- I would struggle emotionally without the boys. It would be awful.
- But it happens all the time. People cope, meet new people.
- Boys would integrate into a new family.
- I'd be happy.

```
Could I handle it? Who knows?
Do I love her? No, I don't.
```

Sophie had read it three times, yet she still wasn't crying.

So, he doesn't love her. Doesn't enjoy her company? Christ, he'd even worked out what happens when he leaves her. How could he leave her? She thought they were trying to work it out, whatever *it* was. She was. He clearly bloody wasn't.

She knew Toby had left the other side of the door and she wasn't surprised he couldn't face her.

There was nothing left to say. She had the answers she'd been waiting months for and there was no point in feeling sorry for herself any longer. Numb with disbelief, she cautiously unlocked the toilet door. Before leaving, she lifted the lid and suspended the hurtful phone over the bowl, longing to let it drop, to watch it sink into the water, bubbles indicating its demise.

But regardless of how much she hated that phone, she could not be that malicious. She left it on the floor.

Carrying a heart of lead but with a reinforced rod of iron through her middle, she held her head high and walked through the impressive hallway of the house she thought she'd never buy and may soon no longer own, then turned to go upstairs.

'Sophie, let me explain.'

Toby rushed out from the lounge and gently caught her arm, but Sophie didn't need, nor want further confirmation of his lack of love for her. There could be no justifiable explanation.

'You're in the spare room … obviously.' She emphasised the last word and threw him every ounce of disgust and pain her face could summon before climbing the stairs to say goodnight to the boys, still engrossed in their games, obeying the rules for the adult-only night.

'Night, boys. I'm going to bed. Thank you for being so good. Daddy will be up soon to tuck you in.' She picked up a mountain of sweet wrappers. 'Don't forget to clean your teeth.'

'I'm sleeping with Daddy tonight,' Michael said. 'He promised me. He said you can sleep in my room.'

Sophie winced at his offer, new tears threatening her resolve. On this adult-only evening, to keep applying sticking tape to the marriage, Toby had agreed in advance that Michael could sleep with him tonight.

Sophie knew their Daddy hadn't changed to them. They had never met the old Toby; the one that was the other half of her. They adored him as he was, wanting to grow up to be just like him.

Sophie knew it was going to be her job to keep it that way, so she smiled sweetly. 'Maybe another night, Michael. Daddy will be up soon. You can talk to him then. Night Boys.'

*

Sophie woke alone, her eyes swollen and bloodshot. Her lips were thin and on the verge of trembling as she recalled the emotions from last night. She looked like she had aged ten years, hiding it all behind sunglasses as she took the boys to school, dashing in and out of the playground on autopilot.

It was ten a.m. when she received the first message regarding the night before.

Toby:
I am so sorry you saw my note. I'm shit scared but want more than anything to work it out. I know I've not tried as hard as I need to. I'm just too caught up in fucking Drema, and I'm so confused. I know I spend too much time on my phone and iPad, so we'll sell them, or lock them away, or smash them up if it helps. I want more than anything for our family unit to be strong again, for you and me to be a fun-loving and happy team. I know we can be. I'm going to write down what needs to be done to change. We can talk about it and start to put things right. I want to save our marriage. I do love you.
Please ignore everything I wrote. It was the wine talking. I know I need help.
Help me mend this, please? X

The more Sophie read as she drank her industrial-strength coffee, the more it chipped away at her worries. Her husband was in a bad place, and she couldn't prevent her overpowering want and need to help him. He was in the midst of a mid-life crisis, emotionally confused but ready to right the wrong.

She needed to remain strong. Besides, she had no idea how to deal with the alternative. That was a place she couldn't imagine entering. Toby had acknowledged the elephant in the marriage, and Sophie knew from her self-help books that the only way to eat an elephant is one bite at a time.

He really means it, she thought. He could still love her, and he does want to change and God, she wants him back.

Maybe tonight they could talk productively, in the Room of Pain, minus the wine. Discuss marriage guidance and find a professional counsellor to help.

That could be bite number one, Sophie thought, and the size of her imaginary elephant began to reduce, just a little.

*

It was 5:30 p.m. when Toby phoned. Sophie was at Study Class, sitting in her usual position in the small, dingy room with three other mums. She felt her silent phone vibrate, and quickly moved outside, holding her breath as she answered.

'Hi, sweetheart. Thanks for picking up.' Toby spoke softly. 'Have you seen my texts?'

'Yes, I have. I can't talk now. I'm at Study Class.' She didn't allow him the privilege of hearing her softened nature. She had struggled not to answer his messages and didn't want him to realise just yet, how ready she was to continue helping him.

'Oh yeah, of course you are. Look, I've had an amazing day. I left work at lunchtime and went walking in Holkham.'

'Holkham? Norfolk?'

'It's bloody lovely here, the dogs would love it. We could

bring the caravan; I could take a week off over Easter. What d'you reckon?'

'You hate the caravan. That's why we haven't used it for months.' Sophie wasn't sure who this was talking on the end of the phone, but it surely wasn't Toby. The caravan had always been *her* little pleasure. Reliving family holidays from when she was a child, loving the freedom it offered. She was convinced she must have been a gypsy in an earlier life. The basic living suited her fine, but Toby had never fully embraced it. Probably only agreed to the trips away because the boys loved it so much.

'I don't hate it, not really. Maybe we could do a long weekend? Anyway, I've been walking in the dunes for miles, and d'you know what?' Toby didn't wait for an answer. 'I've seen the light. I truly know what I need and what's important. I sat on the dunes for hours writing you an email. I've just sent it.' He paused, as if expecting Sophie to check her inbox. 'I'm leaving now, and I'm leaving all this crap behind. I'm coming home, and I promise you, things will be different now.'

'Really? Well I'll see you in a couple of hours then.' Sophie hung up and loaded up the email. It was titled, 'Ramblings from Holkham.' His assertions made her cry within thirty seconds.

> My Darling Sophie,
> I'm going to fight for it, I'm not giving up. We had it before, and we can get it back. I've changed, hit a mid-life crisis where I've questioned everything around me

and think I'm unhappy, but it's blatantly obvious! You get out what you put in, and I just haven't put enough in. You are not the issue here; I am for fucks sake!

You've recognised things weren't right, you've been trying hard to resolve it, and I've not done the same. I've just felt sorry for myself, assumed we don't love each other and feared the worst. Our love is still there, absolutely it is, it just needs uncovering again, and I need to play my part in uncovering it, and all will be great again.

So, what is it I need to 'put in'? Well, I thought hard about this. It's a lot really. For a start, I need to listen, share my thoughts and fears, notice you and enjoy your company again. I need to actually be there when I'm home in person not just in body, but talk, interact, look at you, hug you, kiss you. Make plans to go out, walk the dogs. Make 'together' plans not 'Toby' plans. You haven't changed, I have. Do I really want different things? No, I don't. I need to throw myself into what I've got cos I'm the luckiest bloke alive, good job, lovely wife, great boys. And for me to say I don't enjoy your company, well with what I've put in it's hardly surprising you've not exactly been warm to me, and yet I then say I don't like being with you for fucks sake. I'm surprised you didn't throttle me.

I've been absent and in my own world of Drema, Twitter and the iPad. Well maybe I've finally made some sense of all of this, and it's sat squarely with me and has done all along. You get out what you put in;

you reap what you sow. It's about time I put something in, stopped blaming everything else for how I'm feeling and started to sow some seeds and you never know they might just reap some rewards for all of us in happiness, love and getting back to the way things used to be. I just hope I haven't broken things to the point where I can't repair them.

Sophie finished reading the rest of the email then looked up from the screen, her eyes wet. He said it was his epiphany, out on the dunes. He signed it with a single X.

Bite two.

*

Sophie wiped her eyes as she returned to the waiting room. Abigail had just arrived, ushering her children into the study room before taking a seat. They closed the door behind them, smiling at their mother, and Sophie felt a pang of sorrow for all the changes that were happening in their life right now.

Abigail looked glamourous in her flight attendant uniform, no indication of the turmoil she was facing at home and Sophie wondered if her outward demeanour accurately represented the internal.

'Haven't seen you for ages. You look well. How are things?' Sophie enquired.

'Oh, I'm okay. But what about you? Looked a bit tense out there.' She gestured outside with her head.

'I'm fine. Nothing to worry about. Just Toby being an

arse! You've got more on your plate than me. How's the divorce going?'

Abigail shifted her seat to turn her back on the other mothers in the room. She seemed uneasy. 'It's all progressing fine. Matthew's being a twat, but no surprise there.' She twiddled with the golden buttons on her sleeve. 'But you were crying out there. Is something wrong with Toby?

'Oh no, nothing like that. He's just had a bit of a weird day by all accounts.' Sophie glanced at her watch, willing the boys to hurry up, not wanting to sit any longer making small talk.

'Weird? What sort of weird? Abigail checked her phone, as if trying to find the answer there.

'Just the seven-year itch or whatever it's supposed to be these days. He's struggling, midlife crisis, too much work, not enough sex, you know how it is.' Sophie laughed. 'Even wants to go away in the caravan. He hates that caravan!'

Abigail scraped her chair back into its original position and awkwardly laughed. 'When will you go away then? Soon?'

'Oh, who knows, probably never. It's all just words with Toby. Men, eh? Can't live with them, et cetera!' Sophie dismissively sighed as the boys came out of the study room.

*

It was three weeks before Toby's epiphany was challenged by one simple text message. He knew this test would come, so had been mentally practising how to react to it, how to successfully pass and build on the positivity of his last few weeks of repairing his marriage.

He had been working hard on all of his declarations from his 'Ramblings from Holkham' email but was struggling with the intimacy, the physical closeness to someone who wasn't Abigail, and as he reflected on those lost, lustful moments, he pushed his chair away from his laptop and stared at the lit screen, displaying the new notification.

He failed the test the moment he tapped the message icon.

James B:
I missed you at swimming practice last night. I'm sorry, but I can't stay quiet any longer about what happened between us. I don't believe you are doing the right thing. I know I always said I would never force you to decide, but I can't believe you think this is right. We have something amazing. You will never have that with Sophie. I bet the last few weeks haven't made much difference, have they? I bet you've missed me. I know what you wrote when you were at Holkham, Sophie told me. But you will never get back what you had with her. I'm not going to let you go. I will fight for you. I'm not letting her keep you. Sorry. xxx

The spreadsheet Toby was working on turned blurry. He looked up from his phone, forcing himself to calm his mind and take control of his racing pulse. He gazed out the office window, taking deep, long breaths, watching a chicken bathe in the loose dust under the old willow tree, flapping and rolling around without a care in the world. He envied her simple life.

He knew he should just press delete, but he re-read Abigail's message and saw so many truths in her words that his wavering finger recoiled from the delete button.

Beginning to calm, he realised that perhaps he shouldn't consider it a weakness that was allowing his feelings for Abigail to flourish. Maybe it was a strength. A strength to allow him to be in love with two amazing women he recognised he needed in equal amounts.

Maybe he was strong enough; he might not need to choose. He could have them both.

He knew he could convince Abigail to agree to this proposal. She would be patient; she wouldn't mind sharing if it were for the sake of his boys. She knew how much they meant to him.

Sophie would be harder to deceive. She seemed determined to stick it out to the end and had become far too proficient in her detective work for his liking, but she represented everything he wanted to protect. The boys, the family unit, his identity as a good father.

He would simply have to be careful. Loving, but careful. Fulfilled.

He knew he had to be more present and properly

involved in both women's worlds if this new strategy was going to be successful, and it would start tonight with Sophie. But first, he had to message Abigail.

> Toby:
>
> I know I should have deleted your message, but you know me too well. It's true it's been hard these last few weeks, but I'm not giving up my family. I don't think I can give you up either, so if you are willing and patient, I want to see where things go? We can let time decide what happens in the future and I'm making no promises. You know I love you too, but you also know I love my family. We need to be patient and very careful, so Sophie never finds out. You have to promise me that? What d'you think? X

He smiled to himself as he pressed send. Then he changed his recently divulged password, powered off his phone and with a broad smile, closed his laptop and went to find Sophie.

He knew Abigail would say yes.

18

Sunday, 19th May 2013

Sophie felt they'd made good progress in the resolution of Toby's mid-life crisis following his epiphany two months ago. There were still days when she was submerged into the dark depths of his thoughts, at the bottom of a long list of greater priorities, but the last month had brought many more days of positive optimism.

He would often be in an upbeat mood making spontaneous suggestions for family outings and adult-only nights and had been leaving his phone on the side so that he was more present.

Boosted by his progress, Sophie had contributed to their recovery by applying a work ethic, to which Toby had responded well. She created flow chart exercises for them to work through, followed up with logical action plans and numbered, prioritised steps to resolve any obstacles or barriers.

She encouraged open and honest conversations about

feelings, their past, and their future. Everything was driven by the understanding they would achieve an end goal of a healthier, happier marriage.

Intimacy was still on the flow charts as 'work in progress', but their communication had never been better. Sophie felt they were at last, turning a corner in the marriage. She was working hard to get what she wanted: her old Toby back, and it seemed to be working.

This morning, she had taken the boys to the local boot sale to absorb their time whilst Toby was running a half marathon.

It was gone one p.m. when they returned home, laden with bargains from the biggest fair of the season. The boys were exhausted after walking for miles in the hot sunshine and bouncing for hours on the inflatable castle, so Sophie allowed them the freedom to play on the Wii.

The sunshine was streaming into the conservatory, transforming it into a furnace, so Sophie opened the sliding doors as wide as they could go, letting the fresh air race through the house. The gas barbecue, unused since last year, called out to her from behind the wall of the barn. With a broad smile she dragged it onto the path, deciding that tonight they would have the first barbecue of the year. She checked it was clean, but her inspection was unnecessary. Toby took great pride in his manly gas cooker and she knew it.

Her stomach rumbled as she thought of food, so she went to the kitchen and took some sausages out of the freezer. Then with a little giggle at the indulgence, she placed two bottles of prosecco in the fridge. Noticing the overloaded egg rack (thanks to the chickens being back in full lay), she removed six eggs, deciding to surprise Toby with his favourite pavlova dessert.

This evening was shaping up to be a perfect way to start the week, especially now the conservatory had almost renounced its 'Room of Pain' title. When it cooled down later tonight, they would step inside, close the huge sliding doors, and enjoy the sun setting across their fields whilst sipping an effervescent glass of wine, all under the glow of the twinkling fairy lights.

Toby's car was in the drive, so Sophie knew he was home from his run. As she carried her bargains upstairs, she guessed he hadn't been back long as she could hear the shower running and see him moving behind the frosted glass door.

She unloaded her bags onto the bedroom floor and threw some clothes into the wash basket, smiling contently as she arranged her new books on the shelf. She wondered if he'd be hungry. She was starving and was about to go downstairs to get a late lunch for them all when she heard the quiet vibration of Toby's phone, sitting unnoticed on the bed.

With the shower still running and with no other thoughts in her head, she casually picked it up. The message showed in full view on the locked screen. It showed itself as being from someone called James B.

James B:
Sweetheart, I'm so proud of you. That was a great time. I couldn't think of a better way to celebrate than that last

hour with you. Shame your car wasn't
bigger! LOL. I love you so much. I'm so
glad we have made this work. xxx

Sophie's heart was pounding out of her chest in tiny pieces, like a hundred little hearts all beating at different rates, fighting to escape. How she was still breathing, she didn't know. She read the message several times, sinking to the bed as her knees collapsed, her eyes fixated on the screen, trying to process the words.

She wanted to scream, but she had no sound. Her brain was pounding silently, like a thousand horses galloping in time to the pumping of Toby's shower. She could feel superhuman strength emerging, both physical and emotional, and when she stood her entire world blurred with a darkness she associated with the end of everything. She was quaking, and she could no longer speak, not even to herself.

But then, just as dramatically, the realisation hit her. *This* was what had been driving her recent pain, her true answer. It wasn't a midlife crisis. It hadn't been porn nor her lack of technique in that hotel room. Even Holkham, his epiphany: they had all been lies. Rationally, she began to calm and sat on the bed composing herself, regaining her self-control to give an illusion of calm just as Toby entered the room.

She recognised his relaxed, happy smile, jubilant from his run and momentarily felt sorry for him. For what she was about to disclose.

Toby's smile rapidly transformed as he fixated on his phone in her hands. He shrunk in front of her. As his eyes moved up, registering the look on her face, his smile and euphoria fell through the creaking floorboards along with the drips from his legs.

'Toby.' She spoke calmly, looking up at her husband through steely, dry eyes. 'Who's James?'

'James? … erm … oh, you mean from the club, James?'

'Oh, from the club? Really … then I suggest you think carefully before answering this next question with yet more lies.' She maintained eye contact, unabashed by her dramatics. 'Are you having an affair?'

There was no delay in his response. 'What? Don't be ridiculous.' Then came the expected challenge. 'Why are you asking? What are you doing with my phone?'

If Sophie hadn't been using every ounce of her energy to control her emotions, she would have noticed a slight tremble in Toby's words. 'Really? That's your answer?' She allowed the disbelief to show in her voice. 'I'll ask you again, one more time. Are you having an affair?'

'You're not making any sense. Of course not.' But there was no conviction to his words, and the blush to his cheeks rose higher with the lie.

'Oh, God, you're still lying to me. I can't believe it.' Sophie held the phone out in front of her and read out loud the notification still showing on the locked screen. 'Explain, you lying bastard.' She sat back against the headboard, waiting.

'Sophie, give me my phone. It's nothing. It—'

'Don't you *dare* say nothing.' She slammed the phone into the bed. '*This* is my explanation for everything. All the second-guessing I've been doing, wondering if I'm going mad. All the effort I've put in, trying to be sexier for fuck's sake and all the time you've been seeing someone else? I never stood a chance, did I? Now you owe me. Explain.' Her self-control had vanished, and the look on her face could have killed as she squared up to him.

'Okay. Oh, blimey. It wasn't meant to happen like this.' His face crumbled. 'I'm so sorry, I can explain. It's true. I've met someone. Oh. What have I done?' he collapsed onto the bed seeking sympathy with his head in his hands and his face carrying the guilt like a man at the gallows. Sophie had never seen him look so pathetic and broken, and it bolstered her strength.

'Who is it?'

He didn't answer immediately. Sophie wondered if he would even tell her the truth.

'It's a woman from Study Class. I met her a while ago. She's—'

Sophie gasped; her hand clasped to her mouth. 'It's Abigail, isn't it?' Reading the surprised look on Toby's face as confirmation, she continued. 'I know her. And her kids. I know her husband had an affair, and they're getting divorced and selling their house. I know all about her. Jesus, I even know she's found someone else.' Sophie's breathing was running away with her. 'I've even felt sorry for her these last few months. I've let her bloody cry on my shoulder. Christ, what a bitch!'

Sophie thought back and realised Abigail hadn't been at Study Class recently. Abigail hadn't been squeezed in the dingy waiting room with her because she was squeezing in somewhere else with Toby.

'So, how long?'

'It's only been a couple of months. I don't know. We just sort of hit it off when we met last year. It's really only been text messages and the odd run.' Toby was speaking quietly into his lap, head bowed, still wrapped in just a towel. He looked up and made eye contact. 'She's been through a lot.'

'*She's* been through a lot?' Sophie veered toward him, throwing a threatening stare straight into his eyes. He didn't look away. He was taking his punishment, not disputing it, but he didn't utter those pleading words of forgiveness Sophie was waiting for. 'What the hell Toby? I don't give a rat's arse about *her*!'

Putting his head in his hands, Toby said, 'I'm sorry. How has this happened to me?'

'Happened to *you*?' Sophie spun away, then paced up close again. 'What are you now, the fucking victim in all this?'

Toby didn't answer. The room fell silent as Sophie stormed downstairs without a backward glance. She was surprised she didn't feel like punching his lights out. She was feeling a perverse sense of relief.

Finally, she had the truth and that felt like a success. As she walked through the kitchen, she placed the six eggs back on the rack, one by one, scrapping all thoughts of the barbeque and formulated her next steps. To anyone watching, she was exhibiting the scary calmness that preambles the loud, dramatic music of a horror movie climax.

Her brain, however, was working overtime. She didn't want to talk to Toby, she wanted to be as far away from him as possible. He had lied to her so many times, so consistently, for so long, she would never believe anything he said, ever again.

But Abigail might tell the truth. She knows what it feels like to be cheated on.

Fucking bitch. She owes me.

*

'Wait! Where are you going?' Toby had been watching from the hallway, still just wearing his towel, waiting for her next move. He'd been preparing himself for the fallout and being kicked out of the house, but now Sophie was grabbing her car keys, and that gave him a far greater sense of unease.

She didn't answer. She didn't even look at him as she strode purposefully out the side door to her car. He made a half-hearted attempt to follow her, repeating his question, but she ignored him, shooting out the drive, spinning her wheels as she went.

Toby went back inside with one priority dominating his mind. He had to protect, to forewarn, to prepare. He had no idea how well his wife knew Abigail, and that worried him. He speedily sent a message to 'James'.

> Toby:
> Sophie's seen your message. I've told her. She knows. She's just left the house,

> and I don't know where she's going.
> Does she know where you live? I'm so
> sorry.

*

Sophie's knuckles turned white, gripping the steering wheel as she sped up the motorway. She slammed on the brakes as she approached the services, realising she had no idea where she was actually going. She knew Abigail's house had recently been put up for sale, so she loaded the Right Move website on her phone and began her search.

There were four properties for sale, in a village five miles away she was sure Abigail had mentioned. It housed the secondary school her children attended, so it was a logical place to start. The details of the third property gave Sophie the conviction she'd found it. The photos showed children's bedrooms, and the image of the garden contained the family dog which was most certainly Abigail's black spaniel.

Sophie couldn't see much of the house as she approached from the village centre. It was set on a shared driveway, running downhill, away from the road. The house marked for sale was at the end of the row of three, sunk into the dip below.

She turned onto the gravel drive and parked outside the front door. There were two cars in the open-fronted garage, and Sophie racked her brain to remember the car Abigail drove to Study Class. She was convinced it was that big, black Jeep.

Feeling unexpectedly confident but unsure of her plan,

Sophie stepped out of the car and approached the front door. It wasn't welcoming. Just solid, dark wood, flat panelled with dull, brass furniture. No glass to peer through, no decorative surround, no architectural features at all.

So different from the charm and character of Nettlefield House. For a moment, she forgot why she was there. She'd been so focused on finding a house for sale that she could almost imagine she was there to buy. She would never buy *this* house. The thought calmed her.

The door opened just seconds after the bell sounded. A man stood in the doorway, seemingly unsurprised to see a stranger at his door on a Sunday afternoon.

Sophie had never met Matthew, but she did know he was still sharing the family home, so she stood tall, assured it was the right house.

'Can I help you?' he said.

They were total strangers, but it was obvious he had been expecting her.

'Is Abigail in, please?' She spoke brightly, giving away nothing.

'No, she's out.'

Sophie didn't believe him. He didn't open the door wide enough for her to see past, and she didn't like his controlled, rehearsed manner. Trying to get a foot forward, she said, 'You must be Matthew? Perhaps you could tell Abigail I called. It's Sophie. She knows what it's about. What time will she be back?' Sophie hoped her clarity of voice and absolute authority would show she would not be brushed aside.

Of course, she realised. Toby would have messaged

Abigail to tell her what had happened.

Sophie hoped she was trembling inside the house, trying to glimpse unnoticed through the curtains, questioning what a betrayed, irrational wife would do to the adulterous mistress of her husband.

Hang on a minute. Sophie's thoughts continued as she glanced up at the windows above the front door. *Of course she knows. She's been that woman. Jesus, what a bitch!*

'She won't be back till later.' Matthew replied evasively.

'That's fine. I'll come back. What time?' She was not letting this drop.

Matthew's eyes flicked behind him, his fingers drumming the door frame. 'I'm not sure. Maybe seven?'

'Great. Sorry you've been dragged into this.' Sophie raised one eyebrow. 'Perhaps you could message her … or if you see her … let her know I'll be here at seven. Goodbye.'

Sophie turned back to the car, remaining calm and in control, unhindered by this game of charades.

It was only when she got back to the main road, out of sight of the house, that she let her guard down. The delayed adrenaline filled her body, making her palms sweat and her heart race.

'Bugger,' she said. 'Bugger, bugger, bugger.' She hit the steering wheel with both hands, oblivious to the speed she was travelling. Now she'd have to do it all again.

With her adrenaline driving the car on autopilot, she approached home, prepared for the inevitable confrontation with her husband, or at least with the man who used to fill that role. She didn't quite know what Toby was to her anymore.

The large Victorian house with the flowering rose, climbing over the ornate door and the five-bar gate leading to the cobbled courtyard, loomed in front of her.

She stepped through the door and into the kitchen, holding her head high, expecting at any moment to come face to face with her remorseful husband.

Her eyes were blinking quickly, adjusting to the light, fighting off the nerves as she continued to search the house for signs of her family. She may have felt a lack of achievement from failing to meet with Abigail, but she wanted to portray a strong mental state for facing Toby. She was not going to let him evade her as Abigail had done.

Instinctively, given the silence of the house, she walked into the garden, clenching and unclenching her fists to release the tension in her body. She saw Toby sitting on the Olympic size trampoline, his long legs nearly touching the ground. From a distance, he looked like a man in despair, his head hung in shame, blankly staring at his palms facing up, questions running through his muddled mind.

But he wasn't. His phone was in his hands, and he had a deep furrow across his brow, his lips tightly drawn, and as she strode towards him, his head flew up, his eyes narrowed and he jumped to the ground.

'Where have you been?' He bellowed.

Sophie stopped short, shocked she wasn't the first to shout. She was convinced the woman-scorned mentality would take over her body and voice to carry her through this unwanted conversation, but now he had spoken first and it had thrown her.

His words hadn't carried overtones of sorrow, nor any of the apologetic, pleading nuances she'd expected. She didn't understand how he felt he had the right to use that tone of voice, but she knew she had every right to use the tone she was now going to adopt for this conversation.

'You know where I've been, don't you?' Sophie squared up to him, shoulders back and head high.

'Yes, I do. But how could you? How could you go to her *house*?' He stood directly in front of her, glaring.

Sophie stepped back, momentarily lost for words. He was saying all the wrong things in all the wrong ways. There were no visible tears in his eyes, no sheepish glances or weak apologies.

He continued with his inappropriate onslaught. 'You should talk to me, not her. Leave her out of it. For God's sake. You're not going back you know. Her kids were in the house. What were you thinking?'

Sophie's internal sledgehammer began smashing her heart as her strength returned. 'What about our fucking kids?' She took a step forward, eyes wide, flinging her hands out to the side. 'How the hell can I talk to you? You're a lying bastard of epic proportions. I'm never gonna believe a word you say ever again.'

Sophie was on a roll now, and although tears were forming in her eyes, she was oblivious to the path they took down her cheeks.

'How can you stand there protecting *her* Toby? Protecting *her* kids? What about *our* boys, in there?' She gestured over her shoulder to the big, red brick Victorian house with its grand new conservatory.

Wiping the tears from her cheeks, she continued. 'Why would you be calling her, whilst your wife and mother of your children has just had her heart cut open, bleeding in pain and confusion? Where was *my* phone call? Why weren't you looking out for *me*?'

Sophie's anger was multiheaded, it wasn't now just for the affair. He had thwarted her plan to catch his mistress off-guard, and he was now showing a total lack of concern for her mental state. But most excruciating of all was the anger she now felt at his concern for the boys. His lack of regard for their own children and the backlash they were soon to face shook Sophie's world to a whole new level. A fierce maternal power to protect her children from the actions of someone they should never have needed safeguarding from propelled her forward.

'I *will* go and see her. You can't stop me. I'm going to find out the truth and *she* is going to tell me. If I turn up at her door unexpected and just happen to introduce myself to her children, I will … that would be a shame, wouldn't it?'

Sophie mimicked the imaginary conversation in a jovial, high-pitched voice: 'Hi, guys. William and Michael's mum here. Can I come in? Just need to speak to your mum. She's been sleeping with my husband over the last few months, so I need to slap her face.' Sophie reverted to her own voice, and with as much authority as possible, demanded. 'Tell her she *will* meet me later. Seven p.m.' She turned away, shouting as she went, 'And *you* should stay well away from me.'

Sophie wasn't surprised he didn't follow her back to the house. She suspected it was because he was deep in conversation with Abigail, not because he felt too much guilt and regret to face his family.

Going into autopilot, sensing the massive elephant in their marriage leave of its own accord, she began sorting out the boys' uncompleted homework.

19

Sunday, 19th May 2013

Sophie stood outside the plain wooden door. It was her allotted time to confront the person who had shared such a large part of her life without permission.

Those elusive words, 'It didn't mean anything, it's you I want,' still hadn't come, and now Sophie knew, never would. There was no emotion. Even her adrenaline had left. She had to force herself to stand tall, shoulders back, to combat her feelings of defeat. She was losing a fight she hadn't known she was having, and she felt stupid for her naivety.

The door opened, and Abigail stood silently to one side to let Sophie in. Inside was a large, open plan lounge, with views of the massive lawned garden, framed by long, double-height windows.

Sophie could see Abigail's children playing football. She recognised them from Study Class and could hear them laughing from here. No one should be laughing. The situation of both families was cruel and life-changing, yet no one seemed to be respecting that. Even the black spaniel was softly padding around, offering his friendship by wagging his tail, dispersing the tension that should have been in the room.

Abigail led the way upstairs to another large, open plan seating area, with even longer windows opening to the garden and the uninterrupted countryside beyond. Off this space were bedrooms, with open doors giving a glimpse of what lay behind. A large wood-burning stove dominated the room, giving off a smoky aroma even though it wasn't lit.

Sophie sat on a deep, black leather sofa and petted the dog as he joined their conversation. Abigail sat sideways, turning her body to face her, seemingly devoid of any apprehension of what was to come.

It felt like at any moment Abigail might offer her a glass of wine, and like two old friends they would sit and gossip and laugh. She had no idea how to start this conversation with yet another person who was showing no fear or remorse, nor any ability to diminish her engulfing pain.

Sophie shifted awkwardly in her seat as the spaniel dumped a wet, slobbery toy on her lap, letting it fall unceremoniously to the floor. She looked down as the dog laid his head on her lap, gazing up at her with his kind, black eyes and she smiled in reply, instinctively ruffling his ears. Then remembering who he belonged to, she pushed him away and readjusted her face. 'So. What the hell have you been doing with my husband?'

'I'm sorry,' Abigail began. 'It wasn't planned. It just happened. I've never met anyone like him, not even Matthew,' she confessed, lowering her voice.

Sophie could feel the conviction in her words and shrunk into the sofa. 'How long?' she managed, unable to think of what else to say.

'Long enough to know we can't stop it. I'm sorry. I know it's not what you want to hear.'

Sophie wanted specifics. She wanted to know everything, no matter how awful. Was Abigail the reason for Porngate? Had Toby even run those marathons, or had he been doing a different type of training? How many times had they slept together, in her house, in her bed? She wanted greater justification to hate them both more.

The only emotion she could now control was her hate, and the more reasons Abigail gave her, the more in control Sophie felt. Abigail continued answering in the same painful manner but remained emphatic that the relationship hadn't been physical. Sophie didn't believe her.

'Seriously? You expect me to accept you haven't had sex? How can it be serious then?' Sophie challenged, hopeful that Abigail was disillusioned in her interpretation of Toby's affections. 'He must have shown you strong feelings *somehow*, convinced you, to make you feel so certain he's as into you as you think he is?'

'Yes. I believe he feels the same.'

Sophie could see her trying to control a smile as she said this. Abigail was obviously being honest. She believed Toby was already hers.

'I really am sorry,' she continued.

'Sorry you got caught you mean?'

This word irritated Sophie. Her parents had taught her

that 'Sorry', was a word you use when you mean you wouldn't do it again. It was the wrong use of the word in this situation. She wasn't sorry at all, and Sophie's silence meant Abigail carried on talking.

'Look, I've told Toby I'm not going to influence his decision. He has to decide for himself, and I'm not pressurizing him. I won't break up your marriage. That's down to him.'

'Wow, that's big of you, Abigail. Cheers,' Sophie raised her hand as if it contained a glass of wine. 'Thanks for your kind consideration of my marriage. Very respectful.'

'I know this is all so painful. That's why I agreed to see you, but truly, it's nothing to do with me. You need to speak to Toby. He told me things haven't been great for ages. You both need to talk.'

'Thanks for the marriage guidance. If it's all the same, I'm not going to take advice from you. Your husband left you, so you stole someone else's. Hardly a balanced emotional approach, was it?' Sophie spoke quickly, pushing back her growing anger. There would be no point in losing it with Abigail. 'I've tried talking to him. We've talked heaps over the last few months, but hey, he's a lying, deceitful bastard, so I'm hardly going to believe a word he's said. I'd suggest you do the same.' She waved her hand dismissively and smirked. 'Thanks for what I believe is your honesty. You're a deceitful, shameful bitch, but at least I got the truth from you. I think we're done here. What's the point in talking anymore, the horse has already flipping bolted!'

Sophie stood up, roughly pushing the soppy spaniel as she made her way across the room. She no longer felt bad shoving him away, this was the enemy's dog, so he deserved no affection.

Abigail followed, and the two women made their way down the stairs. They walked to the front door with the stupidly optimistic dog pushing past them both. Abigail held the door open, revealing a large, white leather watch dominating her wrist. Sophie recognised it immediately.

'Nice watch!' Sophie glared into Abigail's eyes. 'Looks even worse on than it did in the box. You're welcome to it. Hope it stops.' She stepped outside, her humour concealing her hurt.

It was as simple as that. The lie had been outed, the discussion had been had, and the door was closed. This was emotional control at its best, and as much as Sophie would have loved to have screamed, shouted, and slapped, she knew this was going to be just the start of the abuse of her strength. This fight would be won on control, not emotion, and that thought empowered her. But right now, she felt like a loser, ganged up on and unloved.

She climbed into her car, reversed out of the drive, and drove home on autopilot looking through eyes that didn't see. Straight lines, bends, gear changes, and braking, all controlled by a part of Sophie's mind not consumed by the unanswerable question: what now?

This whole situation was scary, but Abigail's reaction to being found out was by far the scariest. She hadn't mutated into a nasty human being since she'd become a mistress. She was still softly spoken and kind, with honest emotions totally committed and loyal to her misplaced relationship.

Was she really what Toby wanted? Was she really worth giving up your family for?

Sophie had no idea what to do next. She was worried about the boys and wanted to rush home, but simultaneously, she wanted to run away, miles from anyone, to escape the next few months of her life. She didn't want to face up to the man that was no longer the other half of her, and she felt a massive gaping hole that this left.

She wanted someone to tell her what to do, to give her a plan, a step-by-step list of instructions with the certainty of success at the end. But she didn't even know what success was anymore. She wanted to delay the start of this new life and wondered if Toby would already be planning his.

Abigail would have messaged him by now, letting him know Sophie had left. Torn between wanting to see the boys and not wanting to see Toby, Sophie pulled over at the village pub.

She sat in a dark corner, caressing her pinot grigio, hoping her delayed return would worry him, ignoring the questioning looks from the bar staff. She guessed she looked as bad as she felt.

*

It was gone ten p.m. when Sophie let herself in through the side door of Nettlefield House. She knew she would have been over the limit after two glasses of wine, but it was helping to numb the pain. She poured herself another medicinal glass as soon as she walked in.

'Sophie!' Toby's head jolted upright as she entered the

lounge, but his slumped body didn't follow. 'You've been ages. Where've you been?' He was cradling a large glass of wine in his hands.

Sophie suspected it wasn't his first. He too had the decency to look a dishevelled mess.

There was a long pause before she answered. She wasn't sure she wanted to talk. She had no fight left and no idea what sort of tactics she should be using to win.

They remained like statues, held in each other's gaze, searching each other's tear-stained eyes for answers. Each wondering what winning would look like.

'It doesn't matter where,' Sophie finally answered with a drawn-out sigh. 'I spoke to her, Toby. I spoke to your paramour.' Sophie's words increased in pitch as her bottom lip involuntarily quivered.

Sophie knew she was still looking for the bunch of red roses, a sorry note, and a heartfelt apology for his mistake. Still hoping there would be begging for forgiveness from a man full of determination and conviction to right a wrong.

Instead, there was just Toby looking sad, drinking wine, his top lip, stained red.

'What did she say?'

'You know what. She's probably already told you everything. I didn't smash her face in, you'll be pleased to know. We just spoke. You probably got your stories sorted anyway, but she certainly seems sure of your relationship.'

'What d'you mean, sure?' Toby leant forward, showing the first bit of movement since she had walked into the room. 'What did she say?'

'She said she'd never met a man like you before. Never felt this way about anyone, not even Matthew.'

If Sophie had a tape measure, she could have recorded the subsequent expansion to the size of Toby's chest. He was like a pufferfish blowing out his body, his head now sitting several inches higher on his thickened neck. He even splashed his wine a little.

'Really? She said that?' The sparkle in his eyes gave away the skips in his heart, and with every accentuated beat, a serrated knife turned in Sophie's.

'Christ. Don't look so happy,' Sophie snapped. 'So, is that how you feel too? She seems to think so. Thinks it's all a done deal, and you're hers now. Is that right, you little shit?'

Sophie's bitter anger had taken hold now. Any thoughts of the red roses, the apologies, were dispelled by his reaction to his mistress's declaration of love.

'I have strong feelings for her, yes. I've tried to stop them. You must believe me. Please don't look at me like that, I'm so ashamed. I know I have to stop it. I want to stop it. I can't lose you, Sophie. I've been such an idiot. Please don't hate me.'

Sophie took a large swig of her wine, emptying her glass.

Toby continued. 'I've been on a slippery slope, and I've tried to get off, I really have. Remember that night before I went to Holkham? I was mortified when you'd read my note. I felt so strong and convinced then that I wanted to save our marriage. I ended it with her that day. Oh, God, Sophie.' He ran his fingers through the hair he had left and looked at his wife with tears in his eyes. 'I know there was nothing wrong in our marriage that couldn't be fixed. I've been tainted by my conversations with her, condemning her marriage, foolishly believing ours was the same. It isn't though. I know it isn't. She convinced me it was.' He wiped away a tear. 'Seeing you now, your face, feeling this pain ... I can't lose you. I love you, Sophie. I have to finish it with her. I will, right now, tonight.' He moved towards Sophie, holding out his hands, widening his arms as if to embrace.

Sophie recoiled. 'How the hell are you going to do that, given you have 'strong' feelings for her?' Sophie emphasized the words with air quotes. 'I've had enough. I'm going to bed. I can't listen to your crap anymore.'

'I'm sorry,' Toby uttered pathetically as she left the room.

And there it is again, Sophie thought. *That bloody useless word. Sorry.*

*

Toby sat alone, in despair, drinking his wine. The house was silent, but his mind wouldn't stop the chatter, replaying so many scenes, conversations, and deceptions. His heart felt dead. It had loved too much, and he hated it. He knew there was only one action that could put things right. There was just one choice, and for the first time in months, he truly felt that it was the right one.

Earlier, as he'd put the boys to bed, he'd had to explain their mother's absence. He had struggled to hold back the truth and the tears as he gazed at their innocent faces, believing all his lies. He had painful visions of all the lies to come if this deceit continued. He could never tell them the truth; they were too young to understand, and he would be too weak to explain. If Sophie ever told them, he would just die. He had to choose the boys over his affair, and he had to do it now, before it was too late. He was choosing the boys.

He wasn't strong enough to tell Abigail face to face, or even over the phone. She had always said she would accept his choice, so now he was going to find out how true to her word she was.

He drained the last of his wine and picked up his phone.

> Toby:
> I'm so sorry. I can't believe Sophie found out. I'm such an idiot. I've let everyone down. I should never have let it get this far. I'm sorry. It's over. It has to be. I can't speak to you again. I'm deleting you from my phone. Please don't call me anymore. It's my only option. I'm so scared but I have to choose the boys. I know you'll understand. Goodbye.

He drained the last of his wine and stared at his phone, watching for the sign she had read it. He could visualise her now, sobbing gently, hugging the dog for comfort, until slowly she would dry her eyes, sweeping her long hair off her face, accepting that the pull of his family, of the boys, was too powerful a force after all.

His heart skipped as her reply appeared, reminding him it was going to take a lot longer to rationalise his own feelings in this situation.

James B:
I know the boys have to be your priority, but please don't forget me. If things don't work out, I'll always be here, I promise. I won't call you again. You're kidding yourself if you think you can get your marriage back. But I'll wait for you. I'll always love you. xxx

Toby purposefully took a deep breath as his finger hovered over his phone, intensifying the feelings and power of his conviction and certainty. He closed his eyes, struggling to reinstate the face he knew he still loved, eradicating the one that had caused so much pain. He opened his eyes and his finger purposefully pressed the 'delete contact' symbol.

James B disappeared.

Toby then messaged his wife, asleep in her bedroom and for the first time in a long time, pressed send without guilt or self-loathing.

Toby:
You've known for a while that something was up. I developed feelings I shouldn't have, and I'll always regret that. What I wrote that day in

Holkham, I meant, but I allowed other things to influence me, which meant I was crap at making the changes. I can't forgive myself for that, but I need you to. That external influence has now gone. I've deleted her from my phone, and I will do what I should have done months ago and focus on what's right. I want so much to put things back together. You have to let me try. X

20

Monday, 20th May 2013

Sophie woke feeling as if her world had stopped, but a glance at the clock showed it was still moving. She staggered out of bed to bravely face the first day of her new life, thankful that Toby had left early for work.

She hastened the boys to school, carefully concealing her distress, then quickly tended to the animals. By 9:45 a.m., she was sitting in the doctor's surgery, waiting for the appointment she'd booked the moment the surgery online system went live.

So far, she had maintained her outward composure, protected by the routine of a Monday morning, but inside she felt as close to the edge of her reality as ever. As it was, it was the simple words, 'How can I help?' that pushed her over.

Sophie allowed herself to tumble down in a spasm of tears and discharged emotions until she found herself at the bottom with an unexpected smile on her face. She looked up into the eyes of the young Indian doctor and saw this comical scene for what it was. A trained medical professional, too young to have any real experience of marriage or children, being asked to mend a broken heart by a distraught, middle-aged female, collapsed in a puddle of tears, with a smile on her face.

He must think I'm an idiot, Sophie thought as she came to her senses. She explained that she knew there was nothing medically he could do to change her situation, but maybe there was something he could prescribe to ensure nights like the last would not be as infinite as they felt.

He wrote her a prescription for non-addictive sleeping pills, handed her some leaflets and some information about marriage guidance counselling and asked her to come back to see him in four weeks.

Sophie left the room, realizing that her genuine smile represented relief that everything could now get better. Releasing her emotions and sharing her problems so openly with a stranger, gave her new optimism for her future. She reminded herself that she finally knew what the problem in their marriage had been, and now it had gone, she simply needed a plan to fix what was left.

She just had to decide what, and if, she wanted to fix.

*

Sophie had just sat down with a single piece of toast she wasn't sure she could eat and was googling, 'how to recover from an affair,' when the house phone rang. She considered ignoring it as she was mid-way through an article entitled: 'Affairs: the best thing that can happen to a marriage?' Apparently, if the numerous case studies were to be believed, an affair can create such massive demands for communication and the sharing of emotions, that the relationship can actually become stronger as a result. You *can* forgive and fall back in love again and Sophie was keenly digesting the methods how.

Nevertheless, she picked up the phone.

'Sophie, it's me, Dot. I'm so sorry. I can't believe he's done this. I hope you're okay?' She didn't pause for an answer. 'He's been on the phone all morning, and we've told him straight. He should never have done this to you and the boys. Oh, the poor boys,' she wailed, not covering the phone as she sobbed.

Sophie swallowed her own silent tears and soothed her mother-in-law with awkward words of reassurance that she would forgive her son, he would stop the affair, and the boys would be okay. The certainty her voice commanded, comforted them both and Sophie believed now, more than ever, that this would be a recoverable situation.

As they said their goodbyes and Sophie returned to Google, she was hit with the realisation she would now have to tell her own parents. All four of them were supposed to be staying in Sussex for a few days this half term so she would have to tell them something, she was certain Toby wouldn't be coming with them now.

Sophie's parents had been happily married for over fifty years and expected the same long-term commitment from all of their daughter's marriages. The thought of having to tell them she had failed at the one thing that should have lasted forever, filled her with dread.

They would probably think she was joking or would make assumptions it had been her fault Toby had strayed. As she picked up the phone and dialled the number, she wiped her sweaty palms down her jeans.

'Mum, Dad, can you both hear me? I don't want to have to repeat this. Are you sitting down?'

'Yes, yes, we're both here. Hang on. I'll put you on speakerphone … Right, okay, what is it?' her mother asked without any idea of the potential bomb her daughter was about to drop.

Sophie could imagine her now, busily tidying up the kitchen, emptying the dishwasher whilst shouting back into the speakerphone. Her father would be sitting at the breakfast bar, reading a paper, frequently looking out the window, itching to start the days mowing on his prized sit-on lawnmower.

'It's Toby. He's had an affair.'

The background noise of clanking crockery continued for a few moments, until its cessation and ensuing silence signalled her mother's delayed reaction.

'What d'you mean? Are you sure? Toby wouldn't do that,' her mother defended her favourite son-in-law.

'Really?' her dad spoke with uncertainty and doubt. 'Don't be silly. Are you sure you're not imagining things?'

But as Sophie retold the story of the last few months leading up to her apocalyptic day, both parents accepted the reality of it. Sophie's dad was less angry and disappointed than Sophie thought he should be. Surely, he should defend his second daughter with primal aggression and protectiveness from this man he had walked her down the aisle to.

But he simply said, 'I saw it all the time at work. Men reach a certain age, have a bit of a midlife crisis, leave their wives, then come back with their tail between their legs, begging to take them back. The grass is never greener. Just be patient. He'll be back.'

'He wouldn't do anything to hurt the boys,' Sophie's mother added with certainty.

'Yeah, I know. Maybe you're right. It's just so shit.' Sophie could feel wet tears of emotion creeping up behind her nose and throat, threatening to burst out her eyes again.

'Never give up, Sophie, not if it's what you want. Marriage isn't always easy. I told you both that the day you got married, didn't I?'

And to Sophie's parents, that was the end of it.

*

The next few days were full of emotional extremes. Sophie never quite knew what mood Toby would adopt since ending the affair: positive and focused on repair or despondent and miserable, missing Abigail?

They had some good times, moments when they could act as if nothing bad had happened. The ease at which they still slotted together as a family reassured Sophie of the strength of the bonds holding them there, emboldened by Google, they *could* make this marriage better than ever.

She couldn't allow herself to carry any doubts or insecurities. It was Toby who was suffering, Toby needing consoling, and however ridiculous it seemed, she had to maintain her resilience and hold them all together whenever he would allow if she was going to make this work.

Her father's words were never far from mind; she really did want this marriage to succeed. She couldn't give up before she had really tried. She wanted to raise her protective walls as high as she could against Toby's rejection, but she could never let it show.

She became tireless in creating opportunities for loving conversations and sympathetic consoling, even buying the bestselling self-help books on relationships. To her, knowledge was power, so they formed an essential part of her recovery. She would digest every piece of advice and repair her marriage.

Even the boys remained oblivious to the wreckage around them as their parents continued a journey neither knew where, or when it might end.

Finally, the longest week ever ended with the arrival of the school break and Sophie and the boys could escape for a few days to her parents' home. Instead of being a family break as originally intended, it would now form part of her healing process, spending time with the people who loved her the most, some time away from Toby.

*

As Sophie unloaded the car at the end of the long journey, the boys dashed off and the dogs disappeared into the dusk of the Sussex countryside. Sophie's parents had moved four years ago from a lifetime spent in London, and the contrast couldn't have been greater. Sophie fondly remembered a comment Toby made when they'd first visited. He'd exclaimed how he woke up during the night, thinking he had gone deaf and blind because it was so quiet and dark.

Now the silence was being challenged by the shrieks from ten grandchildren excitedly reuniting and with the rustling and jangling of the two dogs as they hunted around the old Sussex farmhouse. Regardless of the circumstances, Sophie was happy to be here and was looking forward to the first (and inevitably one of many), gin and tonics.

Sophie's three sisters had all arrived earlier, travelling from a much shorter distance, and Sophie could bet their main discussion so far had been about her. The family had never shied away from gossip. They talked about everything and as a result rarely fell out. It was laughable the way they all stood now, around the large granite breakfast bar in the middle of the expansive kitchen.

They made idle small talk, none brave enough to open the discussion on the most sensational bit of gossip since Lisa, the eldest of the four, secretly eloped to get married on an elephant in Sri Lanka. Her bravery in hiding this from their parents was admirable, and surprisingly, the fallout had been short-lived.

It was Sophie's youngest, still-single sister, Amber, who ended up kicking the covers off the elephant in the room. She put her arms out to Sophie and embraced her sister. 'So, are you alright?' That was Sophie's cue to open her war chest and take her family through it. By now, her mother had joined the sisterly group. They spoke and drank for hours, laughing, crying, bitching about Toby and his paramour, and generally giving each of their marriages a verbal overhaul.

Their mother was quite matter-a-fact about it. 'Well, of all my sons-in-law, Toby was the last one I'd have thought would do this. Oh well, darling, I'm sure it doesn't mean too much. If they haven't had sex yet, then it hasn't been a proper affair, has it?'

As she spoke, several raised eyebrows were thrown from one sister to another. Not having sex was something they did not believe. 'No, it wasn't a proper affair,' her mother concluded as she exited the room.

Bloody was, Sophie mouthed to her sisters, then threw the empty gin bottle into the recycling bin with a loud, satisfying clunk.

*

Sophie climbed into the double bed, with a vintage, hand-crocheted eiderdown and old, battered, feather pillows and picked up her new books. She was unlikely to sleep anyway, given the storytelling that had just unfolded and the emotion that had spilt, lubricated by the gin.

She flicked through the pages of the first book, about loving someone but not being *in* love with them, to try to understand how Toby might be feeling. As she did so, she instantly recognised Toby's handwriting as a folded piece of paper fell out.

> I'm going to miss you all like crazy the next few days. I will reflect on what I've done with utter remorse I have hurt you so much. I can only hope you can find it in yourself to look at the wonderful things we have in our

> life, which I have needlessly put at risk, and find it in your heart to give me a chance at redemption. I cannot change what I've done, but I can change how we recover from it and I am going to really try.
>
> I've always loved your ability to make rational judgements when all around you is irrational and emotional. I never realised I would need that so much. My judgement and outlook have been totally wrong, and I am the only one to blame.
>
> Ultimately, the great reasons why we got together are still there.
>
> I just really love you.
>
> Toby X

Sophie's eyes were wet as she re-read the note, to make sure his certainty was still there. She was going to read the self-help books, check out the marriage counsellor's details the doctor had given her and devise a solid plan to get them back on track.

There was a mountain to climb, and she was going to carry her husband up that mountain if she had to. She wasn't giving up. She'd get what she wanted if she worked hard enough and she wanted her old Toby back.

Feeling more content and understanding about her future than she had for nearly a year, she gratefully gave into her alcohol-induced sleep, first popping a sleeping pill for good measure.

21

Tuesday, 28th May 2013

Sophie had to return to Nettlefield House a few days later, emotionally boosted by the many conversations with her sisters and parents. She kissed them all goodbye, momentarily forgetting her challenge ahead, and drove off, loudly singing to a CD of children's party songs with the boys happily joining in. Gradually the singing subsided as the boys fell asleep and Sophie drove the remaining miles in silence, her mind working overtime.

As she spotted the motorway services in the distance, the butterflies in her stomach woke up and took flight, spooked by her developing thoughts and recognition of the size of the mountain in front of them.

Why does no one teach you how to stay happily married? There should be compulsory night school courses. You should at least have to pass a test before you say, 'I do'!

As she pulled onto the driveway she closed her eyes, listening to the silence of the deadened engine and took a moment to imagine herself and Toby, holding hands on the mountain's summit, gazing at the horizon with the rambling countryside and simple happiness in-between. She would start climbing that mountain tonight.

Excited at being home, the boys had taken ages to go to bed and Sophie worried that Toby had purposefully encouraged it. Her butterflies would flutter every time he looked at her, as if he was about to say something loving, then he would just turn his attention back to the boys, leaving her hanging.

Eventually, William and Michael succumbed to sleep, and Toby came downstairs. Sophie put on a recording of the latest period drama and the dogs took up their usual positions on the sofa, before Toby completed the familiar picture.

Sophie watched the television, yearning for contentment, trying to ignore the elephant that was back in the room. She didn't want to taint this scene she had longed for by bringing up the reality of their situation, but she had to start at some point.

As the adverts began, she took a deep breath and turned to face Toby, painting on a gentle smile, ready to talk. Then her face dropped.

He was asleep.

She watched him a moment, suspicious he was faking, trying to avoid the conversation he would have known was coming. She pressed pause and gently prodded his side.

'I know you're not asleep. I can tell. Your mouth's not open, catching flies.' She was attempting humour, encouraging Toby's amenable side.

He smiled as he opened his eyes. 'I'm just tired. Shall we

go to bed?' They may have still been sleeping separately, but they tried to go to bed at the same time.

'Wait.' Sophie turned to directly face him, pondering the intelligence of her next question. The self-help books spoke of absolute honesty and asking questions you might not like the answer to in order to move forward. The books said everything you want, all the desirable things, can only be found outside your comfort zone and Sophie's impatience encouraged her to step outside hers. 'Have you seen her … you know … since?' she asked, widening her eyes, getting straight to the point.

Toby gazed into the space beyond the television and said, 'No, of course not. You've seen her more recently than me. I told you it's over.'

'Have you messaged her? Been in touch?'

He was quick to answer. 'No. I told you. I'm not going there again. I've finished it.' His affirmation had a harsher edge than Sophie would have liked.

She paused before her next question, less for effect and more to gain confidence. 'Are you going to miss her?'

There, she had said it. She had asked the question she didn't want the answer to, but she knew it had to be asked if they were to heal. The books had said so.

'Yes. Of course I am.' Toby paused, creating a dramatic silence. 'I've just got to try and get over her. I've got to go cold turkey. You have to understand, it's not going to be easy for me.' His words carried less conviction and strength than a feather drifting in a summer breeze.

Internally, Sophie screamed, *Get over it? What about me? How the hell do I get over it?*

She remained outwardly calm, but inside she was fuming. God, she loved the honesty of the man, but wow, it hurt.

His words were like rejection, kicking the butterflies dead. She wanted to run back to her parents, pretend she'd never returned home. She wanted to kick herself for having the optimism that this would be a simple process and she wanted to kick her father for always insisting she never give up.

Doesn't matter how hard I work, Dad, if Toby doesn't work at it too.

She replied as unemotionally as possible. 'There is no 'try', Toby. You either get over her, or you don't.'

Once again, the familiar heat of her tears replaced the sorrow the moment she left the room.

One of the dogs had followed her into the kitchen, sitting watching as she made herself a tea. Sophie looked at his little black face, watching his tail wag as their eyes connected, enticing her to take her drink outside.

As she opened the boot room door, she was joined by the other dog and the three of them went into the dusk. Sophie sat on the trampoline, cupping her mug for warmth, and watched the shadows of the dogs' race off into the orchard, wishing her life was as simple as theirs.

Her tears had stopped, they were achieving nothing. In some funny warped way, she now understood how hard it might be for Toby to give up his mistress. If she was going to get her marriage back, she was going to have to accept this and give some allowance for it.

Just as Toby was going to have to allow her to have her

own difficulties in forgiving him and learning to trust again. She knew she could overcome her obstacles; the books had said so and she really did still love the man and everything he stood for. Maintaining the vision of the two of them, side by side at the top of that mountain would help her, to help him.

Her mug had lost its warmth and without a coat, she was beginning to shiver, so she called for the dogs, deciding to go back to face the conversation she knew they had to continue. Her footsteps were subconsciously silent, and her pulse quickened as she approached the lounge, reminding her of the many times before when she'd acted like a private investigator.

She hated this paranoia; it was like poison in her veins, and she knew she would have to get rid of it if they were to heal. She stopped short of the door and peered through the gap at the hinges directly in line with where Toby was still sitting and squinted at the colourful little thumbnails flashing across the screen of the iPad.

Suddenly, a larger icon appeared and she immediately recognised it from so many house searches from the past. Before Nettlefield House. Before it had all gone so horribly wrong.

'Christ, you bastard. How is that going to sort out our marriage?'

Sophie's sudden entry caused Toby to hurriedly turn over the iPad.

He meekly looked up as his face flushed. 'I'm just looking at options. I've got a lot to consider.'

'Nothing like rebuilding a marriage based on *your* options. Thanks a million for considering mine and the boys! We're supposed to be a team. How is moving into a—' and she stopped as she flipped over the iPad before continuing. 'Oh, I see. A two-bedroom flat for £950 a month. How exactly is that going to help?'

'I'm sorry, Sophie. I'm just looking. It means nothing. Please just give me time. I want this to work too. I really do.'

'By moving out? Seriously?'

Sophie's anger took over her remaining forgiveness. 'I hope you find something a million miles away. Go fuck yourself.' And she turned abruptly leaving the room.

Definitely a night for a pill, she thought as she made her way alone to bed.

*

Sophie woke to her phone, incessantly vibrating on the side and answered it just as Rani hung up. She looked at the clock and bolted upright as she registered it was past nine o'clock.

Her first panicked thought was about the boys being late for school, until she remembered it was half term. Her mind began to race again as she thought of the poor dogs and chickens, still locked inside. She swung her legs out of bed and stood quickly. Her head rushed with stars, momentarily going black, slowly clearing again as her racing heart returned to normal.

As she bustled about the morning's chores before taking her tea upstairs, her thoughts turned again to the challenge ahead of her. She wished she hadn't told anyone about the affair. Now her whole family knew, she felt a ridiculous obligation to keep fighting for this marriage, to not let them down.

She had massive respect for her parents' long, happy marriage and significant gratitude that they had succeeded. Emulating that success, ensuring she gave the boys the same stability and love of a family unit that she'd had, was never far from her mind.

She picked up her phone to call back Rani, taking a sip of tea as she answered.

'Morning. Hope it's good to be back? Ant said Toby was really miserable whilst you were away. Really missed you all.'

'I doubt it.' Sophie replied. 'He was missing Abigail more.' Sophie went on to tell her about Toby going cold turkey and how hard it was going to be for him. 'I've got to understand, you know! He's going to try!' Sophie laughed at how ridiculous this sounded.

Rani didn't disagree. 'It astounds me that you're putting up with it. It's like you're the one in the wrong, waiting for him to accept you back.'

Sophie imagined her pacing up and down, arms gesticulating in time to her words, not pausing for breath.

'Jesus, you're the one drugging yourself to sleep at night, crying down the phone. It's you keeping the house going and looking after the boys. How do you know he's not off with her every spare minute? I thought you were tough and strong. Get tough and kick him out.'

'Don't think I haven't thought about it … But I still love him, Rani. I still have to try and make this work. I owe it to the boys.' She took another sip of tea feeling close to tears. 'What have I got to lose? I can't bear to think of the alternative.'

'Well, you're braver than I am … or more stupid.' Rani laughed.

'Probably both.' And Sophie laughed too.

'Don't tell me you're still going on that work trip with him Friday? You are, aren't you!?'

'Yup, I'm a glutton for punishment, but wives are kind of expected to go and I have to keep trying. Maybe he does just need more time. There's too much at stake to just throw it all in.'

Sophie began to believe it. The upcoming work do at another extravagant hotel, could offer a distraction, a break from everything still hanging in the balance, a chance to properly talk. She wasn't going to let Rani's heavy sigh or her painful memories of the last Drema work do, drag her down.

She wasn't giving up. Not yet.

*

The day of the Drema event brought with it a deluge of heavy rain and dark skies. Sophie hoped it wasn't an ominous sign of the night to come.

There had been no other opportunities for further conversations due to Toby's heavy workload and the arrival of his parents, who were staying for a few days at the end of half term.

Sophie had, however, devoted some time to reading the self-help books, mentally storing a series of exercises on how to communicate better and reintroduce intimacy. She had done her homework and felt sure the luxurious hotel room and romantic grounds could only add to her success.

Besides, she had lost four kilos in two weeks. Heartbreak was the best diet she had ever tried, so she finally felt she may look the part too.

Before leaving, Sophie checked that her in-laws had understood the instructions for the animals. They would be fine with the boys; they'd had their own children after all, but coping with a disappearing dog or a chicken not cooperating at bedtime would be less familiar.

Reassured they knew how to deal with all potential problems, Sophie made her way to join Toby, who had been at the hotel since morning, on a team-building day with his boss and twelve of his colleagues.

The hotel was a stunning piece of architecture, with a pillared and stepped entrance and massive sash windows with Georgian bars. The rooms were large, with thick velvet curtains and a substantial leather sofa with numerous feather cushions scattered along its length. The bathroom was fully kitted out with toiletries, robes and an inbuilt media centre that at the press of a button emerged from its secret hiding place in the wall. The grounds were probably equally as impressive, but with the heavy mist and rain, she could only imagine them as she read the glossy magazines and drank the boutique tea with handmade biscuits.

Sophie decided to make use of the pool and spa while she waited for Toby to finish his team meeting. She sent him a text before she left, suggesting he join her. He couldn't be much longer now.

Sophie's leisurely swim was cut short as the four o'clock deadline for the adults-only session ended. She was disappointed as the pool had been virtually empty, and it would have been a great time for Toby to have joined her. A great group of noisy children plunged into the water creating a massive splash and tidal wave, and Sophie vacated quickly.

Back in the room, she ran a bath to take advantage of the luxury toiletries. She had been soaking and watching television for nearly an hour, slowly turning into a prune, when Toby finally arrived just before six. He didn't mention the scented candles she had lit, nor the melodic music streaming through the Bose sound system. He barely acknowledged his naked wife sitting in a deep and bubbly bath as he ducked his head around the door.

'So, have you been swimming?'

'Yeah,' Sophie answered to the vacant space as he retreated, pulling off his tie.

A few moments passed in silence, then he returned, seemingly unaware of his wife's answer. 'Did you go swimming?'

'Yes. I just said Yes. I texted you too. I thought you might have joined me?' Sophie struggled to keep the annoyance out of her voice. 'What's wrong, you seem distracted? How was your team day?'

'Yeah, good. Sorry, it went on a bit longer than I hoped. Some of the team are such hard work, just couldn't wrap it up any earlier.'

Toby continued changing out of his work clothes in the bedroom, chatting about his colleagues through the en suite walls.

Sophie knew she would be meeting them later, so she asked appropriately prising questions in preparation.

When Toby returned, he was fully dressed in jeans and a shirt, not in a bathrobe, naked, ready to join her in the warm water as she had hoped.

'So, did you go for a swim?' he inquired again, and Sophie screamed inside. Not waiting for her answer, he added, 'Think I'll go for one now.'

'Seriously?' Sophie said, eyebrows raised. 'Why don't you get in the bath with me? It's massive.'

'No, it's okay. I won't be long.' And he left.

Sophie screwed up her face and groaned, swiping the little bottles off the side of the bath, watching them roll around the floor, seeping shampoo onto the tiles. So much for the first part of her homework:

Create a time and a place for your memories, removing all distractions. Don't just leave it to chance, otherwise it might never happen.

She looked down at her wrinkled hands as she retrieved a fallen bottle from the depths of the bath, randomly remembering it was nature's way to ensure you could grip things underwater. Nature never failed to impress Sophie, but all she wanted to grip now was the bottle of champagne, patiently waiting in the ice bucket, two cut glass flutes by its side.

He probably hadn't noticed them either.

*

Sophie worked hard during dinner on the illusion of being a happily married couple, pretending to be Toby's trophy wife. She was glad she hadn't cut corners on her outfit, and she knew she was playing the part well from the way he placed his hand across the small of her back as they chatted to the male-dominated group, his gesture of ownership.

She got the impression that Toby's team thought highly of him, and she knew how important that was for any sort of career progression. She could so easily turn the tables tonight, telling everyone what he had done, highlighting his failings, but somehow, she didn't think they would mind. The way they were all talking about the HR department and the hormonal women that worked there, they would probably think more of him as a result.

The seating plan at dinner positioned Sophie next to Toby's elderly, rather drunk boss, who effused complements at what a good catch she was, whilst frequently placing his wrinkled hand on her knee.

Sophie froze, sickened but not surprised at the chauvinistic attitude of the old man.

'So, you little minx.' He winked. 'Had to drag Toby away from the golf earlier, did you? Wanted him all to yourself for a few hours in that lovely hotel room, eh?'

Sophie had no idea what he meant but smiled and responded with a coy look. 'I don't know *what* you mean.' But the forced, flirty tone of her voice implied that she did.

'I'd give up nine holes of golf for you too!' He squeezed her leg, higher up, laughing raucously.

Sophie's stomach churned at his touch. She glanced across at Toby, looking for reassurance or an expression of gratitude for her tolerance, but he quickly looked away, avoiding her stare. Hoping to prevent the old man's hand from rising any further up her leg, she said. 'Well, I'd never ask you to, so no need to worry about that!'

She politely laughed, took a sip of her wine, then quickly excused herself from the table, allowing his hand to drop so abruptly that he wobbled in his chair.

Why hadn't Toby played golf with his team? What had he been doing instead? And why had he lied to his boss?

Finally, the end of the evening arrived, and they retired to their luxury room. Toby quickly undressed before collapsing naked onto the bed, falling into his wine-induced sleep, taking away any chance Sophie had of interrogating him.

Feeling as if she cared a little less, she popped a pill and pulled the duvet over them both, then allowed her drug-induced sleep to carry her away from tonight's worries.

*

It was nine a.m. when Sophie had the chance to practise her second piece of homework. She was desperate to quiz Toby about the missing hours from the day before, but she would do that later; damaging the mood now would make her homework impossible.

Her task was to selflessly reintroduce intimacy, simply by asking for a kiss. A proper kiss, full of love, passion and longing. As he stirred, she rolled over to embrace him, then dutifully delivered it, fully and completely.

Whilst she may have got an A+ for effort, it was clearly an E- in results. He felt nothing, not a stir nor a skip, and he told her so. Sophie was reminded of her similar failings in the hotel room a few months before when his apparent problem was simply an overindulgence of wine.

We know differently now, though, don't we? Sophie thought to herself bitterly.

Toby picked up her hand from the duvet, squeezing it, gazing into her face. 'It's just going to take time, Sophie. You need to be patient.'

'Really? Just for a kiss?'

'It's so difficult. I feel so guilty.' He kissed her hand, holding it tight.

'You've no need to feel guilty anymore. What's done is done. I'm learning to forgive you. I'm reading the books, but you need to read them too.' Sophie squeezed back and held his gaze, longing for him to lean in and kiss her. Properly this time.

'You don't understand. My guilt, it's like I'm cheating on Abigail. I know I should be able to forget her, but I just can't, not yet. Please understand. I need more time.'

Sophie snatched her hand away. 'Wow ... d'you realise how messed up that is?'

Toby remained silent.

'How can you just not love me anymore? I haven't changed. I'm still just me.' She wasn't expecting an answer. 'It's unbelievable, Toby. It's heartbreaking and unbelievably wrong.'

Sophie threw the covers off her naked body and with zero embarrassment, stood tall over the stranger in the bed. 'I'm going home. Do whatever you want. I'm not gonna be second choice. I'm not trailing around like a lovesick puppy waiting for you any longer. I've had enough. Go stick your golf clubs up your a—'

She stormed into the bathroom, slamming the door behind her, drowning out the last of her words.

*

Sophie surprised Dot with her early return home without any explanation. Dot could tell something was wrong and was probing her daughter-in-law for answers. Sophie had considered talking to Rani on the drive home but knew she would probably have just said, 'I told you so'. So instead, Sophie confided in Dot.

'He's no different. Nothing's improved. He's making no effort. I guarantee you he's still seeing her, still talking to her, and goodness knows what else. He must be. Why else would he feel like he was cheating on her? *I'm* his wife for goodness sake.'

'I ... I don't think that's true, Sophie. Surely not.' Dot sat down at the kitchen table, unable to make eye contact.

'He's a lying, deceitful man. He cannot decide, and I've had enough.' Sophie no longer cared she was talking about this woman's beloved son. 'I deserve more, and the boys need a happy mum, not this miserable mess he's turned me into. I won't let him carry on doing this to me. I should kick him out.'

Dot pulled out a tissue from her sleeve and dabbed her eyes. Sophie wanted his parents to understand exactly how little effort their son was putting into righting the wrong.

'D'you know I caught him looking for flats to rent last week? He's probably already got one lined up and moving her in.' Sophie's voice broke as her tears started. 'He loves her, and he can't get over her, and I'd bet money he's still seeing her.'

That was too much for Dot, and she gave in to tears with her head in her hands.

Sophie sat opposite and joined in with the sobs and both women took a moment to privately absorb themselves in their emotions

'Oh, you're back early.' Frank walked in, pulling off his coat, presumably having just walked the dogs. 'Oh. What's happened? This can't be good news.' His brow creased and his eyes darted from woman to woman, trying to understand why both had tears rolling down their cheeks.

Dot was the first to speak, with a voice stronger than any Sophie had heard before. 'It's Toby. He's still seeing her. He's looking at flats to rent, he's going to leave them!' She put her hands up to her face, hiding behind them.

'He can't be! Those poor boys. Oh, God. Why is he doing this?'

His question went unanswered, and just like any well-scripted episode of *EastEnders*, Toby walked in with perfect timing, stopping dead due to the emotion in the room.

'Tell me it's not true,' his dad demanded in a shaking but powerful voice. 'Are you still seeing her?'

'What! No, of course not,' Toby answered immediately, looking around at the three adults he should have loved most in the world. 'Of course not,' he repeated. 'I swear it. I swear it on the boys' lives. I haven't even spoken to her. It's over. It's been over since Sophie found out. I promise.'

The boys' entrance abruptly ended the conversation. Dot disappeared silently, and Sophie mumbled that she needed to do the horses. Michael had already stolen Daddy's unguarded phone and was playing Candy Crush. William likely sensed something was wrong, but confident it wasn't himself at fault, wandered off to play on the Wii.

As Sophie left the men alone in the kitchen, she heard the stern voice of Frank echo through the hallway.

'Don't do this. Don't you *dare* do this to those poor boys!'

She didn't hear Toby's reply.

22

Saturday, 1st June 2013

That night, when they went up to bed, Toby asked Sophie for the self-help books. She had been suggesting, unsuccessfully, that he should read them for ages. Perhaps now, following the confrontation with his dad, he finally accepted he would, so she left them in full view, side by side under his bedside light.

Totally exhausted from the night before, Sophie collapsed into bed, mildly comforted by the thought that Toby was about to take responsibility for his mess, finally giving himself this much-needed self-help.

A few hours later, she was still awake, her mind unable to mimic the physical exhaustion of her body. She was trying not to become reliant on the pills. This was going to be a long-term battle, and drugs, even if they were non-addictive, would not be the solution.

Sophie took a pen and paper and applied her own therapy, putting her midnight thoughts into words. Her journal allowed her the therapeutic time to record the day's events, but the last few months, her notes had been excessive and incoherent, with emotions all over the place, often scrawled late at night.

When she had nothing positive to write, she would force herself to start with, 'Today, the best thing that happened to me was …' and the words and emotions would flow, releasing pent-up worries and worthless thoughts, inducing sleep.

Tonight, she wrote: 'Why are thoughts in the middle of the night so much more intense than during the day? Problems become greater; solutions become harder. The simple fact I shouldn't be awake is a massive complication to falling asleep!'

Before she realised, she was penning a poem, putting emotions into rhythmic phrasing to create soothing peace in her mind. It was a love poem. It was written to Toby. The first draft needed no editing.

The Other Half of Me

I never thought love could hurt this bad.
Words can't describe my pain, so sad.
Because of you, love's ripped apart
my home, my life, my world, my heart.

I never thought it could be you,
so mean, so weak, so heartless, so cruel.
Your dishonesty has driven me insane.
My world will never be the same again.

THE OTHER HALF OF ME

Each minute of each and every day,
I relive my torture with aching dismay.
My torment is all because of you,
you selfish, dishonest, uncaring fool.

Did you think you could have the both of us?
Did you think with time, your choice would be thrust
by one or another of your female friends?
The final destination, the final end.

Well, prematurely it's come to pass.
Your love affair I caught at last.
You made the choice; you made your bed.
Now face those demons in your head.

I no longer see the man I loved.
He's long since gone, my mate, my love,
the one that would never dream of hurting me,
the one that was the other half of me.

I now have to choose which path to take:
Real but lonely, together but fake?
The one thing I am that you could never be
is trustful, honest, with strong loyalty.

You have to live for the rest of your years
knowing you caused these continual tears,
knowing you changed the course of my life,
knowing me once, your beautiful wife.

Do I love you more now than I did before?
Do I see our future, roses round the door?
Did my silver cloud burst, or implode with a bang?
Till death do us part? Forever?
Amen

This may have been her own form of therapy, but she desperately wanted it to work for Toby too, so she went to see if his bedroom light was on. It was. Sophie took it as a hopeful sign he was reading the books. Once she had begun reading, she hadn't been able to put them down. The sooner she absorbed the information they divulged, the sooner she could correct the wrong in her life.

Maybe Toby was finding the same now.

She crept silently along the corridor, through habit rather than suspicion, and tapped gently on the door before walking in. He was sitting, propped up with all four pillows from the king-size bed. The bedside light was on, and Sophie's eyes were immediately drawn to the books, seemingly untouched, highlighted in the soft downlight from the shade.

Perhaps he had finished reading and was now writing down his thoughts on the open laptop. Or, more likely, he hadn't even opened the pages, and Drema was receiving all his attention. As Sophie ran through the scenarios in her head, the opposing emotions were painful.

She knew instinctively which one was true.

'Why are you still up?' Toby questioned, shutting the laptop as she walked in.

Sophie didn't answer. *Stupid question, all things considered.*

She reached down for the books, looking for a bookmark or a fold in the corner of the page, indicating he had at least started to read. She found nothing.

'Have you read *anything*?' She didn't wait for a response. 'What have you been doing?'

'Emails. There's so much going on, and China's just started working. I'm trying to keep up.'

'But it's past midnight. You were meant to read the damn books.' Sophie picked them up and tossed them onto the duvet. 'I've been in bed, unable to sleep, so full of emotion that I've written you a poem, and you're in bed with Drema.'

She collapsed onto the edge of the mattress, sighing noisily and handed him the poem, hugging her knees defensively. 'You've got to stop. It's not worth it. You've broken our marriage, and we have to resolve things. I can't do it on my own.'

Sophie went to remove the laptop, implying this was the end of Drema's time. In her mind, Toby would read her poem, tears slowly forming. He would feel a massive surge of guilt and regret as he re-read the heartfelt lines and would vow to sort things out. Promise to revert to the old Toby, bringing back their old life. Hugging her close with his conviction.

The actual scenario couldn't have been more different.

The moment she placed her hand on the laptop, Toby grabbed it, pulling it aside. The poem slid to the floor, unnoticed. His sudden movement, the cold black eyes, the tight lips, and the defensive, protective attitude gave him away. Sophie received another virtual twist of the knife in her stomach as she realised that, once again, he was hiding something. Something on his laptop. Something he was doing instead of reading the books, instead of working with China.

'Open your laptop, Toby. Show me what you were doing,' she demanded. Her voice was strong, and her body language was not taking no for an answer.

'Jeez, Sophie.' He sighed. 'I'm just doing emails.'

'Sorry, but I don't believe you. I'm not good at trusting you now, for some reason,' she added, raising her eyebrows and standing up. 'Open it then and show me if you've nothing to hide.'

Toby did so without the anticipated fight. He just handed the laptop over: defeated or innocent, Sophie couldn't tell. She scrolled through his inbox. There were many emails sent over the last few hours to various addresses at Drema Ltd, all very dull. To hasten her search, she placed Abigail's name in the search bar. Nothing. Nothing in deleted folders either. She tried James. Nothing.

'Satisfied? Then pass it back. I told you, it's just emails.' He held out his hand to regain possession.

But Sophie wasn't satisfied. She sensed his agitation. If there was nothing to find, then why would he care? Why was he hovering over her?

As she methodically moved the cursor across the various thumbnails, she could sense his growing agitation, as if they were silently playing the childhood game of warmer or colder. Sophie read his body language as she searched for the hot spot. It didn't take long. She noticed the Facebook icon in the toolbar, which surprised her. She didn't even realise he had an account. He certainly didn't have her as a friend if he did.

The icon jumped to life and as Sophie scrolled through his personal profile, she found what she hadn't known she was looking for. Abigail, boldly filling the screen, barely covered by a skimpy black dress, with her long, blonde hair loose around her coquettish face. The photo was taken at some grand function room; there was a large table in front of her with numerous empty glasses and bottles.

Taking pride of place was a large ice sculpture of a penis, four feet tall in all its erect glory and detail. Abigail was half-facing the camera and half-turned towards the phallic structure. She was leaning into it with her hands around its base, her back arched, and her head tilted up. She was licking it.

Sophie felt disgusted, yet slightly amused. *Not something I wouldn't have done myself, drunk and face to face with a huge penis*, she thought. Her breath caught as she spotted the message from Toby underneath.

'Gorgeous. Keep them coming!'

'Yeah, nothing to see here, was there? Jesus, look at all these!' Sophie's anger smothered her pain as she continued to scroll. She found many more photos and comments throughout the last part of 2012, sent privately to Toby, when Abigail was still 'happily' married to her husband.

Had Matthew got the penis photo too?

'Seriously, I didn't know they were still there. It was ages ago. I'd forgotten about them, honestly.' Toby pleaded his warped innocence.

'Of course you didn't remember. I don't believe you for a second. Look at your response to this one. What the hell did that mean, asking a married woman licking a giant ice penis to keep the photos coming? God, you're pathetic. What d'you do? Look at them every night before falling into an erotic sleep?'

'Oh, God, I'm sorry. I promise, I haven't seen them for ages.'

'Really? Forgotten about them, had you? So, what were you so anxious about just now? Have I not found it all then? It's just lies, lies, lies. I can't even be bothered to look anymore, and you want me to believe you've ended it!'

Sophie slammed the laptop closed, leaving him to his electronic fantasies. She held her head high as she walked out of the room, giving the illusion she couldn't care less.

She did care, though. She had no idea how to deal with this amount of care. It would be so much easier if she was like Abigail and just gave up on her marriage without a fight. She had enough justification to. But she just couldn't accept she would ever give up on her future of a happy ever after, fighting for the family unit the boys deserved, what she had as a child, and that was a powerful drug flowing through her veins.

Besides, she still loved her Toby, the Toby he used to be, the Toby she had dedicated the poem to, but she doubted he would remember the slip of paper on the floor under the bed, with her heart opened wide on top.

A heart with a core of infinite strength.

*

Toby opened the laptop and reloaded the photo that had caused Sophie to explode. He loved that image and did look at it sometimes. It was one of many she had sent him, but he hadn't been looking at that one tonight. Abigail put loads on Facebook, shouting about what her kids were up to and about her feelings, so tonight he had been innocently surfing her public profile.

It made him feel close to her when he couldn't physically be. He would never comment publicly, of course, but he knew that she knew he looked. He was grateful that Sophie hadn't been an accomplished user of Facebook. If she had been, she might have noticed the time stamp of the last photo to Toby.

Feeling twinges of guilt, Toby reached down to find the poem. He read through the verses, surprised at her poetic skill but not at the emotions in the words. He only read it once, ashamed of the way it made him feel. Why couldn't she just give up? No one had ever fought as hard for him before. Why could he not be that strong? How could he switch allegiances so quickly?

One minute, he was convinced Abigail was his future, and it would just be a matter of time. Then the reality would hit that of course, it was, and always would be Sophie he would spend the rest of his life with. That's what he had sworn on oath to nearly twelve years ago. That's what he saw every time he looked into William and Michael's eyes.

God, this doesn't get any easier.

He placed the slip of paper inside the top book, reading its title about learning to trust again after an affair, and groaned at the challenge ahead of him. He could barely trust himself.

How was Sophie supposed to?

*

The next morning, there was no paper love heart slipped under Sophie's door.

Toby's room appeared the same as it had the night before, with his recently vacated bed left unmade and the books still at the side, unread. The only difference was that the poem was no longer on the floor. He had placed it inside one of the books, presumably meaning he had read it.

How Sophie wished she had been there to see his reactions. She pulled it out from the book and re-read her words, unable to prevent the wetness from forming in her eyes. She wondered if it had affected Toby in the same way, but suspected it hadn't. Leaving the poem where she found it, she shook off her impending tears and began the day's tasks of getting the boys off to school.

Today, Sophie was planning on confirming their first counselling session. She had contacted the counsellor recommended by the doctor, so now just had to get Toby to agree to the dates. Marriage guidance seemed such a poor description for what they needed, but it would be another small step on their way to resolving the situation and Sophie had run out of other ideas.

*

Toby didn't hide his reluctance when she discussed the dates with him later that night.

They were sitting in the lounge, neither really watching the programme on the television. Toby's crossed arms gave her an infuriating message, causing her own arms to wildly flail about as she spoke.

'You have to do *something*. Why am I trying so hard, while you keep messing it all up? It's all me, me, me sorting this out, and you're not bloody doing anything.'

'Seriously, Sophie, how is a total stranger going to help? It'll be a waste of my time.' Toby stood abruptly and switched off the television, nearly pushing it backwards with the force of his touch. The veins in his neck were standing proud and his tired eyes had come alive. His mouth, the blackest of holes, was spitting out his words. 'Just leave it. I'm tired. I've been at work all day. I'm *not* going to have this conversation now. I've told you I'm not seeing her anymore. Why do you have to be so flipping righteous about this goddamn marriage?'

Sophie stood to face him as he paced across the room, her voice raised. 'Because someone's got to do someth—'

'Christ. Just leave me alone.' Toby interrupted. 'Stop going on about it all,' and with a burst of movement, he grabbed the ironing board from where it was permanently erected. As the iron slid to the floor with an audible crack, he propelled the board through the air, directly at Sophie's head.

She reacted quickly, darting out of the way as it collided with solid brick, metal buckling under the force and removing a chunk of plaster as it fell to the ground.

Toby let out a roar, a cry of desperation and confusion

directed at Sophie as she retreated behind the door, holding it as a shield, poised to run if he moved towards her. He didn't. He simply stood in the middle of the room, staring at her, arms down by his side, suddenly depleted of energy.

Anyone looking in would have concluded that the man inside hated his wife and Sophie's pounding heart would have concurred. But she knew this outburst had come from a deep, agonising place and was her confirmation that this affair was not over.

It was more than just limerence, that lustful, surface-level affection the books kept reassuring her was the love of affairs, which never lasts and is rarely serious. These were not the actions of a man trying to rescue his marriage and put his family first. These were the actions of a desperate man in a tangle of lies and deceits, driven by contrasting love, with no strength or guts to get out of it.

Sophie locked eyes with him, scared but defiant, then silently left the room with more physical impact to the broken man than any amount of retaliatory hostility would have achieved.

He had crossed a line she had no idea they'd been so close to. She would not let him abuse her feelings any longer with his lies. Like moves in a game of chess, she had been spending too long moving little pawns up and down. Now she was going to play her queen and she knew exactly how. She was going to take control of the game, forcing him into checkmate.

There would be nowhere for Toby to hide.

23

Saturday, 15th June 2013

The timing had to be right for Sophie's planned move, but her impatience led to her getting it wrong. She should never have attempted such a thing the day before Father's Day.

Toby was against such commercialism—he barely even sent birthday cards—but ever since the boys started school, he was unable to ignore these dedicated days. They would lovingly create Father's Day cards with vast quantities of glue, stuck-on pasta, and felt-tip exclamations of 'Best Dad Ever'. They would proudly deliver them early in the morning, with tea and biscuits, watching as he read their loving words, exclaiming at their clever handwriting and creativity. Sophie would be secretly trying to retrieve fallen pasta and randomly stuck on pieces before the dogs hoovered them up. It was always special.

This year, Sophie knew she had ruined it before the day even began.

She executed her plan at nine a.m. the day before Father's

Day. Everything was as normal as normal now was. She'd just come back from sorting out the horses. Toby was in the office, on his laptop, and the boys were in the lounge, playing on the Wii.

The plan was simple: she would walk into the office and ask a straightforward question, receive a compliant response, then be able to decide what would happen next.

Every time Sophie ran through the delivery in her mind, her heart rate increased, and its rhythm fluctuated. She had planned for two possible scenarios. Scenario one would bring little change to her life, and whilst frustrating, was preferred.

Scenario two, suspected to be the most probable, would challenge her ability to keep fighting for this marriage to a level she wasn't sure she was brave enough to face.

Her question was simple: 'Show me your itemized phone bill.'

'W … What?' Toby faltered, looking up from his spreadsheet, then quickly closing his laptop before moving to escape the office. But Sophie stood firm, she had already shut the door and her back was against it, trapping him inside.

'You're being stupid.' The vein in his neck was pulsing. 'Open the door.'

He didn't grab her and exert his strength to push through. Sensing this, Sophie continued applying pressure.

'Toby. Log onto your account and show me your itemized bills. I know you have them from work. You have no choice.' Her voice was strong as she felt the higher ground she stood on. 'Refuse to show me, and I will know for sure you have something to hide. Show me, then with any luck, I'll find nothing and look stupid.' Sophie's strength surprised her. No tears had begun to form; her voice stayed strong. She was strengthening, second by second by Toby's lack of response.

He didn't shout or get forceful. He just turned away from the door and sat heavily in the office chair, causing it to spin. She had expected a loud voice, his refusal, the normal adrenaline, not this complacency.

'Sophie, I know what you're looking for. Yes, I've been in touch with her. She's been so unhappy, and she's rung me a few times. I've had to ring her back. You don't need to look.' He rubbed his hand back and forth over his head.

'You shouldn't be in touch with her at all Toby. *At all.*' Sophie emphasized the last words with an abruptness that caused her to spit a little. She didn't want to hear excuses. Abigail's unhappiness was irrelevant to her and should have remained irrelevant to Toby.

'Well, I need to look anyway. Log on.' She spoke with a firmness that meant she wouldn't remain calm for long.

Toby obediently logged into his Drema expense account, then left the room with his head bent low, refusing to make eye contact as he said, 'It's only words. We've not met up.' Then as an afterthought he added, 'I promise.'

Sophie took the laptop upstairs and tried to make herself comfortable on the bed, but her tense shoulders could barely control her arms, shaking the laptop in front of her.

The accounts page was open, displaying the thumbnails for the last several months of expenses. She felt euphoric, as if she was about to climb inside Toby's mind, about to be vindicated.

The most recent O2 bill uploaded to his expense account was from two weeks ago. She opened it, glancing up and down the list of unknown numbers. One number jumped out from the pages and pelted Sophie in the eyes with the pain of real bullets. Tens of calls, several times a day. She knew who it belonged to.

Grabbing her diary from the bedside table, she began logically moving through the dates of the phone calls, cross-checking them with her emotional words on the pages. Her hands were shaking violently, unable to control the curser as she acknowledged the correlation of Toby's erratic behaviour to the secret hours spent on his phone. And these were just the outgoing calls. There must have been just as many, if not more, incoming. The text messages were worse: hundreds across a week. How Sophie would have loved to read their content.

She stopped scanning the lines of print and looked out the window, watching the horses graze, squinting as a memory slowly formed.

A summer day. A happy day. A picnic. Orange juice was everywhere … the dog disappeared.

'That's it!', Sophie slapped her head as she joined the dots from the last few years. 'That mystery caller. My phone number changing. She told me he was lying. The *bastard*. He's done this before.' Sophie slammed the laptop shut and with a growing rage, went to find her husband. The shaky hands that could barely control a cursor a few moments ago now had the strength to strangle a man.

She raced down the stairs, phone numbers and memories flooding her mind and stormed into the old barn, where she instinctively knew he would have retreated.

As she left the brightness of the day, her eyes adjusted to see Toby in the back, nervously fiddling with some tools. He tentatively made his way towards her, eyes wide, daring to display a sheepish smile. Sophie's anger overflowed, bursting through the space between them. She laid into his chest with her clenched fists as many times as she could, half-crying, half-shouting, blinded by the reality of her stupidity. The words now coming out of her mouth took no care of the listening ears of the children within the house, the neighbours over the fence, nor the lorry drivers in the service station.

'*Get out.* Leave. Go. I hate you. Disgust isn't a strong enough word for what I now feel. How many other women were there? *How many?*' She didn't wait for an answer. 'You pack your stuff, and you leave. *Now.*'

*

Toby had control of her hands but could not stop the verbal abuse from her mouth. The fists had been easy to bear compared to the way his wife now spoke. He had never experienced such raw emotion and hatred directed at him, and he was frightened of what she might do next.

He was certain if he had not been six-foot-two, he would have serious facial injuries, and he knew he deserved them. He didn't say a word. He took it all, and secretly felt relieved that maybe now things would change. Maybe now Sophie would give up her fight, knowing he had continued deceiving her. Knowing he had done so before.

He remembered back to that day. The day he'd insisted she change her mobile number after that stupid bitch from work had got hold of it and began divulging his secrets. He'd been so shocked at Sophie's faith in his fidelity and their marriage, it was all he had needed to stop the affair at once. He remembered the vow he then made to himself and how certain he was he would never do it again.

This time was different though. That woman meant nothing to him. Abigail meant everything. Maybe now, Sophie would give up, push him away, release him from his torment.

But as Toby watched her tortured face, deformed with rage, he felt desperate to hang onto what they had. Sophie had been everything he ever wanted and their family unit and life at Nettlefield House was a thing of dreams.

He watched as Sophie, anger spent, turned suddenly, leaving him alone and felt a gap in his life he didn't recognise nor welcome. A gap even Abigail couldn't fill.

He turned towards the back of the barn, into the shadows and clenched his fist, smashing it into the wooden workbench, oblivious to the pain. He held the throbbing hand and stared up into the roof feeling the warmth of his tears slide under his chin. He missed the old Toby, the one that married Sophie, the one that made her smile. He'd been a man worth a thousand of this man he had become. The vow he made now was to get this man back.

This time his vow would be like concrete.

*

Sophie retreated into the house, locking the door behind her. The outburst had physically exhausted her, but mentally, she was still on fire. She logged onto Facebook, taking her anger onto social media, and wrote a message to Abigail.

YOU ARE A FUCKING BITCH.

Sophie knew Toby would have informed Abigail of the situation. She would have known what the message meant. Sophie didn't expect a reply. She needed to get out of the house to deal with her emotional turmoil alone, in the only way she knew could not cause further harm to anyone.

Toby had re-entered the house through the side door, courtesy of William. He made his way to the kettle and began making some tea, trying to calm her down. She pushed past him, out the side door and into the barn, grabbing her bike and a slightly worried dog.

'Where are you going? We need to talk. Don't do anything stupid.' Toby pleaded.

Ignoring him, she pushed off on her bike before hearing William's worried voice cry out.

'Mummy, what's wrong? Where are you going?'

Sophie stopped and glanced back, seeing the tense wrinkled frown across William's face. Her heart shattered under her fake smile. 'Don't worry William. I'll be back soon. Before daddy leaves. He's going away.' She glared at Toby. '… and he won't be back, *will* you?'

*

It had been a pill night, and Sophie woke early feeling like somebody else. Today was Father's Day, and she immediately gave into tears as she realised how it should normally start. Not like this, alone in her bed, whilst Toby was in a hotel somewhere. He had needed no encouragement to leave.

Sophie hated herself for the way she had told William that Daddy wouldn't be back. She had spent ages last night, reassuring him that of course Daddy would be home for Father's Day. For the boys' sake, Sophie was not going to upset the day. The story had been planned.

Daddy had spent the night at Ant's for reasons unexplained. Tonight's excuse would be created later.

Sophie lay in the bed, considering the easiest way to get through this day without the boys picking up on the knife-edge of their lives. She wanted to sink under the covers and not come up for at least a month. Instead, she rang Rani.

'Morning. Happy Father's Day.' Sophie imagined the happy family scene at Rani's house. 'Sorry to call but it all kicked off last night and I booted him out. The boys think he stayed with you. Just thought I should tell you.'

Sophie preceded to divulge the events of the day before, twiddling the duvet, creating an ever-tightening knot as she spoke.

'Good. Glad you've finally kicked him out. You were trying too hard Sophie. He's been having his cake and eating it too!'

'Yeah, I know. Hope his 'piece of cake' is having a shit Father's Day.' She smoothed out the tightly wrinkled cotton.

'I should think his 'piece of cake' is quite happy this has happened. She's probably invited him over for dinner.'

'Don't say that!' Sophie gasped, propping herself up

against the headboard. 'But you're right. She probably would, the bitch.'

Sophie had a sudden whoosh of adrenaline as an idea for revenge hit her. 'Look, I'll leave you to your day. Don't worry about me. I've just had a great idea. I'll talk to you soon,' and without waiting for a reply Sophie hung up, immediately logging onto Facebook.

Since uncovering that Toby was a Facebook user, Sophie had been educating herself on its applications. Abigail's public profile was now willingly divulging details of all six hundred of her friends and family, and Sophie was writing them down individually in her diary. She knew she could have screenshot the pages, but the cloud would have carried them straight to Toby and she had no idea how to stop that. She felt an overwhelming power at how easily she could inflict significant pain on another human being, like a criminal in possession of some illicit information that could start a war.

These six hundred friends would be offering Abigail support and love on this emotive day, erasing the pain and hurt, telling her children what a strong and selfless mother she was after her husband's affair tore their life apart.

Abigail meanwhile was dishing out the same poison to another wife and family and Sophie couldn't let that go by unpunished. Her friends and family should know the truth, and Sophie could tell them. She could tell them all, right now on Facebook on this special day. But perhaps, she deduced, there was more power in *not* doing it.

The message she sent instead was blackmail, but Sophie couldn't have cared less.

> Sophie:
>
> If you go near my husband again, I promise I will make your life hell. I have a list of all your friends and family from Facebook and will tell them all what a home-wrecking bitch you are if you so much as speak to him again. You should have known better and stayed away. I am now having to lie to my two little boys about where their dad is and when he will be back. I will never forget this, and although in time I may forgive Toby, I will never forgive you. Stay away from my husband and go to hell.

Would she carry out the threat? Sophie knew immediately that she wouldn't. She knew Abigail's children, and she couldn't, as a mother, hurt them that way. It was a shame Abigail didn't share the same morals.

Sophie re-read the message as she waited for the symbol to appear, showing that Abigail had read it. She could feel the return of her strength; her tenacity to never give up. Abigail couldn't have Toby anymore because *he* would no longer exist. Sophie *would* get her old Toby back, the other half of her.

It was simply too soon to give up on that.

24

Friday, 21ˢᵗ June 2013

It was forecast to be a glorious weekend. The heatwave that had been promised for so long was finally here and Toby was due home any moment from his week in a bed and breakfast. Sophie hoped it had been as basic as it looked in the photos when she'd booked it. This was not a reward; it was his punishment and he had accepted it silently, disappearing at the end of Father's Day, once the boys were in bed. The rooms didn't have en suites, and the building stood on a main road near his office. Sophie suspected it was full of half-broken, adulterous men, and she had happily added Toby to the pot.

Ever since he had left, Sophie had been working to understand her emotions. Being honest with herself and trusting them to carry her in the right direction, unafraid of her vulnerability. She frowned as she watched the driveway, unwillingly accepting how she was looking forward to his return. She couldn't stop the hope emanating from her every pore that he would, if she allowed him, beg her to reconcile their marriage. She calmly turned away from the door as Toby let himself in.

'It's so good to be back. I've had so much time to think. We're going to be okay, Sophie.' He said as he spotted her standing, waiting. 'I'm going to make it okay. For you, for me, for the boys. We're gonna be good again, I promise.'

If he had a tail, it would have been tightly tucked between his legs, with just the end quivering in nervousness. He had a sorrowful look, a deeply sad droop to his whole face, but with a gentle smile, sucking her back in.

'Is it?' Sophie stared him straight in the eyes and her stomach flipped as she saw her old Toby deep within. She couldn't hate this man as she knew she should. She wanted to carry on loving him and carry on having the life she had mapped out in front of her. The life she had dreamt of for her and her boys. The invisible winch kept winding her towards him and she was powerless to stop.

'I've booked us a counselling session. It's next week. I know I said I didn't want to but you're right, we need professional help.' His smile creased his eyes and they sparkled in response.

'Help to mend us. Or help to end us?' Sophie couldn't help the sarcasm.

Toby didn't answer. 'We're gonna be okay. I haven't started things up again with her. I never did. It was only ever over the phone. I promise. You must believe me. I'm begging you.' He offered his arms to her. 'Can I give you a hug?'

The invisible winch retracted the rest of its line and

Sophie felt as secure and strong in his arms as the tightly wound metal rope in its coil.

*

The morning of the counselling session came amid a heatwave that was scorching the earth and shrivelling up what little grass was left in the fields at Nettlefield House. The last few days since his return home had been consumed with the boys' activities and Toby's work, with little opportunity for further discussion. Sophie couldn't help but think they were both holding off any true actions for reconciliation till after today's session.

The session started where all therapy seems to commence, in childhood. This hadn't worried Sophie. Apart from her disappointment that no present under the Christmas tree ever barked, she'd had a happy childhood.

However, it soon transpired to the three people in the little windowless room that Toby hadn't. He cried as he recounted how he felt a lack of love, a lack of physical touch as a child. He spoke of parents who retreated into separate lives and separate bedrooms from as early as he could remember, to the detriment of his emotional balance. It wasn't a sad childhood, but it had a massive chunk missing that Sophie's had in abundance.

Her heart went out to him, crying as he was in front of a stranger, wondering how she had never known this before; never realised the significance behind his parents' choice of bedroom at Nettlefield house. She moved her chair closer, taking his hand in her lap, showing her sympathy.

They discussed their early marriage and how absolutely

right it had been. There were no doubts or hesitations about their commitment and life had been kind, leading them easily into Sophie's dream of a country house with land and stables. It was what they had both come to want, but somewhere along the way, they had forgotten about each other. They had forgotten how to communicate, how to speak each other's language. Sophie was surprised to hear there were five different languages of love you needed to speak to have a fulfilling relationship.

'How do we not know this?' Sophie questioned. 'Why do they not teach this at school or at least give it out in a leaflet at the wedding.' Sophie laughed, relieved to find there was something they were doing wrong, which simply meant they could put it right.

'Well, it's not too late to learn. It's a bit more than a leaflet but all the information is here, including an exercise for you to complete. It'll explain your preferred language of love, then you will both be able to speak and understand each other perfectly. It's powerful stuff!' The counsellor handed them both the paper.

Toby looked across at Sophie and smiled, seemingly pleased there was something powerful they could share. 'I know it was your dream, Sophie. But truthfully, I found it all rather overwhelming, owning that house. What with my job and the boys being so young. I think I'd have been happy with just the sit-on lawnmower and the gas barbecue!'

'But you never said. You loved the house? It was you that persuaded me to buy it! How did it all go so wrong?'

The counsellor waited patiently for them to stop talking,

then turned to Sophie and said, 'Sophie, you are right, he should have said, but perhaps he didn't think he could. You are a strong character with a determined mind and your dream had come true. Maybe Toby didn't get a chance to vocalise his concerns. He should have, but he didn't. Perhaps your dominance, over time, may have begun to rule the relationship. I'm not placing blame anywhere, but I've a lovely story to tell you to illustrate what I mean. Would you like to hear it?'

The story was from the book, Men are from Mars, by John Grey. It was about a knight in shining armour who rescued a damsel in distress from a dragon. Like all good fairy tales, they fell in love and were meant to live happily ever after. However, when the next dragon came, the now less distressed damsel, insisted her knight use a different method to slay it. He did as she instructed and was successful, but he felt less worthy of her admiration as a result. As the dragons came and went, the knight became annoyed with his interfering princess. After several more months, he was drawn to the cries of another damsel in distress and resorted to his original, trusted method of slaying the dragon. He felt proud, confident, and alive again, so he never returned. Instead, he lived happily ever after with this new, non-interfering damsel.

'You have to drop the reins, Sophie.' The counsellor stated. 'Allow Toby to pick them up. When he does, and you need to give him the time, then balance will be restored. Then you can repair.'

The realisation of this dynamic in the relationship made

Sophie accept, totally, the concept of letting go of the reins. Perhaps her dominance *had* been destructive. Maybe she *was* emasculating him. Perhaps within every man there should always be a knight in shining armour. She desperately wanted to find Toby's.

Maybe that's what Abigail had found. She made him feel like an adored man.

I make him feel like an unloved wimp. Sophie felt a renewed hope that perhaps if Toby drove the marriage without her interference or pressure, they could correct the imbalance that may have contributed to Toby seeking fulfilment elsewhere. It wouldn't be all they needed but the counsellor had apparently lived through exactly that and was still successfully married twenty-five-years later.

It was a powerful beam of hope that Sophie clung to as they left the session. She wouldn't give up. She had to give him another chance. He had begged for it, the counsellor supported it, and the boys deserved it.

*

Later that night, motivated by the desire to do it right, Sophie encouraged Toby into the Room of Pain, with its fairy lights twinkling in the setting sun. Their homework from the session was to encourage each other to be honest and strong. To be that knight in shining armour and to be that damsel in distress.

Toby admitted to Sophie that although he had not had face-to-face contact with Abigail since the affair was uncovered, he *had* been tempted to meet up. As he spoke,

Sophie could see his body language changing, the slump in his shoulders and the saddened tone of his voice.

He put his legs up on the chair beside him, reclined back, and stared out into the dark as he owned up to his temptation, looking nothing like the knight in shining armour she was waiting for.

Sophie was desperate to stick to the counsellor's plan, so she became the damsel and told Toby about her distress. She admitted how close she had come to telling William everything, when he'd accidentally spilt his milk last week. She told Toby how she had reacted to this accident by smashing the glass into the table with a howl of anger and pain, nearly cutting her hand in two.

'Has Daddy done something wrong?' William had said, so quietly, yet with so much maturity and thought. He must have known it was not the milk that caused the anger and tears.

Sophie's mind had spoken its silent revenge. *Yes, he has. He's done this to me, to us. He loves her more.* But she'd mopped up the milk and the tears she couldn't hide, and instead had said, 'Don't be silly. Of course Daddy hasn't done anything wrong.'

Taking revenge at that time would have been a pleasurable power, but it was not a feeling she would permit when her children would suffer because of it.

She hoped, by making Toby aware of how close she had come to telling the boys, he would have more reason to destroy the part of his brain oblivious to feelings other than Abigail. But sitting here now in the Room of Pain, after hours of discussion about the marriage, he didn't even react to her story. He didn't adjust his position; his eyes displayed no fear at what she had nearly divulged to his children.

'D'you not care if I tell the boys?' Sophie watched his expressionless face and lowered her voice. 'I could tell them so easily. I could make them hate you. How can you not care?'

Toby slowly raised his eyes and said, 'Because I deserve it.' His face began to crumble. 'I don't deserve to be your knight in shining armour. I don't deserve to be their dad.' His lips were trembling, and he turned to stare out the window.

'But you can stop this, Toby. You can make this all okay. Why won't you just make this all okay?'

The reins Sophie had optimistically dropped earlier today were hanging as loose as ever. They were on the verge of being snapped by the proverbial grazing pony, about to step on them. Sophie followed his stare and looked out into the night too, a single tear rolling down her cheek.

'I miss you so much. Not who you are now. I miss my old Toby. Has he truly gone? I'm so lonely without him. Will he ever be back?'

Across the table, the knight in shining armour looked as rusty as ever and would still not pick up his steed's reins. He could offer nothing more than his pondering stare into the dark night beyond. For the first time ever, looking across at him now, Sophie accepted that her Toby may never be back. It was quite probable that he was gone and lost forever.

'I can't do this on my own, Toby. How many more times

can I pick myself up and dust myself down?' She willed him to look at her.

He didn't react. He just kept staring into the nothingness.

'I hate this house; I hate this damn conservatory. You've made this dream a flipping nightmare. You've ruined everything. I don't want it anymore.' She had an overwhelming need to leave him in Nettlefield House. To find a new reality, her new future, for her and the boys. She walked out of the conservatory without saying another word and in her peripheral vision, caught Toby finally move. But it was simply to top up his half-empty glass of wine.

Sophie crept into the boys' room, where they lay sleeping, oblivious. William's eyes twitched as she kissed his head, and she willed for him to wake. She longed to tell him what she was planning. How the roller coaster of emotions from today's events had led her to a re-evaluation of their situation. He would sense things were changing. He would worry about her. She hated leaving them in the middle of the night, without explanation, but she had an overwhelming need to get out of the house, to plan and protect against the worst possible scenario that now didn't seem far away.

She wouldn't drop the reins on the protection and care of the boys. She needed contingency against Toby's irrational, changeable decisions and just a few rapidly sent text messages settled the arrangements.

She went into her bedroom and without much thought, threw a few items of clothing and cosmetics into a bag. She spotted her diary on the bedside table and ripped out a page. She felt compelled to write.

Toby,

Tonight, I've handed over the reins, and you didn't even flinch. (Do you even want them?) I'm worried that you won't ever pick them up and I cannot leave the fate of me and the boys in your hands if that's the case. I hate this house now. I feel so lonely, I want to go home to Bromford. To work out what options there might be, for me, for the boys… and maybe… one day … for you?

I don't want to regret anything or think I could have done more. Please become my knight in shining armour and let me be your damsel in distress. I know I can do it, but can you? Be the man you'd like your boys to become. I know you can become a great knight. Be proud of what you have achieved before all this, and what you have in your life. Gain massive strength and belief from knowing that even after everything, I'm still here. Be confident, be committed, and have conviction. No half measures, no what-ifs, no buts. There is no try. Just do it or don't.

I don't know what's at the end of this. I'm giving no guarantees. I've never done this before. it's just you and me … how can that be hard? Ultimately, I can't show you I love you any more than with the fact I'm still here. Embrace this challenge and take all my love or let me go. It's your choice. Either way, be bold and choose!

I love this quote by Goethe:

'Whatever you can do or dream you can begin it. Boldness has genius, power, and magic in it. Begin it now.'

(I doubt you know who Goethe is, but he's basically Germany's equivalent to Shakespeare and was a very wise man!)

So please. Be like Goethe. Begin it!

Just writing these words made Sophie feel bold and brave. She didn't want to have any regrets that she could have done more, dreamt harder. She wanted Toby to see it as an inspiring, motivational note, empowering him to make a choice, any choice, either choice, instead of this nothingness in-between.

She left the note on his pillow. Whatever happened next, Sophie needed the power and magic that Goethe promised, and she needed Toby to find it too.

She walked back into the Room of Pain with a small bag over her shoulder and found Toby caressing the bottle of red wine that was his refuge. He didn't look up.

'I'm going away. I'll take the dogs. The horses will be fine but please keep an eye on them and do the chickens. I'll call the boys in the morning. There's only one football match tomorrow so you'll manage. There's food in the fridge. I'll be back Sunday night. I need to get out of this house.' Sophie turned as soon as she had spoken, not wanting to see his lack of reaction or feel any further rejection.

As she walked through the kitchen and out the side door, she thought she heard him scrape back his chair. She paused, walked slowly to the car, and waited a moment before encouraging the dogs to jump in the back. Then she climbed in and started the ignition. As she pulled out onto the road, she glanced over her shoulder and could see no sign of any movement from the house. Toby had not pushed back his chair to stop her from leaving.

As she flew down the motorway, she contemplated how this sudden departure felt like a research mission for a new action plan or was it simply her protection policy? She wasn't sure which. She would need to look at schools for the boys, stables for the horses, and availability and pricing of rental houses before a new life in her hometown of Bromford became an option either way.

Nettlefield House was a dream that had turned into a nightmare, and she didn't want to stay there a second longer. That was the place where new Toby lived, where her heart had been broken, each room carrying a different painful reminder. She felt a tear escape from her eye as she remembered the little thatched cottage on the bridleway where old Toby used to live. They had been happy there; it had been a simpler life.

Sophie would give anything to be able to go back, but she knew that the past is not somewhere you should live. She sniffed hard and wiped her eyes, refusing to let the emotions out, instead she spoke sternly to the dogs.

'The only thing that lasts forever is change and positive

change is what this trip is about, so I don't want any moaning about the lack of rabbits from you two!'

She smiled to herself as the light pollution of London encroached.

25

Sunday, 30th June 2013

Sophie's research mission to Bromford was a success. The rental market was expensive but plentiful, the schools were excellent, and the stables, whilst currently full, had willingly placed two of her three horses onto its waiting list.

Her three sisters had been unanimous in their belief that she should return south, with or without Toby, and Sophie had been caught up in their enthusiasm for her potential new life. It had all felt like a guilty pleasure, creating plans without Toby, and the hint of release simultaneously scared and excited her in its possibilities.

The long drive back to Nettlefield House flew by as each possibility whirled around Sophie's head, clearly mapping out a new path.

Bolstered by her newfound confidence, Sophie cheerily shared her findings to Toby over a late dinner, emphasizing her preference that this move south *could* be as a family, as a team. She didn't want him to think she was giving up on the marriage. It wouldn't be easy, but a move to Bromford, away from the memories and the presence of Abigail could be the first step in repairing this marriage.

She hoped her enthusiasm gave Toby a similar conviction, but he remained in the same impassive stupor he had been in when she had left. Sophie wasn't surprised, and to a certain extent, felt vindicated that her research mission had in fact been absolutely necessary. She was doing everything she could to protect the boys and provide a future. He was still doing nothing and tonight, Sophie cared a little less.

As they were walking towards their separate bedrooms, Sophie played devil's advocate.

'Come to bed with me tonight?' She paused at the top landing, feeling vulnerable and slightly scared he might agree. She tilted her head and smouldered, a damsel in distress. 'Just tonight? I need you. Let's just be close for once?'

Toby didn't make eye contact. He spoke quietly, lacking conviction. 'I can't ... It wouldn't be right.'

'Right? It's fine. Really, it is. I want you to. I need you.' Sophie was surprised he hadn't grabbed her olive branch with both hands and pulled her in tight, but he was already walking towards his bedroom. 'Why not?' she said to his back.

'It just feels wrong,' he said, without turning around. Then more quietly, '... as though I was betraying Abigail.'

Sophie wanted to take her olive branch and flail him around the head with it. 'Oh, yes, silly me. Don't want to upset Abigail, do we? And you think I should believe you that you're not still seeing her?' She glared at the back of his balding head. 'What am I? A flipping idiot?' She hushed the last words so as not to wake the boys then turned to her room, mentally snapping the olive branch in two before tossing it over her shoulder along with her feelings of guilt at making such extensive plans without the other half of her.

*

When Sophie woke, she reached for her diary and began filling in the gaps from the last few days in Bromford. She spotted the large, black number at the top of the page, not quite believing that today was the first day of July. That meant there were just nineteen days till the boys broke up for their school summer holidays and she smiled. Her research mission to Bromford had not managed to jolt Toby into a decision or choice, but maybe her newly formed plan, to commence in nineteen days, would.

She looked out the window to her beloved horses and the realisation of what this plan meant, made her chest tighten and her smile disappear. She willed herself to breathe deeply, as she accepted, she had every reason to do this. No one would blame her. She wasn't giving up on the marriage, she was simply giving him the space and freedom to choose.

Once the boys were at school, Sophie called Rani. She needed extra endorsement for her new plan, to help alleviate her guilt and she knew Rani would willingly oblige.

'So, what d'you think? Should I take the boys away for the whole summer? Threaten not to return? Is that too cruel?'

'I can't believe you're even asking. If it was me, I'd have left him ages ago. What exactly are you waiting for?'

'He has to make the choice. I'm not choosing for him. But you're right. I *shouldn't* stay here a moment longer waiting for his decision. Not with the man he's become.' Sophie looked around as she spoke, noticing the empty bottles of wine to the side of the bin. An indication as to how Toby had consoled himself over the weekend. The sight made her sad. Sad that he found his solace in five bottles of wine instead of in his forgiving wife, still hoping to make everything okay. 'Yes, it'll be good for the boys and summer at Granny's will be good for me too. Who knows where we'll end up after that?'

'What do you want me to say, Sophie? I don't want you to move, of course I don't, but I really feel like Bromford is where you'll end up, with or without Toby, together or apart. It's where your family are, and it's only natural you'll want to be close to them. I know you, and you'll succeed, whatever you do. Wow, I'll miss you though. Can't believe I'm telling you to go.'

Sophie could hear the tremble in her voice. 'Listen, don't say anything to Ant, I don't want Toby to find out just yet. I need time to work out how to tell him. I wish I knew for sure he was still seeing Abigail. I wish I had something more to give me the justification it's the right decision.'

'Ask for his phone bill again, that worked last time, didn't it?' Rani's voice had returned to full strength.

'Yeah, but he promised he hasn't spoken to her since. He swore it. Oh why can't he just sort himself out? Argh!' Sophie picked up a bottle and tossed it in the recycling bin, dispelling some of her frustration through the satisfying clink of glass on glass. 'D'you think he's depressed? He's drinking too much. Shall I book a doctor's appointment for him?'

'Oh, don't be stupid, he knows exactly what he's doing. Pushing you away, waiting for *you* to end the marriage then he'll go running to her. Ask for his bill, Sophie. Or better still, intercept it. My bills are all online now, his could be too. Could you guess his passwords? Get your evidence, then for God's sake give up on the marriage. I'm sorry I know I shouldn't say this but you are driving me mad.'

Sophie laughed at Rani's frustrations with a pang of regret she would be moving so far away from her best friend and confidant.

Once they had hung up. Sophie went into the office to find an old paper bill, one from before Abigail, at a time when Toby had no need to cover his steps. His filing system had always been meticulous, so she found one easily, hoping to find something that would enable her to log into his account. She entered Toby's email address into the O2 homepage and made her first attempt at his password. The computer beeped and an error message popped up; Email address not registered.

Sophie tried another, older email address, Toby used occasionally. But the same error message appeared. Then her heart quickened as she foolishly realised it would be his work email. It was after all his work phone. 'God you're stupid,' she said out loud as she typed it in.

'Email address not registered', reappeared.

Sophie slumped back in the chair, quizzically studying the screen, when she spotted the flashing words, 'sign up now for online billing'. She couldn't believe it would be true but maybe Toby had never signed up to begin with. She quickly typed in all the relevant details, rapidly filling the blank boxes with personal information a loving wife would know but feeling more like a naughty child. Mother's maiden name, date of birth, payment method on account. She held her breath as she clicked 'submit.'

Magically, a page loaded, shouting at the top, 'View latest bill. Download PDF '. It was dated two days ago.

Sophie did view it. And it filled in all the gaps. The number she knew so well still repeatedly called, still repeatedly messaged. Sophie wanted to find the evidence they had been meeting too but O2 billing didn't itemise that. Regardless, it gave her all the authority she needed to justify leaving for the summer.

Evidence collected, she had the foresight to redirect the notification emails to her own address, covering up all traces of her forced deceit. Toby would never know, and she wanted to keep it that way. She wasn't going to confront him with it, she wanted him to be honest, own up to it without the evidence in black and white. She wanted to see just how far his lies went and for how long.

Just nineteen more days.

*

Over the next few weeks, Sophie realised Toby was reading her diaries. She didn't care; he was pretty much writing her story for her, but the lack of any significant verbal conversation gave extra weight to their written words. Whether he read them on paper or listened to them, Sophie knew from experience it would make no difference, but the simple fact he was bothered enough to comment pleased her. Their new method of communication, from the 8th July, suited her fine.

> I know I shouldn't read your diary, but I want to say I'm not giving up on us. I know I'm in a world of confusion and I'm driving you mad, but I really do want to snap out of it. I'm trying hard. Please let me keep trying. Please be patient. I love you. Sleep well. T

Sophie took up the dialogue that night, sarcastically questioning him as to what trying 'soft' would look like if his current actions were trying 'hard'? Her words crossed over to fill the pages of two whole days. They were simply a summary of everything he had put her through; all the situations she had endured, all the pain he had caused, and all the reasons why he had no right to ask for patience. She had written them for her own cathartic therapy as well as for him to read. Her words ended by formally confirming her plans for the summer.

> *So, I'm going away at the end of term. I'm taking the boys and the dogs and I'm leaving you to sort out your confusion and decide once and for all. I refuse to do it for you. I'm not giving up on this marriage, it has to be*

your choice. I'm going to Mum's, and I can't guarantee when we will be back, if at all.

The scribbled dialogues continued, each capturing their innermost thoughts and feelings under the fake presumption of a diary's privacy. But no one wrote a conclusion. Even their latest marriage guidance session ended without a positive result.

The counsellor didn't seem to know what to do with them. She had tried and failed to correct the wrong and concluded that perhaps a separation was, in fact, the right thing to do. To give credibility to this solution, she booked their next appointment for three months' time.

Sophie knew she wouldn't be attending. With this professional approval, she now knew for certain she would be over a hundred miles away by then, with or without Toby.

Sophie was not surprised to read the last diary entry from Toby on the 18th July. Abigail had just left for a two-week holiday, so understandably, he was feeling lonely and unloved. Her damaged heart healed just a little at his timely misfortune as she read his words.

> I want to leave the last few months behind me and bury it. I know you can never forget it, and I'm so scared I've lost you. I beg you not to close the door on us. Please don't punish me. The bloke I am is the person you've known for the last 13 years, not the monster I've become. I want more than anything to fix our marriage, to show you how much I love you. Please give me a

chance to finally be the man, husband, and friend I was before and can be again.

I know you want to move to Bromford permanently, I want to come with you. We can all start again, build a simpler life, and be happy. I know we can. Please keep the door open for me, Sophie. I love you with all my heart. I want you, not Abigail. How could I ever think otherwise?

All my love, always, Toby xxx

Sophie didn't write a response. Nothing was going to change her plans, and in just over a week she would have the next black and white PDF displaying line by line, number by number, exactly how much he really wanted her over Abigail.

*

Ten days later, happily ensconced in the comfort and love of her parent's home; Sophie gazed out across the valley. The scorching summer had meant an early harvest, leaving the fields covered in stripes as the evening sun cast its long shadows on the mounds of discarded straw. Sophie would never tire of this dynamic view, changing with the seasons and was content to think she would see a little more of it once she had moved to Bromford.

Even her parents seemed to support her decision to spend the summer away from Toby. Her dad viewed it as taking a break, time to breathe, in order to put things right. Her mum simply referenced the pleasures of living a simpler life and how happy she would be to help if they ultimately moved to Bromford.

Sophie hadn't spoken to Toby since she'd left, hadn't even answered his messages, she'd just allowed the transfer of her phone to the boys when he called, before quickly leaving the room so as not to hear how much they missed him.

As the boys handed back her phone after one such call, she suddenly remembered something pressing she should have done a few days before. Her adrenaline spiked as she ran upstairs to her laptop, willing the old machine to come to life quicker. She lay on the bed, legs crossed, her feet tapping against each other as she typed in her password and watched impatiently for the screen to load.

Letting out a bigger breath than she realised she was holding, the PDF eventually appeared. She rapidly scanned through the lines of print and numbers, noticing the unusual frequency of her own number appearing, but couldn't see Abigail's. Her first thought was that Toby had stuck to his word and had stopped all contact.

Or maybe Rani *had* told Ant about the online billing and he'd told Toby, who was now secretly calling Abigail on a new phone the second he had finished talking to the boys. But then her memory kicked in. 'Damn. She's in flipping Spain, no wonder he keeps ringing me.'

Sophie slammed the laptop, frustrated she would now have to wait another four weeks till she could search for new evidence, then went downstairs to catch the last of the sunset over the stripey fields.

*

It was mid-August when Sophie received a detailed communication from Toby. His obvious frustration at not being able to speak to her meant his words arrived securely via Royal Mail Special Delivery. The premium paper was cream, with an embossed, orange butterfly at the top of each page. There were seven pages of A5, written in blue fountain pen.

Special writing paper for his special words, Sophie mocked. She doubted she would be reading anything she hadn't read or heard before.

Taking herself away from the boys and her parents, carrying a large mug of sympathetic tea, she began to read.

> To My Dearest Darling Sophie,
>
> Well, I don't know if you approve of my paper. I thought the butterfly was a great symbol of our transformation, of being whole again. Two halves coming together in perfect symmetry. Plus this will likely be the most important letter I ever write, so the least I can do is use a decent pen and paper!
>
> I've spent a long time the last few weeks, without you here, thinking about our early days and how wonderful and happy we were. Everything felt so natural. We were soulmates, and we used to say, 'We're the same,' then laugh. I still think we are. I'm laughing now just thinking of our sameness back then. We just lost focus on the amazing relationship we had. But throughout it all, I loved you totally.
>
> I then made the biggest mistake of my entire life. I can't stand to even write about it. I look back on it now,

dumbfounded by what I did. I thought I wanted something else. I retract everything I've ever said to you about not being in love with you. I sit here in total disbelief that I—a good man, a dependable father, and husband—could do what I did and take so long to get out of it.

Well, it's been four weeks, and the old Toby is back for good. The best of me has finally come after the worst of me has finally gone. All I want to do now is show you how sorry I am for the pain and suffering I put you through and make us right again. You can push me away again and again, but I <u>will</u> take it, and I <u>will</u> get back up again to support you and get us through it. I'm so remorseful, I'm determined to go through whatever is necessary to put our family back together.

It's been the hardest few weeks of my life not being with you all, but I know that pales compared to the pain I've put you through. Why did I need so many chances from you? Why the hell has it taken me so long to get back to being me? How could I possibly ever put everything at risk and even suggest that I wanted out of it? I will never truly get my head around it, but I do know beyond a shadow of a doubt that the real me is back. I think you have always been convinced that, at some point, the good, solid, dependable Toby would reappear and say it's all okay. Well, he has and I'm here! I want to start afresh nearer our families too. I can change my job to something less stressful and focus purely on us as a family, with you and me being the most important part. Please give me this final chance to

> be the man, husband and father I should have been. I'm a good bloke deep down, and I'll finally put things right.
>
> I love you with all my heart, Sophie Cooper, and one day, I want to put a proper, big ring on your finger and recommit to you for the next forty years.
>
> All my love,
>
> Toby xxx

His words seemed genuine, making decisions, pushing for change. It was everything Sophie wanted to hear. He seemed to be truly recognising the extent of what he was giving up, repenting every action, suffering. She took unexpected pleasure from that.

She stored it in her diary. Knowing that every night she would glimpse the orange embossed butterfly, knowing what was written beneath and her feelings of hope would grow. Maybe Toby *had* committed one hundred per cent to his new ways, and maybe things *would* be different in Bromford. Even the most recent O2 inquiry concurred, as it produced another PDF displaying a multitude of calls to herself with none to Abigail.

Who knows? By Christmas this year we could all be in Bromford, and this nightmare could be a distant memory.

Sophie knew she had to return to Nettlefield House for the start of the school term, but she was more optimistic than ever that she could at last plan and instigate positive, lasting change. The novelty of feeling back in control was intoxicating.

But novelties wear off.

26

Tuesday, 1ˢᵗ October 2013

A month had passed since Sophie's return to Nettlefield House and the damsel in distress act had to go. She needed to pick up the reins of this marriage if they were going to make a successful move south and as Demanding Drema still took all of Toby's time, it was left to her.

She tried to involve Toby in the discussions, usually over dinner once the boys were in bed, but he rarely had anything to add or any requests for change. It was as if he was relieved someone else was taking control, making all the decisions for him, until the physical move to Bromford would force his head out of the sand.

They were still in their separate bedrooms, coexisting in the expansive house, but with the PDFs from the phone bill continuing to show Toby's abstinence, Sophie was positive and optimistic. Now she had hold of the reins, she wasn't letting them go.

'The only problem is the schools.' She began tonight's

conversation over a pizza dinner, overcooked due to the massive preoccupation in her mind. 'You can't even begin to put their names down till you're physically living within the catchment area, and for that good school, it's less than a fifth of a mile.' She paused, waiting for his reaction, but received none.

'It's a nightmare. We're going to have to rent that little house I told you about, take the boys out of school before the end of term, and move in. Then, with any luck, they'll get a place for the New Year. If they don't, I'll home-school them.'

Toby came to life with a grin on his face. 'Best of luck with that, home-schooling Michael. Rather you than me!'

'I'll have nothing else to do. Will I?' she couldn't help the bitterness. 'It's not like I've got a job, and I'm hardly going to be busy looking after the house and animals, am I?'

'What was the rental figure for here again?' Toby gestured with his head to the large house he sat in, ignoring his wife's question. 'We need to be careful how we financially cover this place and Bromford.'

Sophie knew the rental income from Nettlefield House would be more than enough. She had done her sums and had shared them with Toby a few days ago. If he'd forgotten that was his problem, she was getting fed up with his lack of attention to what was the single most important change in their world right now.

She didn't hide her thoughts. 'That's *so* not the most important thing here Toby. I've already told you it's financially comfortable.' She hated repeating herself and even now could see his mind wandering, picking the burnt bits of pepperoni off his pizza. She wanted to poke him with a pin. 'Listen. I'm taking the boys and all the animals to a tiny, crappy house, just so we can be in the catchment for the good school because you've made staying here impossible. That's it. That's the priority. It's the only decision available to us.' She spoke faster and louder as her emotions built. 'If it means a few months of minor hardship, then I'm not sure you have the right to complain. Either you're with us, or you're not. The priority is getting out of here and getting the boys into the school. That's it,' and she slashed her hand through the air to reinforce her point.

'Right. Yes, of course,' was Toby's answer.

Without expecting further contribution to the plans, Sophie went to say goodnight to the boys. As she climbed the stairs, she felt a new emotion creeping up her chest and realised with satisfaction and a smile what it was. Apathy.

She had read in the self-help books that the opposite of love isn't hate as everyone believes. Hatred means there are still strong emotions attached. Hate is only there because of the love; one cannot exist without the other. Now she felt apathy; the true, exact opposite of love.

Finally, she no longer held enough love for the man downstairs to fuel her hatred. This new emotion was going to be essential to ensure the smooth transfer of their life down south. What would happen to it once they were settled, she would worry about then.

*

Toby watched his wife leave the room; glad the conversation was over. He didn't want to talk anymore. Every night there was a new plan, a suggestion, or a new decision to make. He was tired of it. She was moving to Bromford; he would stay in Nettlefield House till they found a tenant and to be close to work, *then* he would worry about what came next.

He had been so certain over the summer; so convinced he knew what he wanted. He had deleted Abigail from his phone and would only answer calls with caller ID. He had only ridden his bike with Ant and was no longer part of the triathlon club. He had done everything he should have done months ago, and whilst Sophie had been away it had felt good.

So why now she's back does it feel so wrong? He looked into the depths of his red wine.

Since Sophie had returned from the summer, he felt shackled and chained to a dominant force he couldn't escape. He felt trapped, craving his freedom. He knew it was his fault he hadn't picked up the reins, that they were moving south, and he knew the right thing to do would be to go with them, but at times it just felt so wrong. He was in two minds about what freedom really meant to him.

Freedom to get back with Abigail, or freedom to resolve this crisis and get back to being the man he used to be? He took a large swig of wine, looking for the answer in the bottom of the glass before topping it up with the last of the bottle. He knew Sophie frowned on his drinking, especially on a school night, so he quietly put the empty bottle straight into the recycling, hidden under the mountain of empty plastic milk bottles.

*

Sophie worked tirelessly over the next few weeks, moving the contents of Nettlefield House into their temporary storage area in the barn, cleaning the house from top to bottom as she went. She held onto a large quantity of furniture and antique items, ever hopeful that another large, country house would be in her future and prayed that the barn would keep them dry and free from rats.

Many people had turned up over the past few weeks to collect items placed for sale on Facebook or eBay, each taking with them a different part of her dream. There was the sale of her brightly coloured show jumps, usually set up as a mini-course in the field, which she loved looking at through her bedroom window.

Dear old Snowy had already gone. Sold very cheaply to a close friend as a companion pony. The Bromford stables didn't have the space for three new residents and the expense wasn't justified for what would simply become an expensive lawnmower. Breaking the news to the boys and the subsequent sad goodbye to such a large part of her old dream broke off a different piece of her heart.

But the most heartbreaking sale was the five-berth caravan Sophie loved. As she stepped inside to remove their personal belongings, its nostalgic smell twisted her stomach with sorrow. She gazed at the wall behind the boys' bunk beds and their many colourful drawings, haphazardly stuck up with Blu Tack. They had painted such innocent, childish scenes of each place they had visited, complete with out of proportion people and extra-large dogs. As she carefully prised them from the wall, she was cruelly reminded of the happy family trips they had made and the future memories that would no longer be theirs to have.

Toby put his arms around her as it was hitched off the drive by its new owners and whispered, 'Don't be sad. We'll get another one. A better one. And we'll have loads of lovely family holidays again, I promise.'

Sophie allowed herself a moment of hope and silently agreed. She knew he had chosen someone else over her, over the caravan, over the family holidays to come. His words, like so many before, were quickly null and void, yet they could never entirely erase the hope in Sophie's mind.

*

By the beginning of December, Sophie was ready for their move south and Nettlefield House and grounds were finally ready for a tenant. She'd left behind some essential items for Toby, for when he might return to be nearer to work, but essentially, her work was done.

In just a few days, Sophie and the boys would be moving into the two-bedroom, squashed Victorian terrace in Bromford. It had a downstairs bathroom straight off the kitchen, which meant both rooms had mould on the walls and a wet floor that moved when you stood on it. The smell of damp was masked by the stale smoke from the previous tenants, and Sophie prayed the agent was correct in saying the smell would dissipate in time.

There was no parking, so she would have to fight the thousand other neighbours for the nearest permit place, which could mean finally settling on a location five minutes' walk away. The garden was minuscule, overlooked from every angle. It had the luxury of a patch of rough grass and one tree, plus an old wooden shed, smaller than the toilet in their caravan.

The house was a massive compromise, but the rent was cheap, and most importantly, it was within the catchment of the good school. Plus, it was less than a five-minute walk to all three of Sophie's sisters.

*

The day before the move, under a dark and drizzly sky, Sophie took Juno out on his last ride around the open countryside. She had been trying to be enthusiastic about closing the door on her old dream, hopeful that she might uncover a different dream in her new life, but she was riddled with doubt and the miserable weather seemed to concur.

'Thank goodness you're coming with me, Juno. It's gonna be different, but there'll always be a place for you, just won't be in my back garden!' Sophie spoke out loud to the horse as she tightened up his girth and got ready to mount.

'We've got to stay happy. We're gonna have a great Christmas in Bromford and I like positive numbers, so 2014 is going to be a great year. Flipping 2013 has been really shit, don't know how I'd have coped without you,' and she swung her leg over, landing gently in the saddle and rode off through the orchard, out onto the road.

As she listened to the calming, rhythmic sound of Juno's hooves hitting the tarmac, she remembered back to last year's Christmas with Rani and Ant, when life was more as she had planned. She had barely spoken to Rani over the last few months. It was as if their friendship couldn't survive the fracture of the marriage, and now with the move a hundred miles away, it was likely they would rarely see each other anymore.

This loss of a friend and the sadness of the journey that had brought her to this point, compressed the wet drizzle into a cloud of doom, which followed Sophie as she turned off the main road and kicked off for her last ride across the fields.

'Make the most of this, Juno,' she spoke out loud. 'Next week, it's all gonna be concrete paths, lorries, fumes and going round in circles on rubberised surfaces.'

She rode out toward the long track that wrapped around the back of Nettlefield House, taking her favourite circular route across fields and byways that eventually crossed over the motorway and bypassed the services, before returning through the quaint village. It had begun raining heavily, and the ground underfoot was slippery with the surface moisture.

Sophie felt like releasing her reins, letting go completely, and galloping across the fields, unhindered by what was safe or indeed permitted. Equally, she wanted to take her time. She didn't want her last ride to be over too soon and held her face up to the sky allowing the rain to pound her cheeks.

They trotted slowly, Juno's head down low to the rain, and approached the beginning of the footbridge over the motorway.

Sophie pulled Juno up short, listening to the roar below, feeling the shuddering of concrete as lorries stormed underneath.

Usually, Juno became scatty at this point, fidgeting in anticipation of the thundering traffic beneath his feet. Today, however, perhaps sensing the sadness of his rider, he stood still, taking the uncharacteristic, mature role in their relationship. Sophie simply sat and absorbed the latent energy in the half-ton of warm muscle beneath her and became mesmerised by the traffic below.

Sophie had always held some trepidation at crossing this footbridge. Somehow, the six-foot-high fencing seemed insignificant when she was already five feet in the air. She recognised how easy it would be to 'accidentally' throw herself over, allowing her horse to run free and her problems to disappear.

Her whole body shuddered as her thoughts turned dark. She roughly kicked Juno on, clearing the footway onto solid ground, away from the temptation below.

She was surprised at how depressed she was feeling about the move, about giving up the dream she had worked so hard for so long to achieve. At least she wasn't giving up on her marriage. This sadness wouldn't last forever, she wouldn't let it.

Perhaps that was her saviour. Some people couldn't see an end to their depression, couldn't make the changes they knew they should. She may not know the circumstances of her ending, nor which path fate would take, but with everything in her life, she knew it would be positive. She wouldn't allow it any other way.

'Everything will be okay in the end, Juno,' she hollered over the noise of the traffic. 'If it's not okay, it's not the end.'

Boosted by her outspoken words, she kicked on across the field into a gallop without any more thought to a grisly ending. As the racing wind transformed the rain hitting her face into tiny pellets of lead, she smirked wickedly at what a deep twist of the knife it would have been if Toby had to live with the guilt, following his wife's 'release' from the situation he had forced her into.

Thank goodness, for Toby's sake, she was strong.

The windy, wet ride continued and Juno, reassured by his now more responsive rider, returned to his scatty self, leaping four feet in the air at the little brown leaf that dared to blow across his path.

27

Monday, 9th December 2013

As Sophie pulled out her diary, the realisation hit her that over the last twenty years, there had never been such a lack of commentary on her life. As she flicked through the empty pages of the last few months, she found her last entry on 1st October.

> *Toby's still got his head in the sand. Life's still shit. When is it ever gonna get better????*

She smiled weakly and sighed. At least things *had* got a little better since then. There had been some positive changes. It was a long way from being over, but they were taking decisive steps in the right direction.

Looking out of her new bedroom window across a hundred regimented chimney pots of Bromford, she longed for her old vista of grass, hedges, and horses. In their place, were cars, houses, and tarmac, with strangers walking along the pavement just a step from her front door, and in that moment she hated Toby for it.

The boys were in their bunk bed, still fast asleep, happy to have been pulled out of school a few weeks before the Christmas break. The dogs were sleeping contently downstairs, unaware of how different their walks would now be. The two chickens were dominating the tiny garden, probably fighting over the small patch of morning sun that might occasionally peep between the numerous rooftops and trees.

The horses had also settled well, just a mile up the road, luxuriating in a livery yard that cost nearly as much as Sophie's rent.

They had established new boundaries for their marriage, focused on making the transition as smooth as possible for the boys, yet without explaining why. Such was the innocence and adaptability of youth; they barely questioned their new routine.

Toby would stay in Bromford for weekends and occasionally during the week, whenever work and emotions allowed. Sophie accepted this, mostly for the boys' stability but also so she and Toby could begin to rekindle whatever might be left from their marriage.

Sophie had been blown away by her family's reaction to Toby being part of her move to Bromford. Apart from her older sister, Lisa, who retained her hostility, they had supported him, shown him forgiveness, and welcomed him back.

Toby had oiled his wheels by writing an elaborate letter on the orange butterfly paper, delivered via Royal Mail, to

Sophie's parents. They had been smiling when they showed it to her, proud of what he had written.

Sophie had read it quickly, scanning over the similar phrases she had read so many times before. It talked about going off the rails and shattered dreams, about treadmills and a midlife crisis. It had asked them for forgiveness and space to rebuild. It talked about doing the right thing, about loving his wife. It talked about a happy family Christmas altogether and a positive new year ahead.

Her parents saw this as Toby's declaration of love and certainty of actions. Sophie pretended to agree, they weren't to know any better, they hadn't read what had been written before.

As she sat in bed on this cold December morning, drinking tea and waiting for the boys to wake up, she thought ahead to Christmas. It was just a few weeks away and usually so exciting, but this year, it was unrecognisable. She closed her eyes, trying to visualise a freshly cut tree, surrounded by presents, somewhere in this tiny house. She concluded that the only space was in front of the Victorian fireplace in the lounge. It would take up half of the floor, but it was one tradition she was not prepared to sacrifice.

She swallowed a lump, refusing to allow the threatening tears a pathway through as her thoughts turned to Nettlefield House, devoid of any festive cheer. She visualised the conservatory, cold and empty, minus its twinkling lights, with the views across the frosty grass marred by the unwashed panes of glass. Her sorrow increased as she reflected how they had only been able to enjoy one year of eating Christmas dinner under the stars and as she closed her eyes and breathed in, she could now smell the smoky hot wood, burning on the open fires and see the boys' happy faces as they toasted marshmallows. She couldn't swallow quickly enough to halt the heavy tears that now silently rolled down her cheeks.

The memories she was deliberately conjuring up, effortlessly brought back her pain and she focused on enjoying the fresh release they allowed.

She had been so strong for so many weeks to secure this move, that now she was here, she was allowing herself a moment to indulge in this self-pity and sorrow, enjoying the weakness if just for a moment. She cried more softly now, looking out across the rooftops, squinting to blend them into a mass of brown, speckled by the coloured spots in her eyes. Being weak and succumbing to her emotions gave her new strength, so when the boys woke, excitedly jumping on the bed in Mummy's new room, she shoved her bad feelings back in their place and released the visible strong ones back out front.

'Can I have an iPad for Christmas, Mummy?' Michael said. 'Daddy said I could if you said yes too.'

'Well, Daddy shouldn't be—' Sophie quickly halted her admonishment. 'Let's just see, shall we? Daddy and I haven't talked about Christmas presents yet.

'Will Father Christmas know we've moved?' Michael screwed up his face in concern.

'Course he will. He knows where everyone lives, stupid.' William confirmed. 'Where will Daddy be?' he added. 'Will he be living here too?'

'Daddy will be here for Christmas. Of course he will.' Sophie hoped for the boys' sake this was true. 'Shall we get a real tree and decorate it before he comes home this weekend? We could make some mince pies too.'

'Yes, yes, yes! Can we do it today please, please, please?' Michael pressed his palms together and held them in front of her face.

'Do we really not have to go to school today?' William double-checked.

'Yup, no school for ages. Let's go buy a tree and make some mince pies.' Sophie threw the covers off the bed to show her commitment.

Her happiness returned so quickly when she was with the boys and as she climbed out of bed, she imagined their happy faces as they opened their presents on Christmas day, unhindered by the cramped setting. She would be watching them with a massive tub of Quality Street on her lap, a pile of mince pies in the oven, and several bottles of fizzy wine in the fridge.

Yes. Christmas this year was going to be great, she convinced herself.

*

The card from Toby on Christmas day was simple. He handed it to her with the traditional glass of Bucks Fizz, shortly after the boys had opened all their stocking presents.

He'd arrived the night before and now had a week off work to spend as a family. The new tenants were moving into Nettlefield House on the 1st of January, so finally, money would be less of a worry.

The card he handed her was small and square. There were no Christmas pictures, no festive messages. Just a plain black front with contrasting white writing in capitals stating:

I CAN.

I WILL.

WATCH ME.

Inside, it read:

> Sophie. I _can_ and I _will_ get through this and put us back together. _Watch_ me. I love you with all my heart.
> Toby xxxx

The simplicity and understated nature were exactly what Sophie needed during this time of transition. There were no extravagant gifts to win her over, no obscure boxes from John Lewis. No gift at all. Just this clear and precise message on a small piece of card, delivered by a strong hand.

*

The New Year came and went, and although the blow-up mattress downstairs was a continual reminder of what was wrong, everything felt like it was going right. Whilst January may have been wintery and dismal outside, Sophie felt a normality that brought warmth and comfort into the small, surreal environment she now called home.

They had all faced significant change, and now they were living it, she wasn't sure who, if anyone, was holding the reins. The simplicity of their daily life was working, and Sophie didn't feel any pressure to change it. If anything, demanding more frightened her. She wanted to enjoy this little bit of stability for a bit longer.

Now that Nettlefield House was let, Toby had moved his base to his parents' house, thirty minutes away. The little Bromford house was simply too small and their relationship too precarious to both share the same limited space full-time.

When he came home, and he frequently did, they chatted, laughed, and acted like a normal family, creating the optimism that everything was going to be okay.

Of course it will be, she'd say to herself. *Eventually.* She was never quite sure if she believed it, but the hope in her veins was still a powerful drug.

The boys were happy, securing a place in the good school, much to Sophie's relief, so she could start looking for a part-time job. They had made new friends with amazing ease, and Sophie admired them for it. She herself was finding it awkward making friends at the school gate and avoided couple's occasions, of which there were many, giving the excuse that her husband worked away a lot. No one in Bromford knew her background, and that was the way she wanted to keep it.

Only the animals had been adversely affected by the changes in housing. William's pony, Chicco, had to be sold due to the exorbitant cost of the livery bill, and one chicken had decided enough was enough and declined to survive urbanization, dramatically presenting herself, legs in the air, early one frosty morning.

Sophie's late January birthday delivered another simple and meaningful card. It was larger, with black writing in capitals on a white background and had little diamante studs punctuating the words. It read:

> SOME PEOPLE
> ARE BEAUTIFUL
> JUST BECAUSE OF
> WHO THEY ARE.

Inside, Toby had written on elaborate cream paper with a brightly embossed orange butterfly.

> You've shown amazing strength and beauty through all of this. You've held the door open time and time again for the man you love to come back through it, whole and consistent. I've tested that love just about as far as I could, but I'm begging you to keep holding it open for me. I'm going to come back through as the man I know I can be, to love the woman I took my vows with, through thick and thin, sickness and health, till death do us part.
>
> I've booked a series of life coaching sessions, and they are helping me see what's important. Sophie, I know the right path. I really do, and I hope and pray we can put this last year behind us. I honestly believe we can be so much stronger than we ever were because of what's happened. I've said it before, but 'the best of me has finally come after the worst of me' and I truly believe it. I need you to believe it too.
>
> I want to move back in with you properly. We can

stop renting, sell Nettlefield House, and buy a new, nice house in Bromford. I'll change my job, so I'm at home more and less stressed. I want to come back home. I want to move back in with you.

   I love you, Sophie Cooper. Xxx

The card and note were accompanied by a little jewellery box from John Lewis, held in a gift bag with a large, red bow. Inside was a silver, heart-shaped locket on a long chain, a diamond dominating its centre. Sophie had always loved the nostalgic idea of wearing tiny images of her family close to her heart and was amazed that Toby had remembered.

As she unclasped the clips to open the little locket, and glimpsed the photos inside, she glanced up at Toby and saw his expression of love and compassion as he watched her. The photos he had chosen were from their wedding day, happy faces, one on each side of the heart, looking inwards as if in loving conversation. It touched a part of Sophie's heart she hadn't thought it would reach, so she rapidly put it back in the box and thanked Toby, then left the room with tears he couldn't see.

*

That night, once Toby had gone home to his parents' house, Sophie pulled out her new, unopened diary for 2014 and made her first entry of the year.

> *The last year has been so shit, I have stopped writing about it. When your whole life's been*

tipped upside-down, it's hard to put the pieces back. Somehow, they don't fit the way they used to, and some pieces have completely disappeared. Others seem to be from a completely different puzzle.

But I'm grateful the worst is behind us. We are all fit and healthy, and the boys are happy in their Bromford life. My new life is such a contrast to the old, but perhaps that's why it's beginning to feel right. Perhaps this normality and simplicity is how it's supposed to be. How we are supposed to mend. Leaving my dream behind at Nettlefield house could be worth it in the end!

I can finally see the end in sight. Yes, Onwards and Upwards. The next dream is coming so bring it on! I'm ready!

Before settling down to sleep, Sophie opened her locket to indulge in the warm feelings the photos emitted. Then, with an optimistic smile, she carefully returned it to its satin encasement and shut it away in her bedside table.

The necklace never left the box again.

28

Monday, 10th February 2014

The optimism in Sophie's diary and the words she religiously wrote each day spoke of hope and genuine belief that this marriage was getting back on track. Her dream had been abandoned at Nettlefield House, but she was learning to accept that. There may still be a mountain to climb but she could create new dreams. She couldn't create the security of a new family.

It was the second week of February, approaching Valentine's Day, when her mountain unexpectedly grew.

'It's over. I can't do this anymore.' Toby spoke quietly as he skulked through the front door, home from work.

'I'm sorry. *What?*' Sophie said raising both eyebrows, forgetting to close the door, stunned by the change in Toby's disposition.

'I can't keep coming back here. It's not working.' His eyes fell to the floor like little pellets of rock.

Sophie felt every nerve in her body jolt. Her emotions

towards this man switched with lightning speed from tempered love to raging hate.

'*What?*' But instinctively she knew and as she saw the tears fill his eyes, her vindictive streak pushed the question harder. '*You* can't? What about *me*? How the hell can it be you who can't do this anymore?' She knew raising her voice may reach a level where the boys might hear, but she was out of practice with her self-control, so she pushed Toby through to the kitchen, closing the door behind them.

'I don't understand. After all this time, all the progress we've made, everything I've done to make this work. We've just had a great weekend, haven't we?' They had been to Ikea, a place of hell for many men, but Toby had bought them all meatballs and ice creams and helped select scented candles and new cushions for the little house.

She glared at him, watching his tears roll down his cheeks, waiting for what came next. An explanation, an admission, but nothing did, Toby couldn't look her in the eyes.

Even the lights in the small kitchen seemed to suddenly dim as the black of the night cascaded into the room.

It was William, as always, who picked up on the charged atmosphere crackling through the little house as he came, unnoticed, into the kitchen.

'Daddy, why are you crying?'

Sophie crouched down, level with William's face, brushing his hair out of his eyes as Toby retreated to the bathroom, but she couldn't find a quick enough lie. She had used so many over the months she couldn't even find a white one. She wasn't even sure he was waiting for a response, as he followed his first question with a far more answerable one.

'Can I have an ice lolly?'

As he disappeared into the lounge with a lolly for him and his brother, Sophie walked into the bathroom where Toby, less skilled in the art of brightly smiling through the tears, was composing himself in privacy. He was sitting on the edge of the bath with a look of wretched destruction on his face.

Sophie refused to see him as the victim. She just saw in his eyes that her optimistic plans for onwards and upwards had taken a turn backwards and downwards and she had no idea how to reverse the trend.

'I'm sorry, Sophie. I thought I was okay. I was managing. I've just had a life coaching session, and I'm now so confused. I'm not sure I'm strong enough to do this anymore.'

'Do what, Toby? What exactly are you doing? I'm the one doing everything.' Sophie moved to the doorway, holding it wide open, with her hands on her hips. 'Just get out. Go back to your mum's. I don't want you here.'

But as William walked into the bathroom, lolly hanging out his mouth with a proffered game of Battleship, Sophie knew she had to selflessly relinquish Toby to his boys, preserving the illusion of a happy family unit for a little bit longer.

*

The following morning, as Sophie drank her cup of tea, a text message from Toby appeared. They hadn't spoken any more last night. She couldn't see the point. She'd left him to play with the boys and removed herself from the painful scene, blaming a headache for her retreat to her bedroom.

Sophie didn't want to read this new message. She wouldn't believe the contrived rubbish anyway. But like a moth to a flame, she couldn't resist. She was held under his spell as tightly as a coiled spring, never knowing when release would come, nor the force or direction with which it would unwind.

Toby's note spoke of being back in his tough place, facing tough decisions, unable to stop the cycle of destruction and depression. A cry for help. But Sophie saw the truth behind his words, and it was the re-emergence of Abigail's face she saw.

He continued to call throughout the next few days, but Sophie didn't respond. He had undone several months of repairing the marriage with last night's defeatist words, so had strict instructions not to return home.

She remained the facilitator between him and the boys, using as little verbal communication as possible. Her life was in limbo. She couldn't understand how this move to Bromford had suddenly turned so sour, and she was out of ideas to resolve it.

*

It was Sunday night before Toby provided her with a proper explanation.

Toby:

I'm sorry for my wobble the other night. I was back in body but not in mind. I've had another life coaching session and he's helped me refocus on what I really want. I've been to the doctor too and he's prescribed me some pills. I haven't taken them yet. I want to come home first. I know I can do what we need! Please let me try? X

She laughed at his definition of what constituted a wobble. *A total emotional meltdown was more appropriate,* but she clenched her teeth, deleted the message, and continued getting the boys bathed and ready for bed. An hour later, another message continued his explanations.

Toby:

I'm coming home. Please let me? My wobbles are over, and it's my demons that caused them. Nothing to do with Abigail. I've banished them (and her), for good. I've made mistakes, but I've always wanted to undo the hurt and pain. I know I have the strength now. My life coach has sorted me out! I can do this. I know I can. I just need you to keep helping me. Like you have been. Please help? I love you so much. X

Sophie couldn't stop the hope from swelling as she read his pleas for help. She knew she was a sucker for someone in need, but she wanted to rip out these feelings and slap herself around the face for allowing them to impact her this way.

How many more times, you silly cow? She rolled her eyes.

She still loved the man, or at least the man he used to be. The one he had so nearly become over the last few months, the one that was the other half of her, and she absolutely loved her boys, desperate for them to remain part of a loving family unit.

Enough that she could power through months' more pain if there was a chance they'd be a happy family again? Possibly.

Toby said he now had the strength, and Sophie had the guts and stamina to try.

*

At eight p.m., there was a knock and Sophie opened the door to a smiling face gazing sheepishly back at her. She was accompanied from behind by gleeful squeals from the boys as they realised bedtime was about to be extended.

She could no more tell Toby to leave than she could tell her right foot to leave her right leg, so she stepped back and allowed the boys to claim him. Whatever happened between them, however they navigated his wobbles, she would have to endure this union forever. Keeping things amicable was the only way forward.

She watched the happy scene in her warmly lit lounge, of a father playing with his two young sons in their pyjamas, happily delaying bedtime with their random, trivial games.

She could do no more than pull out another strand of her inner strength to wrap them all in, before leaving Toby alone with the deflated blow-up bed and his wobbles.

Her night, as expected, was fitful and spent largely awake. It was made even more arduous when at two a.m., Toby slid in beside her. Sophie pretended to be asleep and made a few quiet sniffles and movements, enough to indicate her displeasure at his invasion but not enough to eject him. She was torn between kicking him out unceremoniously and hugging him tight, intertwining toes, feeling the memories of past times through his warm skin, pretending things were all good, that the bad things hadn't happened, just for a bit.

*

It was early when Sophie became aware of Toby leaving the bedroom, fully dressed, off to work.

He leant in close and whispered, 'I love you, Sophie. I've made you a tea. I'll see you tonight.'

She stirred, but not enough to appear awake, then waited till she heard the scuffle of paws as the dogs scrambled to say goodbye, followed by the loud clunk of the front door. She turned, half-sitting to drink her tea and saw his signature heart-shaped piece of paper propped up beside the mug.

I love you. I WILL sort myself out. X

Sophie berated herself for letting the warm glow spread beyond the area the hot tea reached. How could he pull her back in again so easily? For the last few months, their relationship was travelling onwards and upwards, yet since then, his wobbles had reverted the direction. Now he wanted to come back, and she was allowing him to. She felt foolish for permitting his wobbles to unbalance her life so effortlessly.

It can't be normal. Why am I being so forgiving? Maybe it's me who's being weak?

Sophie corrected her thoughts out loud: 'No. It's because you're so strong.'

For the first time this year, she wondered if perhaps she should use this strength and force Toby to accept what he quite obviously wanted. He didn't have the strength to end their marriage, so had been repeatedly trying, unsuccessfully, to repair it.

Could she break it for him? End it? Could she be the one who calls time and files for divorce? Would that shock him, finally into sorting himself out? She said the D-word out loud, several times. A word so unfamiliar, with so much stigma attached, yet a word with the power to now solve her problems.

Sophie hated these thoughts, surprised they were bringing feelings of relief, knowing she had the power to end her pain, the uncertainty.

'Yes,' she said out loud, 'I've had enough. I can end it.'

She longed for something evidential to justify these horrible thoughts of giving up on the marriage and was reminded of a time before when she had uncovered the evidence she craved. She reached for her phone and re-loaded the familiar page, surprised how easily she remembered her password. She put down the phone and calmly drank some tea, waiting for the screen to load, then pressed the button she hadn't pressed for a long time, 'Download PDF'.

She couldn't imagine she would see the familiar numbers of Abigail's mobile, still etched on her inner eyelids, but she couldn't quell her detective mind that was asking the questions she didn't want the answers to.

Why can't he decide? Why's he so hot and cold? What the hell's a bloody wobble?

The unfamiliar number that pierced her eyes with its regular occurrence was a landline. Sophie saw many conversations, stretching back from before Christmas, and she knew instinctively who they were with. Her heart rate quickened, but it wasn't in fear. It was in expectation of what she might find; confirmation as to why everything was still wrong. If her assumptions were correct, it would give justification that her option to officially end things was the right one. No one could blame her for that, not even the boys.

She entered the area code into Google and found it belonged to a village she'd never heard of, just a few miles away from Nettlefield House. She flicked between the screens on her phone, memorising three or four numbers at a time, duplicating them into the call screen.

It was just seven a.m. when Sophie pressed the green phone symbol. It rang twice before a woman's voice brightly answered, 'Hello?'

Sophie had her confirmation. Each time Toby had wobbled, he had wobbled through a haze of lies to Abigail. The image of her weak, plasticine husband wobbling back and forth would have made her laugh if she hadn't been frozen in apprehension of what to say now.

29

Monday, 17th February 2014

Sophie couldn't speak as she allowed the voice she recognised to reverberate inside her head. Her vocal cords were melting as hot pressure from her chest rose into her throat, pulsating, resisting as she tried to swallow it down. She hadn't rehearsed this, and now wished she had thought through her approach more carefully.

'Hello. Who is this?' Abigail asked.

'Hi.' Sophie managed, pausing to permit her enemy the time to associate a face to the voice. 'It's Sophie.'

'Oh.' Abigail's irritation was audible, and her deep sigh took away her earlier brightness. 'What d'you want? You shouldn't be calling me. Please don't.'

Sophie was unable to step into the silence. She had no idea what she should be saying.

Abigail's voice continued to fill the void. 'This has nothing to do with me. Not anymore. You both need to leave me out of it. I've had enough of being in the middle. I've told Toby the same thing.'

Sophie felt silly and embarrassed. Abigail's words were contradicting her assumptions. Dispelling her theory of Toby's wobbles being a result of Abigail. She was obviously having nothing more to do with him.

So why was he ringing her then? Had she been rejecting him, refusing to take him back? Was that why he was wobbling to and fro?

The silence persisted, so Abigail continued. 'I need to get to work now. I really am sorry for everything that's happened, but please, don't ring me anymore. You need to speak to Toby. Your divorce has nothing to do with me.'

The silence took on a different sound as the D-word, spoken by another person, echoed in the air around Sophie's bed.

'Divorce? What divorce?'

'Divorce. Separation, or whatever you want to call it. Can't you finally accept things now and move on without him? It will help us all, especially your boys.'

Sophie sat up straight, rigid with adrenaline, astounded that Abigail was bringing the welfare of the boys into the discussion. The room began to enclose around her, and she threw off the covers to breathe more easily, swinging her legs out of the bed. Thirty seconds ago, she felt pathetic and weak; a paranoid wife in the presence of a disinterested mistress. Now, the reality of what Abigail was saying hit her with emotions she was more equipped to deal with.

'Let me just clear something up for you.' Sophie walked over to the window and looked beyond the rooftops, into the weak rising sun. 'Tell me. Why has my husband been ringing you?'

'He rings me all the time. What d'you mean? Why shouldn't he?' Abigail gave another audible sigh, and Sophie could hear her moving through the house.

'Well, because apparently, he's not seeing you anymore. He isn't even thinking of you. I'm paraphrasing here, but he wants nothing more to do with you, and he's trying to sort out his marriage.'

It was Abigail's turn to be on the receiving side of this tennis game of emotions. 'But you're separated. You're getting divorced. I don't understand.'

'Nope, we are not. Toby is back with me and our very *happy* boys. He was in my bed last night, and we are making it work.' There was a pause, and Sophie heard a door close.

'I don't believe you. He told me you'd separated. At Christmas. He's been staying at his mum's, hasn't he? He's only in Bromford to see the boys. He's with *me* now.'

'Erm, I'm not sure he actually is I'm afraid.' Sophie couldn't help but smirk.

'Has he been lying to me? I don't understand. Why would he lie? To *me?*'

'Because he's a coward, and somehow he's found himself in the fortunate position of having two women allowing him to play at being God.' Sophie felt unexpected pity towards Abigail as she recognised, perhaps for the first time, that she was a victim too. Her emotions were also being juggled.

Abigail's voice was breaking. 'I ... I've been ironing all his work shirts, for goodness' sake. I've been cooking his meals. He's been eating in my kitchen, with my kids, and yet you say he's been lying to me all this time?' She asked this as a question but didn't wait for confirmation. 'I thought you separated when you moved to Bromford. Honestly Sophie, I did. That's what he told me. I can't believe he's done this to me. To both of us.'

'We've been doormats, Abigail. As bad as each other. Two doormats for one pathetic, weak, immoral man.'

Abigail didn't disagree.

It was surprisingly good to talk to the one person who knew Toby was no longer the nice, decent guy. The women hadn't spoken on such friendly terms for so long, it was as if they were back in the Study Class waiting room, gossiping. Their conversation eased by memories from before their lives were so ungraciously entwined.

But eventually, the surreal conversation was forced into reality, and it was Sophie's that was voiced first.

'I think I'm done, Abigail. I can't come back from this now. You're welcome to him. I knew it was you behind his wobbles, but I never believed for one moment it would be as a couple, living together like that. I give up. I'm going to message him now and tell him we've spoken.'

Abigail sniffed and took a moment to answer. 'Yeah, but don't tell him what we've discussed, how much we both know. Let's make him suffer for a bit. I want to see what he owns up to.' Her voice became stronger. 'But seriously, I'm not sure I want him back either. I still can't believe it. Listen, I need to get off to work now, but let's keep talking? Please?'

The friendly enemies said their farewells, neither truly knowing what would happen next. Sophie sat back on the bed, head-spinning, and re-read the lie she had seen so many times before on the little paper heart: 'I love you. I will sort myself out. X'

She screwed it into a tiny ball and hurled it at the window, but its pathetic tap was powerless to dispel the pain or halt the tears that now flowed more ferociously, with a darker, more powerful form of rejection and heartbreak.

*

Getting the boys to school was a blur. Sophie had forced her tears to stop and pasted on a smile before going into their bedroom to wake them. She forced them a little more harshly than usual to eat their breakfast and clean their teeth, and when they decided to flick toothpaste at each other, Sophie jostled them out of the bathroom with a roughness she wasn't proud of.

She wanted to yell at them that their daddy had caused this change in their mother. He was the one living the double life. He wasn't thinking about *them* when he was eating his dinner cooked by Abigail. He wasn't thinking of *them* when he was laughing with her, or in bed with her. He certainly wasn't thinking of their mother, getting them to school, wearing her brave face, keeping everything tightly held together, protecting them from his actions.

The boys were all Sophie thought about. They were the main reason she was still fighting. But this morning, she cared a little less about fighting on their behalf and forced them out of the house earlier than necessary. She needed them away from her. She needed to confront Toby.

She watched the clock on the car dashboard as she drove

them to school, trying to speed up their journey, willing the seconds to run faster. The boys were mucking about in the back, play fighting across the seats and the traffic kept stopping. Sophie was becoming less and less able to control the anger threatening to overtake her. The kisses goodbye at the school gate were brief and lacked any accompanying hugs. As she turned back to the car, she let loose the tears that had built up behind her eyes.

She sat in the driver's seat and took out her phone with hands shaking so violently she could barely type. Her anger was like an animal, escaping from beneath her skin, ready to pounce. It was no surprise he had lied to her, but to now know he was lying to the boys as well, happily indulging in a life without them, made Sophie's heart bleed for everything they didn't yet know.

Sophie:

COME HOME, YOU BASTARD. NOW

The roads to the stables were viewed through a hazy mist of wetness, and her autopilot mechanism drove the car. When she walked into the stable and Juno's face greeted her with his horse's smile and his horse's voice, she cried into his neck, breathing in the comforting, musty smell.

Fortunately, the yard was empty; most owners had left for the day. Sophie sat on the bank of wood shavings, a quizzical Juno nuzzling her for attention.

Her phone beeped.

Toby:
I'm sorry. I know you've spoken to
Abigail. I can explain. I'm on my way.
60 minutes.

Sophie knew Toby would have panicked when he read her message. He probably rang Abigail and would have panicked a lot more if she had divulged what was shared. He might have felt relieved, Sophie surmised. Like a coward, unable to own up to his mistakes, but welcoming the relief at being found out.

Sophie:
Come to the stables.

She took her time changing Juno's rugs, turning him out into the field, before mucking out his stable. Then sat silently in the clean shavings, holding the pitchfork, and waited. The only sounds were a dripping tap and a distant horse's whinny. It was as if the world had stopped and was waiting for this confrontation.

Surprisingly, she felt at peace, sitting in her stable, calmed by the rhythm of the drips. One moment there would be a perfect, synchronised pattern then abruptly, a rogue drip would mess it up and the orchestral score in Sophie's head would be re-written. The drips seemed to stop altogether as the noise of a car splashing through the puddles drowned out the sounds. The car stopped and a door slammed. Sophie stood and held her breath in the sudden silence, frozen to the spot. Footsteps moved towards Juno's stable with the distinctive sound of a hard heel; a business work shoe, not the rubber wellies mostly heard here. The drips were now reaching a climax in Sophie's head, resolutely dripping in time with the thumping of her heart.

Toby appeared in the stable doorway, smiling. Weakly.

All the anger from the morning's revelations and the emotion from the last nine months took over Sophie's mind and body and propelled her to the doorway, her pitchfork horizontal as she ran.

'You bastard!' she screeched as she lunged straight for his body. She shut her eyes, bracing for the impact of metal penetrating flesh. Maybe there would be resistance, some bone.

There would be blood. Lots of blood.

But there was no impact. She felt the fork dragged from her hands as Toby caught its shaft and sidestepped away. She unscrewed her eyes, coming back to consciousness, shocked at how easily she could have murdered him right there in the stable. Premeditated, they would have said. Attempted murder, at least. No one would have understood the extent of what drove her to it. It wasn't self-defence, at least not against a physical weapon.

It was self-defence against an emotion: love, the most powerful weapon there was and impossible to truly build a defence against.

Released from her metal dagger, Sophie continued her assault by pummelling his body, shoving him out of the stable doorway, causing the fork to noisily clatter to the floor. She herded him out of the stable block, backing him through muddy puddles and remnants of unavoidable manure and to his car, shouting hurtful obscenities.

Toby said just one word in reply, 'Sorry.' He had no comeback, just the tears in his eyes as he closed the car door behind him. Her fists hit the window, the door, anything within reach as the engine started. She didn't want or need his explanations.

'Go. Go on, get out. Piss off. *Never* come back again. *Go.*'

Toby was probably too afraid to reply. He could do nothing more than retreat with his tail between his legs, carrying massive shame and an aroma of horse to remind him why. As the car reversed out of its space, Sophie threw a double handful of wet, lumpy manure, freshly deposited by a recent horse, as hard as she could into the rear window. Oblivious to the mess on her hands, she stuck up two fingers and smiled at the sight of the muck running down the glass.

That shit's gonna stay with him all the way to the office, she thought, and a small smile escaped her distraught face.

As Toby's car disappeared around the corner, the fight and massive height Sophie had grown to suddenly diminished and she collapsed to the floor, wimping.

The lady from the next block, an obvious witness to the whole event, sheepishly asked if everything was okay.

In words as weak as the sunrise that morning, Sophie stood and said, 'I've no idea. Could you please tell the yard I won't be around for a few days? Can they put Juno on full livery? I'll text them the details. Thanks.'

Without waiting for a reply or lifting her face from the ground, Sophie left the yard.

*

Toby slammed his hands on the steering wheel as the traffic lights stopped him at the entrance to the tunnel on the M25. He didn't want to be left stationary with his thoughts. He couldn't get Sophie's contorted face out of his mind as she had lunged toward him.

He had been genuinely scared at the force she had behind that fork, and he knew at that moment she meant to hurt him. He wouldn't have blamed her if she had, but he knew the law would have taken a different view, and he was grateful for her sake he had been unharmed.

Those prongs were sharp as hell. Selfishly though, he felt like it might have been an end to his torment. Death would solve his current indecisiveness, rid him of his demons and that thought took him to a dark place he knew he shouldn't be.

A massive line of fuel lorries got ready to be escorted through the tunnel ahead, so with a sigh, Toby turned off his ignition, knowing he would be here a while. As he tried to get his mind into a more positive place, he became aware of the aroma of horse coming up from his feet. He glanced at his back windscreen, at the dark swash of dried muck, and felt stupid for having a damn sports car with no back windscreen wipers.

Hopefully, it would rain before he arrived in the office car park.

He watched as the convoy began to move and imagined what would happen if they all blew up inside the tunnel.

Would the blast reach him? Would it be quick? Who would miss him more, Sophie or Abigail?

But as soon as he thought of how the boys would grieve for their father, he gained increased courage and conviction to straighten out his mess. He loaded up his messages and began to compose what was intended as a white flag.

The message was sent to Abigail.

> Toby:
>
> I can absolutely see how much this has hurt you, sweetheart, but I need you to know my words were never attached to actions with Sophie. What matters is how you show someone you love them, with actions, and I'm going to show you right now. I know it's raw, and you are hurting, but please give it time. We can have a real relationship now that everything is in the open. We've waited so long, don't give up now. This is the last hurdle but the biggest one. Deep breath, and let's jump it together. X

Unknown:
I told you earlier, you need to leave me alone. I'm at work. You are very confused. You didn't need to lie to me.

Please stop messaging me. I need
more time.

The lights were still red. The convoy had disappeared, and there was no sign of an imminent explosion. Toby re-read Abigail's message, tears pricking his eyes as he recognised the truth behind her words. He *was* confused but somehow this confusion was clearer now. There was no need to hide anymore. He went into the settings on his phone and added the number he had memorised, reinstating Abigail as its truthful owner.

Toby:
I know I've messed things up, but who I am with you is who I am. I know I've been keeping my options open, but that was for fear of losing the boys. My feelings for Sophie are done. Like I said, they were words not supported by actions. I know you're hurting, and I'm so sorry about that, but I'm not giving up the fight for you, Abigail. I will never give you up. I love you too much. Please can I come and see you? X

Abigail:
I'm not home till 5. You can call me then. I know the boys are your priority, and you've worried about losing them.

I love that you are such a devoted father. Matthew is absolutely shit in comparison! X

> Toby:
> Yay, a kiss at the end! That's progress!! I know you've seen me wobble and get upset, but that's cos I was thinking just about the boys. Once the routine is settled, it'll be fine. I'll cherish time with you, and I'll cherish time with the boys, then at the right time, we can merge. I will not let you go. Have a good day at work. I'll speak to you later. X

*

No messages came for Sophie. She was half-expecting a text begging for forgiveness, or a phone call begging for help, but neither came. She convinced herself she wouldn't have answered anyway.

In defiance, she collected the boys from school early and took off to Granny's. Her retreat, her place to heal. She had no plans to tell Toby she had gone and had no idea when she would be back.

As she began the hour-long drive, she considered using the boys to punish him. She could tell them exactly what was happening and why they were missing school. Tell them why they'd had to leave Nettlefield House and all their friends. Tell them they were unexpectedly visiting Granny for half-term because Daddy didn't want them anymore; he wanted Abigail instead.

He had been making his choice every time he went north, giving up his rights to them. Sophie took pleasure in her thoughts as she glanced in her rear-view mirror, watching the boys, imagining the despair on Toby's face when he realised they knew it all.

She considered all the different scenarios she could use to enact this new plan. But every time, she came to the same conclusion. She could never tell the boys what Toby had done. They would never understand the adult emotions causing Mummy and Daddy to no longer exist as a team, causing Daddy to be so unkind and Mummy to be so sad.

She remembered back to one of the marriage counsellor's lessons. 'One of the best things we can teach our children is how to have a healthy marriage'. Sophie hated the fact she had not achieved this. How would they learn this lesson now?

But she did know for sure she could teach the boys how to have a healthy divorce, and that became her new goal. She would not make a mess of the end of their marriage. Toby may have broken their home, but Sophie would make sure they didn't notice.

When the car stopped at Granny's, William woke from dozing. 'Is Daddy coming later? Can we go fishing?'

With this simple inquiry, carrying so much innocence, Sophie knew for sure she would have the strength to achieve her new goal. Their marriage may have failed but she was going to ensure their divorce was a success.

30

Thursday, 27th February 2014

Sophie had been able to spend hours over the following days, gazing out across the valleys, mindlessly wandering the tracks and fields with the two dogs. She had enviously watched the tips of the spring grass burst into new life, trying not to think of her old fields at Nettlefield House. How had they recovered from the winter? What animals were eating her grass? Had the rabbits finally taken over the barn in her absence? All questions she knew she would never have the answers to.

She longed to be one of the stable mice, contentedly curled up in a hole, sleeping through the long, winter nights. Not that she had slept much recently, even with the total darkness and silence that staying in the middle of nowhere allowed. Keeping your eyes wide open, yet still unable to see anything, it was like not being there at all.

Sophie indulged in the release it provided, however brief. It reminded her of Toby's comment years before, comparing London's light and noise pollution to here, where you were hypothetically blind and deaf. This memory came from a happy time when she knew exactly where her life was going and with whom.

Now she knew nothing of what her future held, it felt empty. It was becoming easier to imagine a future without Toby, without Nettlefield House, without all the pain, but she couldn't imagine it without the family unit she had taken for granted, never before realising its true significance.

She hadn't had any contact with Toby since the pitchfork incident ten days before, other than his daily messages and conversations with the boys. She dreaded it when he called, and she had to hand over her phone. They would put him on loudspeaker, or even worse, Facetime, and Sophie would have to listen to the outpouring of love and devotion that gushed both ways.

He would pick inappropriate times to call, not considering the life they were living without him. Sophie would shout out how it was dinnertime or bedtime, or they were just leaving to go for a walk, but if he heard, he took no notice and carried on his conversations regardless.

This morning, she'd woken early to a calendar notification on her phone, painfully reminding her of their caravan holiday they had booked months ago. As she quickly sent an email to cancel their pitch, knowing it would be too late for a refund, the hurtful image of the caravan being pulled off the driveway invaded her mind. She wondered where it was now, and humanised it, hoping it was having a nice time, wherever it had gone instead for this half-term weekend.

Sophie crept downstairs, trying to remember which floorboards creaked and flicked the switch on the kettle before releasing the impatient Jack Russells for their morning altercation with the rabbits, praying they didn't wake the rest of the house with their yelps. She stood at the back door and gazed across the fields she had come to know so well. The heavy morning mist lurked in the valleys, waiting for the rising sun to burn it off, swaddling the new lambs, temporarily concealed from view. She was deep in thought, not noticing the kettle had long since boiled.

She wondered where Toby was waking up this morning. Had he remembered to cancel his leave from work? Did he get the same reminder for their weekend away? What emotions did it bring to him? Had Abigail given in and taken him back? Was he with her now, enjoying a different type of weekend away?

Sophie hoped Abigail hadn't weakened, hadn't relented, hadn't forgiven. She finished making her tea and took it upstairs, climbed into bed and began typing a message, hoping to hijack Toby's happy weekend plans if she had.

> Sophie:
>
> I'm not trying to be cruel, but I'm going to send you the messages Toby sent me whilst he was sleeping with you. I think you need to read them. It's definitely over between us, I nearly killed him before, so I'm guessing if he hasn't already, he'll try and come

> back to you. He admitted he loves you but said it was limerence and wouldn't last, and he would always resent you for what happened. You are therefore welcome to the mess that is my husband if you are stupid enough to still want him. He will never be your rock. I was always the rock in our relationship, he was the weak one. You and I, more than ever, need a rock. I am convinced they are out there. It isn't Toby. Best of luck if you choose him. You're gonna need it! I'm sending you the messages now. Sorry.

Sophie followed up the message with screenshots of the many communications Toby had sent when his marriage was supposedly still important. One by one, they flew across the internet.

Back in body and mind ... prodigal son ... biggest mistake ... actions are what matters ... I'm going to show you ... I love you ... I'm so sorry ... amazing strength and beauty ... desperate to do the right thing ... stronger than ever ...

For a moment revenge felt good and a tight twisted smile stretched across Sophie's face. She paused as she re-read the last message. Toby's words ended with, 'Our cloud may be grey now, but there's still a silver lining, and I promise I'm going to make it brighter than ever.' Sophie didn't press send. Her eyes welled up as she remembered a time, years before when words about silver linings had carried so many hopes and dreams of a future, together forever.

Shaking off her memories, Sophie quickly stood and drank the last of her tea. It was still very early, and it could be ages till Abigail woke to read her messages. Deciding to take the dogs for an early morning walk across the fields, she began to get dressed when her phone vibrated.

Emotions were potentially waking Abigail up early too.

Abigail:
OMG, he sent me the same messages! The strength and beauty through all of this I have shown as well, apparently! He probably cut and pasted the same texts. He has asked to come and see me several times, but I have said no. I can't face him yet and what he has done. I'm so sorry, Sophie. We have both been played well. Everyone else saw it. I didn't! Thank you for forwarding them. I only believe you! I'm so sorry for allowing all this to happen. You've been so strong. I don't know how you do it. You're amazing, Sophie! Please forgive me.

Sophie collapsed on the bed, half undressed as the recognition hit her, that Toby's eloquent lies had not been written exclusively for her. He was sharing them with his mistress too, and whilst it pained her she would never know who the more deserving recipient was, her decreasing heartbeat was an indication that now, perhaps, she cared a little less.

> Sophie:
> I think I kind of already have forgiven you. I found my birthday card in my diary earlier. It said, 'I can. I will. Watch me.' Well, he can't, he won't, and I've stopped looking! I'm going to pin it to my front door as a reminder of his deceit and to keep me strong!

There was no point in seeing Abigail as the enemy anymore. Whilst Sophie was belligerently hanging on to her marriage, Abigail had also been hanging onto her version of a relationship and Sophie couldn't hold it against her. She might have forgiven Abigail, but she knew Abigail would struggle to forgive herself. Sophie recognised the empowering significance of being part of this love triangle without any blame or guilt and without the demons that Toby and Abigail were carrying.

Since that heartbreaking day last May, Sophie felt she had done everything she could to become the very best version of herself, and she was surprised at how strong that now made her feel. She had forgiven Toby's mistress and been consistently strong for the boys, emerging with a significant boost to her pride and self-esteem. If she had forgiven Abigail, then maybe she could forgive Toby, and this could all be over.

Perhaps forgiveness was going to play a large part in her

journey of repair, to escape this existence of living a life she didn't want nor felt she deserved. This ability to forgive might now carry her forward to a better life, and for that, Sophie felt grateful to them both.

*

As half term quickly came to an end, Sophie had to leave her adopted retreat and return home. She had been keen for the boys to relinquish their free-range lifestyle, to gain back the routine to their days. Plus, she didn't want to think of the small fortune Juno would be costing her in livery fees. The time at her parents had provided an essential bit of emotional rehab, permitting her a complete lack of pressure to pretend.

But life had to go on, and she had to take on the responsibility of pulling herself together, to get back to a normality she hadn't yet created.

The boys had fallen asleep within minutes on the journey home, such was their exhaustion from their mini-break in the countryside. Sophie had played the radio extra loud and sang along to Sunday night classics all the way home. It had uplifted her mood and motivated her to kick arse and sort out her life.

She had begun the very next day, the moment the boys were at school, by ringing a solicitor and booking an appointment. She had been confidently researching the divorce process over the last week, but the thought of discussing how to end her marriage with a stranger, scared her. How would she explain to the boys she was divorcing their dad? They would end up blaming her. They wouldn't know the truth that drove her to it.

Her Google research had eventually led her to a solution she was more comfortable with. If the grounds for divorce were cited as adultery, then all blame would be on Toby. *He* would be the official reason the boys came from a broken home, not her. She could accept that, so she had asked Toby to come over to discuss, hoping to reach an amicable understanding before her solicitor's meeting tomorrow.

The boys were so excited when Sophie collected them from school, informing them that Daddy was coming over for tea. William immediately asked if he should get the blow-up bed out, and Michael rushed upstairs as soon as they got home, arranging in a neat pile the books that Daddy would read to him before bed.

It broke Sophie's heart multiple times as she recognised how much they had missed their father over the last two weeks and what the full impact of tomorrow's meeting could mean to them in the future.

*

After dinner, Sophie left Toby in charge of the bedtime routine and disappeared to the stables for some valuable alone time with Juno. The horse was beginning to look like a luxury she could no longer afford. It had been a cold winter, and the cost of his hay, feed, and livery had depleted her savings.

She couldn't see how he would fit into her new future. Toby was hardly going to make an allowance for a horse in his maintenance payments. Even finding herself a job after so long out of work, with the boys still so young, looked extremely unlikely, and the money would never stretch to the expense of a horse.

Once enough time had passed and she knew the boys would be in bed, Sophie kissed Juno goodnight on his soft muzzle, wistfully remembering a time when just a small orchard separated her horses from her back door. With apprehension growing inside her, she climbed into the car and drove home, finding a lucky parking space just eight doors away.

'Thanks for letting me put them to bed. Michael's reading is coming on well, isn't it?' Toby spoke like an uncle, not a father.

'Listen, it's late. We need to talk.' Sophie couldn't look Toby in the eyes as she spoke. She busied herself putting away the toys. 'It's about my solicitor appointment tomorrow.'

Toby was hovering on the threshold of the hallway, glancing at his watch, running his hand over his balding head, a slight nod the only indication he had heard.

'I've made my decision. I'm *not* filing for divorce.' Sophie continued, watching for his response.

His head jolted up and she saw the fleeting surprise on his face turn to worry.

'But I thought a divorce was what you wanted. That's why I'm here, isn't it?'

'It is. We *are* getting divorced.' Sophie explained. But *you're* going to do it. *You're* going to accept all the blame on the grounds of adultery, officially.'

'What d'you mean? I'm not seeing a solicitor. How am I going to do it?' He began pacing the room.

'By making a choice tonight. I'm permitting you to end

this marriage now. Then, tomorrow, I can discuss your decision with the solicitor and see what we do next. But it's your choice, your decision, not mine. Tonight.'

Sophie felt empowered. She was not giving up, he was. She was orchestrating it, but he was going to be the one to take all the blame for ending the marriage. He had struggled to do this for so long, she was simply giving him the permission. Whether it was the relief of forgiveness or the unfamiliar experience of giving up, Sophie knew she wanted to create a time, a place, a memory for the night he decided to finally end the marriage and she could begin to forget.

Toby stopped pacing and leaned on the door frame. 'I can't believe it's come to this. I … I can't believe we're doing this. Do we have to say adultery?' Tears were forming in his eyes.

'You're doing it, Toby. Remember that. I'm giving you permission to, but you're the one making the decision. And yes, I think citing adultery means it can be quick.'

The corners of Toby's mouth turned down, trembling, but Sophie locked her eyes into his. She wanted to see, not just hear, his response. The kitchen clock was ticking loudly in the silence and someone slammed a car door right outside, making Sophie jump, but she kept her eyes boring into his.

Eventually, he looked away as he feebly answered. 'Okay, I promise I'll make sure you're alright, financially. I'll do it properly. I'll do what I need to do to make it all amicable.' His voice was breaking as he spoke.

'Good, because we have to keep it amicable for the boys' sake. And we need to tell them soon, I can't carry on with all the lies.'

'Oh, Sophie. How do we do that?'

Sophie had read the books and consulted Google on this, so responded with authority. 'We do it together and we make it clear it's not their fault. We tell them we'll always love them, as much as before, and that you and I will remain friends. I think we just have to listen really carefully and answer their concerns honestly.'

Toby slid onto the sofa his head in his hands. 'I'm so sorry, I can't believe this is happening to me. How has it come to this? What have I done?'

Sophie could stand no more. 'Come on, get up. You need to go. I'll let you know what the solicitor says. We'll tell the boys tomorrow night,' and without waiting for an answer, she opened the front door, standing aside to let him through. As she watched him walk away from the little house she called home, neither saying a proper goodbye, she held her head high, proud of her dry eyes, but with a debilitating pain in her stomach.

She walked into the lounge and collapsed on the sofa, wondering how many minutes would pass before she would be physically able to move. She felt totally abandoned, on her own, rejected, and tomorrow her loneliness would be made official.

The eventual thought that enabled her to get up from the sofa was that maybe, finally, this now meant she could begin the process of trying to forget and put her life back together. She had no idea what this new life would look like, or even what she wanted from it, but one part she felt compelled to get right, for the sake of the boys, was her ongoing relationship with Abigail, if indeed there would be the need for one. She pulled out her phone from her back pocket and typed.

> Sophie:
> I did the bravest thing I could tonight to finally end this for all of us. I made Toby make his choice, and he has officially chosen to end his marriage, which I will be discussing tomorrow with the solicitor. Finally, you can have him back (if you even want him?) knowing it's because he didn't want me. I now hope we can all be adults and mature enough through the next phase to help the boys adjust. I know that as time passes, if you take Toby back, I will warm to you as a person and not see you as the horrendous thing that has caused all this pain. I wonder if your new relationship, without the secrecy/guilt/thrill of being caught will dwindle and die. I hope not. I don't want it all to have been a waste. I'm going to struggle massively when I'm left without the boys, if he takes them to be with you. But this is the start of my new chapter too, and there is some excitement about what it will be like. So

> take him back, please. He wants you,
> I'm sure. Keep him happy. A happy
> Toby means a secure father for the
> boys. I'm sure I'll see you in the future
> for that glass of pinot! Remember,
> everything will be okay in the end. If it's
> not okay, it's not the end. Be happy.
> Look after him and my boys.

It felt good to put positive feelings into words and share them with Abigail. This woman had turned from the adulterous mistress Sophie was permitted to hate, to the person who may now become an integral part of her boys' lives, potentially sharing in all of their life events and memories.

Sophie would not waste negative emotions on this relationship with Abigail. This had to be a positive one. This was going to be one of the lessons she needed to master in order to teach the boys how to have a good divorce.

Switching off her phone, she went upstairs to kiss the boys goodnight, and stood for a moment, watching them sleep. The last few weeks, she had been well educated in the challenges that love can bring and felt confident she would eventually find a new way to love Toby. But there was an alarming, ominous emotion hammering her heart as she watched the boys' rising chests, moving in sync with their little breaths in and out. An emotion she knew she would struggle to accept or even begin to comprehend.

Motherhood. Alone. As a divorced, single parent.

31

Tuesday, 4th March 2014

Armed with Toby's decision from last night to end their marriage, Sophie walked into the solicitor's meeting with a guilt-free conscience and a confidence that surprised her. The solicitor relayed the simple, factual advice she had likely given a hundred times before, to a hundred similar women, offering various scenarios of what their divorce might look like.

She advised Sophie to act as the petitioner, divorcing Toby on official grounds of adultery. Assuming he accepted, it meant she could begin proceedings immediately and remain in control of the process. It was a positive start to the meeting.

'So, best case scenario then, is that Toby and I agree everything out of the courts?'

'Yes, if at all possible, it will be cheaper, quicker, and less painful for all. However, be aware the custody arrangements and finances can cause conflict in even the most amicable of couples.'

'I don't think Toby's got a leg to stand on. He's brought this all on himself so he's not exactly in a position of power, is he.' Sophie spoke this as a statement. No doubt in her mind that as the innocent party, she would have the upper hand in any negotiations about finance and the boys. 'What d'you think a fair split of our finances would look like?'

The solicitor answered immediately. 'A judge will always start at fifty-fifty. Even if Toby accepts the adultery, he would not, at least financially, be penalised for it.'

'Seriously?' Sophie's eyebrows rose high enough to ache. 'So, even though he has behaved appallingly, there is no penalty for him breaking our marriage contract?'

What's the point in the witnesses and their signatures? In the stupid photos of them all signing the register if you can commit adultery without penalty? How can that go unpunished? The questions raced through Sophie's mind.

'What about everything I brought to the marriage? I started us off with a house and my career. He didn't even have a job for goodness' sake. They'll allow for that, won't they?'

'No, they won't. You can appeal to his guilt? You can appeal on behalf of the children that you need more than fifty per cent to keep them in the manner to which they're accustomed, but in principle, he's under no obligation to agree. You've been married more than seven years. That's a long-term marriage in the court's eyes, therefore it's fifty-fifty, but a good judge would argue for you to get more. You'd get to keep the house.'

'I don't want to go through a bloody judge. And I don't

want the damn house. What a bloody stupid law marriage is. I bet it was a man who made it!'

Sophie could feel the emotions threatening to catch in her throat, her confidence waning. She could no longer stop her lips tightening across her teeth, and she wished the solicitor would step in to break the silence. She noticed there was no ring on *her* finger.

Not surprised you're not married. You know it's a waste of paper.

Gaining some composure, she continued, 'Well, the law *is* bloody stupid. Who's ever heard of a legal contract with no penalty for breaking it? They didn't tell me *that* when I signed on the dotted line. Where was it? In the small print?'

Remaining professional, the solicitor reaffirmed. 'His guilt, Sophie. That's your best means of financial security. Play to his guilt.'

'He hasn't bloody got any.'

*

Sophie thanked the solicitor for all the negative news and left with a significant amount of fear regarding her next steps. Her mind was in a spin as she walked to the bus stop, questions and doubts somersaulting inside. She watched her bus pull into its stop up ahead, debating whether to run to catch it, but even that decision was beyond her.

Her legs felt heavy as she continued dawdling, feeling the weight of the world on her shoulders. A world she didn't recognise and didn't want to be part of. She reached the bus shelter and sat down, watching the bus disappear around the corner and began to cry. Her fear was allowing the weakness in, a total contrast to how strong she had felt just a few hours before. She wiped her arm across her eyes and phoned her sister. She needed to offload.

'Hiya, how was it? Did you take him for every penny then!' Lisa laughed.

'Not even close. Apparently, if I'm lucky, I'll get enough money to buy the shitty little house I'm in now!' She sniffed loudly, searching in her bag for a tissue.

'Seriously? But he had nothing when he met you? The house you had before you were married was bigger than that one.'

'Yup, apparently so. Unless I go through a judge, that's the best I'm gonna get. All that signing of the legal stuff, the, 'thou shalt not commit adultery', God what a joke. D'you remember? You were our witness, weren't you?'

'Was I? But seriously, does anyone even know what those signatures are for? It's just a piece of—'

'And then the bastard breaks that contract by having an almighty affair and there's no legal ramifications. No penalty at all. I can't believe it.' Sophie stood abruptly, interrupting as if addressing everyone at the bus stop. 'He married me with bugger all, not even a dream, and he's allowed to get off scot-free after shattering my whole life. Plus, he's got his six-figure career. What have I got? How can I ever get my career back now? It's so unfair.' The tears began again, this time with an anger attached and the old lady sitting next to her stood and moved behind the shelter.

'Then go through a judge Sophie. How else are you going

to manage? Losing that lovely house, your stables. Oh, Sophie, I'm so sorry. At least you're near us all now. He's a total bastard, come over later for a glass of wine, I'll cheer you up!'

Sophie blew her nose and allowed a little smile. Lisa's answer to everything was a glass of wine, and today, she felt it might just be true. 'Think I'll need the whole bottle, not just a glass. But no, I can't, I've got to collect the boys from school. We're telling them about the divorce tonight. Maybe I'll see you at the weekend. Got to go, my bus is coming.'

She put her wet tissue in the bin and allowing the older lady on first, climbed on board. As the bus drove through the streets of suburbia, Sophie enviously watched the expensive Victorian houses flash by. With their electronic gates and knocked through lounges, displaying massive bifold doors and open-plan kitchens, all illuminated by their impressive feature lights.

Bromford was an expensive borough. If she was going to live here, to be close to her family, how would she cope without a career, a job, or any income other than that which the Child Support Agency dictated by law? How would she be able to teach the boys how to have a good divorce when she felt so wronged?

She knew *she* could adjust, but the boys knew nothing of the changes to come. They would have to reduce their expectations in life, at least when they were with her, and the thought of their enforced sacrifices tore at strings that were only just holding her heart in place.

Getting off the bus, she made her way to the little house,

and walked through the door, trying to see it as her future, as her best-case scenario. Then, taking her sister's medicine she poured herself a glass of wine and checked her silenced phone.

There was a message from Toby.

> Toby:
> We don't need a solicitor. I'm coming back. I decided too fast. I was being a coward; it was the wrong decision; I can make this work. I can't lose you. I should always have chosen you. I'll be home at 6 p.m. Please let's hold off telling the boys? X

Sophie didn't reply but downed the wine and made her way to the school, unable to stop herself from visualising a new, happy scene in the grand Victorian houses. Herself, Toby, and the boys, sitting in an open plan kitchen, repaired, mended. Her future worries and problems solved by one simple message.

'You stupid woman,' her inner voice chastised herself out loud. 'Remember those texts? He sent them to her too, at the same time probably. You weren't special, he didn't want you. At least not enough.'

'Yes, but they might have been sent to me first. Doesn't that stand for something? She answered herself, meekly.

'Oh, shut up. It's the wine talking. You're worth more than that and you know it. That big open plan kitchen (she glanced across the road at the lit window), that *is* your happy scene, but without Toby in it. You don't need him. You. Are. Enough.' And her inner voice won the argument as she arrived at the school gates.

*

Toby drove to Bromford straight from work, later than he wanted. He had been messaging Sophie all afternoon, without a response, frightened of what the solicitor was encouraging her to do. Would she take the house and the boys? Could that happen? Would he then have to provide for her? She had no income; she might take him to the cleaners leaving him with nothing? Could she do that? Would she? Surely he could rescue this situation?

Abigail wasn't answering his calls anyway. She probably wouldn't take him back either, now she knew those messages had been sent to Sophie too. At the time he had genuinely felt the messages applied to both women, it had simply saved him time in typing. 'Jeez, I'm stupid,' he said out loud as he parked the car in the nearest space, two streets away from Sophie's house. 'At this rate, I'm gonna end up with no one.'

As he stood at what was now Sophie's front door, no longer the holder of his own key, he could hear the dogs barking in response to his knock and his heart raced with the anticipation and love of what was inside. He hated the way his conflicting feelings so easily changed his mind and he longed to be stronger, to sort out this mess.

It was William who opened the door, immediately thrusting a Wii controller in his hand. Toby had missed the boys so much over this last week, that he willingly took the gadget, even though Sophie's stern face suggested he shouldn't. Using hand signals and mouthing the words silently, he managed to convince her it would be five minutes, just one quick game, and he sat cross-legged on the lounge floor, feeling like he totally belonged. Sophie seemed to have accepted this delay to their conversation and as he played with his son, racing through the imaginary countryside, dodging obstacles, and flying through the air in his little Mario racing car, he vowed that from now on, there would be no lies, no deceit, and no more giving up. He felt compelled to tell Sophie everything, all those things she didn't know, however painful. She deserved to know the truth. As he played his third game, this time with Michael, Toby sensed Sophie had softened. Maybe she was as uncertain and worried about the conversation with the boys as he was. Maybe she was going to give him one more chance. Tonight, he had to tell her everything, in order to put things right, and as soon as the boys were in the bath he did.

'God, this feels good, Sophie. It's a weight off my chest. I can't bear to hear myself own up to it all. I've been such a bastard.'

Sophie was casually sitting back, sipping wine, listening but giving away nothing. She had obviously had a few glasses already, and her relaxed facial expression barely changed as he divulged his dirty secrets.

'Yes, you have,' she complained. 'You really have. I can't believe Abigail let that happen ... in my bed too, whilst I was crying my eyes out at Rani's. What a bitch.'

This honesty felt good, and it was outpouring in buckets, releasing his demons. 'Oh, and while I'm telling you everything, you know that polo day you bought me?' He didn't wait. 'I took Abigail. When you were at your mum's. Gosh, I'm sorry. I know how much you were looking forward to it.'

Sophie sipped her wine nonchalantly, but he saw her eyes wince. 'I'd forgotten all about that present. You like giving her things that are mine, don't you? Like that horrible white watch, you gave her that too, didn't you?'

'Oh. Yes, I did, she helped me pick it for you. She got that wrong, didn't she?' He allowed a smile and felt a sense of achievement in finding yet another secret, another demon to release. 'I'll buy you another watch. A better one, it wasn't a great make anyway and I'll book another polo weekend, maybe at the posh London polo grounds.' But seeing the scowl cross her face, he thought twice. 'Or something different. It wasn't all that great anyway. The horses were slow. You'd have gotten annoyed with them.'

'Well, I hope you both bloody fell off!' She didn't laugh but he sensed it was said in jest, as though she were softening following all of his divulged secrets. He wasn't sure if it was simply the light, but her hair seemed to sparkle as she animated her words with movement. He hadn't noticed before what a beautiful shade of rich mahogany it was, with so much greater depth of colour than Abigail's plain blonde.

'I'm going to show you how much I mean this. Right now. This text is going to be the last one.' Toby typed a few words into his phone, then held it across the space in front of them. 'Press send, Sophie. We're doing this together.'

> Toby:
>
> I'm sorry. I've told Sophie everything. Everything. I refuse to give up fighting for my marriage. Sorry. This is my final goodbye. Sorry.

Sophie read his words but made no attempt to press the symbol. 'Whatever. Least there was no kiss at the end of that one. But you're pressing it on your own Toby. And we're still getting divorced. This marriage is tainted, and I don't want it anymore. We still have to tell the boys. They need to know what's going on. We have to at least get that bit right. For them.'

Toby hesitated, then pressed the button before he could change his mind. It wasn't quite the response he had hoped for, but for now, he felt like he was home, and he knew he should be grateful for these warm feelings. He squeezed Sophie's hand as she stood, and caught her gaze, with his best effort at making loving puppy dog eyes.

'Look, Toby. It's too close to bedtime now to tell the boys. You can stay here tonight, on the blow-up, but tomorrow we are telling them. Please don't start playing Wii games again, eh?' She smiled. 'I'm going upstairs. Can you put them to bed? You know where everything is.'

Toby agreed, then said his goodnights as he watched her climb the stairs, ignoring the small pain in his chest he knew still had Abigail's name on it.

*

Sophie woke the next morning to all evidence of the blow-up bed tidied away and with a comfortable contentment she hadn't felt for a long time. Toby had admitted so much, so many lies, all those things O2 billing hadn't told her. He was desperately trying to wipe the slate clean and had even joked that maybe they *should* get divorced, if only to end this horrible period, this thing he had irrefutably damaged. Then maybe, they could start again, slowly dating and rebuilding their family unit from a new base.

'Who knows how good we could be after all this?' he had said but Sophie hadn't answered. She had spent too many nights tossing and turning trying to understand what was going on in Toby's turbulent world. Now she had to focus on her own mind. On gaining peace with her own decisions. To be at her best with this whole situation. She needed to forgive and forget.

She spent several hours whilst the boys were at school, re-reading her self-help books, learning about forgiveness, trying to understand the meaning behind the words of the famous poet that 'to err is human, to forgive divine'. She reaffirmed to herself that forgiveness is a gift you give to yourself, it takes the pain out of the past and is the best way to move forward.

Forgetting what Toby had done would be harder, but apparently, the books said she didn't have to 'forget'. The memories could remain, but by reaching forgiveness, their power to hurt would be removed. Sophie underlined that part of the book, she desperately wanted to show the boys how to have a good divorce, so bitterness of any sort had to be banished. Only by forgiving and forgetting could she shield them from the painful truths that led to mummy and daddy living separately, ensuring they could securely join newly blended families. They would never know what their father had done. Their future well-being would be protected, and so too, therefore, would hers.

*

When Toby returned home from work that night, he had lost a little of last night's happiness. Whether from a day at work or his worry about telling the boys, Sophie wasn't sure, but it took her by surprise regardless. She was cooking lasagne and garlic bread for dinner. It was easy and comforting, and the boys loved it. It would help set the right mood for their difficult conversation. Kiss FM was playing on the radio as she let him in.

'Turn that off. It's really loud.' He threw his bag on the table, ignoring how it had been set. The knives and forks fell out of place as the bag slid roughly along its short length.

'What? Turn off what? The radio?' Sophie was enjoying the uplifting songs and had been singing along, boosting her strength for the conversation.

'Yes ... well, no. Just this station. Turn off *Kiss FM*.'

'What on earth is wrong with *Kiss*? It's just the radio.' Sophie turned the volume down a little. He was right; it was loud, and they were having to shout over it.

'Just damn well change the channel. Sorry, but it reminds me—' His face contorted as he stumbled over his words. 'Of her. Abigail listens to *Kiss*. She has it on everywhere, all the time. Please, just turn it off?'

With the obvious assumption that Sophie would do as he bid, he calmly left the room to say hello to the boys.

Sophie was fuming as she pulled the lasagne out of the oven, hot steam enveloping her already heated face. *How dare you tell me to turn it off. It was making me feel good whilst cooking your flipping dinner. I don't give a damn what Abigail listens to.*

She wanted to turn up the volume in defiance, but all she could visualise was an ominous scene of Abigail listening to *Kiss FM* in Nettlefield House, giving the boys their dinner at the large kitchen table. She took a deep, controlled breath, and followed him into the lounge, turning off the radio as she went.

Toby was sitting on the sofa, his head in his phone. The boys sat to his side, watching cartoons. He didn't acknowledge her walking in, nor appreciate the silenced radio. She bit her tongue, pushing aside his insolence, and chastened the boys to wash their hands for dinner, worried about how they were going to attempt this devastating conversation whilst Toby was so morose.

*

After dinner, and with as yet, no mention of the elephant in the room, Sophie left the boys to their bath and went through to the lounge to face Toby. He was sat motionless, staring at the TV, not flinching as she switched it off. 'You don't seem very chatty. I thought we were going to tell the boys. You've barely said anything to me all night.' She sat next to him, not quite touching. 'What's wrong, Toby?'

There was a long pause. Toby turned to face her, decreasing the gap between them and took hold of her hand, looking directly into her eyes.

'I wanted to distance myself from her so much. I wanted to forget her, move on from everything that's happened and focus on the boys, and make peace with you. I wanted to take some time to be just by myself, to re-evaluate everything. I really did.' His voice trembled and he turned his head away as he wiped a tear from his cheek.

'So what's wrong? What's changed?' She pulled her hand out of his.

'I'm worried. I'm just so worried I'm never going to stop loving her. We spoke today. She came to my office. She said she would take me back. She said you'd messaged her, asking her to. Did you really?' His sudden flood of tears couldn't wash away his demons. Sophie could see them sitting in the front of his mind. She took his sobbing body against her and held him close, rubbing his back as if calming a child. She wanted for all the world to make things right but knew she couldn't.

Why did she love him so much that she could forgive him for everything? He was so caught up in his own, sad emotions he couldn't see that he had to forgive himself too.

She knew all the horrors, yet still wanted to help. Still felt she could if he wanted it too. But the person with all the decisions to make was the weakest.

She held him away from her. 'Why are you here Toby? Why didn't you just accept what the solicitor said and agree to end this thing? Go to Abigail if that's what you want.' The books had said that loving someone properly, carries significant self-sacrifice, and Sophie was feeling the full brunt of it now. She couldn't deny him the chance to be happy, even if it made her so sad.

'I'm sorry. I just never seem to know what to do. I love you both.'

'Oh just go, Toby. I think we both know you need to see where things can go with her. We can't talk to the boys when you're like this, I'll tell them you had to go back to work. We'll talk to them another time. Please just go.'

'I can't believe I'm still wobbling. How do I stop?' The sobbing had ended, but he looked a hundred years older.

'You stop by doing what *you* want to do. Don't be influenced by me, your parents, the solicitor, or even the boys. The best thing to do is what you want. Do what makes *you* happy. Nothing will be easy until you do.'

Toby wiped his sleeve across his face. 'That's funny, that's exactly what my life coach said.' He smiled.

Sophie stood up from the sofa and held out her hand. 'I knew you couldn't leave her.' She took his hand tightly, guiding him through the door, agitated by his presence, desperately trying to extend her forgiveness, to stop the memories from hurting. 'Go. Be with her. Just leave me alone.' She handed him his bag and felt ridiculous, like his counsellor encouraging him to destroy his family, again, pushing him away.

He left.

*

It was Wednesday, 5th March 2014, and Toby left his wife and children to be with his paramour. The time, the place, and the memory had been made, but it felt different this time, it felt final. She had put her emotions on the line, time and time again and now, at last, he was going to stop asking her to. She gently shut the door behind him then leant her back against it, looked up to the ceiling and forced herself to smile.

Ensuring the boys were content in the bath, she poured the last glass of wine and messaged Abigail.

> Sophie:
>
> Toby has officially left me for good, and the divorce is happening. Please forgive him for his wobble yesterday. It was simply the fear of me talking to the solicitor. You have always been on his mind, and I couldn't compete. He loves you enough to give up on his family, something I cannot ever imagine doing. I don't know if he's already messaged you, he's probably on his way to see you now, but allow him back, please. This is 100% his choice. I grieved for him a long time ago, so I'm just relieved he's finally made a choice he can stick with. I'm in pieces about the boys and how the hell divorce will affect them, but I plan

> on doing everything I can to show them what a good divorce looks like. Please help me with this. I want this to be amicable and I guess that has to include you? Please don't feel you need to text back. This message was just to get some closure. All the best.

Abigail's reply was immediate.

Abigail:
This text must have been so difficult to write. I really appreciate it. Thank you.

32

Wednesday, 2nd April 2014

Throughout March, Sophie and Toby's relationship existed only as was necessary for the boys. Sophie no longer wondered what had become of his relationship with Abigail. She never asked and she made no further mention of her pain in her diaries.

Her entries of late were deliberately positive. Her success stories of finally shifting her surplus weight and her surprise at how much she had been enjoying the local gym. But mostly they were entries about her admiration for her boys, who'd been so accepting of their new lives. Accepting the changes, not challenging the reasons why, partly due, Sophie felt, to the well-managed conversation about their parents' separation that had finally taken place.

Toby had come over on a Saturday morning for brunch, aiming to create a warm and secure environment for the talk. The boys knew there was to be an announcement but neither had thought it would be a big deal. Sophie had tried to keep it that way.

'So, boys. Sit still for a minute. Mummy and Daddy need to talk to you.' Both boys had finished eating and were keen to leave the table and drag Toby into the lounge to play on the Wii.

'You know how we moved house, and Daddy hasn't been here all the time? It's because Mummy and Daddy don't want to live together anymore. We're happier living in separate houses.'

William stopped cutting his crusts into tiny pieces, surreptitiously dropping the odd one to the waiting dog below and looked up. 'Where are we going to live then?' he'd asked.

'We both love you so much, we've agreed to share. Daddy's getting a new flat, not far from here.' It had been the first sensible decision Toby had made in a long time, deciding to rent a two-bedroom flat twenty minutes away as a base for himself. 'Sometimes you'll be here with me and sometimes with Daddy. But you'll still go to the same school, nothing else will change, we promise.' They had mutually agreed for Toby to have the boys every other weekend, plus one night in the week which according to Google, was the 'usual' share of time.

'But what about the Wii? Which house will the Wii be in?' Michael had said, climbing on Toby's lap.

'You can have two Wii's, one in each house.' Toby finally joined the conversation.

'Two Wii's?' William asked, raising an eyebrow. 'That's like Elliot, he's got two Wii's. He gets two birthdays. Will we get two birthdays?' Elliot was William's newest friend and presumably had separated parents too.

They had agreed not to mention the D-word, deeming it unnecessary to discuss at this stage as the word would carry no meaning for the boys. 'Yes, I guess. Like Elliot.' Sophie said. 'Two of everything.'

'But why? I want us all to stay together. I don't want to be like Elliot.' William looked from Toby to Sophie, as if at a tennis match, unsure who was going to give the answer he was looking for.

'Well, I want two Wii's *and* two birthdays,' Michael had said, not likely understanding the full implication of what was being discussed. 'I'll be eight soon, can I have two parties as well?'

'Yes, Michael, and two cakes. We'll make it super special.' Toby elaborated.

Sophie could see William's bottom lip quivering as they listened to Michael running Toby through his extensive birthday list. It had broken her heart to see the innocence of devastation, the understanding that things would never be the same again and the uncertainty of what that all meant. His eyes were wet, and he'd looked like a rabbit caught in headlights.

'William. Michael. We both love you so much. We will never, ever leave you. We will always look after you, forever. We'll just do it in separate houses. Mummy and Daddy will always be friends and we'll always be able to do things together, if that's what you want.' Sophie had gone off-piste from what the books had said but she had no other words for her desolate son.

'I've got a viewing at the flat tomorrow, why don't we all

go and have a look?' Toby had said, brightening the mood, going on to describe the high-tech lift and the large balcony. The distraction technique had worked, and the boys appeared more accepting, that whatever this change was going to bring, there would be some good things in there too.

Now the changes were fully in place and Toby had moved into the flat, the new routine became the new normality and the boys had accepted it in the same resilient way they had dealt with everything. Sophie would have loved to see Toby fail to maintain his part of the schedule, his commitment to school runs and weekends, but it was better for the boys if he didn't. He seemed to be adapting well too.

Only occasionally, would Sophie have to collect them from school on his behalf (due to work or traffic). They would meet her at the school gates, unable to hide their disappointment when they saw her in place of Toby, but she forgave them.

The weekends were harder to forgive. Sophie had never felt like a martyr before, but the three nights without them every other week brought out her victim mentality. She had to constantly remind herself that suffering in silence was the only way the boys could enjoy life with their Daddy, undamaged.

The fun and laughter of each weekend without her were evident in their brief, disinterested responses to her phone calls. Just a few seconds of conversation to show she was thinking of them, missing them, returned with the briefest of replies.

If she cracked, they would be the ones to suffer, and her

puffy, red eyes were her bi-weekly indication that her boys were making memories without her. Sophie had no idea if Abigail was back on the scene and didn't ask, but she was dreading the day their union might be announced and another delicate conversation with the boys would be needed. The idea of Abigail calling William and Michael 'sweethearts' riled her, but it hadn't come, and she was grateful for that.

*

It was the 2nd of April, thirty-three days since Toby had chosen the time, the place, and the memory for the end of their marriage when a phone call rudely interrupted Sophie's morning coffee.

'Sophie. Hi. I'm sorry to ring. You're probably trying to forget all this, but you need to know. Toby and I have been trying to make it work these last few weeks, but he's just finished with me. It's over.'

Sophie expelled the breath she had been holding since recognising Abigail's number, hoping it came across as a disinterested sigh, but there was a joyous little jump in there too. She remained silent, as if to reinforce her disinterest.

Abigail continued, 'He can't stop crying about what he's done. He said he's tried—he gave it a go—but all he wants now is to get his family back. The man's a mess. I feel I owe it to you to let you know.'

'Well, he's said nothing to me. I didn't even know you two were back together. Whatever happens, our marriage is over, so I've no interest in listening to your problems.'

Whilst that statement was true, to know he had been crying, pulled at her heart strings. Sophie suspected being a martyr on alternate weekends was not working for Toby either, and she couldn't shake the compassion invading her thoughts.

Abigail's voice caught as she continued, 'We really were making a go of it. I thought we were all out the other side, getting on with our lives. He was going to introduce me to the boys. I felt I had to let you know. You were brave enough to tell me when he left you, so I'm returning the favour. I guess our *EastEnders* saga continues.'

'Well, yours might, but I'm done with mine. I'm not running any more episodes; I can assure you!'

The conversation between the damaged women ended politely, on a companionable note, but Sophie suspected that neither found release from their torment.

She sat in silence with the cold remains of her coffee, straining to hear her rational thoughts over the din of her irrational mind. Why was she feeling uplifted about this news? Why was she smiling? Could she be contemplating this as a positive thing for her future relationship with Toby?

She had told him to go and try with Abigail. Nothing was going to be clear until he did. But now he knew the grass wasn't greener, could that mean they would finally work? He's got her out of his system, that's got to make a difference, hasn't it? But I'd just be laying myself on those train tracks once again. Wouldn't I?

She slapped herself round the face and physically shook herself off, then went into the kitchen to make a new coffee, finding it hard not to reach for the wine instead of milk. Abigail's pain had been palpable and as she gazed out across the tiny garden, she contemplated the depth of emotion Abigail must be dealing with.

If it hadn't been for the past fourteen years, the dreams of the next fourteen, and the boys' starring roles, Sophie didn't think she would even consider reconciling with Toby. Abigail had none of that, yet she always seemed to be there for him.

Sophie's conflicted mind took up the dialogue. Could this mean Abigail loved Toby more? Was this highlighting a deficiency in the strength of her own love for him? Is that why she forgave him with relative ease? Was it easier to forgive if she never truly loved?

Abandoning the coffee, Sophie grabbed the dogs and went for a walk to escape her meddlesome thoughts.

*

Toby hadn't come back to her, begging for more forgiveness, hoping to try again. He continued to be full of heartfelt apologies whenever discussions about the settlement or custody were needed, but he never talked about reconciliation.

Sophie maintained her determination to achieve a good divorce, regardless of the ever more frequent glimpses of the old Toby, which threatened to break her resolve.

She had discarded her self-help books, no longer feeling the need for the information within and had turned her attention instead to books on divorce and being a single parent. She had read a Facebook article on how to be happy again after divorce. It described how it takes twenty-eight days of consistency to break the old habits or create the new ones, then had immediately counted back to the day of Abigail's phone call.

Toby had reached day twenty-one, and Sophie allowed herself a feeling of pride that potentially, he could be near the end of breaking his habit of Abigail. The last few weeks he *had* seemed happier. He was playing more golf and would Facetime the boys from his flat, rather than his car which had perhaps been a way to avoid Abigail coming into view.

Reaching for a red pen, she wrote the number '21', inside a circle, at the top of her diary page for 23rd April 2014.

*

Day forty-four, recorded in red ink at the top of Sophie's diary, was Michael's birthday. As she wrestled with the Sellotape and finally wrapped his present, she couldn't stop the gloomy thoughts that Michael might never remember a birthday, shared jointly with his parents. As she wrote, 'Love Mummy,' in his card, she just managed to stop a falling tear from smearing the ink.

She imagined all the special occasions where there might be just one invited parent, or just one choice of parental home to visit. No child should have to make those decisions. Divorcing amicably was the only way to limit the emotional damage to the boys and so far, they had managed this well. Sophie had accepted her fate and begun the acceptance part of the grieving process, but her boys and their unknown future regularly brought her to tears.

She may still have doubts as to what right was anymore, but she knew she couldn't have tried harder to find it. Tonight, Toby was treating them all to a trip to the circus, so for Michael, she was going to work intently at not noticing the wrongs.

*

Sophie felt proud as they walked to the showground, pleased they could appear, at least from the outside, a happy family group, blending in with the crowds. Toby had been attentive, almost suffocating in his consideration of her, taking hold of her hand as they walked across the field. Sophie wanted to pull away, but a glance across at the boys reminded her of the memory she was creating for Michael, so she left her hand limp in his.

The tent was busy, with no allocated seating, so everyone was jostling for the best spots at the edge of the ring. Sophie watched Michael determinedly race round to the far side and saw the beam spread across his face as he triumphed in securing four seats at the ringside.

The boys excitedly fidgeted in their folding seats, catching glimpses of the colourful chaos behind the curtain and Sophie's smile was as happy and obvious as everyone else's in the tent.

Looking around at the audience, Sophie couldn't help her internal scepticism. It probably wasn't all as it seemed. Everyone would have a sad story somewhere behind the smiles. They may still be living it. Broken families, relationship traumas, shattered dreams, and unfulfilled promises all playing out in their own unique way.

As the music increased in volume and the lights dimmed, she felt a rogue tear slide down her face. Involuntarily released in the cover of darkness, it served simply to remind her that this was just another act in her own production of a show she didn't understand, and to which she hadn't been given the script.

*

At the end of the night, Toby stood by the front door of his flat, not yet making the effort to open it. 'It's been lovely having you here tonight. Thank you for being so good about all this.'

Sophie remained silent. She wanted to reply with, 'Thank you for having me. It's been fun,' but her mood was rapidly declining by her upcoming weekend, alone. The boys were in the lounge, playing their new Wii game, disinterested in the fact their mother was leaving. She knew they wouldn't understand her need for a big hug and kiss to stave off the loss she would feel over the next few days. They had no idea of the hurt she would be carrying, so she left them to play.

Toby's eyes locked onto Sophie's, daring her to move her gaze. 'This flat's really cosy. D'you know it makes me think of a little holiday let.'

He laid his hand gently on her shoulder. 'We could sort all this out, Sophie. We could pretend this is our weekend retreat and use it to mend everything. There are some great restaurants and bars around the corner.' His words were tumbling out faster. 'We could get a babysitter and recreate things the way they used to be when we first met. What d'you think? We could go back to before. We can start again, I know we can.'

He placed his arm over Sophie's shoulder, hugging her to him. She remained silent, but couldn't stop a natural, soft smile from escaping her composure. He was pulling her back in, and she was unable to resist. It felt so easy and so right, and now his words about reigniting the early days with the old Toby resonated with what she had wanted for so long. His eyes were sparkling with conviction and she could sense power in his words, a significant contrast to his previous cowardly notes in a message.

Plus, she remembered, he was now on day forty-four, sixteen days more than the gurus at Facebook said he had needed to break his habit.

As if reading her mind Toby said, 'Listen. Abigail's gone. She's miles away and I'm never going back. I'm in a really good place now. Near you. Near the boys. I know the divorce is happening, and that's fine, but you and I were always meant to be together. I know I've messed up, but I feel like my old self and it's you that's allowed me to get here. You've given up everything for me and I promise I won't let you down again.'

There was an eruption of noise from the lounge as the two boys fought over the controller, and Toby went to referee. Sophie took the opportunity to escape from her brainwashing. She opened the door and stepped outside.

'Wait.' Toby rushed backed. 'Wait.' He put his head low to Sophie's and kissed her on the cheek. 'Come away with us?' he whispered into her hair. 'Come away with me and the boys. I can get you on the flight. It'll be so good for us.'

Sophie knew this holiday was coming. She was dreading the thought of being so far apart from the boys for two weeks. It was a painful reminder and prompted her first response to this odd conversation.

'Don't be silly. How is that a good idea? We have to finish this before we can start it again. I'm nowhere near finishing this, and I cannot believe for one minute you are. Let's not confuse things further. It won't be fair on the boys.'

Toby didn't argue. Stroking her arm, he said, 'Just think about it. Please. See how good the next few weeks will be. I'm back Sophie, I really am. This *is* going to get better.'

Sophie turned away from his words. She shouted her goodbyes, along with a final 'happy birthday,' and walked down the two flights of stairs to the main door, feeling him watch her go.

Only once inside her car did she allow the smile to stretch her face. Five minutes. Just five minutes and one conversation, and he had turned her convictions so effortlessly into jelly. He had done it again. He had pulled her back in, giving her back the hope, and she had taken it.

Hope had a lot to answer for. Expecting the best in the future, believing that it can, with hard work, be brought about. Over the last few months, Sophie had managed to control her hope, kept a lid on it, but now it was oozing out all around her. Toby had tried his relationship with Abigail, the grass hadn't been greener, and now *hope* was suggesting he might finally, be returning to the other half of her once again.

She remembered the 'twenty-eight days to break a habit', wondering if maybe this was to become her day one. The first day of believing that hope was to be believed. She knew she was allowing herself to be sucked in, but it felt so good, so easy, and was a path so well-trodden, she accepted that maybe, it was the only direction she could take.

That night, in her diary, she wrote, 'My Day 1', in red ink, with a large exclamation mark encased in a circle. As she closed the pages and laid back on the pillow, a great, unexpected sigh left her body, as the magnitude of forgiveness wrapped in hope engulfed her.

It was going to have a lot to answer for.

33

Saturday, 7th June 2014

Nothing more had been said about that moment in Toby's flat, yet the possibility of being part of their holiday never left Sophie's mind. Over the last three weeks, they had spoken formally about the divorce, their decision to finally sell Nettlefield House, and the daily details of the boys' activities.

They were in total alignment on the end goal of finalising the marriage before either would consider starting anything new. No matter how gradual their progress had felt, they were mutually moving this thing forward, positively verified by the ascending red numbers on the pages of Sophie's diary and the reinforcing, caring messages from Toby.

Day 6:
Toby:
Just a note to say I love you. Hope
you've had a lovely day. Remember

how excited the boys were on
Michael's birthday when we were all
together. It was lovely to be back that
way again. Let's make it like that the
whole time, eh? Ring if you want to
speak to the boys. They're not in bed
yet. We're just lazing about! X

Sophie did speak to the boys, often. And their happiness when they were with Toby, whilst painful, was exactly what she wanted. They moved effortlessly from house to house, each time packing a little bag of personal items, and apart from missing the dogs, showed no outward sign of distress. *Hope* gave no timeline, nor came with any guarantees, but for now, the days were progressing with companionable ease.

Day 12:
Toby:
Feels such a relief to be in this place.
Long way to go, I know, but finally, I've
found the right path, and I'm so excited
by it. I know you're probably shit scared
but have faith. Hold my hand, and I'll
be your guide through our next exciting
chapter. X

Sophie had allowed herself the odd reply. A bit of humour, minus the kisses.

> Sophie:
>
> Blimey, you have been practising your poetic language! Either that or you've turned to religion? Sleep well.

Toby:

Thought you'd like that! All my own words too! I'm determined this story will have a happy ending, and I'm going to write it! X

Their messages had become a night-time event. Both imagining the other alone in bed, clinging onto hope which became stronger with each passing day. Sophie was reminded of her last birthday card, when so much was waiting to unfold. She remembered the words, 'I can. I will. Watch me.' But the affirmation had long since been removed from the front door. She had put it in an old laptop bag, with all her other cards, paper hearts, handwritten notes, letters, and the neglected self-help books, displaying her numerous annotations in their margins.

She'd wanted to hold onto it all because it helped keep her hope for a better future alive. It was all evidence that this journey had been complicated and emotional, and because of that, their destination, wherever they ended up, would be victorious.

They had contentedly slipped into a happy end to their marriage, whereupon they could clearly define what they both wanted and whether that involved each other. Sophie's old habit of doubt and distrust was leading to a new habit of hope and belief, giving Toby permission to take all the time he needed to fulfil his promises. Sophie didn't want to hurry the process; they couldn't afford to make any more mistakes, so she held her expectations low and was never disappointed.

It may have felt like a tentative approach, but so long as she didn't force it, how could it go wrong?

Sophie's twenty-eight days to break her habit were nearly over, and every message Toby sent broke off a little more.

Day 19:
Toby:
It will be lovely to meet you. I've heard you have two beautiful boys and used to be with a nice bloke who became a bit of a twat. Maybe I can come over and treat you properly, be a great dad to your boys, and show you a future of how it could and should be. Look forwards and not back, eh? Can't wait to take you out on a date if you'd like? X

*

Day twenty-three arrived with the optimistic warmth of a sunny June morning. Sophie took a deep breath of fragrant air as she let the dogs out and opened the chicken run. She had no idea how the last chicken was still alive in this fox-saturated suburbia, but today the freshly laid egg was testament that she was positively thriving.

'You old bird you. First egg of the year! Kept me waiting

for that one, didn't you! That's got to be the most expensive egg ever.' Sophie loved chatting to the chicken, pretending to decipher her gentle, clucked replies. 'Okay, yes, I guess that deserves some mealworms,' she answered and threw a handful from the storage bin to the frantic chicken, rushing to hoover them up. 'I love your robust resilience, you old bird.'

Sophie had missed her abundant supply of fresh eggs and the boys had abandoned their morning egg hunts a long time ago.

'This garden's not that bad really, is it? Maybe I should get you a friend or two? You'd like that wouldn't you?'

Leaving the chicken clucking away with the remaining worms, Sophie went inside and placed the fresh, warm egg on the empty rack. Today, she had a greater reason for her uplifted feeling.

Toby was coming over to finalise the last cog in the divorce documents, which involved reviewing the financial order. She was planning an informal family meal, to be eaten outside if the generous June weather allowed.

As she pulled the plethora of horse paraphernalia from the shed in order to reach the garden chairs at the back, she contemplated her ownership of Juno. She loved him to bits, but apart from the amount of stuff he came with and the extortionate cost of his livery, he would always remind her of everything she had lost.

She didn't want those memories; those times she had hung around his neck, crying into his mane. Time had done its healing. She would find him a good, loving home, free from the emotion and make do with a dog for any ongoing therapy.

With the table and chairs set up outside, Sophie grabbed some carrots and stood over the sink, singing to *Kiss FM*, loudly. She was amazed that her decision to sell Juno hadn't subdued her mood. Maybe her emotions were becoming more resilient. Maybe she was simply accepting her life in Bromford, seeing the contrast to her old life as a modification rather than a disaster.

She wanted today to be a symbolic moment when the divorce was concluded. Then, finally, she could begin thinking about what came next, perhaps beginning with that holiday, all four of them, together. What better way to show the boys we are still a team, than going on a joint holiday? She finished peeling the carrots then placed a bottle of wine in the fridge, laughing that there couldn't be many couples who celebrated together in this way when they finalised their divorce. She wasn't quite confident enough to chill the bottle of champagne, leftover from Christmas; she would save that for their decree absolute.

*

Toby lagged behind the boys as they approached Sophie's front door, dirty and hungry from their football match. He could smell the roast chicken before he got there, and it made his stomach turn. He couldn't eat a thing.

As Sophie opened the door, he noticed she'd made an effort with her hair and makeup. He hadn't seen her in lipstick for a long time and knew it was for his benefit. His stomach lurched, reminding him of what he was about to say, and it was all he could do to not run away.

The boys rushed straight inside, excitedly chatting about free kicks and goals, but Toby didn't move from the doorstep. The hot June sun was causing sweat to form on his balding head, and he swiftly wiped it away before it dripped down his face.

'Wow, you look really hot, I thought we'd eat in the garden it's such a lovely day. Come in, it's nearly ready.' Sophie said and stood aside to let him through.

'I'm sorry. I can't stop. Boys, come and say goodbye.' He avoided her narrowing eyes as he shouted across the hallway, not daring to step across the threshold.

'What d'you mean? What about lunch? I've cooked roast chicken.' Sophie gestured towards the kitchen, opening the door wider.

'I'm so sorry. I wish this wasn't happening.'

'What? What's happening?' She frowned, then moved towards him, smiling. 'I've put a bottle of fizz in the fridge to celebrate us finalising the figures. Come on. Come in.'

'I can't.' He took a step backwards, onto the pavement. 'I'll email you some numbers.'

'Woah … What d'you mean? We can't do it over email. That was the whole point of today. That's what *you* wanted.'

'I know. I've ruined everything and I can't stop it. It's all gone wrong.' Toby fought back the tears. He didn't want sympathy; he didn't deserve it.

'You look awful. What's happened?' Sophie held out her hand, still trying to usher him in. Still trying to help him.

Toby looked into her sympathetic, puzzled eyes and said, 'I've really tried. I think I've tried too hard.' His sweat had turned cold, and he felt a shiver traverse his spine. 'I saw Abigail yesterday. It's broken me. I can't pretend anymore. This isn't what I want. Not really.'

Surprised by her silence he continued. 'I've been lying to myself. Abigail is going to take me back. I should never have left. I'm really sorry Sophie.'

Sophie didn't move. She threw no fists nor shouted any angry words. He knew he had convinced her over the last few months he was happy by himself, that there might be a chance for them to mend once the divorce was finalised, but she was still not reacting. Not at all.

He glanced into the house, ensuring the boys couldn't hear. 'I … I've also got to tell you th … that I'm introducing Abigail to the boys. And her kids. Properly. I wanted you to know b … because they are coming on the holiday with us. I'm so sorry.' He took another step backwards, unnerved by the lack of any response, but as his last few words sunk in, she flew at him.

'You have got to be kidding me! Are you for real?' She lunged at him, pushing him down the street, forcing him off the pavement.

He regained his balance and quickly began walking away. 'I really am sorry,' he said, but he doubted she would have heard him over the blasphemous words hurtling down the street behind him.

His car was parked a few streets away and he was thankful for the distance between them. Before he rounded the corner he stole a glance back and saw her, collapsed on the pavement, with her head in her hands, her hair wildly hanging down across her face and his heart contracted in pain at what he had done. Again.

*

Sophie slammed the door, then punched the back of it as hard as she could, wishing it had connected with Toby's face. Welcoming the pain, she went into the kitchen to run her throbbing hand under the cold tap. As she passed the sideboard, she grabbed the newly laid egg with her undamaged hand and launched it against the closed front door, listening to its satisfactory smash.

She watched the oozing, orange goo slide down the door, effortlessly traversing over its lumps and bumps, and took deep calming breaths as it formed globules on the floor.

Sophie maintained her composure whilst encouraging the boys into the shower. She washed away the mud and sweat from football, then put them straight into pyjamas. She then responded the same way as before; each time life had been pulled from under her feet. She messaged the yard, threw some clothes in a bag, packed a complete roast dinner for four in foil, and drove her depleted family to her parents' retreat.

*

Sophie collapsed into her father's arms, breathless as he opened the door in surprise. 'He's done it again. I just can't cope anymore.'

Her mother hurried past, to gather up the boys, still in

the car, and brought them into the house. They had no idea why they were quickly driven to Granny's for another impromptu visit this Saturday afternoon.

They were now so accustomed to being within the care of just one parent, they hadn't realised Daddy had vanished. They hadn't noticed their mother's bandaged hand, nor the smashed shell and partly licked up egg. All they complained about was the aroma of roast chicken that had not yet turned up on their plates. Granny removed them from the sight of their distressed mother, crying pitifully into her father's chest, and distracted them with the desired food.

Sophie was trying to explain, through the sobs, how amicable her relationship with Toby had become. How much they were both looking forward to ending the marriage, so that there may be hope they could start again. How she was now having to deal with the unimaginable process of blending her boys into a new family.

She had come so close to trusting and believing in him, that she now felt more foolish, rejected, and abused than at any other time.

She begged her father to make it all better. 'I can't do this anymore. I can't do it.' She was crying hard now and repeating the only words she could vocalise through the sobs. She stared into her father's eyes. 'I just can't.'

'Then don't. Don't do it anymore.' The simple words were delivered with authority. 'I'm going to tell you something. Something my father told me, listen carefully, it will help you, I promise.'

He sat her on the sofa and moved beside her before

speaking. 'There's a word, 'portage.' It's the practice of taking your canoe out of the water and carrying it along the riverbank to avoid an obstacle. When faced with rapids, for example, a guide would inspect ahead and decide between the heavy work of portage, or the life-threatening risks of running the rapids.'

'What? What *are* you going on about? They're going on holiday by plane, not boat!' Sophie's eyes dried a little as she gazed at her father, thinking he had gone ever so slightly mad.

He looked deep in thought for a moment, then continued, 'You've been on the same river for so long, but it's not your river. It's Toby's. He's controlling it. Sometimes he forces you to portage. Sometimes he motivates you to take the risk on the rapids. It all depends on how he feels, not how you feel. You've responded like this for so long, you think it's your only choice.'

Her father paused, perhaps lost in thoughts of where his own river had produced rapids in the past.

'You've been asked to take the rapids, so you tried, then you're told to portage, and you do. It's all based on Toby's whims. You've done it again and again, and you're taking the boys and your whole life with you. It's never been sustainable. You say you can't, and yet you always do. Well, now, don't. Pick up the boys and carry them to *your* river. Get off Toby's once and for all. Decide by yourself when you'll portage and when you'll risk the rapids, disregarding where his river is going. Leave him on it.'

Sophie began to see the relevance. 'But I still want my

marriage, Dad. I wanted to grow old together like you and Mum, why couldn't I make that happen? I never wanted to fail, I did what you said, I tried really hard, I never gave up. It didn't work. Why didn't it work, Dad? The tears returned.

'You're trying so hard but on the wrong river. You have to do it from yours, not his. You can still care for him, love him even if you really must, but from a different perspective, on a different river. Going where you want it to go. Each time you make your own decision, you'll get stronger. You'll travel further down, getting closer to where *you* want to be. Toby won't be able to trigger the old feelings with the same intensity as before because you're not on his river. Whether your rivers ever cross again, God only knows, but if you want to be strong and able for if they do, then you need to portage now. That's not failing, that's succeeding.' He hugged her close and kissed her head. 'Find your new river, darling.'

*

Sophie found her river that night with the help of a couple of gins and the peace and darkness of her parents' home. With her father's words muddled around in her head, her dreams focussed on creating the hypothetical river she wanted to travel. She dreamt of her river as wide and blue, with banks lined with vibrant wildflowers. As the wind blew gently downstream, it carried the aroma of freshly cut hay. Occasionally, a wild, black horse cantered alongside, whickering across the crystal clear water.

She made the colours brighter, allowing the river to flow faster as she visualised her large canoe, a little like a caravan, carrying her and the boys, the dogs, and a chicken. Everyone was giggling as they traversed a small rapid with ease. Toby's river was visible in the distance, travelling off course to hers, with many more twists and turns, forcing his water to quicken, churning up the silt and black from below into aggressive, dark rapids.

It felt good being on her river. She was in full control of everything, and every part of her body relaxed with the relief that there was no bridge across to Toby's.

Being on her river meant she could begin to work on herself and who she might now become, regardless of Toby's decisions. She didn't realise until now just how much he had been defining her, emotionally, mentally and physically. She thought she had been strong and brave, and she may well have been sometimes, but she was being strong on the wrong river. Her new sense of power was coming not from the fight to succeed, but from the unaccustomed act of giving in, accepting failure. Hope was still there, it just looked different now.

This new hope was her empowerment. She could see many rapids ahead on her river but they were inviting, welcoming, and she would tackle them with confidence. That was what success looked like. That was going to be the way to get what you really want.

Sophie was grateful that whilst she had been negotiating Toby's river, she had managed to protect the boys from the emotional rapids he had forced her through. Each moment he had convinced her to portage she had carefully carried them with her, allowing them back once the rapids had subsided.

The boys would still love being on Toby's river, with its exciting twists and turns, and Sophie would never diminish that. Daddy could stay on his river, but Mummy's river was going to be a journey dedicated to herself and to becoming the best single mother possible, and everything else would become irrelevant. She wouldn't fail at that.

Nothing was going to pollute her river.

34

Wednesday, 25th June 2014

On this bright, sunny day in June, William skipped out of school, chatting excitedly. 'We're going to Adventure World. Daddy's booked the special passes too, so we won't have to queue. *And* he said we can have candyfloss.'

'What? When did he say that? When are you going?' Sophie pursed her lips, taking hold of his hand. Adventure World Play Park was in Abigail's territory. 'Who are you going with? Daddy hasn't asked me. No one's going anywhere.'

'He's already booked it. Daddy said we can go.' William pulled his hand away. 'Stop being a fun sponge.'

Sophie baulked at the unfamiliar expression and instinctively knew where he'd learnt it. She guessed this was going to be the big introduction to Abigail and whilst a fun sponge was not something she aspired to, there was no way the boys were meeting Abigail before she had a chance to prepare them first. 'No one's going anywhere near Abi—'

She quickly stopped her words, took a deep breath, then

pasted on the smile reserved for the school gates, and said, 'I'll have to call Daddy. I know nothing about it.'

Taking this as authorisation for the trip, William ran off ahead to discuss the imminent adventure with his younger brother.

*

Sophie slipped into the garden, out of earshot of the boys, and rang Toby. He had indeed told them they were going away, and yes; they would be staying with Abigail. They would be meeting her kids, sleeping in her beds, and eating her dinners. They were going to have a weekend of outrageous fun and excitement.

Abigail was probably the opposite of a fun sponge, whatever that might be. Sophie managed to remember the river she was on and kept the animosity out of her voice as she requested how in the future, these events should be discussed between them first, before telling the boys. Toby apologised but refused to accept these discussions would be about permission. His only concession to Sophie's requests was an agreement that they would tell the boys about Abigail, together.

Sophie hung up, devastated that he could do anything he wanted with *her* boys on *his* river, and she just had to accept it. She may have maintained her strength during the call, but the rapids brought tears to her eyes as she realised how her river didn't offer an exciting new partner. Her river couldn't provide a set of stepsiblings for fun weekends away and might never be equipped with the same resources as Toby's, picking up the tab from adventure parks and two-week holidays along its route.

She allowed herself a private moment to indulge in self-pity and despair, tinged with jealousy, allowing her tears to fall unabated, with just the dogs looking on in sympathy.

Moments later, drying her eyes, Sophie walked back indoors. Her thoughts had rationalised this situation to be just another part of the journey on her river. Now she just had to build a bridge, to allow the boys to effortlessly cross over onto Toby's river and she had to be the one carrying their bags.

*

The agreed discussion took place on Sunday night. Toby and the boys were squeezed onto the two-seater sofa, playing piggy in the middle with a tiny bouncy ball, causing Michael to flip out in annoyance, unable to grab it.

Sophie walked in, standing rigid in the door frame, hoping to emphasize how this was to be a functional and brief discussion. She didn't want Toby in her house any longer than was necessary, so caught his eye and gave him a nod, accompanied with a stern look to indicate he should stop messing about and get this discussion going. It wasn't her conversation to start, so she was curious to see how he would manage such an awkward, sensitive topic.

'So, boys. You know we are going to Adventure World soon? It's going to be great fun.' Toby smiled broadly to back up his words. 'Well, Daddy's got a special friend coming with us, and we're going to be staying at her house.'

William looked up from retrieving the ball from under the sofa. Michael's attention was now on the television, he probably hadn't even heard.

'Is Mummy staying there too?' William asked Toby but looked directly at his mother.

Sophie smiled reassuringly, trying to relax her tense stance, knowing she had to give the illusion that this was all okay with her.

'Well, no. Mummy can't come. It's just us staying. You actually know my friend. Her name's Abigail,' Toby offered. 'Is that okay? It'll be fun, won't it?'

The boys both looked at him, seemingly confused as to what exactly, they were being asked. William's eyes darted between them, and he opened his mouth as if to say something, but quickly shut it.

Sophie couldn't help but step into the silence. 'Look, boys, here's her picture.' She handed them her phone displaying Abigail's photo on Facebook. 'That's Abigail, and those are her kids. D'you remember them from Study Class?'

Michael took a quick glance before satisfying himself he needed no further involvement in this conversation, but William took longer to study the images. After a moment, he raised his head from the phone, staring directly into Toby's eyes. 'Is she your girlfriend now then, Daddy?'

Violent rapids immediately formed on Sophie's river. It broke her heart as she realised her lovely, innocent ten-year-old had joined the dots.

Toby didn't have an answer.

Coming to his own conclusion, William added, 'Has she

been your girlfriend for a long time then? Is that why you don't live with Mummy anymore?'

Sophie felt desperate to say something reassuring, but this was not her answer to impart.

Toby delivered a coward's response. 'Yes. She's a good friend.' Changing the focus, he added, 'She's got a big black spaniel and two cats. It'll be fun, won't it?'

'Is she buying Nettlefield House?' William seemed to be trying to join more dots.

Toby looked up at Sophie at the mention of the house, then quickly turned away from the little room, 'No of course not. Look, I need to go now. I've got an early start tomorrow, but I'll pick you up from school as normal on Friday and we'll go straight from there. Pack your swimming trunks, there's a water park too. You can splash me.' He winked, kissed them both on the head and left, gifting Sophie a gentle smile and a grateful squeeze of her arm as he went.

*

Once Sophie's rapids had subsided and the boys were in bed, she went into their little room to kiss them goodnight. She walked in to find William flicking through old photos in a tatty plastic album. Sophie hadn't seen these for a long time. She remembered the captured memories from a birthday party in the garden of Nettlefield House years before. William had tears streaming down his face.

'I don't want to sell the big house, Mummy,' he said without looking up from the album. 'I love that house. I want us all to go back. I miss the garden.' He looked straight into her eyes from his heightened position on the top bunk. 'I want to get the ponies and all the chickens back as well?'

'Yes, then Daddy can live with us too because there's plenty of room.' Michael offered.

Sophie was lost for words. The earlier reminders of Study Class and times gone by had placed a whirlpool on her river, and she had no idea how to navigate the boys' heartbreak. She wanted to be honest, to tell them exactly why they couldn't go back.

Nettlefield House had sold. The stunning Victorian hallway, their large bedrooms, the desired conservatory, the orchard, the fields, and Sophie's beloved stables. Her dream. All of it gone because Toby took it from them. In that moment she wanted them to dislike their father as much as she did, but she knew this would cause desolation to the two people in the world she had to protect the most. She had come this far without succumbing to this temporary satisfaction. She would not give in now.

Instead, her response focused on distraction. 'Don't be silly. It's great here. We have your cousins all around us and Granny and Grandpa are nearer too. Your school is lovely, look at all your new friends! Listen, we can buy a better house than this, and you'll have your own bedrooms again. You can help me choose. I promise I won't be a fun sponge, and Daddy's only going to be up the road, so you'll see him all the time.'

Her brightness was false, but her optimism wasn't. 'Come on. Cheer up. Give me a kiss,' and she kissed them both noisily on their cheeks. She giggled. 'Now give me a hug,' and she theatrically reached across each bed hugging them close, adding a little tickle until William began to smile. 'Now. Tell me that you love me!' and they all chorused the three little words together, laughing at their little goodnight exchange of words and affection.

Sophie pulled the door to, then went downstairs to listen to *Kiss FM.* Really loud.

*

The next few weeks brought many more challenging questions, followed by edited answers, bringing both tears and laughter into the tiny bedroom.

A torrent of emotion for Sophie came on the night the boys returned from their weekend at Adventure World. Sophie's pleasure at having them home was tainted by a new set of painful emotions she knew she was going to have to get used to.

They were exhausted and hadn't stopped talking about all the exciting things they had done with Abigail and her children. Even their clothes had smelt of the new home, their new family. The one Sophie would know nothing about. She would not form part of those memories.

The boys had brought back with them more than just the new smell. Phrases and behaviour traits trickled out, subtle to an onlooker but like a knife in the chest to Sophie. The boys commented on the games they had played, the restaurant they had visited, and Abigail's daughter's imminent birthday.

Sophie had acted as excited as they had and covertly tried to get intimate information from them. Did Abigail cook nice dinners? Were her kids well behaved? Did Daddy kiss her a lot? Sophie hated the competitive nature it invoked as she quizzed the boys, unable to find fault in Abigail's hospitality.

Sophie didn't want a competition to see who could give her boys a better weekend. She knew she might lose, and that felt so unfair.

*

Tonight, Sophie was feeling particularly sombre. The end of the school term had arrived, and with it the poignant memories of last summer, when she had fled Nettlefield House. She remembered her feelings of hope, attached to a sense of achievement, as they began to make changes, planned to put things right. She thought she had been in control, but of course, she now knew she never had been.

She'd always been on Toby's river, and he had been captain the whole time. Whilst she had, to a certain extent, become more accepting of the changes and influences Toby and Abigail brought to the boys, tonight felt different. Worse.

Tomorrow, they were going on the holiday they had been looking forward to for months. The holiday that, at one point, she had sincerely believed she might be part of, and that might have given the boys the best possible end to their marriage. The holiday that now painfully included Abigail and her children instead.

Sophie went upstairs to say goodnight to William and Michael, a fake smile across her face and a forced enthusiasm to her voice. They were eagerly discussing the seating arrangements for the plane, arguing over the window seat, and had already decided that the four children would sit together, sharing their sweets and iPads. Father Christmas never had delivered the requested iPad into Michael's stocking, so he was quick to bagsy the seat next to Abigail's daughter, who being a few years older, had all the latest electronic gadgets.

Sophie's voice caught as she joked. "D'you think you could fit me in your suitcase? Promise I'll be quiet!"

"Don't be silly Mummy, you have to stay here and look after the dogs and chicken." Michael had it all worked out.

"But maybe we could ask Daddy?" William had likely sensed the pain in his mother's voice.

"Ahh. No, it's okay, Michael's right—who's gonna look after the animals?" Sophie replied, pulling the duvet up to his chin. "It's your holiday. It's for you, Daddy, and Abigail. And you're going to have so much fun. Just don't drink too much beer!" Sophie winked and tickled William. "Now come on, get lots of sleep. Daddy's picking you up early."

Then without mention of her imminent fourteen nights of pain, she gave them her goodnight blessing from her precious river of life.

'Kiss me. Hug me. Tell me that you love me.'

She gently shut the door and let out a shuddering breath, releasing a deluge of tears. As she turned to go downstairs, she was distracted by a sudden strong breeze, gushing through the small landing window, causing the blind to flap noisily. She paused and stuck her head out, smelling the fragrant summer air. The gusts were throwing the bushes and trees around, creating a musical symphony of leaves hitting leaves and twigs hitting twigs.

She listened to Mother Nature and breathed a deep, heavy sigh, allowing the tears to flow, enjoying the sensation as they slid from her face, splashing the bushes below.

The wind suddenly dropped. Mother Nature taking a moment to pause. Sophie heard the tinkle of a cat's bell, daring to come into the garden of the two Jack Russells. She took in another deep breath as all around her, life just kept on going regardless, irrelevant to what was going on in her world. Rivers would keep flowing, and hers was no different.

She silently asked Mother Nature how long would this hurt? How long would the outpouring of love from her boys to the man who had ruined so much for them all, keep breaking her heart? How many more weekends were going to result in a little piece of Abigail returning with her boys? How many more holidays would they enjoy without her?

She knew Mother Nature's answer. The boys loved their father unconditionally, like all boys should, and would do so forevermore. Her only option was to love them as hard and continue to show them what a good divorce looked like. Teaching them a good marriage was now not her lesson to give. Allowing them to learn this from Abigail and Toby might be.

Sophie could feel the warm wind drying her tears against her skin, and she closed her eyes tight against the light, pushing her neck out further, holding her head up high. Taking a few deep mouthfuls of air, she allowed the sweetness to inflate her lungs, encouraging the resurgence of strength that came after releasing such emotions. Forcing herself to believe that sometimes the dreams that come true are the dreams you never knew you had. She opened her eyes and glimpsed the sudden orange flash of a striking butterfly just inches from her face. Mother nature's endorsement that she *could* keep transforming, keep on dreaming. The hope for her new life was still pulsing through her veins so she would never give up striving to achieve it.

She was strong enough to do this; she knew it.

'I never knew how strong I was until I had to forgive someone who wasn't sorry and accept an apology I never truly received.'

Unknown

Epilogue

Sunday, 23rd December 2014

Sophie reacted with lightning reflexes as the letter dropped through the door, grabbing the little dog by her collar. A fraction later and the overly excited Jack Russell would have beaten her to it, ripping the white envelope to shreds. Sophie wanted that piece of paper intact. She had been on high alert to the postman for what felt like weeks. Finally, her wait was over. It was here.

She had no idea how she was expected to feel now she held it in her hand. She turned it over, inspecting it, checking it, waiting for the emotion, making sure it was real. It was, it was here, so now her marriage had officially ended. She felt success. She had spent two years on the greatest tidal wave of her life, finally, it had ended.

Her success turned to relief. She no longer needed to fear those early morning emotions that agitated her mind, nor experience the nauseating, fearful anticipation at every email or message of Toby's compliance or dispute. They could be banished now. His changing mind could not affect her again.

Her worries were over. This piece of paper had ended them.

Sophie's relief gave way to sadness. She knew the sadness would come. It had never been far from her thoughts. Probably would be for a while to come. But for now, there were no tears to accompany it. Just a heavy, dull sadness and loss of what had been and what was now not to come.

The little dog, Sophie's last living remnant from her previous menagerie, ran into the tiny garden to stalk the magpies and pigeons. Sophie made herself a coffee and followed, needing space to think, still holding the unopened letter. She sat huddled on the hammock frame, bare of its cushions, and held her coffee warming her hands, focusing on a tree in the distance. The tree reminded her of a happier moment, sitting in the new conservatory of Nettlefield House before it earned its painful nickname.

The memory was of a towering tree in the distance, across their expanse of lawn. It had surprised her; she couldn't have imagined owning such a large tree. It looked so far away, and it had made her feel so proud that it was theirs, as was everything in between. This tree she now looked at across the rooftops struck her as being at a disadvantage against its dull backdrop of suburbia. If trees could talk, Sophie was sure this one would reveal two major stages of its life.

The first took its canopy to the expected height, opening up to its deserved expanse of sky, in proportion to the rest of the chimney-dominated skyline. Then there was the second part, enabling it to soar another twenty feet in the air, as if creating a new tree sitting on top of the first. It had risen above itself not with a sprawl of branches and leaves but with a single, strong, isolated trunk. The secondary canopy it gave life to was not as large as its relation below, but it likely had years to mature.

Uncaring as to whether the neighbours would hear, Sophie spoke out loud to the tree. She spent so much time alone now, that talking to herself was a habit she considered the norm.

'I'm a bit like you, Tree. My old life was full of branches, leaves, and twigs and I've had to push up a second trunk too. I'm managing to sprout new leaves and little twigs, might even manage a whole branch soon.' She laughed at her joke and took a sip of coffee.

'What made you have to start your new life?'

She turned away, distracted by the noise of the little dog, digging at the corner of the shed, desperate to reach the mice wintering deep beneath. She watched the mud flying in all directions, momentarily mesmerised, remembering how much she had once longed to be a wintering mouse, now so grateful that she wasn't.

'I reckon it was the building of those new houses around you.' She spoke to the tree again. 'Bet that caused you to have to portage on your river, didn't it? That must have been, what? Twenty years ago? You've done well, I hope I'm as successful as you.'

She envied the resilience and longevity of the tree and contemplated how she could leave such a legacy. She had certainly taught the boys how to have a good divorce and that could be considered a gift, but what else had she contributed to this world. What other lessons would she learn from her new direction in life?

Sophie was reminded of the unopened letter, still in her hand. Its document within, the reason she was talking to a tree, thinking of legacies. The person who typed it probably gave no thought to its importance or relevance. Just one of a hundred every week, a generic letter printed by a generic computer. She momentarily considered giving it to the little dog, to enjoy watching her ceremoniously rip it to shreds.

Sophie held it up high as if showing the tree, trying to see inside, contemplating everything it stood for. She was amazed when she looked back at the journey that had cumulated with this letter, she could see things now without the emotion. She had allowed herself to be emotionally tortured, yet she couldn't see it so kept going back for more.

Was that really love?

She decided it was simply tenacity. She would have fought it to the end, which she did, and the resilience she now carried, as a result, was her reward. She'd never given up on anything before, so this marriage was her first defeat. It had changed her, not fundamentally in who she was but in how she dealt with life. She had been forced to accept changes that changed her, yet she was now a better version of herself. She had learnt that the only relationship you have a hundred percent control over is the one you have with yourself; so she was going to make it the best one.

She hoped she would have the strength to trust again. To love as hard. There were plenty of times she longed for another half of her, and she knew someone would come, but time still needed to do its healing. Loneliness delivered a cruel lesson, every other weekend, but there was a certain type of contentment that came from learning to be whole and complete, all by yourself.

Sophie felt an almost spiritual warmth rise up her spine as she recognised a desperate need to capture her past. She owed it to the boys to tell the story behind the life they might have had, which subsequently defined the life they ended up with. The story wouldn't be about discrediting Toby. He had done that by himself. It would be a story to credit herself, highlighting her as the amazing person and mother she felt she was and would continue to be.

Taking her gaze away from the tree, Sophie carried the letter back into the house and pulled out her old laptop bag from under the stairs. She looked through her old diaries, written at a time when the strength of her hope was driving her emotions. She pulled out the plethora of love notes and heart-shaped paper cut-outs, several ripped in half and ran her finger over the embossed orange butterfly that adorned the elaborate letters, full of hope, wrapped up in lies.

She knew she had more of the story encapsulated electronically in texts, voicemails, and emails. She marvelled at just how much all this constituted and formed her life up to now.

It felt like her gift, waiting to be unwrapped. A story to tell that may help others to grow. She could pull it all together, into a coherent format for everyone to read, to understand what happened to her and her boys and all that now defined them. This was all hers. Her legacy.

She placed the unopened letter to one side and began.

I am Sophie. I am stronger and truer than I ever knew was possible, and I am amazing. I am enough. I love me. This is my story.

Chapter One

Get Exclusive Cut Chapters and Scenes

Building good relationships and encouraging others to do the same, is something I am passionate about. I regularly share experiences from my own broken marriage and emotional divorce, alongside my learnings from years of writing about Sophie and Toby.

I'd therefore love it if you'd be happy to receive my regular newsletters containing advice and support on how you too can recover from heartbreak. As a special thank you I will send you the cut chapters and scenes from 'The Other Half of Me', that didn't quite make it into the final book.

Just visit the link below.

https://ebook.lovicklifecoach.co.uk/theotherhalfofme

I hope you've enjoyed reading 'The Other Half of Me'

I love reading reviews from my readers so I would be very grateful if you could spend just a few minutes to leave yours on Amazon.

Good honest reviews of my book will help to bring it to the attention of others, so thank you.

About the Author

Annabel Lovick never planned on becoming an author—but then she never planned on becoming a divorced, single mother either.

Throughout her emotional breakup, Annabel realised that you can't control what happens to you, but you can control and change how you react to it. Her chosen reaction to what happened to her, positively changed her direction in life, motivating her to retrain as a Divorce and Breakup Recovery Life Coach and Neuro Linguistic Programming (NLP) practitioner.

She is now passionately helping others reach the other side of heartbreak, by encouraging them to believe that everything unwanted in life happens 'for' you, not 'to' you. With her coaching and support, she ensures clients learn and grow from their past, building a resilience they can be proud of and achieve a life they may never have dreamt was possible.

Annabel lives just outside London with her two teenage boys and crazy Jack Russell terrier and runs her successful life coaching business—Lovick Life Coach.

If you'd like to learn more about Annabel's work and her available coaching programs, please visit: www.lovicklifecoach.co.uk

Printed in Great Britain
by Amazon